HER PERSONAL DEMONS

HER PERSONAL DEMONS

THE SEVEN SINNERS OF HELL'S KINGDOM, BOOK ONE

To MJ,
Enjoy riding the devils
down!
XOXO,
Ginna Moran

by

GINNA MORAN

SUNNY PALMS
PRESS

ISBN 978-1-951314-41-5 (soft cover)
ISBN 978-1-951314-42-2 (hard cover)

This is a work of fiction. All of the characters, organizations, and events
portrayed in this novel are either products of the author's imagination or
are used fictitiously.

Cover design by Silver Starlight Designs
Cover images copyright Depositphotos

For Inquiries Contact:
Sunny Palms Press
9663 Santa Monica Blvd Suite 1158
Beverly Hills, CA 90210, USA
www.sunnypalmspress.com
www.GinnaMoran.com

DEAR DAUGHTER,

If you are reading this, put the book back on the shelf. Just because you can read higher than your grade level doesn't mean you can read Mommy's books yet. Let's save this one for when you're an adult.

BUT,

If you have disobeyed me, because let's face it, you are my child, take this to your dad and stop reading right now.

I MEAN IT.

REAL DEDICATION

To my husband, this book is for you.

I figured this might be the best way to get you to see this dedication. It's a good thing our kid listens to you or else you would have to explain such things as butt plugs, bondage, and the appeal of horns on a demon. You're flustered now, aren't you? I'm happy to explain to you—better yet, show you—what I'm talking about above.

LASTLY,

Dear readers,

If you don't want to know more about the above, close this book now. But if you're curious, I'd love to try to convince you why demon sex could be fun. But don't take my word for it. I've never banged a demon...maybe.

1

FOR ALL THINGS UNHOLY

RAVEN

I CAN'T BELIEVE I'm dying on the floor of a dirty bathroom. I know it. I feel it deep inside me, and I regret not sucking it up and cleaning the damn place. I don't know what bullshit I've done in my life to deserve an end like this, but here I am, hanging onto a toilet, sweating and crying with no one around willing to save me.

I wish I could say my impending death was due to partying too much and drinking over my limit. At least then I'd have an explanation for my body betraying me. But no. This is something else. I'm sick without an explanation, and it's been a never-ending cycle the last few months.

This time feels worse, though. My body can't take it. I need help from someone who actually cares about me. If only my cousin would answer my calls.

Clutching my phone, I listen as my cousin sends me straight to voicemail for the third time. "Tamia, I'm sorry. I know I fucked up, but I need you. Please call me back. Please." Closing my eyes, I disconnect the line and rest my head on the side of the tub.

I know I shouldn't expect much after our last fight, but I thought that maybe she'd give me another chance if I apologized. I was just so mad at her for yelling at me for moving back in with my ex. She didn't believe me when I told her we weren't back together, and it just...it's pointless to think about it now.

Dizziness washes over me in another intense wave. I blink through the strange haze in my vision and smear the sweat prickling on my forehead with my arm. Fuck. What is wrong with me?

Lifting my phone, I tap my finger on the screen and call my parents next. They haven't answered since Christmas, but maybe today will be different. They can't ignore me forever, right?

It goes straight to voicemail too.

I groan and lie on the bathroom floor.

"Joel," I call, shielding my eyes from the vanity lights over the wall mirror. I didn't want to have to yell for my ex-fiancé, but I don't know what else to do. He's all I have despite not wanting anything to do with him. "Joel, I need to go to Urgent Care. I can't wait it out this time. I feel as if I'm dying."

Joel's voice muffles through the door, annoyance lacing his voice. I can't hear what he's saying, but he's pissed. Maybe drunk. I don't know. I've been in the bathroom for hours. He never took me seriously before we broke up, always shrugging me off like I make things up to inconvenience him on purpose, so I don't know why I even try now.

"Joel, please," I beg, groaning. "Please. Please. Please. I'll do whatever you want if you take me."

He mutters from outside the door too lowly for me to hear but doesn't come in.

I sigh.

I've been feeling sick on and off for months now. At first I thought it was food poisoning or a stomach virus. Maybe too much drinking to deal with Joel's asshole behavior over refusing to take his lying ass back and accept his engagement ring again. But even after I quit drowning myself in alcohol, the sickness still comes back.

Without medical insurance, it's been tough. I can't afford all the tests I know my doctor would want to run. Joel says it'll be in the thousands. It doesn't help that he also makes me feel as if I'm going crazy. He thinks I get sick because of the stress over losing my job as the office manager at Tony's Construction and having to move out of my apartment in North Angel Canyon. It was always like him to brush me off, which is why even though I could make things easier and give him what he wants by taking him back, I don't.

I don't even like being here.

The shitty circumstances made me swallow my pride and call Joel for help. I didn't want to, but I had nowhere else to go. He only hassled me over not calling him sooner and told me he loved me still. He claimed that our breakup made him appreciate me more and that he'd do better. That it was our destiny to overcome the drama that split us up...

My stomach clenches at the thought. I can't think about it. I'm sick enough as it is. Joel's been generous, allowing me to sleep on the couch, rent-free. He's taken care of me, even when he didn't have to, but I can't imagine spending my life with him because he holds things over my head and makes me doubt myself.

It's one of the things that always starts an argument between us. I'm too stubborn for my own good—according to him. I wouldn't be in this situation if I'd accept his ring already. He claims he wants to take care of me, but I know it's not about that. I see the shit he does more clearly, no matter how nice I know he can be. Things could be worse. They have been. If only he was a dick all the time, I wouldn't feel so conflicted.

A soft knock sounds on the bathroom door, and Joel cracks the door open without waiting for me to respond. "I brought you some water, baby. You need to stay hydrated."

I bob my head and hold my arms out, silently asking for help. Setting the glass on the edge of the tub, Joel ignores my request and crosses his arms over his chest. He tightens his jaw and gives me a long once-over. His frown deepens like I'm the last person he wants to be with.

I prop myself up on my elbow and reach for the glass of water. "Can you please take me to Urgent Care? I don't think I can drive myself. I'm feeling worse."

"Because you're dehydrated. Come on. Drink." Joel points at the glass. "You'll feel better. I know the last week has been rough, but you can't let the stress get to you, baby. You'll get a call back for a job soon. I know it."

Maybe Joel's right. I'm sick because of the stress. He always said I overthink things.

My hand shakes as I bring it to my mouth, and I accidentally drop the glass. It cracks on the bathroom floor, spilling across the tiles. I scramble to pick up the pieces. Sharp pain swells across my thumb as I cut myself on the shard. Blood drips from my hand and splashes into the puddle soaking my pajama pants.

"Damn it, Raven! I swear to God I think you pull this bullshit just so you can live here and mooch off me while fucking around with other guys. You're taking advantage of my love for you, and I've had it! If I'm going to have to constantly take care of you, then you need to fucking take care of me how I want. Would it fucking kill you to give me a blowjob every now and then? It drives me crazy that you won't even sleep in my bed after everything I've done for you even though you threw my fucking ring in my face." Joel stomps on the broken glass with his boot, crushing it into tiny pieces. He throws a towel from the cupboard at me next. "Soak this up. I'll call Rob and see if he'll prescribe you some anti-nausea meds, and I'll pick them up at work."

I tuck my legs closer to me and grab my phone. "I can't wait that long. I'll just call a ride to take me to Urgent Care if you can't."

"With what fucking money?" Joel leans over and snatches my phone from me. "You're overreacting. You're going to be fine. Just clean up, and I'll get you another glass of water. Try not to ruin the bathroom even more."

Without waiting for my response, Joel exits and slams the door behind him. A bang sounds on the wall as he punches it, a sound I've become familiar with. I groan and shift, my body aching. I sweep the towel across the sopping water and drape my arms over the edge of the tub.

I close my eyes and say a silent prayer for strength. I don't know how much time passes by, but it feels like Joel has been gone forever. Long enough that I manage to take a few deep breaths without feeling like my insides want to escape me. Reaching for the tub faucet, I turn it on and pool a handful of water in my palm. I sip it slowly, dribbling it down my chin with the effort, but my stomach doesn't reject it.

I kind of hate that Joel might've been right. Maybe I am being dramatic and this is nothing serious. People get sick all the time...no. It's more. I know it is. The only one stressing me out is Joel and only when I feel like shit. Nothing makes sense.

I think about last night's dinner, wondering if maybe this really is food poisoning this time. Except I ate the same thing as Joel apart from the glass of wine where he drank whiskey.

A thought nags at me the more I think about every time I've been sick. He wouldn't do anything to hurt me, especially if he's trying to get back together, right? He brushes me off because he works in the medical field. He's always so calm, ready with some sort of diagnosis or assurance from his doctor best friend. It's not like he's making stuff up. He's a pharmacist at the same hospital and can ask a number of people for off-the-record advice.

Why don't I believe the thoughts, though?

Why am I questioning every kind gesture and focusing on his asshole attitude? How he berates me. How he just said he thinks I'm faking it to stay here, when in fact, right now, I have the urge to run. My gut knows something is wrong, and I've been ignoring it. But what can I do? My parents refuse to talk to me. My cousin Tamia won't call me back. I haven't spoken to my old friends in so long that I can't remember the last time.

"Fuck. You're overthinking. You're paranoid," I whisper to myself.

But what if I'm not?

Confronting Joel will only piss him off. He could kick me out, and then what? I'm broke. I have twenty bucks to my name after eating through my savings. I need it for gas money to go on my non-existent job interviews. It's been weeks since I've heard a call back.

I push the thoughts away and swallow my nerves, using the tub to get to my feet. My body trembles, and I shiver through my disgusting sweating, but I manage to stay on my feet. I'll just let Joel know he was right and apologize. Hopefully he'll drop the attitude. I just want to plop my ass on the couch and sleep the rest of the sickness off.

Cracking the bathroom door open, I peek into the hallway and spot the brand new crater in the wall. That's the fourth one in as many weeks that I'll have to fill and spackle because he won't. He'll say if I didn't piss him off all

14

the time, they wouldn't be there.

"Come on, man. It's for a couple of pills. I don't want to miss work," Joel murmurs, standing in the kitchen with his elbows on the counter. He sighs and rubs his hand across the back of his neck. "Yeah, yeah. I get it. No one will know. All that other stuff is just for fun. You and Ky should join us sometime. Makes for a helluva good time with Raven. She's been so tense lately and they chill us both out." He laughs. "You're a saint, bro. I appreciate it. I can't be sick if I'm going to take care of my girl. She's going to take my ring back soon. I know it."

I blink at his words, my body tensing. What the hell is Joel talking about?

He chuckles again. "Shit, yeah. I'll try that next time. The hangovers make her useless, but she doesn't care. She knows she can always count on me as long as she doesn't pull that trying to move out shit again."

My legs wobble the longer I clutch onto the hallway wall for support. I can't hear Rob's side of the conversation, but the trash Joel spews shocks the hell out of me. He makes it sound like we get high and drunk together or something. And he needs pills for himself? He was supposed to get me anti-nausea meds. What the actual fuck?

"Right," Joel says, stretching his back with a groan, drawing my attention back to his conversation with Rob. "I'm telling you. It works. Try it. You'll never have to worry about things like the shit Raven put me through. Train Ky now, man. If she doesn't follow your lead, then find another woman who will. It's too fucking exhausting. I didn't waste two damn years of my life to just let her think she can leave me." Anger deepens his voice. "I'm not putting up with that. She'll learn."

Joel stands in silence, clutching the phone. The murmur of Rob's voice trickles through the quiet. I hold my breath and listen.

"...Jesus, Joel. Are you drunk?" Rob asks, though I miss the other part of what he tells Joel.

Joel barks a laugh. "Fuck. That obvious? Sorry, man. Raven's been a pain in my ass all night. Needy and coming down. You know how it is."

"Just be careful what you say. People don't know you guys like I do."

"You're right, Rob. They don't." Joel sighs. "Anyway, send the script to Bell's this time. Anna's working and won't give us any problems like Rita would." Rita's the Chief Pharmacist at the hospital he works at. As for Anna? I have no idea. "I have to get back to Raven before she starts screaming for me to hurry back to bed. She gets lazy and acts like a fucking useless bitch when she's annoyed."

With a laugh, Joel sets his phone on the counter and turns toward the cupboard, grabbing a bowl from the shelf. My heartbeat pounds in my ears, and I try to process his

16

conversation with Rob. Anger burns through me, repeating all the lies Joel told. I knew he had a temper, but he made it sound as if I'm some needy, worthless bitch who is only tolerable high. I haven't done any recreational drugs in years, since my early twenties. The most medicine I even take is for a headache...

I scratch my nails into the wall, staring in shock as Joel pops open an orange pill bottle from inside an oatmeal container on the top shelf out of my reach without a stool. He smashes a pill on the counter before adding it to the bowl and mixing applesauce from a pouch of snacks he keeps for his niece when she comes over.

Scooping up the bowl, he spins on his feet. I can't move out of his view fast enough, and he narrows his eyes in annoyance.

"What are you doing up? I don't want you fucking puking on the carpet," Joel says, striding closer.

Panic squeezes my chest, my mind whirling. "I won't. I'm feeling better. You were right. It must've just been stress. Maybe something I ate. I'm going to rest on the couch."

"The hell you are, Raven. You're disgusting. I don't want your filth on my furniture," he snaps, stopping a foot away to tower over me. "Now take this and get your ass in the shower." Shoving the bowl at me, he pushes it against my stomach. "If you can keep this down, then maybe I'll let you sleep on the floor next to the couch."

I stare down at the applesauce. "I'm okay. I swear."

Glowering, he grabs me by the shoulder and digs his fingers into my skin. I wince in pain, trying to pull back, but he only squeezes tighter. "Don't be a fucking pain and eat it. It's what Rob said to do. You want to feel better, don't you?"

I keep my gaze locked on the bowl, my body shaking under his heated glower penetrating my forehead. Tears burn my eyes. He sounds so angry like this is all my fault, but I know it's his. Everything starts connecting together in my mind. How could I be so foolish?

Joel shakes me. "Raven, don't you?" he repeats.

Still, I can't get myself to look up or respond.

Grabbing me by the back of the head, Joel yanks my hair, forcing my gaze up to his. I drop the bowl of applesauce on the floor, and it splashes all over our feet. Fear seizes my chest with his rage. I don't know what comes over me, but I swing my hand out and slap him.

"You've been drugging m-me," I say, stumbling away from him.

His surprise over my slap only makes him hesitate for a moment.

I scream and try to get out of the way, grabbing onto the torch lamp just outside the hallway and in the living room to knock it in his path. "Stay the fuck back, Joel! If you don't, I'll go to the police. I'll tell them what you've done."

I regret my threat immediately. I should've known better than to piss him off even more.

Lunging at me, Joel grabs the front of my shirt and forces me against the wall. I squeeze my eyes shut as he swings in anger, punching me in the cheek. Pain swells through me, and I lose my footing, my body wanting nothing more than to cower.

"Don't you ever fucking threaten me, you crazy bitch," Joel mutters, a deep guttural noise escaping his mouth. "I'm trying to take care of your damn ass. Whatever the fuck you think you saw is in your damn head. You're sick. Seeing things."

Tears leak down my cheeks, and I heave a shuddering breath. "You're r-right." I can barely get the words out. "I'm sorry."

The fury in his brown gaze diminishes, and a cocky-bastard smile tugs at the corner of his lips. If I know one thing about Joel, it's that he always thinks he's in the right. I don't even care if he isn't. All I want is for him to back up and leave me alone. I want the chance to get up and run. He's fucking drugging me. Making me sick. I saw him do it with my own eyes.

But if I leave...

I can't stay here. I can't.

I slowly shift to my elbow. "I'm sorry," I repeat. "I'm just feeling sick. It's making me crazy."

Grabbing my hand, Joel yanks me off the floor and sets me on my feet. He drags his gaze over my body like he's looking for another part of my body he can hurt next. I can only imagine what he'll do later.

Joel touches my cheek, pushing my hair behind my ear. It takes everything in me not to recoil from his touch. "I'm only trying to take care of you, baby. You know that I love you. I want to marry you for fuck's sake. I don't know why you always have to give me a hard time. Have you been talking to Tamia again? She putting thoughts in your head?"

My bottom lip trembles uncontrollably. "No."

His eyes narrow. "You're lying. I saw her calling your phone."

My heart beats in overdrive, his silent glower daring me to argue. I can almost feel the sting of his berating and the pain of his fist all over again. It twists my insides and shadows my vision. Panic steals my breath. I feel like I'm going to die at any second. If Joel doesn't kill me, then my heart still might, exploding to escape this misery.

"Raven," Joel grumbles.

My stomach heaves, and I puke all over the front of his shirt.

Baring his teeth, Joel hollers and swings his fist, hitting the wall inches away from my head. I panic and shove him back, twisting out of his hold on my shirt, not even caring that he yanks it off in his attempt to catch me. I bolt toward the door in my bra and sweatpants, my feet bare and my black hair an out of control mess. Joel hollers behind me, but it only pushes me to run harder, my feet slapping the cement pathway as I head to the parking lot.

"Raven, damn it! Get back here!" Joel yells from behind me.

I give up on running to the parking lot and instead cut between the last two buildings in our apartment complex and scream for help. I rush to the door of the apartment on the right, which is the only one lit up inside.

I raise my hand to bang on the wood, but a hand slaps over my mouth and another one hooks around my waist, yanking me back. Joel shoves me to the grass and kicks me so hard in the stomach that I can't even cry out in pain. Shadows crowd my vision as I open and close my mouth, trying to suck in air that doesn't come.

I try to push up, to fight, to do anything to protect myself from Joel. He's too fast and livid, kicking me again until I roll on my back. I lie defenseless on the ground. Joel towers over me and punches me in the face again. And then again.

Blood pours from my nose and my split lips, dripping down my cheeks. It pools in my ears and stains my hair. I close my eyes, cutting off my view of Joel's scowling face, his rage turning him more into a monster than I ever knew possible.

I pray for the pain to stop.

I pray for a quick death.

My life is over, and there is nothing more I can do.

Joel beats the fight out of me.

"Hey, asshole! What the fuck are you doing?" a rich, smooth voice shouts. "You can't do that here."

Joel's hand loosens from around my throat, and he shoves himself off. "You better not fucking say it was me, Raven," he mutters in my ear. "I will kill you."

"Hey!" a man shouts. "You can't just leave her."

My mind refuses to process what's going on.

All I can do is stare up at a strange man as he looks down at me.

His eyes glow red.

2

RAVEN

AS THE WORLD BURNS

"THAT FUCKER. I'M going to rip out his bowels and feed them to him." A man peers down at me like I'm the grossest thing he's ever seen. Scruff covers his sharp jaw, and it's hard to get a good look at him because of the broken lamp-post. "What a damn mess. Shitty mortals."

The glowing red of his eyes flickers and dims, turning into an indistinguishable shade I can't seem to recognize.

They're just dark, shadowed by the low light of the world around me. Fisting his hands, he flexes his biceps, and the colorful lion tattoo on his arm looks as if it comes alive with his movements.

"Save it for later, Kase. We don't have time for that. They made too much of a commotion." Another man steps to my other side and peers down at me. "If a savior doesn't show up, then some fucking flesh bag with a hero-complex will."

Emerald green eyes pop against his tan skin and ruggedly handsome features, obscured somewhat by his beard. His hair is dark like mine in the lighting from the orange glow of one of the porchlights flicking on, but I think it might be more brown than black with warm undertones instead of the midnight shade that makes my hair look bluish in the sun.

"Then what do you think we should do, Dante?" Kase asks, locking his gaze to mine. His eyes glow red again, and I wonder if what I'm seeing is from head trauma. Because fuck. It's unnatural.

I try to shift under Kase's scrutiny. His stare burns over me but leaves me cold. His skin ripples and he flares his nostrils, inhaling a deep breath. He drinks me in from my head to my bare feet and has the nerve to nudge me with his boot. Who is he? Am I that injured that I'm seeing things?

Ice floods through me at the thought, the intensity of

his eyes making my skin crawl. My whole body screams that these men are dangerous, and I should fear for my life. If I were on my feet, I'd get the hell away from them. But I can't move. My body hurts too badly. My vision blurs no matter how much I blink. I realize how wrong I was, thinking I was dying before. I'm certain I'm dying now. It's hard to even breathe.

Squatting down, Dante hovers his hand over my bra like he's contemplating touching my boobs. But he doesn't. Heat radiates from his palm, sending a strange glow illuminating from his hand. "She's a pretty broken soul, but pure. Too pure. If I didn't know any better, I'd think she was assigned a savior, but she's not blessed. Only a pathetic mess probably too boring to do anything fun or naughty. Useless to us. We should just let her die."

"Die?" I open and close my mouth, trying to process his comment. What does he even mean? "No. Please, help me," I whisper, tasting the tangy metallic grossness of my blood on my lips. "Please."

Dante doesn't react to my words, training his gaze on Kase.

"We should move her. It could take a couple hours for her to drop dead," Kase says, nudging my ribcage with his boot. He ignores my pleas, despite keeping his eyes on mine. "The fucker could've at least put her out of her misery."

A whimper escapes my mouth. Who the fuck are these monsters?

"There's a dumpster around the corner. Drop her inside, and I'll go make sure everyone else in the complex minds their damn business." Dante swipes his finger over my cheek, rubbing his finger over my blood, sweat, and tears. He pops it in his mouth and sucks on it. "Throw some of the trash on her. She's disgusting enough that she'll fit right in."

"No," I whisper, their conversation igniting full-blown panic in my chest. I thought these men were here to help me, not finish what Joel started. "Please. I don't want to die."

Two hot arms sink beneath me, and I gasp as pain shocks me to my soul. Kase lifts me up and dangles me in his arms a foot away. Every inch of me screams in anguish. Sobbing, I cry out, my voice finally echoing through the cool night with my desperation. What have I done so badly in my life to deserve this? Who are these monstrous men, and why are they doing this?

"God, please. Help me. Save me." I sputter and hiccup, my panic giving me the strength to fight as best as I can, even if I can't move a muscle. "Please, Lord. I can't die like this."

Kase stiffens, his eyes blasting with red light. His nostrils flare and hot fingers sear my lips as Dante slaps his hand across my mouth from behind. Heat radiates from their bodies like they sandwich me between two furnaces, but it doesn't burn me. It helps ease the cold ice shivering through my body. Now that they're so close, I can smell the warm fragrances of burning pine needles, leather, the woodiness of vetiver, and something sweetly gourmand like vanilla. I can't distinguish and separate the array of scents between them, but they're seductively intoxicating to my senses.

"What the fuck? Are you praying?" Dante asks, his hot breath tickling the hair around my ear. "That's not going to change anything."

It's my turn to ignore them. "God, please. Give me the strength. I need your protection," I mumble against Dante's hand. Whoever—whatever—they are, obviously don't like me begging God for help. It makes me want to rebel and yell louder, fighting with my voice instead of my broken body.

"Fuck. Make her stop." Kase shakes me with a growl. His hands pinch my skin, but instead of hurting me, it distracts me from my aching chest. "You're just pissing us off, broken soul. Keep that up, and I'll shove something in your mouth to shut you up. You won't like what I choose."

"Please, God. I'll do anything. Don't let it end like this," I say, continuing to pray. Because fuck these psycho assholes. I might not have a strong relationship with the

Almighty, but I have faith, and right now, it's all I have left.

Kase's face sharpens with anger, and the heat of his body intensifies. Red light flickers in his gaze, casting an eerie glow over his features. He looks evil, demonic. Scarier than Joel ever could look. I tremble uncontrollably, terror snaking around my body, watching as his features shift. I've never seen anything like it. It prods at my human rationale. This can't be possible. The guy can't be changing in front of me with the tips of three horns breaking through the skin on his forehead.

"Oh, fuck," I squeak, my body obeying my command to fight. My adrenaline suppresses the pain, leaving me breathless, but a new, more intense agony bursts through me right to my core. I thrash and buck my body. "Help! Please, help me!"

"Shit. She's fucking determined, isn't she?" Dante drags me away from Kase and hugs me to him, pressing his chiseled chest to my back. His skin warms me even more, sending beads of sweat dripping from my hairline. His smoky, sweet scent engulfs me, and he tightens his grip on me, waiting until I lose some of my fight.

It doesn't take long.

Fatigue and exhaustion leave me bleary-eyed and slack in his arms. The spark of hope I cling to snuffs out with the rest of my will to fight.

"That's a good girl," Dante murmurs, loosening his

fingers in my hair. "Don't fight the inevitable."

Inevitable? Like his comment gives me a second wind, I thrash again, breaking from his hold. He drops me, and I land on my knees and fall over from unbearable agony. I crawl forward, each burst of pain reminding me that I'm still alive. I still have a chance. There is no fucking way I'm letting them do this for Joel. If I die, he deserves to rot in prison.

"Please, God. Help me," I whisper, summoning energy from my adrenaline rush. "Give me the strength. I'll do anything."

"That's enough fucking praying. The Higher Power doesn't barter with mortals." Footsteps clomp toward me as Dante closes the space. Swearing under his breath, he steps in front of me and blocks my path.

I swing my arm out, socking him in the shin but it does nothing to stop him. Snatching me from the ground, he carries me toward the end of the building, purposefully swinging me back and forth. A smile crosses his face and he hums under his breath, enjoying playing around with me like I'm just weak, defenseless prey to his vicious predatory side. Even his scent messes with my fear instincts, and I can't stop thinking about the warm fragrances engulfing me or the strength of this monstrous man's arms. His diamond-shaped pupils hypnotize me until he breaks his gaze and looks past me.

"That's a good, pretty soul. Just relax. It'll be over soon," he murmurs, his alluring voice like a soft melody in my ears.

But then two fangs peek from beneath his full top lip like a snake's, shocking me out of my hazy mind. Panic explodes through my essence, and I can't stop envisioning how awful it'll be to die alone in a dumpster. How Joel probably packs his bags right now, getting ready to leave. This is so messed up. How is it that men like him get away with horrible acts such as this? I don't understand.

This is it. I know it. I feel it deep in my soul.

"Please, you don't have to do this," I beg, my body more desperate than ever to survive. If praying to God doesn't work, then I'll resort to begging and bartering with this beastly psycho. He's obviously annoyed that he has to clean up Joel's mess. Maybe I can use it to my advantage. "I'll do anything. I don't want to die. Please. I know you're not human. There has to be something you can do. I can't die in a dumpster. Fucking Joel can't get away with this. Please."

Dante's footsteps slow with my words, and he stops a dozen feet away from an overflowing dumpster. I release a soft breath, my heart pounding in my ears. "Fuck. Fucking flesh bags and their trash."

And like that, my hope crushes into a million pieces. I'm not even sure he was listening to me, more concerned about how inconvenient the tenants of the complex make it for him to throw me away like garbage. Who knew a heaping, smelly pile of trash would be a small miracle to me?

Dante lets go of me, and I hit my ass on the ground, pain radiating through my body. Striding away, he flips the lid up and starts throwing trash and garbage bags on the ground. I don't waste more than a second watching him. Instead, I find my will to live and crawl away on my hands and knees. I can make it to a neighbor's. I just have to keep moving.

I grind my teeth. "God, pleas—"

Two hot hands rip me from the ground, and I scream and flail, trying to make as much commotion as I can. These monsters are crazy to think they can just leave me in a fucking dumpster. I'm not ready to die.

"Let me go, you fucking asshole! You can't just throw me in a dumpster!" I buck and slap Kase's face over and over again without getting a reaction from him.

"Fuck, Dante. She's got too much fight. I don't think she'll stay in the dumpster. We can't leave her here," Kase says, flipping me onto his shoulder. It's like they have some special ability that allows them to ignore me, and it's really starting to piss me off. "We'll take her home and get her out of sight until we figure out how we should proceed."

Oh no.

Hell no.

"Help!" I scream, pounding my fists on Kase's back. "Help!"

Fingers lock into my hair, yanking my head up. Dante bends my neck to meet his startling green gaze. His eyes do this weird, filmy second eyelid blinking thing, and his pupils morph into diamonds again. Slipping his tongue between his lips, he shows off two silver barbells on each side...and then his tongue splits into a fork and flicks at me with a hiss, grazing my cheek. I cringe at the freaky sensation and try to recoil before he does it again.

"Pretty soul, are you afraid of me?" he asks, the strange hissing noise coming from his mouth again. I don't know what should freak me out more: the fact that he turns more animalistic by the second or that I'm not as scared as I should be. The dissipation of my fear surprises me. He obviously desires for me to scream and cry in fear but I don't.

My mouth slackens the longer he stares at me, my heartbeat slowing. A strange sensation buzzes across my skin, numbing me. I can't move my limbs or anything like I'm trapped in his glowing green stare.

"Tell me," he says, leaning closer. His warm breath tickles me with his command.

My mind whirls with a dozen thoughts. Why am I not terrified? My heart should feel as if it wants to explode from my chest. But the only thing I feel is the inviting electricity between us. I can't take my eyes from his, the darkness in the depths far more intense than the glowing green of his irises. He's strikingly handsome—too handsome—even in this weird half-beast state. It's enough that the vain part of me can overlook his monstrous features trying to frighten me.

His brows furrow at my lack of response, and he gets so close that I can feel the soft touch of his tongue caress my lip but not in a sexual way. It's almost like he's sensing me in the same way some animals do.

"Tell me you're afraid of me, broken soul," Dante repeats, revealing his two long fangs from beneath his lips.

It snaps me out of the dizzying haze entrancing me. "No!"

I try to thrash on Kase's shoulder to throw myself off, but a weird-ass rope slides out from beneath his jacket and wraps around me, restraining me to him. Fuck. It literally might be an ass rope and not just extremely weird. I don't know whether to laugh or cry. So I shriek and struggle.

Dante tears his shirt sleeve off like the cotton is made of tissue paper and shoves it in my mouth, silencing my screams. "Fuck, we gotta get her inside. She can resist my influence," Dante says, releasing another hiss.

The two men stride back into the complex without glancing around. Nothing I do affects them or gets them to let me go. Panic turns me wild, and I buck and thrash, knowing if they take me inside their apartment, I'm going to die. They'll kill me and finish what Joel couldn't.

Kase kicks an apartment door open, sending it clattering against the wall. Warm air engulfs me along with the collection of fragrances lingering on the two of them. It's their apartment for sure. I try to look around, but Dante blocks my view, and I can only stare at the dark wood of the floors far nicer than the ones in Joel's place.

"Take her to the bathroom. Make her get cleaned up. I'm summoning Lucian." The strange black rope uncurls from my body, and Kase flips me into Dante's arms. "Be quick. The saviors might've picked up on her calls if she is what I think she is. I need him to verify."

Verify? I use my tongue to push the balled up fabric from my mouth, spitting it on the floor. "I'm no o-one and n-nothing." I wish my voice would stop stuttering and cracking. "Please, let me leave. I won't tell anyone. I won't ever come back. Please. I don't understand what you want from me."

"We might not want anything, so shut up before I make you. It'll be far less pleasant than a gag," Kase says, pointing his finger at me. His eyes glow red with his scowl and he turns to Dante. "Go now. We need to hurry. Our window to put things in place shrinks by the second."

Tears burn my eyes. "Just let me go. Please." I've never begged someone so much in my life, not even Joel when I crawled back to him in desperation.

But begging doesn't work. Neither does praying.

Without arguing, Dante stomps his way down the hall and to the first door on the left. I spot a display case of strange weapons and trinkets at the end of the hall situated between two open doors that face each other. Knocking open the cracked bathroom door with his knuckles, he carries me into the bathroom and drops me in the tub. I flail, trying to orient myself to what's happening. Going from his arms and into the bath freaks me out even more.

I sit up and grab ahold of the washcloth rack on the wall, trying to pull myself up. Dante latches his fingers to my shoulder and stops me from getting to my feet, touching his hot fingers to the center of my back over my bra clasp.

"Hold still," he commands, hissing under his breath. "Don't make me burn it off you."

I stiffen as he goes to unhook my bra and swing my hand, slapping him across the face. "Don't you dare fucking touch me!" I scream, fisting my hand to fight like hell against him. I don't care if he's a foot taller and twice as heavy. I've had e-fucking-nough of assholes treating me any way they want.

Dante groans and takes a step back, raising his hands in surrender. "You think I want to touch your filth? That I want to fuck you in this tub? You look like that nasty thing might be the only one you have. You should appreciate my thoughtfulness. I was trying to help you."

"Help me by taking off my damn bra? You kidnapped me, you psycho!" I heave a few breaths, angry tears branding hot streaks through the sticky blood staining my cheeks. "Just stay away. I didn't ask for your help. I asked you to let me go."

Dante curls his fingers into his palms at his side, his muscles rippling with the movements. It's the first time I notice the half-sleeve tattoo of snakeskin decorating his bicep on the side with his missing sleeve. I can't take my eyes away from the mesmerizing pattern, sheening with gold on the scales, as he glowers at me in silence like he doesn't know what to do besides gawk at me.

"Dante, please. You said it yourself that you were pissed that Joel just abandoned me to die and you didn't want to clean up his mess. You don't have to. I can handle myself," I say, keeping my voice low to keep it from shaking. "Please. You can just forget about me."

He grumbles under his breath. "Why do mortals always beg when they think they're going to die? It's pointless. If you fucking say please one more time—"

The world rumbles around us, the strange vibrations dancing across my skin. It kicks my heart into overdrive. I grab a hold of the rack again and hoist myself up, taking advantage of the fact that Dante shifts to look at the door.

Scooping up the bottle of shampoo, I clutch it in my hand. It's not exactly my weapon of choice, not that I know how to use anything in particular, but I've been using what I've been given my whole life. I can't exactly kill a monster with tea-tree and mint soap, but damn it if I won't try anyway.

The soft rumbling shaking the room turns more frantic, and I nearly lose my footing at the floor quaking. Dante still keeps his back toward me, staring at the door, and I half expect him to leave.

Untwisting the cap, I squeeze shampoo into my palm and whisper a quiet prayer that this works.

Dante jerks around like he can sense what I'm about to do. I scream and chuck the bottle of shampoo at him, clocking him in the chest. It does nothing to stop him from rushing me. I try to swing my hand out to slap the soap into his eyes, but he catches my wrist. Yanking my hand over my head, he forces me to wipe the shampoo on my hair before flicking on the faucet. Cool water sprays on me, shocking me. I scream and fight, slipping on the soap I spilled everywhere. I land on my back, the air knocking from my lungs.

Fangs flash from beneath Dante's lips and he strikes his hand forward, lacing it around my neck to pin me to the tub. "Get cleaned up, pretty broken soul. You can wear the robe hanging on the door. If you pray again, it will be the last thing you ever do, and not one fucking savior will hear. Got it?"

My bottom lip trembles as I nod my head.

"Good. Now be an obedient little mortal, and you might get something you want in return. Lucian is coming. He will decide your worth." Dante releases my neck and adjusts the water temperature, changing it from cold to warm with a flick of his fingers. Turning his back on me, he exits the bathroom and slams the door shut behind him.

I lie frozen and in shock, my whole body begging me to rest and catch my breath. Because if I get up now, I'll fall back down. My adrenaline washes away with the blood, tears, and sweat, leaving me a sobbing mess. I don't understand what's going on and who these men are—what these men are—but I'm not even sure I want to know. I just want to leave and spend my last twenty bucks getting anywhere else in the world.

If a deep, guttural roar didn't filter through the door, I would. The lights flicker and the awful smell of something rotting wafts through the air. Strange black smoke trickles from beneath the door. I panic at the sight and force myself to get up. There's a fire somewhere, and I didn't go through complete hell just to die in this dark bathroom with two psycho monsters plotting my imprisonment.

Without drying off, I rush to the door and press my hand to the wood, feeling the warmth radiating from the other side. I run the basic survival skills my parents instilled in me growing up and grab a towel, wetting it in the sink. I cover my mouth and nose with it and use the other end to cover the doorknob in case it's hot.

I try to twist it open, but nothing happens.

The smoke grows thicker in the bathroom, and an orange and red glow fills the room.

"Help!" I yell, pounding my fist on the door. "Help!"

No one responds.

I'm locked in.

There's nothing I can do as I wait for my world to burn.

3

RAVEN

MONSTERS AND MADNESS

I COUGH AND spit into the towel, trying to rid my lungs of the billowing smoke. Heat radiates from the door, and I scramble back, climbing into the tub. Twisting the knob on the faucet, I adjust the temperature as if a cold shower could possibly save me. Even if the fire doesn't eat away this room, the smoke will suffocate me.

I lower myself down and clutch the drenched towel,

covering up with it the best I can. I've always had a fear of burning alive after one of my childhood next-door neighbor's houses burned down, but I never truly believed something like that would happen to me. I was just afraid it would.

And now it is.

Closing my eyes, I lace my fingers together and tilt my head toward the ceiling. I've never prayed more than I have tonight in my life, and a part of me fears speaking to the universe, hoping that some almighty power might listen and help me, because of Dante's threat. He's made it quite clear that he's not human. Even if he hadn't, a deep-seated part of me knows that the two guys are far from mortals. What they are exactly? I have no idea. I doubt I'll ever find out.

An explosion shakes the room, and I scream and clutch onto the tub as the walls around me split and open. Fire eats away the walls of this small bathroom and drifts across the ceiling. Smoke and red and orange light fill the room and I kick my heel on the drain plug, pushing it into place. Water begins to fill the tub. Scooping it into my hands, I fling it at the walls, hoping to put the flames out before they reach me. My chest tightens with each of my breaths, and I try my best to breathe slowly instead of gulping for air that'll only be tainted by the smoldering room.

I blink through the haze, staring at the fiery ceiling. Soft chants call my name, inviting me to join them in the burning world appearing above my head but looking as if I look down on it instead of looking up. It's disorienting and terrifying. I can't process what I'm seeing. Fear clenches my heart, and I squeeze my eyes shut, so I can pretend to be somewhere else. I'm hallucinating, seeing the vision of the damned and burning. The smoke's getting to my head.

"Hurry up, pretty soul," Dante snaps, the door creaking open. "You should've been done by now."

I bolt upright and splash water everywhere, the bathroom empty and clean with no signs of fire or smoke anywhere. What the fucking shit? I scramble to pull myself from the blood-tinted tub and roll over the edge, crashing to the floor. I gasp and feel across the floor, the heat that was clinging to the air nothing more than the steamy warmth of the still-running shower.

"Fuck," he says, clomping into the bathroom. Stepping over me, Dante turns the shower off and pulls the plug, draining the tub before more water cascades over the edge. "What the hell are you doing? We don't have time for you to take a damn spa day."

"There was a fire," I say, groaning with my confusion, my thoughts refusing to let me think clearly. "I was going to burn alive. Why did you lock me in here?"

Dante's brows lower on his forehead, and he combs his hand through his dark hair. "You saw the gateway." Surprise lines his words. He remains expressionless as he studies me

42

like I will confirm he's right about whatever he's referring to.

"The what?" I ask, shifting onto my side. I struggle not to give in to my body's need to rest. I'm so achingly tired.

He tightens his jaw and shakes his head. A muffled rumbling noise sounds through the door. It trembles on its hinges, jerking Dante's attention away from me. "Never mind about that. It's not imperative information for you to know." Swiveling, he motions to the robe hanging on a hook. "Get out of those wet clothes and put on the robe. Lucian is ready to see you."

"Lucian?" The name sounds harsh coming from my lips. He keeps mentioning this man like he might be his boss or something. "I'm not seeing anyone."

"You don't have a choice, pretty soul. If you don't, I'll carry you out like the unruly mortal you are. Lucian likes that, but only because the disobedient are that much more fun to break," Dante says gruffly, grabbing a towel from the cabinet. He throws it in my face, not giving me a chance to take it from him. "Now don't make me help you get un-dressed. You made it clear you don't like that right now."

Right now? He's delusional to imply that I might even-tually like it. Because fuck.

I shudder at the thought, imagining him transforming into his monster façade. This guy is crazy. Psychotic. He's out of his damn mind if he thinks he can just drag me out of here and force me to meet—

Dante steps forward and looms over me, his arms folded across his broad chest. He starts to kneel, staring at my boobs with more intensity than any man has ever looked at my chest. But it's not sexual. It's in determination. He plans to follow through with his threat, reaching his hand out, ready to rip my bra right off me. He stops short, his fingers open and waiting to strike like a snake if I give him an opening.

I whack his muscular arm away and wince. The bone-hard denseness of his bulging bicep is like hitting my hand against a concrete wall. The pain doesn't stop me from doing it again. I will not make anything easy for this asshole, but especially when it comes to this twisted game of take my clothes off or else.

"Don't you dare touch me!" I yell, raising my voice even louder. Maybe the neighbors sharing a wall will hear and call the cops. If not out of concern, then hopefully out of annoyance. "I swear to God, Dante. You will regret it!"

His whole body shudders, and he bares two sharp fangs with a hiss. "Then fucking obey me and get changed! Now!"

Hot air blows in my face with his holler, and I scramble back, hitting the side of the tub. Fear stops me from arguing. I slowly reach behind me and unhook my bra but don't pull it off my boobs. Dante only watches me until he's sure I'll do as he says before he spins on his feet and strides out of the bathroom. I swallow the pain and exhaustion inside me and force myself back to my feet. I keep my bra firmly in place with my hand, shuffling across the room to grab the robe hanging behind the door.

Voices drift into the bathroom from the living room, and I wonder which of the bedrooms has the backdoor slider. The layout is different than Joel's place, two bedrooms instead of one, but every ground level apartment has a patio. If I can pick the right room, I can make a run for it.

I hook my bra back on and shrug into the robe to cover up. The last thing I want is for another man to see me in this state of undress, and if I don't make it, I know whoever this fucker Lucian is will get a look as well.

Gathering my nerves, I focus on the low voices coming to me from down the hall. The gross rotting smell still permeates the air, consuming the warm scents of Dante and Kase, and I pinch my nose, praying I don't gag and make noise. I peek my head from the bathroom and get a clear view of the living room from my spot. My mouth dries at the sight of a towering beast with a sleek, shiny red body and a long black tail. Three thick horns protrude from its forehead, jutting out several inches in a crown. It stalks forward on two legs like a human. The unsettling sight worsens as I watch its long claws penetrate the wood floors, sending flames shooting around each talon. And that's not the freakiest part. The monster doesn't leave a single mark behind.

No scratches or anything. It makes me question reality.

This can't possibly be real. Maybe I'll wake up at any second, hungover and tripping on whatever pills Joel had been drugging me with. If I didn't bang my elbow on the doorframe, sending a jolt of pain ricocheting through me, I might've just attempted to run to see what would happen.

I cover my mouth with my hand, muffling any noise I can make. "Oh, God. Help me. Please let this be a bad trip."

I immediately regret the prayer, hearing the vicious roar of the beast rumble through the air. Instead of retreating back into the bathroom to lock myself in, I rush toward the end of the hall and the bedrooms. I whip my head from one to the other, spotting the slider in the one on the left.

I bolt into it and slam the door closed, turning the tiny lock. It's no deadbolt, but I don't think it matters. There is no way the door will keep a determined beast of that monstrous size out, but it will hopefully slow it down. Rushing across the room, I grab a desk chair and roll it towards the door, using it to block my path. I fling the blinds open, ripping a few down in the process. My heart hammers against my ribcage, and I flick the lock open on the slider, gasping as cool air engulfs me. I can't believe I'm going to make it...or not.

An arm blocks my exit, stopping me from running outside. How the fuck did this asshole know what I would do?

Has he been waiting for me to try to escape?

"Where do you think you're going, angel-girl?" Kase's hulking form startles me, and I trip backwards and fall onto the bed. He steps through the back slider and closes it behind him, slowly shaking his head in annoyance. Narrowing his eyes on me, he strolls closer, clicking his tongue like I'm some sort of disobedient pet needing correction.

I grab the pillow and throw it at him, trying to get him to stay the hell away from me. He looks even more determined to grab at me than Dante was to rip my bra off. It strikes a nerve, his handsome features leering like he hungers to punish me. A psycho like him shouldn't be so attractive. It makes it harder to see him as a threat. It's in this moment that I understand just a little how some women can fall for serial killers. Because he looks so damn hot, it makes me hope a little bit that maybe I'll be different and not his victim. Maybe he'll be the type to kill for the sake of love like some psychotic romance...fuck. I need to take a long look at my taste in men—if I can even call him that.

"You shouldn't stare at me on my bed like that. Don't you know I'm a devil and can sense your darkest desires?" he says, mapping his gaze over my body. "You want me even though I scare you. Isn't that right?"

Shit. His words prod at my human rationale, reminding me that he might be hot, but I'm not an exception to his brand of torment. If I were, he wouldn't push me. He wouldn't tease and taunt me. He wouldn't look ready to climb into bed with me and pin me down...

I'm so fucking twisted. My vagina clenches in anticipation, loving the idea of being beneath him.

"We'll have time to discover how dark you truly can be soon enough, but for now, it's time to meet Lucian." Kase holds his hand out. "Be a naughty girl. I dare you."

I spot a weird curved blade on the nightstand and reach for it, holding it out in front of me protectively. Did I take him up on his dare? Fuck yeah, I did. But what exactly am I going to do? Can I brave stabbing him? I guess I'll find out. "I don't want to hurt you, but I will. You can't keep me here."

Kase surprises me with a bellow of a laugh, his broad shoulders shaking as if I've said the funniest thing he's ever heard. "Hurt me? You think that's a threat, angel-girl?"

He's trying to get to me. I know it.

I swing the blade at him, expecting him to jump out of the way. He remains stiffly in place, staring down as the blade slices across his shirt. The fabric droops with the gaping hole I leave behind, showing off his tight six-pack and the edge of some sort of black tattoo hugging his side. Before I can react, Kase lunges at me and grabs my hand gripping the blade. I flinch away, shielding my head and throat, waiting for him to rip the weapon from my fingers. I expect for agony to burn through me with his stab, but he doesn't hurt me.

Instead, he bends my arm and forces me to shove the blade right into his gut. I screech as it sinks in and his blood pours down and soaks the fabric of the robe. A cocky smile lights up his features as he lets my hand go. I automatically yank the blade out and drop it on the bed next to me.

I open my mouth to scream, but Kase covers my lips with his hand and leans in. His warm breath tickles my skin as we breathe in the same space. The intoxicating scent of woody vetiver and warm vanilla overpowers my senses, and I can't stop inhaling shallow breaths through my nose. My emotions wage a war with my insides. A part of me fears his all-consuming presence, but another weaker, whispering part of me begs me to remain calm. That the darkness rolling over me is from Joel, and while this monstrous man has scared me with his threats, he hasn't actually hurt me.

Screw that rationale. Just because he hasn't done anything yet doesn't mean he won't. It's taken Joel years to show this violent side of him. I talked myself out of the possibility with him too, and look where it has left me.

I blink my eyes a dozen times, trying to stop the tears from spilling. This is so fucked up. What is wrong with me? I know it's crazy to rationalize any of this, but it's like a part of me doesn't care. A part of me wants to ignore the fact that a terrifying creature waits in the living room and that Kase and Dante aren't human. They can't be.

Tears splash my cheeks as my wild, hurricane of emotions wreak havoc inside me. It doesn't even matter what I think about this situation because nothing will change. The fight in me dwindles the longer Kase stares at me in silence, like he knows if he doesn't do anything, my body will accept that he's somehow not a threat and I won't fight back. And then he'll get me.

Bringing his hand up to my cheek, Kase gently smears away my tears with the pad of his thumb. "Fighting is pointless," he says, stroking his warm thumb across my other cheek. Damn. I was right. "So is praying and trying to escape. Finders keepers, pretty angel-girl. You belong to Lucian now."

My lip quivers with his words, and I think of a thousand horrible scenarios about what his comment could possibly mean. I don't know what's worse. Dying in a dumpster or being what sounds like a slave to a monster. With dying, at least there would be some sort of reprieve from this screwy world. But with being someone's slave? There's a chance I can escape and fight back. I sniffle and close my eyes, wanting to shut out the world. Either option doesn't work for me, but what else am I supposed to do?

"I won't ask you to be a good girl, because that's not my thing, but you really need to fucking stop with this shit. You're not going to die yet, and the only thing you should be afraid of is what will happen if you try to escape," Kase says, easing away from me. He pats the top of my head like a pet. "We didn't go through all this trouble tonight just to see you slip from our fingers. You are a tricky soul. It took some prodding to distinguish what you were. I bet you don't even know, do you? Did the asshole? Where has the bastard mortal been keeping you? I haven't seen you around the apartment complex. If I had, we'd have taken you much sooner."

"Taken me sooner?" What is he talking about? I'm so confused. He's right that I don't know anything he's talking about. "You have to be mistaken about whatever it is you think about me. No one's been hiding me. It's called being depressed, jobless, and unknowingly drugged into being sick."

"Drugged? Of course. It makes perfect sense he'd become a pharmacist to enable his dark deeds. It's less messy. If I had found you sooner, I'd have never allowed that bastard to lay his hands on you," he adds, not even trying to answer my questions. He acts like his comment somehow makes any of this okay. "In fact, I plan to make sure he doesn't ever use his hands again at all."

My tongue sticks to the roof of my mouth. I couldn't respond even if I wanted to.

"I will bring them to you." Kase smirks at his thought as if he thinks such a thing is some sort of acceptable gift. "You would like that, wouldn't you? Or would you prefer for me to hold him down so you can start by breaking his fingers? Add a little revenge to his punishment."

Again, I don't respond.

A knock sounds on the doorframe, interrupting my attempt to try to say something, anything. "What's taking so long, Kase? Lucian is growing impatient. This must be handled now. If she's not marked, they will come. We can't let that happen. We've been waiting so long."

I whip my attention to Dante, his comment knocking a reaction into me. I manage to pull my attention away from Kase's psychobabble and scoot away from him. My gaze darts to the front of his cut shirt to where he forced me to stab him. Disbelief turns me mushy-headed again. While dark ruby blood stains his skin, the wound has disappeared.

Reaching up, I caress my fingers over his tight abs. "What the—"

Kase snatches my wrist and drags me to my feet. "All right, angel-girl. You can touch me all you want later if you let me touch you back. But right now, you're Lucian's. Let's go."

My eyes widen, my body kicking into action. I scream out and swing my fist, trying to hit him away. Dante laughs and steps forward. He grabs my free hand, and the two of them tug me along like a doll. Shrieking, I skid my bare feet on the wood floors, trying to gain traction to resist. Nothing works. There is nothing stopping them. I feel so utterly helpless—worse than when I had to rebuild my life after I broke things off with Joel. Worse than losing my job and having it taken away from me. Possibly worse than being left to die.

"I love when they realize they're powerless," Dante says, swinging me by my wrist. "You'll feel better when you know your place, pretty soul. I think you'll like it."

The rotting smell grows more intense, and panic tightens my chest. I'm going to die. I know it. Heat simmers in the hallway, hazing the air. Gasping, I struggle to breathe in the thickening air. Sweat prickles across my skin and soaks through the robe. I can't do anything at all as these two fuckers drag me into the living room and drop me on the floor.

I push up on my hands and gawk at the horned beast standing within a burning circle right in the middle of the floor. I do the one damn thing I swore I'd never do after watching horror movies. I freeze and scream like a banshee.

Trying to scramble away, I bump into Dante's shins. He remains sturdy in place behind me. Kase squats next to me and smiles. His handsome face lights up, and I can't help wondering why the hell this asshole has to be so damn hot.

"Aw, come on, angel-girl. Don't be a rude bitch. That bastard mortal you were banging can't even compare to the sexiness that Lucian encompasses. Look at those horns.

They're perfect to clutch onto if he likes you enough to let you ride his face." Kase chuckles at my reaction, his suggestion the absolute last thing in the universe I need crossing my mind right now. Ugh.

Dante laughs from above me and pets his fingers through Kase's light brown hair. "Maybe you should show her some fun with y—"

"Bring the soul to me." The guttural growling voice cuts Dante off and snaps my attention from Kase and to the towering beast nearly as tall as the vaulted ceiling of the living room. The flames dance and grow with his movements, yet he never leaves the circle. "I must see it for myself. I need to touch it." The soul? It? Fuck. This thing is talking about me.

"No," I whisper, my heart crashing against my ribcage. Sweat cools my skin, and my whole body trembles. The idea of the fiery beast's clawed fingers getting within an inch of me terrifies me on a deep-seated level. He's not just a monstrous beast. He's evil. Dark. Demonic. Nothing good can ever come from him. "God, ple—"

Dante covers my mouth from behind at the same time the beast roars. The circle of fire burns brighter, hotter, and I try everything I can to break free. Lifting me up, Dante restrains me in front of him, carrying me toward the creature. It stomps its giant hooved feet to the floor and stretches out its humanoid hands. Long curled claws shine like onyx stones in the fire. I can't take my eyes off the creature, traveling my gaze up the length of his body. Molten orange veins climb the beast's muscular arms, the lava-like substance glowing just under his smooth, dark skin. The veins travel through the rest of his body, all gathering to the center of the monster's broad chest, pulsing with power unlike anything I could've ever imagined.

I cringe and recoil, twisting my head to look away as the heat intensifies, burning the soles of my feet. I screech in pain, bucking and fighting, begging anyone who can hear me to help me, to make it stop.

Like some force finally gives in to answer my prayers, the burning sensation fades. A cool gust of wind licks over my heated skin, soothing the agonizing memory of the beast and fire until the spicy-sweet scent of cinnamon and chocolate engulfs me, pushing away the rotting smell permeating the living room.

"Raven Rose, your soul is far lighter and more damaged than the dark beauty your name encompasses." The velvety rich voice hums everywhere and nowhere, caressing my ears while also filling my mind with a powerful, indescribable essence. "I expected more from you."

It takes everything in me to open my eyes. Sucking in a breath, I flutter my lashes open and stare in shock at the startling handsome face of the man cradling me in his arms. His full lips peek from beneath his trimmed beard covering what I suspect is a sharp, angular jawline to match his nose. I rove my gaze over his features, drinking in his shaved hair the same black color as his beard. Black irises blend in with his black pupils, but despite being dark and intense, the depths of his gaze light with the warmth of the fire burning around us. Fire that I realize I can no longer feel.

"How do you know my name?" The question feels wrong coming from my lips, my body and mind feeling disconnected.

"The same way you know mine," the man says, his lips quirking with a smile.

"Lucifer..." Fuck. I did not just say the name I think I said.

"Lucian," he corrects, grazing his fingers along my cheek. "I've abandoned that cursed name long ago." Like it matters.

"I don't understand. I..." My voice trails off.

I never truly believed in Heaven or Hell. I never went to church. Tonight, I prayed out of desperation, like I somehow knew what I was facing. But Lucifer? Satan? The fucking devil or whatever the hell he goes by? I'm losing my mind. This can't be real. I never thought I was a bad person. I never even cheated on a damn test.

"You have a lot of questions we don't have time for," Lucian says, stroking my cheek again like he can read my mind. Maybe he can. "And I have to be certain you're the one I want."

"Want?" My voice rises with my question.

He only smiles. "It will only take a second."

I blink, my body tensing. "What will?"

Fire flashes in his eyes. "I'd like to touch your beautifully broken, irresistible soul."

4

DANTE

GIVE HER HELL

FOR FUCK'S SAKE.

My nuts tighten just at the thought of penetrating that sexy, beautifully broken mortal's soul the way Lucian does. Her achingly bright essence twirls and twists as the void of darkness radiating from Lucian sinks and blends with her light in a way I haven't felt since—I can't even remember.

Time passes in the Earth Realm without me. All I know

for certain is that I've seen the cycle of wars, plagues, natural disasters, and the destruction of different civilizations over and over again. Hell, I've been blamed for them too.

A soft moan escapes from the mortal, and she tips her head back, sending her black hair cascading toward the floor. Her hands press into Lucian's chest like her soul wants to resist the one thing the rest of her body wants—the closeness of Lucian's power pulsing from his heart. Power strong enough to make the saviors scatter like the pigeon-brains they are when it comes to mortals.

"This is giving me a fucking boner," I mutter, adjusting my cock in my pants. "He's taking his damn sweet time with her."

"Can you blame him?" Kase stands with his arms crossed, keeping his gaze locked on Lucian and the broken soul. He whistles lowly and lifts an eyebrow. "Shit, look at her. She's going for his horns."

Damn.

My boner jabs harder against my zipper, threatening to poke through the tough fabric of my jeans. I shift my junk again, considering just whipping out my damn cock to rub one out. I don't give a fuck. If Lucian gets to enjoy her hands traveling up his neck to lace her fingers around his horns, stroking them like they're the sexiest things she's ever seen, then I'm going to enjoy the hell out of this too.

I grab my zipper. My skin ripples in anticipation. If I

don't satiate my burning desire soon, my true body will explode free from this form. And damn it. I really fucking want what Lucian has. I yearn to feel that mortal's body wrapped around me so much so that I step closer. He's taking too long, and I saw her first. He has enough souls. This one should be mine.

Lucian suddenly roars as the light of the broken soul rips free from his all-consuming darkness, and the beautiful mortal throws herself back and out of the Hell circle. Before she can scramble to her feet, I charge and scoop her up, covering her mouth with my hand. Like the power of Hell still clings to her, she presses my fingers harder to her lips until she sucks my middle one into her mouth and chomps down. Fuck, do I enjoy it.

I jerk my hand away more in surprise than pain, and I flip her around and capture her with my gaze. Fire flickers in the blue-green depths of her irises before it vanishes. She blinks and gasps a few breaths, her tits pressing into my chest. Our closeness does nothing for my raging boner, and she widens her eyes as she realizes what exactly keeps space between us. Without having to hear her thoughts, I know what she plans to attack next on me. But this time, it won't be with her pouty mouth.

I don't let her hand get within an inch of my junk and drop her on her ass. Laughing, I say, "Don't tease me, broken soul. You touch my cock and I won't want you to stop.

Control yourself. We will have time for this later."

Her face flushes and she tries to kick me, but her leg isn't quite long enough to get close and personal with my throbbing shaft. I wish it was. Either she'll kill my boner or bring me the fucking desperate release I need—I don't fucking care which one. I want her body pressing against mine. Lucian enjoyed their soul bonding far more than I'd have liked. He doesn't hold the only key to our kingdom, and it's time mortals realize that just because he made the biggest scene doesn't mean my jump from grace didn't create its own level of Hell.

"You went too far, Lucian," Kase snaps, fisting his hands.

His true body fissures his skin, peeking through. The red devil is far more impressive than Lucian, and I can't wait to see the pretty soul's face when she gets the chance to confront him. She'll piss her pants...unless she realizes all the fun she can have with him and me. I don't mind working her up to it.

"Now look at her. She's a fucking mess. What did you tell her? You know we must be careful with revelations in her state of uncertainty," Kase adds, touching the pretty soul's tear-stained cheek.

Like Lucian and I, Kase also fought and abandoned the Higher Power set on controlling us while all its playthings ruined a world that could've been ours. It still can as long as

Lucian didn't do what Kase accused and break the mind of the pretty damaged soul. Mortals are fragile—pathetic even—but this one is different. She's who we've been waiting all our eternities for to come along. She might be a savior's biggest mistake, but she's perfect for what we have planned.

"Do not question my judgment!" Lucian yells, dragging me from my thoughts of the power I hunger for. He rubs his hands over his horns like he savors the memory of the broken soul touching him in fascination instead of fear. "I had to be certain she was the one we want. You know it takes a special kind of angel-kissed soul to do what we need."

"And?" I ask, anticipation coursing through me.

I already know the answer. I glimpsed it for myself even without familiarizing myself the way I crave, especially now. The pretty soul might be broken and damaged from this particular life, but she's strong. Her light comes from a powerful savior—stolen like she would have stolen his wings.

Fire lights his obsidian eyes. "What do you think?"

Fucking Lucian. He takes his current hellish state for granted. The circle gives him more power and is why he doesn't come to this realm completely because he is the current anchor and power source in Hell. He can't leave because of this, but he only bitches about it—fuck, all the time. But he wanted the infamy. Kase and I, on the other hand, prefer to be a bit more inconspicuous and a lot more involved in flesh bag affairs.

Lucian doesn't take his eyes off the mortal as she crawls away from us, the little firecracker lit by the flames of Hell, turning her more into an explosive on the verge of destroying the world. "Raven is perf—"

"God? Angels? Hello?" the broken soul asks, raising her voice through the room. She slaps her palms together and looks toward the ceiling in the most ridiculous sight. Praying in a room full of devils is like brushing your teeth while eating a stack of Oreos. It isn't going to do shit. "I know you can hear me! Help me! I don't—"

Kase tips his head back and laughs. I haven't seen him so amused in a long time. He usually wears a glower and cusses out the world every second of every day. But this soul, Raven, she does something to his wrathful ass. "No one can hear you, angel-girl. You've got Lucian's darkness all over you from that little soul bonding you looked like you enjoyed. Have you ever experienced a spiritual orgasm before? It's quite the out-of-body experience. You would cream at the thought if you knew. Why'd you stop?"

She glares and scrunches her nose. "Because I'm not giving my soul to the devil to get revenge for the shit Joel pulled. That's the worst offer anyone has ever made me. He's not fucking worth it, especially if I'll end up wherever the hell he does. God, I'm not stupid."

Fucking Lucian. He will always go for the shittiest deals first, testing just how much work it will take to break and mold a mortal into the perfect energy source for our kingdom. But this soul is different, and we all know it. Broken yet pure—bright and angel-kissed to balance out the darkness. A light even Hell can't distinguish since it was a gift and can't be taken by the Higher Power.

"And none of us here is God, angel-girl," Kase quips, enjoying this as much as I am as she calls Lucian out. So feisty. Hot. Red light glows in Kase's irises, and I watch his tail sneak from behind him, knowing he plans to use it to touch her inconspicuously until he feels he must tie her up like earlier.

"Stop calling me that. It's Raven, and whoever it is you think I am, I'm not them, okay?" she says, a new fight rising in her.

I step closer and lock my hand around Kase's tail, twisting the smooth, tough black appendage around my knuckles. He grunts and grinds his teeth, shivering under the pressure of my hand, and not because I hurt him. He would never admit it, but the fucker loves it. His tail is as sensitive as his damn cock. I bet he already fantasizes about the broken soul playing with it.

Damn it. Now I am. I wish I had a tail now too.

I drop it, humming under my breath as I step closer to

her, slowly drawing my eyes down her body, making her squirm. She's not afraid of me—I'd sense it—but she doesn't like how she can't take her eyes away from me. She feels guilty for finding me attractive and can't help rubbing her legs together like my gaze alone turns her on. I love it.

"How can you be so certain you aren't who we've been looking for? I mean, look at you, *Raven*." I trace my finger around the silhouette of her frame, savoring her name on my tongue. "You were dying when we found you. Unable to get to your feet. A sobbing and sputtering mess. Weak. Desperate. But now...mmm." I flick my tongue at her, drawing her attention to my mouth as I split my tongue into a fork, slightly transforming, and move each side.

She closes her eyes like it's the only thing she can do to stop staring. If I could listen to her thoughts, I bet she'd be thinking of everything I could possibly do to her with it. How I could rub her clit between it, letting her experience my piercing. She has no idea what kind of pleasure she can have, but she'll learn soon enough. She'll give in when she gets over her human rationale and morals.

Swallowing, she pulls herself together and meets my gaze. I flick my tongue again, slower this time so she can see how well I can work it. Blush burns across her cheeks and she crosses her legs and averts her eyes. I was right. I can read mortals fairly well, and this one is an open book. She's curious.

"You did something to me," she snaps, hugging her arms over her chest. "You're still trying to do something to me. But it won't work. My soul isn't for sale, so don't you expect anything from me just because you sort of saved me."

I grin and look at Kase. "She can't make up her mind, can she? First we're kidnapping monsters. Now, we fucking saved her. Is she insinuating we can perform miracles?"

Raven tries to kick me for what seems like the hundredth time tonight. I hope she keeps this up for the rest of eternity. It's so much fun. "You're worse than monsters. You're kidnapping demons!"

Lucian growls in annoyance and sends hellfire billowing around him. She screeches, her eyes widening, clearly still gripping tightly to the fear the saviors instilled in mortals over the millennia. And that fucking uptight, impatient bastard of a devil. He needs to decide which direction he wants to take things with her. I thought I was the jealous one, but he doesn't enjoy the fact that the broken soul—that Raven—gives us her attention, refusing to look at Lucian in all his sexy, hellish glory. It's obvious he revealed himself as his former self, because she would've never grabbed at his horns any other way. Kase will have to convince her otherwise if he hopes for her to ride his.

"Enough! If the mortal refuses a deal, then she will return to where she belongs and we will continue to search for someone else like her." Lucian's deep voice rumbles through the room, and he bares his sharp fangs. I try not to smirk at his threat. He's so full of shit and everyone except for Raven knows it. We've waited long enough already for this perfect, angel-kissed soul. He's not going to give her up so easily. Waving his hand at me, he adds, "Offer the mortal man a deal instead. I'm sure he'd be willing to do what we need in return for giving him what he wants. He won't be able to resist."

That evil, brilliant bastard. Raven is afraid of us, but damn, I can smell the scent of her terror from here. It's intoxicating. Lucian was always far better at manipulation through figuring out someone's worst fear and using it against them. It's not often that it happens to be another flesh bag either.

"I know I couldn't," I say, winking at Raven. She's so much fun to tease. The perfect plaything to pass time by once she's in my hands, and I'm in her. "Come on, pretty soul. Time to get you home. I'm sure you're missed and we don't want the dumb shit to think you've gotten away." If I didn't think the plan would work, I'd despise even the thought of returning her to the asshole flesh bag. She's far too alluring, sexy, and feisty to waste on him.

Raven doesn't have a chance to open her mouth to respond before I scoop her up and toss her on my shoulder. She screams out and whacks her hands to my back, trying to get me to let her go. Kase watches me carry Raven from our apartment, and I flip her into my arms when we're out of sight. I shouldn't, but Lucian shouldn't get all the credit for cornering her and putting her into a position she can't refuse.

"You can change your mind at any time, Raven," I say, leaning in close as to not give her space to head-butt me. She might knock herself out and force me to actually follow through with Lucian's plan. "The saviors ensure those of us who seek justice and balance with the soul...mortal population look like evil douchebag monsters. We only punish and torment those wicked enough to deserve it."

"You were going to leave me to die in a dumpster. You are a fucking monster." She slaps her hand to my shoulder with her words. "Evil incarnate. A liar. You said it yourself that you punish the wicked. I want to speak to whoever is really in charge if that's the case. I'm not a bad person."

I chuckle. "That's subjective. Plus, I was speaking about your average flesh bag. You, pretty soul, are an exception."

I ease away a bit, inviting her to do her worst to me. Maybe she'll sink her nails into my skin and let me feel her envy over not having the power I do. I don't control those souls who let envy consume their existence without a reason. I can feel Raven's annoyance and resentment over basically every mortal in the world. She'll learn soon enough that it'll be them envious of her and everything she will acquire...if she accepts Lucian's deal.

"It was nothing personal. I'd have done it to anyone left to die out in the open around here. This isn't a fucking landfill to dump bodies in," I add, tightening my mouth, watching the grimace puckering her brows. "Mortals are a fucking mess. Sloppy."

"And you're a fucking psycho." She smacks her hand to my cheek. "Now let me go! I'm not going back to Joel's. He'll kill me."

I shrug, enjoying her attempts to overpower me. "Probably not for a while. You are obviously not the soul to go down without a fight."

I hate the idea of obeying Lucian and taking her back to the mortal bastard. Just because Lucian thinks putting her in her own personal Hell on Earth will break her and turn her compliant doesn't mean I have to like doing this. I want her here with me, especially with her perfect pet names. I can't wait to hear what else she comes up with. The mortal bastard shouldn't get the power over her I crave, nor should he get to play with her even a second more. He won't appreciate her like I do.

"You fucker!" She smacks me again. "You cocksucker. Bitch ass devil minion. I'll figure out how to send you to Hell."

"See? Pretty souls don't brave challenging and threatening a devil. You won't stand by and do nothing with the flesh bag. You won't be his good girl. Which is exactly what

Lucian expects." I turn the corner and head in a direction that makes Raven tense. Her fingers pinch my shoulders in desperation. I'd love to feel her grip somewhere else.

"Please. You don't have to do this." Gasping, she inhales short, shallow breaths.

"Neither do you. The offer stands. But if you prefer to test your luck...I know you'll put the bastard where he belongs. You've already felt the darkness of a devil, and your misery will feed it and help it grow. You'll bow to it. And when you do, that's when we'll return."

I can see the blue door with the broken porchlight appear in my mind's eye. The energy radiating from the end of the building draws me closer, sending a deep-seated need through me. Fucking Lucian. He loves testing me. It's agonizing having to resist the urge to drop Raven on the pathway and storm forward to ensure the fucker doesn't get the one thing I want in this moment. I've never envied a mortal, and it ignites a rage and hunger inside me. If I don't convince Raven to comply, I'll have to accept Lucian's punishment for devouring the man's soul.

An image of the dark soul swirls through my mind as we draw closer, and Raven shudders. Her worst nightmare currently lives in apartment number thirteen. I should've known.

The lucky bastard is about to get luckier.

Raven flails, trying her hardest to break from my arms.

"Please, don't do this."

"It was an order." I stop in front of apartment thirteen, listening to someone throwing things around inside. "I'm not going to piss off Lucian. If he thinks this will help us, then I trust him as I always have."

"Because you're his little bitch servant," she says, kicking her legs, trying to throw me off balance. "What do you get out of this besides making your master happy?"

"My master? No. Lucian and I are equals," I mutter, thinking about the screwed up job humanity did documenting anything. The saviors ensured it. Just shows how vain all the flesh bags are, running in fear from those of us who seek justice compared to the ones who cast out those who see a bit more gray areas in the divine rules. It's not us who block the gateway to a soul's paradise for breaking silly codes. Souls end up with us because they have nowhere else to go.

"Yeah, right. If you're not a little bitch errand boy, let me go. Prove to me you have the same power as Lucian." Raven stops fighting and meets my gaze. "Because I don't believe it. You're his servant. I bet you'd get on your knees if he asked."

"Like you've gotten on yours for this guy?" I motion at the door, smiling. I love her attempt to get me to question my power. But I'm secure with my position and the place I've chosen. "You bet. Didn't you see his cock with your little bonding session? Almost as big as mine."

Her slack jaw proves she didn't expect that response. "Put me down, you monster! You evil piece of shit!"

Damn it, I fucking like the way she talks to me. Instead of crying, she gets angry. She teases the darkness clinging to my essence, and it's nearly impossible not to give in and show her the extent of my power but also what the fuck she does to my damn cock. I want to see her on her knees for me.

"You want down, pretty soul? Then convince me. Lucian isn't the only one who likes his dick sucked." I smirk, sensing her desperation. Reaching up, I stretch her bottom lip with my thumb. "I might even let you pick out your own lipstick." Because there's nothing sexier than watching as my cock glides in between pouty red-stained lips and seeing the reminder smeared all over her face.

"You'll let me go if I blow you?" she asks softly.

Fuck. Just the thought shoots energy right to my balls. I need space before I see how far I can push her. How far she's willing to go. It'll be my damn eternal punishment, because if she does it out of desperation, she'll automatically put me on her shit list and will never suck my dick by her own free will.

"No. I was gauging your fucking desperation," I say, poking her lip again. "If I'm going to fuck your face, it'll be because you want me to."

I drop her and watch as she flails and hits her ass on the

concrete. Without waiting for her to get up, I kick the door to apartment thirteen open, catching sight of the bastard Raven fears more so than even Lucian.

"Hey, fucker. I have a present for you," I call, sweeping my gaze across the open suitcases on the floor. He was planning to run like the coward he is. "Come and get her before she tries to escape. You'll be the one chasing her. I've done enough for your douche ass with nothing in return."

Raven tries to crawl between my legs, and I shut them, locking her in place by her waist. Her hips shake, flipping up the robe, showing off her tight ass in her damp yoga pants. The light gray color is transparent enough to see she wears a thong. I can't wait until she gives in and to be able to slide my finger under the fabric to snap it.

Screaming out, she punches me and scratches her nails into my ankles. She even sinks her teeth into my calf. And damn. Her bite makes me want to scoop her feisty ass up and carry her home to do the same in return. I'd give her more than a love nip. She'll get to experience the fun that comes with my venom. One bite, and her body will be mine. She'll beg for more.

"R-Raven?" A man with red-rimmed eyes and blood staining his T-shirt steps into view from the hallway. I shouldn't be surprised that he's crying. Fuckers like him always do when they get caught.

"Yes, it's fucking Raven. Now come and get her." I ease

my legs open and let Raven pull herself out.

She pushes up, kneeling in front of me for just a second, which is plenty long enough to imagine her pulling my cock free of my jeans. She twists, and I step back as the force of her hair whips over my groin. Fuck, I want to twist her midnight tresses around my hand and pull her into me, gliding my cock between her lips when she moans in excitement.

Instead, I rub my aching nuts and wait for her to get up and try to run. I lock my arms around her, yanking her against my chest, my raging hard-on pressing into her lower back because it has nowhere else to go. She automatically reaches behind her out of instinct because she feels me poking her. Jerking her hand away so fast, Raven denies me even a second of her touch. I expect her hand to glow with the fires of Hell like I burned her. I hope she can't stop thinking about it.

I push her forward, my whole body buzzing from her accidentally grazing her fingers to my boner. If I don't get space between us, I won't let her go. I'll charge forward, releasing my true form into the world, and swallow this bastard whole like the rat he is. "Your little spectacle nearly caused a damn scene earlier. You need to learn to clean up or hide your damn mess, you fuckhead."

"Is this a trick?" The man meanders closer, digging into his jacket pocket. "Are you trying to fucking set me up, Ra-

ven? You attacked me first. I was protecting myself, you un-
grateful bitch."

Anger ignites inside me at the sight of the pocket knife
before the bastard has a chance to flip it open. I shove Raven
toward the stucco wall and out of the way. Stepping forward, I hiss, revealing my fangs to get the bastard to back
up. I grab the door and slam it shut in his face, crossing my
arms over my chest.

Raven tries to run, but I strike out my hand and snatch
her by the back of the robe, yanking her to me. She slaps her
hands at my face and knees me right in my junk, but I hold
firm. If a little cock aggression incapacitates me, I have far
worse problems.

"Damn it, Raven. Just stop," I say, spinning her from
the porch to cage her to the side of the building. "I want
you to listen to me for a sec."

"No." She slams her hands to my chest, trying to get
me to back away. Firelight crackles in her gaze, her brush
with Lucian awakening her soul to the endless possibilities
she still can't seem to see as a gift we're offering. Her soul
recognizes it, but her mortal mind might never comprehend.

Her stubborn ass gets to me, and I swing my fist and
punch my hand into the wall by the door. The fucker yelps,
watching through the peephole. I wish it was the bastard
mortal on the other side of my fist instead of the blue door,

trying to think of as many ways to kill us and cover up his crimes. His darkness seeps through the wood, humming and swirling, growing with the wrongdoings he's planning to commit.

I growl under my breath and grab the back of Raven's neck, getting her to face me head on instead of resisting. My vision narrows on her eyes, tracing the dark blue circle around her irises over and over as I chisel away at her armor until I see the bright light of her soul. Her heartbeat picks up pace, and her muscles loosen as I ease a tiny bit of my essence into her mind, trying to connect with her on a level where she's more malleable and receptive.

Just like before when I tried to get her to admit she was afraid of me, she builds an imaginary wall around herself and pushes me out. My ability to entrance her falters, proving to me once again that she's who we need for our kingdom.

"I know you don't believe me, but you're destined for Hell." I bend slightly, feeling her thighs squeeze me as she straddles my leg because I'm close and give her nowhere else to go. "Whether you agree on your own terms is up to you. Lucian will not back down. He will get you if you're what he wants. If it's not tonight when you can bargain with him over your eternity, then it'll be after you murder the bastard in there. He will push you until you break."

"Or he'll just kill me and put me out of this fucking

misery." Her eyes glass over with her tears, and she sucks in her bottom lip to stop it from trembling.

"He won't," I say, turning toward the door. "I know souls like his. He craves the power of control. He needs you alive for that, so he can obsess and play with you like his doll every day. Lucian will ensure it with a bargain he won't be able to resist. He'll be the one to get the deal, and I can sense the fucker wants nothing more than seeing you bend and break to his will."

A tear escapes her lashes and trickles down her cheek. "This is so fucked up," she whispers. "What have I done wrong? I don't deserve this."

"You deserve more, pretty soul. You're broken, and we can mend you. Make you stronger, better," I say, wiping her tears away. I prefer her to be angry, but she doesn't give me what I want.

"I will not damn myself to eternal punishment," she snaps, resting her head against the rough texture of the wall.

"You will if you don't make your own deal." I lean in closer, trying to get her to look from the roof of the porch to me. "Think about it. Use Lucian's need to have you to your advantage."

Her lip trembles as she finally looks at me. "You're lying."

I shrug. "You are welcome to find out."

Grabbing her wrist, I tug her from the wall and guide

her to the door. "The bastard is waiting for you. If you want to test your luck, then go on. I'll give your deal to him. You will discover your mistakes soon enough."

I twist the doorknob and fling the door open. Raven screeches as the bastard waits for us on the other side with a knife in his hand. I let him grab the front of her robe and drag her away from me. The guy rushes me, shoving his blade into my gut. I don't fight or do anything to protect myself.

His eyes widen in shock, and he drops his hand away. "What the fuck?"

I lock my eyes on him, shoving my darkness into his soul, making him scream. "What is your name?"

The bastard wobbles on his feet. "Joel."

I flick my gaze to Raven, paralyzed in fear behind him. "Well, Joel. I have a deal for you involving Raven. Want to hear me out?"

"Yes," Joel responds, his voice monotonous as I pry into his essence.

"I will guarantee Raven remains in your possession for the rest of your life in exchange for making her life a living Hell. The cops will never interfere, and you are free to do with her as you please. When the deal is complete, your soul will belong to me." I flare my nostrils with my words. "If you choose not to, I will feed you to my favorite devil."

Joel opens and closes his mouth. "I ag—"

"No!" Raven screams. "No!"

I press my hand to Joel's mouth, cutting off his response. Turning to Raven, I meet her gaze. "Does this mean you're ready to see Lucian again?"

Her lips tremble and she swallows. "Yes."

Swinging my fist, I punch Joel in the temple hard enough to knock him out. I offer my hand to Raven. "Good. Now remember, pretty soul. Think about what you truly want."

"I don't even know what that is besides saving my soul from Hell," she whispers, tilting her face toward the sky.

I bump her shoulder. "I'm sure you'll make one helluva deal with Lucian. He underestimates you. Think big."

"Why are you suddenly helping me?" she asks, grimacing.

Because I want your full lips sucking my cock. Your body bent over so I can fuck you every way I please. I don't say my thoughts out loud. I'll save them for when she's warmed up to me. Instead, I grin. "Because I think I'll enjoy having you around."

5

RAVEN

DEAL WITH THE DEVIL

THE LAST PLACE I want to be is on my knees in front of Lucian—the fucking devil. Satan. Lucifer. Whatever the hell name he goes by—and in a world that isn't quite Earth but it's not Hell either. At least here, I can't see his demonic, horrifying, monstrous form. Here, he looks as breathtakingly handsome as I'd expect from an angel, even an evil one cast from Heaven.

He steps closer, and I shift and train my gaze on the black stone floor. At least his cock isn't at my eye-level as he stands butt-ass naked in front of me. I can't help thinking about my conversation with Dante and how he insinuated he'd give Lucian a blowjob. I have no idea if he was kidding or not, but I wish I could forget it ever happened. Blowing the devil should not be on my mind, even if I definitely don't plan to. I'm only kneeling in my attempt to grovel.

"I'd appreciate it if you looked at me, Raven. I'm in this form only for your benefit." Lucian's fingers touch my chin, guiding my head to peer up. "Show me the same respect and courtesy I'm giving you...unless you don't want me to hear you out."

My heart races as I draw my gaze up his perfect body and how his dick, even flaccid, hangs only inches above his knee. If it were hard...I shudder. His chiseled perfection is far nicer than any statue I've seen, and to be fair, I've always looked at their marble junk too. But unlike the stone statues, Lucian's deep tawny skin has black hair traveling up his happy trail and across his chest. He's handsome, not beautiful, yet something about him scares me on a soul-deep level, like my spirit knows that I'm at the mercy of the one being I've been taught shows no mercy at all.

"You have a lot to learn and understand about the purpose I've given myself." Lucian's voice trickles into my mind.

Shit. He can hear my thoughts.

"I can see your past and your possible futures as well, which is why I know if I place you on the right path, you will help give us what rightfully belongs to us," Lucian continues, "but I also know that you're afraid of what great power can do and what your true purpose is. Since you're only mortal, after all."

"I'm not afraid of power. I'm afraid of burning in Hell for all of eternity." My voice laces with anger. I don't care who he is. He obviously doesn't know me regardless if he can read thoughts or touch my soul or whatever.

"But you so easily let others control you," he quips, bending closer into my personal space.

Am I really going to argue with the devil? Fuck yeah. I guess I am. I already question my sanity, so why the hell not? "How? I had no idea Joel was drugging me. I thought he was being nice to let me stay."

"You can't lie to me. I've touched your soul, Raven." Grabbing the front of the robe, Lucian hoists me to my feet and locks his hands to my shoulders. He closes the space, leaving only an inch between our faces, forcing me to share his breath. "I know you unlike anyone. You are afraid of power. Of the possibility that there might be more to your existence than just surviving. If you didn't think so, you wouldn't have returned to me. You'd have continued to pray to forces who've never responded to you instead of choosing to finally stand up and do with your life as you want."

My heart thrashes, the erratic beats picking up my breathing. His words swirl through my mind, and I find myself hypnotized with his black gaze, the depths fissuring with molten light like obsidian stones turned into charcoal, alit with flames. Lucian's eyes search mine. Caressing his hot fingers along my jaw, he sets my skin ablaze with crackling energy that zings through me, drawing me even closer until my lips brush his. But we don't kiss. It feels as if my very being drifts from me, yearning to be close.

I shudder a breath. "If you know everything about me, then you know I will not give you my soul forever. I won't."

"But you will, Raven. You'll beg to stay with me for all time, especially if you accept your purpose and succeed," he murmurs, keeping a millimeter away, sending tingles across my lips. "You won't be able to resist."

"Which is? If you want my soul, you can't expect me to blindly just accept. My faith is already weak. I will not give you the last remaining ounce of it I carry." Because agreeing to whatever it is he wants is obviously not going to go over well with me if he's bartering my soul for Joel's eternal punishment. He forced me into this. I deserve to know how hopeless this truly is.

"It will be easier to show you. Now hold still." Lucian cups my face and kisses me, setting my soul zinging as his essence tangles with mine, filling me with a strange, all-consuming awareness.

"It must be now," Lucian says, stepping away from seven angels with brilliant wings—some in gold, some white, some even just made purely of light—standing tall and strong, bearing flaming weapons. "Join me."

Two of the angels step forward and bow to Lucian, joining his side. Kase and Dante turn and glare at the other remaining five. The world begins to shake as the ground cracks and breaks. The middle angel of the group bares his teeth and raises his sword. I can't hear anything over the yells. Over the ground quaking.

Then all of a sudden, Lucian stabs himself with a flaming sword, sending his body ablaze. Spinning away from the angels, he expands his brilliant wings, the sheer light turning into hot fire. He holds his hands out to Kase and Dante, and his flames dance from his body to devour the two angels.

The three of them don't fall from the ledge of the cliff they stand on. They jump.

No one cast them from Heaven. They chose to go with a fight.

"A fight that isn't over," Lucian says, his voice pulling me from the vision. "My five brethren failed to see my plan and turned their backs on me."

"But you need them," I whisper.

"And you will bring them to me, one by one. Together we will create a true balance to the universe as our kingdom will have its rulers. Including you, my queen. You are the perfect blend of light and mortality, the perfect match to our darkness for the most important level."

Shit. He doesn't have to say the word. I already know. I feel it in my essence.

"If I help you make your supposed brethren fall from grace, you'll give me Purgatory? I don't understand. Why me? What makes me special? I'm mortal." I pull out of his arms and hug myself.

"You've been angel-kissed in another life, Raven." Lucian squeezes my hand. I've heard the others mention that, but it doesn't explain anything. "It's why your soul shines so brightly."

"I don't even know what that means," I say, frowning.

"It means my brethren won't be the first angels you've ever made fall." Lucian rubs his lips together. "If you want to know more, you must agree to my deal."

"So help you make your brethren fall and you'll ensure I don't suffer for eternity?" This is so hard to wrap my mind around. I didn't even truly believe angels existed. Or demons—devils, whatever. I didn't need the threat of Hell to be a good person. But now? Damn. What he asks feels so utterly wrong, corrupting the supposed purest entities in existence...I think.

"Yes," he says, remaining expressionless, his only reaction being the spark lighting up the onyx depths of his eyes. "You will control Purgatory and distribute souls accordingly. When our plan is completed, the Higher Power won't see any soul first. They will all come to you."

Fuck. What happened to resting in peace? The idea of Purgatory sounds like a lot of work. It still doesn't sound like an eternity I'd want either, but what choice do I have? At least agreeing means that I hopefully won't suffer, which I certainly will if I refuse. Because Dante's right. Lucian will get what he wants regardless. "Fine. I will do as you want, but when I'm done, I'm done. No more. You'll let me live out my human life and leave me alone. If I'm damned regardless, then I'll be damned on my terms."

A smile stretches across his lips. "If you succeed."

I blink. "And if I don't?"

"You will spend eternity serving two devils who desire you," he says, petting my hair. "So don't fail. They will surely rip your soul apart."

Lucian snatches my hand and presses his palm to mine. Pain explodes over my skin, and his beautifully handsome façade cracks and reveals his monstrous form. He releases me and summons fire, turning the temperature hotter in this weird in-between realm. I squeeze my eyes shut, expecting for the fire to consume me.

Gasping, I open my eyes, lying on my side in the middle of the living room of Dante and Kase's apartment. The ring of fire snuffs out, leaving behind a circle of soot and nothing else to indicate Lucian was ever here, yet his presence still lingers.

I press my palms to the ground and wince. Jerking my right hand up, I inspect my palm. My skin glows red with a branding that marks my flesh with a pentagram. The heat grows more intense, crawling up my arm to devour every inch of my skin. I scream out, my body trembling.

But then the heat fades.

So does the light glowing within the branding of my palm.

Lucian's presence abandons me, taking my breath with him.

I lose myself to his lingering darkness.

"All right, angel-girl. Get your ass up. We can't wait any longer. You're not allowed to be the sadist and torture us like this." Kase's vanilla-vetiver scent wafts over me, dragging me from utter darkness.

I snap my eyes open to see him an inch from my face. Ramming my hands against his taut pecs, I shove him away. "Shit! Haven't you heard of personal space?"

"There she is. Fucking finally." Dante's deep tenor voice grumbles from across the room. "What about personal space, pretty soul? We live together now. There's no such thing. Get used to it."

"That's what you think..." My voice trails off as I turn my attention to him.

Unholy Hell.

I slap my hands over my eyes and shield my eyes from Dante's well-endowed cock. He stands naked in the hallway, drying off with a towel. He was right about being bigger than Lucian. Inhaling slow breaths, I focus on controlling my out-of-control body. It enjoys the sight of Dante way more than it should. He's so attractive and muscular, tatted, rugged, and tall. Everything I love about a man.

Kase shakes me again, bending over. His warm breath tickles the backs of my hands. "Come on, angel-girl. You need to get used to this. We're in it for the long haul with you. Don't be shy. There isn't anything wrong with appreciating that sexy beast. He wants you to look."

"I don't want either of you to get any ideas, so no. I'm not looking even if that's what he wants," I mumble against my hands.

Locking his hands around my wrists, Kase pries my hands away from my face. "I don't understand why mortals are so modest. This realm would be a lot more fun if everyone just stripped and partied naked. Which is rule number one in our apartment, so get used to it."

In the light of day trickling in through the blinds of the front window, I notice the burgundy depths of his eyes.

They're not dark brown as I expected, but an unearthly color. Thick lashes cast shadows on his sharp cheeks, and he graces me with a smile, showing off his perfectly straight, white teeth. I break my gaze and flick my attention to his bare chest and the intricately detailed collection of skulls tattooed on his side.

Thank fucking hell he wears pants.

"You like what you see, don't you?" he asks, his voice soft and seductive like he knows if he murmurs the words, I'll have to lean closer to hear them. "I can show you more."

Fuck. Me. I want him to. I really, and I mean really, do. But he looks cocky and ready to tease me.

I thrash my head, sending my hair sweeping around me. "That's not necessary."

"You're not even curious?" he prods, playing with the button of his jeans.

I whack him in the shoulder. "Just stop and give me some space. I feel hungover, and the last thing I want is for the two of you to show off your demon dicks."

"Maybe you should show her your tail. It might be less intimidating," Dante says, amusement lightening his voice.

He strolls closer with the towel now slung across his hips, though it does nothing to stop my wandering gaze from focusing on the bulge of his groin. I can't get over how huge he is. I know the vagina stretches, but really. I wonder if it could ever go all in. He's also attractive beyond comprehension. My mind turns to mush the closer he gets, and once again, I can't stop thinking about how I was fully prepared to suck him off in exchange for my freedom. I mean, what's a little sore throat? Desperate times.

"Would you like that?" Kase asks, sitting on the edge of the couch. "I'll let you touch my tail if you want. It won't whip you unless you're a bad girl."

Acting as if my feet aren't even on the cushion, Dante plops down at the end, forcing me to move my legs or get them crushed by his solid, muscular frame. "Don't fall for that. He likes it as much as getting his cock stroked."

Seriously? How do I respond? They're both loving this too much. "Don't take this the wrong way, but you two act as if you're desperate for sex. Probably because you send women running in terror."

"Hardly, but you don't have to worry about that." Kase sucks in his bottom lip and smiles. "You will have no competition with other souls. I like yours too much. I'd hate to see you get jealous and try to deny us all pleasure."

Okay, I can't deal with them. Maybe the Higher Power will take pity on me now.

"God? Can you hear me? Smite them or something so I can go back to sleep. I don't know how to make it clear that I don't want their sex." Throwing myself back on the couch, I rub the heels of my hands into my eyes. What started off as an absolute nightmare now feels like a crazy drug-high, and I'm seriously tripping.

Nudging me over, Kase lies beside me and rests his head against my shoulder. His closeness awakens something wildly dark and delicious inside me like my soul wants to escape my body to merge with his. I shiver, the thought making me cross my legs. What is up with me? Hell. Of course it's Hell. It has to be Lucian's brand making it easier for me to look past their evil incarnate natures and focus on their sex appeal.

"Aw, come on, angel-girl. You've been asleep for what feels like fifty years. We have shit to do before Lucian comes back." Kase points at the ceiling, tracing his finger in the air in some invisible pattern. "Five feather-heads to break, one bastard human to send to Hell, and hours and hours of getting acquainted. It's important to know each other on every level. It'll make it easier in the long run. You seem so stressed, and I have a cure for that. How about I show you that I'm not some demonic piece of shit and rub your clit for you until you cum? You'll feel better. I won't even make you pay me back later."

I groan and shift toward the back of the couch, hiding my face in the cushions. "I can do that myself, thanks." Maybe if I ignore them, they'll go away.

"Then I'll give you something to fantasize about to help out," Dante says from the end of the couch. The bastard reaches over, snatches the cushions, and tosses the pillows onto the floor. Taking their place, he squishes me between his and Kase's chests. "We're a team now. Might as well try some icebreakers. Get you into shape to boldly seduce a savior. Those fuckers won't make the first move."

"So having sex with an angel will make them fall?" I purse my lips, the heat of their bodies warming me up. I can't believe I'm the meat in this demonic sandwich. If my parents previously disapproved of my life choices—fuck. They'll shun me for eternity.

"Not exactly, angel-girl, but why not have fun when changing their purpose? It won't do anything but help." Kase stretches up to whisper in my ear. "It's easier to start with something...addicting. At least two out of the five of them won't be able to resist coming back to you for more."

Shit. "Why is that?"

"Because of the sins they'll embody. Lust and gluttony won't ever get enough of you, especially with how brightly that broken soul of yours shines, even marked by Lucian." Dante grabs my hand, caressing his fingers over my palm.

I can't bring myself to pull my hand away, the light feathery touch of his finger stirring something exciting inside me. Like he knows, he turns his gaze from my palm and meets my eyes. His emerald irises sparkle in the light, drawing my attention to his oddly-shaped diamond pupils.

I swallow and nod as if his words even make sense. Sins? Gluttony and lust? As far as I know, those are cardinal sins—two of the supposed seven deadliest ones around. What that means in relation to the angels? I have no idea. I'm afraid if I ask, my head might explode or something. It throbs enough as it is. So instead, I focus on something simple. "This is a lot to process, and you two make it hard to think. I have only slept with three men in my life, and now you want me to bang five? How soon?"

"Yesterday would've been best. But I was actually thinking you'd bang six men," Dante says, smirking.

"He means seven," Kase adds, caressing my shoulder. "You should be fair, Purgatory. Give everyone, including us, what they deserve. Fuck, we can even bond in one go. Think of it as a team building exercise."

Oh, my fuck. He did not just suggest what I think he did. "You make this sound like a job."

Dante wags his eyebrows. "Because it is, Raven. Think of this as a perk. The ultimate payday. We can bang and make sure your pussy is nice and ready for a trip to paradise."

"After that, we'll fuck up the bastard in apartment thirteen. Give you the justice included in your bargain with Lucian." Kase aligns his hips with my ass, pressing his hard bulge into me. The excitement in his voice over his twisted words should freak me out, but I struggle to feel anything except the heat and hardness of their bodies. I've never had two hot guys give me this much attention in my life. "We'll make him suffer."

"Then come back here for some more fucking to celebrate. What do you say?" Dante licks his lips with a hiss, a spark of fire lighting in his eyes as he searches my gaze. "Lucian shouldn't be the only one getting to savor that light of yours. We'll be doing all the work since he can't cross the planes."

My mind shuts off, ignoring everything after his idea of returning here after punishing Joel. "I don't know. Your cocks are so huge that I think I might pass. You look better equipped for pain and punishment and not pleasure."

"Thinking you might pass still leaves room for possibility. Don't assume anything until you give it a go. Have you been denied foreplay? Never get to ride someone's face? Play with toys? Slip and slide with lube? Foreplay is the best part, pretty soul." Dante rests his hand on my hip, lightly drawing circles over my side.

Kase groans under his breath. "With enough workup, you can take anything. We can start nice and slow. How does that sound?"

I realize now how thrilling the idea of being adventurous and trying new things truly is for me. Their assessment of me was right. Joel was a wham-bam-thank-you-ma'am sort of lover, and he never cared whether or not I orgasmed. Apparently it was my fault if I took too long to cum.

"I'm in. Are you, Raven?" Dante asks, pinching my hip just enough to make me inhale a soft breath. "Do you want to know what it's like to have your body worshipped by the devils themselves?"

Tingles ignite across my body from their touch as they press in closer. Kase's bulge rubs against my ass, my squirming not helping either of us. And now that they mention sex and foreplay and pleasure, my traitor vagina and her asshole next door neighbor suddenly don't think it sounds so bad.

What am I even thinking? I clench my ass. If Kase is anywhere near as big as Dante...let's just say anal with my ex was like a warm up without even breaking a sweat. These guys would be like trying to slip a wine bottle into a koozie meant for a beer can. It'll take some stretching and a gallon of lube.

I might already be heading to Hell, but getting double penetrated by the rulers of its kingdom after we just met? I'm not ready to start this kind of stuff so early.

I scramble out from the middle of the two of them, not even caring that I ram my hands into Dante's chest or how my knee sinks into Kase's gut. Flipping over him, I land on the floor and gasp in a few deep breaths. Without their intoxicating scents and all-consuming presences surrounding me, I can think again. I can push away the lust they elicit from me like I'm a damn plaything for them to enjoy.

"What'd we do wrong, angel-girl?" Kase asks, sitting up

on the couch. He puckers out his bottom lip, looking a bit more psychotic than pathetic. "You were enjoying the cuddles, weren't you? We're trying to be good to you. Lucian said no eternal torture unless you fail. And even then...I think you might like it." Red light glows in his eyes, his pout creeping into a smile.

Shit. He was playing with me like I thought. They both were.

"You assholes!" I straighten upright and square my shoulders. "We need some ground rules. You can't mess with me like this. I know what you're doing."

Dante chuckles and hugs his arms around Kase from behind, resting his head on his shoulder. "Is that so, pretty soul? What exactly do you think we're doing?"

"Trying to have your way like you're the ones who made a damn deal with Lucian." I lick my lips and raise my palms, motioning for them to stay on the couch. "And you know what? I might be mortal, but I've been pushed around enough. I won't let you do it."

"So now she decides she's going to stand up for herself," Kase mutters, raising an eyebrow.

Dante sighs. "Lucian did give her some of Hell."

"Shut up!" I snap, annoyance rushing through me. "Like you said. We have shit to do, and you're going to let me figure out how to do it. I fucking doubt sleeping with five angels will do anything. If such a plan worked, I bet you my rule of Purgatory that you'd have already finished the task."

"What about fucking only us then? I can promise banging us will help you grow stronger. Maybe we can test the whole Anti-Christ theory and see if maybe getting knocked up by a ruler of Hell will send power popping out of that tight pussy of yours." Kase grins with his words.

I try not to react to his comment and clench my jaw. "The only thing I want to fucking test is if it's possible to drop you hellish fuckers to your knees with a punch to the junk."

"Aw, pretty soul. All you have to do is ask." Dante scoots off the couch and kneels on the floor. His intimidating cock pitches the biggest tent I've ever seen against his towel, spreading the fabric open to give me a view.

I can't control my eyes, so I spin around and storm toward the front door. With each step, energy returns to me, my body feeling as if I just gulped a pot of coffee. I fling open the front door, and my headache fades with the fresh air. I feel better than I have in a long time. Whatever drugs Joel had been poisoning me with have left my system with Lucian's deal. The cuts and bruises no longer decorate my skin like a battle zone from the abuse I survived. And fuck, the more I think about Joel, the angrier I get. He's probably long gone now.

I don't know what comes over me, but I don't bother

waiting to see if Kase and Dante come after me and leave, disregarding the possible consequences. Their murmurs to each other fade with the short amount of distance it takes to get to the walkway.

Striding forward, I head in the direction of Joel's single-bedroom apartment. The sunshine overhead halos my vision, and I blink a dozen times, trying to adjust to the bright rays. I don't know why I haven't noticed before, but the complex looks more rundown than I thought. The paint on the trim peels and flakes, and the grass needs watering. Weeds overrun the flowerbeds. Someone even abandoned a smelly bag of trash right on the walkway.

Footsteps sound behind me, and I ignore Dante and Kase finally choosing to follow me like predatory stalkers. They hang back and out of my sight. How I know it's them? I don't fucking know or care. Call it a psycho-sense. Because I obviously attract the wrong type of guys. Stupid vagina. She's not only a traitor but a damn hellion.

A soft whistle sounds through the air, grabbing my attention. "Raven, what do you think you're doing? You look like you're on a mission of self-destruction," Kase says without closing the distance. "We have rules, you know. You can't just do what you want."

I spin around and nearly crash into Dante's chest. "Are you kidding me?"

Locking his fingers to my shoulders, Dante bows closer,

HER PERSONAL DEMONS

flicking his forked tongue at me like he enjoys the taste of my agitation. "Does it look like we're kidding? We were not ready to get to work yet." He flashes two long fangs at me. "Acting like a righteous brat in our apartment is one thing. You can do who and what you want in the protection of our hellhole as long as it involves us. But leaving without asking? Treating us as if we're not your keepers and that you can take matters into your own hands? These are punishable offenses, pretty soul."

"Now turn your sexy ass around and go home. You will wait there until we do what Lucian included in your deal." Kase motions to the pathway. "If you make one of us drag you back, I promise you that you'll—"

I slam my hands into Dante's chest, trying to knock him into Kase. The bastard doesn't even budge, and I start to wonder what he's really made out of. Because it's not flesh and bones. It's more like concrete, steel, and bullet-proof glass.

"You guys have already taken too damn long in holding up your side of the arrangement. Joel probably ran." I place my hands on my hips, summoning my strongest nerve to keep me from looking away from Dante and Kase's towering presence. "I want to make sure he's gone and never coming back. I also want to grab my stuff. You can't expect me to keep wearing this nasty robe and my dirty clothes."

"We said you could be naked," Dante responds, a

smirk pulling his lips up in the corner.

I glower. "Fuck off. I'm not playing around anymore."

I spin on my feet and stride away from them, picking up my pace into a full-blown sprint. I can hear their quick footsteps as they follow behind me, and I won't put it past the lunatics to go through with their threat to punish me for breaking rules I had no idea were in place.

"Last chance, Raven," Kase calls, his voice rumbling through the air. "If you go in there, you will have to stay to bear witness to the start of Joel's eternal damnation."

"Unless that's something you want. I just didn't think you had the stomach or nerve," Dante adds.

Ignoring them, I rush to Joel's apartment and grip the knob. Like he's been waiting for my return, Joel yanks the door open. I'm caught off guard by him, and he locks his fingers through my hair and drags me inside. Kicking the door shut, he rushes to block it with the dresser he pulled out from the bedroom. He was waiting for me—for us. For something. I can't believe I just walked right into a trap, and the bastard devils didn't bother to tell me. This wasn't in the damn fine print of their warnings.

"You brought them here, you fucking bitch," Joel growls, slamming my back to the wall.

The putrid smell of rotting wafts through the air, and I cover my mouth and nose. The scent reminds me of what the gateway to Hell smelled like. The memory ignites a wave of fire inside me, burning away the fear Joel summons in me.

He grabs my throat. "You're dead—"

The front door explodes open, and the lights pop and shatter as the floor quakes beneath my feet. Dante storms into the apartment, flashing his fangs. His skin ripples and moves and his bones crack as he grows taller, broader—and then the most shocking black wings unfurl from his back.

Joel hollers and releases me, scrambling to run away. A deep, guttural roar echoes through the room, reverberating through my very soul. Dante engulfs me in his arms and lifts me off my feet. His warm fingers graze my neck, but I don't look at him. I can't. My eyes refuse to abandon the majestic beast stalking into the living room from the hallway. Feline in stature, yet massive and with a crown of three jutting horns, the demon roars again as it rises on two legs. Red eyes glow from its massive head, matching the slick ruby color of its skin. A long black tail whips from its backend and wraps around Joel, dragging him forward.

I gasp and cover my mouth, though I can't squeeze my eyes shut as much as I want to. Joel screams like a banshee, flailing his arms to fight against the beast. Widening its jaws, the demonic creature reveals a mouth full of sharp fangs.

"Close your eyes, Raven," Dante whispers, pressing his big hand into my back, trying to force me to turn away.

"You don't have to watch justice being served."

A blood-curdling scream pierces my ears, and I watch in shock as the demonic beast chomps its fangs into Joel's arm and rips it right off. My stomach heaves, but I don't throw up. There is nothing inside of me to expel.

"Oh, God," I whisper, my vision crowding with shadows.

The beast jerks its head up and roars at me. Dante envelops me within the warmth of his devastatingly beautiful black wings, but I grip my fingers and pull one down, unable to take my eyes away from the horrors unfolding before me. Slamming its dagger nails into the floor, the beast causes the apartment to rumble and shake until the carpet splits and opens. Fire billows from the crack, and I tense, knowing exactly what's happening.

"He will never hurt you or anyone ever again," Dante whispers, stroking his fingers up and down the length of my back. He sounds so certain, almost relieved, and I finally manage to break my gaze away from Joel and the beast. "I promise."

I stare at him in awe, his emerald eyes glowing with the fire behind us. The world shakes, and the intensity of the heat burns over me, but I feel no pain. All I feel is utter and complete relief.

Joel's screams cut off, and Dante's eyes dim, returning to normal. His wings unfurl, releasing us from their protective cave, but I don't move. I don't speak either.

A warm hand touches my back between my shoulder blades. "It's done," Kase says, leaning in close enough that I feel the heat of his body. "The bastard will finally get what he deserves."

6

RAVEN

ENVY

"THREE DAYS IS long enough. It's time to get cleaned up, change, and get to work." Kase crosses his arms, towering over me. "I know you're still reeling over the fucker and everything, but you need to suck it up, angel-girl. Lucian will disapprove of our coddling."

Coddling? Neither Kase nor Dante has even said one word to me since the demonic beast devoured Joel and sent him to Hell. Sure, Dante carried me all the way back to the apartment, fed me, and handed me the TV remote and his phone to play with and Kase collected all my belongings and placed them in a pitiful pile in the corner of the room, but this is far from coddling.

"I filled the tub. If you don't get up, I will carry you to it and drop you in. You're starting to smell like Hell," Kase adds, leaning down. The fucker has the nerve to sniff me. "You'll feel better after."

"Better? A fucking demonic beast tore off my ex's arm and sent him to Hell on my behalf. I'm—it was—fuck. Where did that thing even go?" I turn away from his glowing red eyes and roll to my other side.

"That better not be sympathy I'm hearing in your voice. The fucker cemented his place in Hell before you two even met. Remember his last girlfriend? The one who died in a tragic accident?" Dante strolls from the hallway like he wants to always be included in the conversation and has decided to follow Kase's initiative. I'm not exactly certain, but I think Kase might be the one in control of things here.

"How do you know about Davina?" A pit forms in my stomach as I recall what I know about the woman Joel dated before me in his early twenties. She had died in a swimming accident on a lake and it took two weeks to recover her body. I wouldn't have known if Rob hadn't brought it up when the two of them were drinking at a get-together.

"Kase told me. He's the one who reaped that bastard's soul. I'd be envious about it if I didn't get the better end of the deal, getting to cuddle with you during the show." Dante winks at me as if we went to a concert or something.

"You forgot about the chick from his high school." Kase nudges me with his hand, getting me to make room for him to sit on the couch. If this turns into a common occurrence, I'm going to have to start planting my ass on the floor to sleep. "The prom queen."

I frown, furrowing my brows. What the hell?

"Shit, that was brutal." Dante strides closer like me avoiding getting squished under Kase's ass is my offer for him to sit as well. "What did you ever see in the bastard, anyway? I know you're in your early thirties and all, and mortals get antsy for companionship if they haven't had it yet, but for fuck's sake. He wasn't even attractive."

"Maybe she likes the whole dad-bod thing. It would explain why she doesn't throw herself at us." Kase raises an eyebrow at me. "You should really evaluate your standards."

Annoyance rushes through me. "Fuck off, the both of you. You're fucking demonic shitheads and have no room for giving me mortal dating advice. Joel wasn't always bad to—"

"Yes, he fucking was," Dante says, hissing under his voice. "It's time you accept it, get off your sexy bubble-butt, and get naked before I climb in that bath and enjoy all the hard work Kase put forth in an attempt to make you feel better."

"If it means getting away from you, then fine." I shift my legs and manage to get off the couch without touching either of them.

My mind whirls as I snatch some clothes from the corner and head to the bathroom. A part of me wishes they were lying about Joel, but they don't seem like they would, despite the Hell thing. If what they say is true...fuck. I never in a million years ever expected that two demonic bastards would save me from a man I trusted. One I had planned to marry until he showed his true self. Now I can't help wondering if I was somehow set up. What are the probabilities that I would lose my job, have to return to Joel to avoid being homeless, and then have Kase and Dante intervene? It's not divine intervention, but maybe something wilder. Fate? I don't know.

I push the thoughts away upon the sight of the steamy bubble bath that smells as if someone bottled up a delectable dessert to pour in, knowing my love of gourmand scents. I peek over my shoulder at Kase and Dante sitting on the couch. They both smile and wave, way too proud of themselves for getting me to move my ass. Clicking the door closed, I lock it and drop the crusty robe to the floor along with the rest of my grimy clothes. I dunk my hand in the water, groaning at the heat, already dying to get in.

GINNA MORAN

"Need some help, pretty soul?" Dante asks, knocking on the door.

I rush to climb in, splashing water over the side. "No, I—"

The door swings open, and Dante stands in the frame with his hand over his eyes. How did I know he could just come in despite me turning the lock? Or how did I know one of them would barge in?

"Dante, what the fuck? Get out," I snap, flinging soapy water in his direction.

He steps forward. "Aw, come on. I'm not going to look at you unless you let me."

"Seriously?" I chuck a bottle of shampoo at him.

Catching it with his free hand, he shakes the bottle. The fucker. I want to yell at him and chuck another bottle, but I already know it won't stop him. It'll give him an excuse to drop his hand from his gaze.

"You guys talked about rules, but I think you need to follow some of mine if you want to survive another day with me." I sink lower in the tub. "I thought I made it clear I wanted some space. I can't think when I'm around you."

Dante sighs and continues on his mission to close the distance to me. "Would you believe me if I told you I hate the fucking space you want over me? You've had days of space. I just want a couple minutes of your time."

"For what? To make poor attempts at seducing me?

Telling me I have awful taste in men? Or that you're my big bad boss and you can't wait for me to fail so you get to keep my soul for all eternity?" I close my eyes, hearing Dante set down the shampoo bottle.

"You make me sound like a monster," he quips, his voice lowering. He's close. Too close. "All I wanted was to check on you. Wash your hair, if you'd allow it."

Well, if this isn't the weirdest fucking thing.

"If I let you do that, will you then leave me alone?" I ask, sitting up. Bubbles shield my breasts, but I still feel incredibly exposed.

"For an hour," he says, squirting shampoo into his palm. "Maybe two."

I tip my head back and peer at him from upside down. "How can I get three?"

A smirk pulls at the corner of his lips. "Let me shave your legs."

I blink. "Are you for real?"

"You're the one who wants to make a deal. Take it or leave it, Raven. You may never get this sort of arrangement again." Dante sticks out his tongue, flicking it.

I can't stop staring at how it's split in half like a fork with silver barbells on each side. Like my finger takes on a mind of its own, I reach out and touch it. Dante's eyes spark with fire, and his tongue wraps around my finger as he pulls it into his mouth. The sensation surprises the hell out of me.

I jerk my hand away and dunk it underwater.

"Our next deal will be even more fun, though," he teases, rubbing his hands together. Gathering my wet hair, he begins to lather in the shampoo. "You'll cave eventually. Shit gets boring. And with you...I can be my true self."

His words dig into me as he soaps up my hair, gently scratching his fingers into my scalp. I inhale and exhale slowly. I will never admit it out loud, but it feels fucking amazing. I haven't been able to go to a salon in so long that I almost forgot what it's like to have someone else do it for me.

"What? No snarky comment about my true self being a monstrous beast?" he asks, filling my silence.

I shift and peek over my shoulder at him. "I thought it was a given. Now, stop talking. Our deal only included you washing my hair."

"And shaving your legs," he says, wagging his eyebrows.

My cheeks flush, thinking about how weird his desire is. "If I let you talk, will you give me four hours? You have to keep Kase away too."

"Add shaving your pussy to that, and you have a fucking deal." Dante grins, loving the shock slackening my jaw.

"You're crazy. I'll take the damn two hours for the hair washing. The deal is off on everything else, you perv. Now get out." Slapping my hand to the water, I send a wave of it over his head.

Dante howls a laugh and hops to his feet, yanking his wet shirt off. "I said *maybe* two, but you just keep getting more entertaining, so now it's one. You didn't even let me rinse."

Grabbing the conditioner, I chuck it at him. He lets it hit him in the chest and fall to the floor. A cocky-bastard smile lights his face, turning him even more handsome. It only pisses me off more. I stand up, and splash more water at him.

"Hey, God," I call, raising my voice. "Can you bless this water? I could really use some demon repellant."

Dante play-growls, narrowing his eyes. "Stop being so much damn fun, and maybe I wouldn't want to be around your bratty ass."

"If you think this is fun, I feel bad for you. You must've had an awful existence." I can't stop the smile from crossing my face.

"It was dreadful. Pity me, oh pretty broken soul. Wipe off those bubbles from your perky tits so it feels as if I've ascended to Heaven again." Dante unfurls his magnificent black wings and flaps them, sending a gust of wind in my direction.

I screech and scramble to grab the towel hanging on the rod, only giving him a view of my naked body for a split second. Glowering, I stomp the three feet of space it takes to reach him and slap my hand against his taut pec. He flexes his muscles, and for the first time, I can see the details of the tattoo over his heart. A snake slithers around a skull, and I swear the eyes glow at me.

"I'm sorry, Raven. I couldn't help myself. Just the thought of your heavenly body getting ravished by mine..." He shakes out his arms, and his wings disappear. "I'll give you three hours and keep Kase away. You can even punish me."

"No fucking way. You'd enjoy it, you glutton." Am I crazy for not being upset? Maybe. But for the first time in days I've managed to smile and laugh, even if it's because this bastard doesn't understand boundaries.

"Envy is my calling," he responds, smirking. "And you should shove me out of here and get some clothes on. I'm starting to despise the towel hugging you."

Oh, boy.

I do as he says, pushing him out of the bathroom, though he doesn't resist. He grins the whole time as I shut the door in his face. I turn away and rest my back against the door. Why am I okay with this? Is it because I already know these fuckers aren't going anywhere? Is something wrong with me? It's only been a week since Joel left me for dead and even less than that, watching as the beast threw him into Hell. I should be reeling. Panicking. Crying and questioning my existence. Right? What the hell has gotten into me...oh. Maybe that's it. Hell has gotten into me. I don't know exactly what it means, but apparently I can forgive shitheads who planned to throw me in a dumpster.

Fuck me.

Quickly rinsing off the bubble residue, I dry and dress, wondering exactly what a few hours of space will look like. I already know that they don't want me to leave the apartment unsupervised for whatever reason, but it's not like either of them has given up their rooms to me.

"Hey, angel-girl?" Kase asks outside the bathroom door as if he knows I'm hovering on the other side. "We have to run some errands. I picked you up a pizza and some beer from around the corner. Make yourself comfortable in whoever's room you want. If it's Dante's, feel free to go through all his shit. It'll drive him crazy and pay him back for his games. Hell, if you sleep on his bed, he might kick it out of his room because it got to sleep with you first, and he's a whack job when it comes to not getting what others have."

An image of fucking with Dante makes me smile even wider. I consider responding to Kase but decide if I open myself for any sort of conversing, he won't leave. And now that I know they're planning to go out? Fuck. I have shit to do. Angels to find. They think they know what they're doing, but I can't exactly trust them. This is my eternity, and I will not put it in anyone else's hands. They had mentioned before that these supposed saviors were flying around. Maybe all I have to do is embrace this crazy-ass situation and start shouting prayers or something. Who knows? If I'm out of this demonic lair, someone might actually respond to my calls.

A door slams, startling me. I was so lost in my thoughts that I hadn't heard Kase move away from the door. I lick my lips and press my ear to the wood, trying to hear for any noise. I can't be certain this isn't some sort of trick to get me to come out, so I wait five more minutes, gathering my nerve. I crack open the bathroom door and listen for another minute. Silence greets me from the rest of the apartment. Strolling into the hallway, I peek into Kase's room with the sliding glass door to the patio and then into Dante's...sex chambers? I don't know how else to describe it. He has an impressive collection of restraints, paddles, spreader bars, gags, and other toys on full display in cases on his wall. Along his dresser, dozens of different bottles of lubes and other unfamiliar liquids rest in neat lines. His closet door is a mirror with the perfect view of the bed, and another mirror hangs from the damn ceiling. If he didn't admit that he embodies envy, whatever the fuck that means, I'd have pegged him as lust.

I huff under my breath and silently curse Kase. The fucker probably knew there was no way I'd actually step foot in Dante's room and probably just wanted to get me to look. I half-expect the two of them to pop out and surprise me and tease me for the rest of time, but the apartment remains silent.

They're gone.

I almost don't believe it.

They made this too damn easy. Now I feel like this could be a possible trap. I guess there is only one way to find out.

After slipping on my flats, I snag my hoodie from my pile of clothes and shrug it on. The sun will go down soon, and with how hot I've been feeling the last few days, I'm sure the nights will start feeling much, much colder.

I grab my purse, though it's not like I have anything I could possibly use unless I need some lip balm, and head out the door. I don't know what I was expecting, maybe the fires of Hell to light up the world. But nothing happens. The porch is the same as it was the last time. It feels anti-climactic to just exit the apartment without sudden blaring alarms or angry demonic beasts trying to stop me.

Clutching my purse like a safety blanket, I head down the pathway and in the opposite direction of Joel's apartment. I have no idea where I'm going, but the farther I get, the better I feel. The easier it is to think.

I reach the parking lot and spot my old Honda in its assigned spot. I had been planning to walk. I mean, I really should save my quarter tank of gas for an emergency. If only seeing my car didn't bring on a wave of desperate need to escape. I could get more than thirty miles with the gas I have left. That sounds like the perfect amount of space. It would be easier to search for the angels in all the places I can think they'd be hiding.

And when I find one, I can figure out how to make them fall...

What am I even thinking? Make them fall? No. I can beg them for help. Pray for divine intervention. Ask to be saved.

I pick up my pace with the thought and run the rest of the way to my car. Relief floods over me as I start the engine and back out. If Kase and Dante catch me, I'll surely have hell to pay. I push away my hesitation and back out.

Gripping my steering wheel, I brace for one of them to pop up from my backseat, because my life has turned into a horror movie and such scares seem possible. It takes driving two blocks for my body to start relaxing. In another three blocks, I flick on my stereo.

"You got this, Raven," I say to myself, peeking into the rearview mirror at the sun setting behind me. "This is your eternity. Don't let anyone try to fuck it up. You deserve—"

Bright lights flash through my side window.

I don't even have a chance to scream before a truck collides into me.

7

RAVEN

EVIL ANGEL

I CLUTCH ONTO my steering wheel, spinning out of control until I crash into the traffic signal pole. Fuck. So while demons didn't pop up in my backseat, I should've considered an unexpected car crash to be the second thing on my-life-is-a-horror-movie checklist.

Groaning, I smack my hand to my steering wheel and scream in frustration. My airbag didn't go off, which means this could've been a lot worse. It would've been nice had this small miracle been me escaping instead of wasting precious time.

A tap sounds on the window. "Hey, bitch. Get the fuck out of the car. You wrecked my truck."

Bitch? Get out? I wrecked *his* truck? What the actual fuck?

I turn my head, my chest aching from my hitting the seatbelt. "What happened to, 'hey, are you okay?'"

The second our eyes meet, I know something is wrong. The man yanks my car door open and grabs my wrist, attempting to drag me out. My seatbelt keeps me in place. Grabbing my bag from the seat, I swing it at the guy's head. He hollers in anger and bends closer. I punch and hit his head, trying to get him away, but he unlatches my seatbelt and drags me from the car.

"Help!" I scream, locking my hands around the guy's wrists, jabbing my nails into his skin as hard as I can. "Help!"

"Shut up, filthy soul! No one will come for—"

Bright light explodes from above us, and the man freezes mid-sentence. His silhouette morphs before my eyes, and he transforms into a hideous humanoid creature with blood-red antlers, black fur from head-to-toe, and a mouth full of jagged brown teeth. I screech and yank away from him, but he doesn't move. He remains frozen in place in his demonic body.

"Shit. Shit. Shit." I scramble farther back until my back hits...some seriously muscular legs.

Tipping my head back, I peer up at the silhouette haloed in blinding sunlight—no, not sunlight. The sun is just a sliver in the distance. Whatever this light is comes from nowhere and everywhere, and it stings the hell out of my eyes. Tears roll down my cheeks, and I rapidly blink, trying to clear my vision to focus on the being preventing me from moving.

"Don't hurt me," I whisper, my voice hoarse with my burning throat. "Please." God, help me. I didn't go through all this just to die. If I die, my soul will automatically go to the devils, and as strangely attracted as I am to their psycho asses, I don't want to be at their mercy forever. I barely know them. They could be messing with me until I fail. Then, their horns will truly show.

"Heathen prayers don't get answered." A smooth, baritone voice hums through the air above me. "If you want another deal, you'll have to ask your soul keepers."

My eyes widen as glorious bright white wings unfurl and stir a cool breeze through my bath-damp hair. The wings shade the glow emanating from the angel enough for me to catch sight of his achingly perfect features. I mean, talk about the epitome of tall, dark, buff, and handsome beyond this world. And this angel isn't a cherub—no white diaper or billowing white robe like I've seen in paintings and depicted in stained-glass windows. This man is a sex dream come to life. I already feel heat building between my legs, but a part of me knows that there isn't going to be any magical climax. I'll just wake up panting, in need of serious sexual relief, and with a case of lady blue bean.

Thick lashes rim the angel's gold eyes—and not brown-gold. His irises look metallic and shimmery—the perfect complement to his smooth, flawless complexion. I blink in awe, unable to form coherent thoughts. My mind registers what the angel says, but my body and soul refuse to accept hearing anything at all.

And honestly, if I didn't know deep inside me how pure and good this man was, I'd think he was a devil in disguise.

Especially seeing him raise a flaming sword into the air.

Holy shit.

Raising my hands protectively, I brace to get sliced in two under the burning grace of his angelic weapon. "Wait, please! Please, don't! I'm begging you. Don't kill me. I was hoping to find you. I need help. I was manipulated into making a deal with Lucian and—"

"Call him by his true name!" the angel hollers, his voice echoing through the air. "The betrayer must be recognized."

I cringe and try to scoot forward out of his looming shadow, but the angel slams the tip of the sword into the concrete right between my legs. If I had a dick, I'd be sweating in fear. Shoving myself back and harder into the angel's legs, I try to escape the heat of the sword. I thought Kase and Dante radiated heat—fuck, the hellfire used to transport Lucian into their apartment was scorching—but neither of those fiery temperatures compare to the burning flames licking across the surface of this sword.

"I never wanted to be in this position," I whisper, my voice struggling to escape my dry tongue. "I don't want to have a deal with Lucifer, but he manipulated me into it. He was going to put me in a position that would send me to Hell regardless. I was trying to save myself from a worse torment."

"Those worthy of help wouldn't turn their backs on the Higher Power and the good in the world to save themselves. Your selfishness and lack of regard for the greater good would have sent you to Hell, not Lucifer. Not the demons. Not even Joel's pitiful existence. You made your choices and now must live the rest of eternity with the consequences." The angel jerks his sword from the concrete and holds it above me.

I lose my shit.

What the fuck kind of angel just casts me aside and writes me off as a heathen because I discovered there was Heaven and Hell after not believing and was terrified of eternal punishment at the hands of demons? Anger rushes through me at his accusations, and I slam my back hard enough into his legs to send him reeling. It's like the strength of my deal with Lucian gives me power unlike anything I've had before, and now that I once again face a shitty fate, I can access it.

I roll out of the way and push myself to my feet. "You righteous bastard! I'm begging you for help, so I don't have to go through with the task I'm bound to. Maybe if you or whoever else is supposed to be some sort of savior would have, oh, I don't know, given me proper divine intervention when I needed it most, then maybe I wouldn't have agreed to this deal. I'm not selfish. I'm human. If I were truly the heathen you claim me to be, I wouldn't be pleading for your mercy."

I heave a few breaths and clench my fingers into fists. The angel, one who is more evil than Kase and Dante could ever be, stares at me with unblinking eyes. I shift under his scrutiny, feeling his gaze penetrate me on a soul-deep level, and it leaves me wanting more and more space between us.

I step back, listening to my instincts. I have no idea how I'm going to get out of this mess. I either have to run and hope he lets me go, fight and face the fact that I'm no match for a warrior of the Almighty, or I have five seconds to try to make him fall.

Shuffling back, I grab the hem of my shirt and yank it up, flashing him my boobs. And fuck. It doesn't work. The pure bastard doesn't even glance at my naked breasts as he strides closer. I screech and try to get out of his reach, but I'm not fast enough. My back hits against something solid, and the angel scowls, baring his teeth, his handsome features turning dangerous.

A strong, hairy arm grabs me from behind, and the frozen demon comes to life, launching itself at the angel. Bending his knees, the angel launches in the air and takes flight. My eyes burn at the brightness of his form ascending into the purpling sky of twilight, and I squint, peering at him through my lashes. I'm afraid he'll come nosediving at me, sword pointed, and dead-set on sending my soul to Hell.

But the angel disappears.

The hairy arms don't though, and the demon tightens his hold on me from behind. Growling under his breath, the demon blows strands of my hair from my throat. His disgusting breath permeates the air, twisting my stomach. It smells like death and far from Kase and Dante's irresistible fragrances.

"Lucian's going to be pissed that your soul keepers let you out of their sight. That bastard angel almost ruined everything." His grumbly voice vibrates across my back. "You can tell Lucian I saved you. If you do that, I won't kill you myself. You can be my filthy soul. Wouldn't you like that? Not being shared?"

I stiffen at his attempt to manipulate me. This fucker is

out of his demented mind if he thinks I'm going to just give in to his ultimatum. I've already been pushed around enough and forced into shitty deals. But even my deal now is better than the one he tries to offer. If I agree, I'll lose what little of a fighting chance I have.

"You want me to give you my soul in exchange to live? But also for you to keep my soul for eternity? Are you fucking kidding me? No. I'd rather die and end up with—"

The demon screeches, startling the words out of me. The intense sound of his wail pierces my ear, and I wince in pain. He shoves me away from him. Stumbling, I land on my hands, scraping my palms on the gritty asphalt. Shadows crowd my vision as I try to look around. Soft light emanates from a yellow lamppost overhead. I would've thought onlookers might be watching this freak show go down, but it's eerily empty.

And then a familiar beast roars.

I catch sight of the blood red, feline-like beast lashing its long black tail at the demon man, slashing his skin. Smoke wafts from the hairy demon as he tries to dodge out of the way. Instead of fighting, the demon looks like he's trying to run.

"Please, my liege, I saved the soul. She's alive because of me. Don't hurt me." The demon turns toward me, flashing his gross teeth. "Tell him. The angel was trying to send you to Hell."

Fury rushes through me. I don't know where I find the nerve, but I suck up my trepidation over getting within feet of the same beast that sent Joel to Hell. The same beast that was in Kase and Dante's apartment when they summoned Lucian...shit. Is that—

The monstrous demonic beast rises onto two legs and whips its tail around the demon's ankles, flipping it upside down. "Raven will not lie on your behalf."

Oh shit. I recognize the voice despite its throaty, guttural growl. I thought the beast might've been Lucian in another form than the one I saw, but it's Kase. This is his true demonic form. The guys don't summon some Hell beast to do their bidding. They take care of things themselves. I don't know why I didn't consider it.

"She would be lying if she didn't tell you the truth!" the demonic man screeches, thrashing in an attempt to break free. "You can't trust a mortal. You know this."

While recognizing Kase in this form threw me off, this bastard demon drags me right back on my mission to...I don't know. I'm not a good fighter and definitely not great at facing gross creatures. But damn it. I won't allow him to speak against me.

"Oh, shut the fuck up, you asshole! You couldn't even stop the righteous shithead if you wanted to. Your godforsaken bastard self was frozen in time or some shit. I'm the one who saved you—by accident. You were the one who crashed my car. You wanted to use me against my demons in an attempt to bow before Lucian and suck his cock, hoping you get the piece of Hell you'd never deserve." I fist my hands and meet the demon's scowling face straight on as he dangles in front of me. Swinging my arm, I punch him in the side of the head.

"Gotta do it harder than that, angel-girl," Kase says, whipping the demon back and forth before slamming him to the ground. Dragging him up again with his tail, Kase bobs him in front of me like a monster in a trap. "Show me what you got. Teach this asshole where his place is."

Kase's words of encouragement ignite something dark inside me, and I step back and glance around the ground. I spot a piece of sharp metal debris from the wreck and scoop it up. The demon roars, watching me from upside down, hanging like the perfect evil piñata, waiting to have his insides spilled.

Grinding my teeth, I yell out as I rush the demon. Darkness laces around me, squeezing my chest and possessing my body until it consumes me. The world slows and my movements feel as if I fight through jelly until I watch myself from another pair of eyes. Light and shadows blend and merge around me as my figure rushes forward and jams the metal fragment into the demon's stomach and drags it down to his chest.

A shockwave of energy zaps through me, jolting me

back into my body as hot liquid spills over me. The ground shakes and cracks, and I shriek and scramble away as pieces of the demon dissolve into a molten pit of fire. Kase's beast roars and whips the demon around, sending his insides raining through the air. I cover my face and heave a few breaths.

A loud screech echoes through the dusky world, and I peek through my fingers as Kase slams the demon into the pit and it closes up as if the burning fire never existed at all. He stretches his enormous form and gathers fire into his clawed fingers, igniting himself ablaze. My eyes widen, watching the red flames engulf him. My heart pounds in my ears, my body humming.

Kase's demonic beast form burns away, leaving him behind as his breathtakingly sexy self. His chest heaves with his deep breaths, and he curls and uncurls his fingers. Red light glows in his eyes, and he jerks his attention in my direction. Trembles shudder through me, and I hug myself, trying to suppress the fear rattling my soul. I take an automatic step back.

Kase hesitates, tilting his head to the side. "What's the matter, angel-girl? You afraid of me?"

I blink a few times. A strange glowing light shines in the distance behind him, and I realize it's not Kase setting off my panic. I spot the righteous evil angel peeping at us like a damn creeper.

"You should be, Raven," Kase says, cracking his knuckles. "What the fuck did I tell you? What was the one rule you were supposed to follow?"

I don't respond to him, keeping my gaze locked on the angel.

Closing the space to me, Kase towers over me, his muscles rippling. "Answer me."

Kase grabs my chin and guides my gaze away from the angel until I meet his glowing eyes. Heat radiates between us, and I can't stop myself from sliding my hand up his bare chest until I clutch his shoulder. Like he can sense my innate need to be in the protection I had no idea truly existed in his arms until this moment, Kase hooks his free hand to my hip and pulls me to him until I'm flush against him. I feel every hot muscle of his body, but especially his raging boner pressing against my stomach through his pants, which is the only thing he wears.

"Don't make me force you to tell me," he mutters, his voice low but loud enough that I'm sure the angel can hear. The righteous bastard probably gets off on Kase's threat of punishment.

My bottom lip quivers as I summon my voice to speak. "You told me not to leave the apartment."

"And what is the first fucking thing you did the second we gave you a moment of freedom?" he prods, his handsome features sharpening.

"I ran," I whisper.

Releasing my face only to grab me by the neck, Kase leans into my face and grins. His wicked smile should freak me the fuck out, but I suck my trembling lip into my mouth and inhale shallow breaths of his delectable scent.

"I'm sorry," I add. "I thought—"

"You didn't think! You put yourself in unnecessary danger, and for what? To pray for help? To seek divine intervention? And after everything I've done for you." Kase's nostrils flare, his smile widening with his words. Leaning in even more, he brushes his lips to my ear. "You're a fucking naughty girl. I want to bend you over the wreckage, tug down your panties, and bang you from behind as that bastard angel watches. A little reward for bringing Micah out of hiding. He's already hooked, and I hate it."

I try to remain expressionless under the whisper of his words. If only my vagina didn't love the sound of his desire enough to turn me on. I never thought I was much of an exhibitionist, but the thrill of knowing that Kase won't let anything happen to me and feeling the power radiating from him so strongly that the angel stays away—I almost nod my head in agreement.

But if I do? It'll ruin my plan.

"Please, no," I say, forcing my voice louder. "I won't do it again. I've learned my lesson. I'll obey you. Just don't punish me."

Kase smirks, raising his eyebrow. "You will obey me as

I punish you. Do you understand?"

I lick my lips, drawing Kase's attention to my mouth. "Yes."

"You will let me do whatever I want. Your soul is mine." Kase loosens his hold on my neck and slides his hot fingers into my hair, tilting my head up. "Mine."

Something crazy intense comes over me like a rush of electricity zinging from my core to travel up to my chest and down my legs until I'm buzzing all over. Standing on my tiptoes, I brush my lips to Kase's, devouring what it's like to kiss such power and survive. His hand tightens on my hip, his fingers digging harder into the skin peeking out from the hem of my shirt. I nearly expect him to do what he craves and rip my pants open to screw me right in the middle of the empty street.

He breaks away first and searches my face, his demonic form peeking from his expression. I pant with my building desire. If he didn't tug my hair, keeping me back, I would kiss him again, harder and more desperately. I'd slip my tongue into his mouth and find out if his kiss tastes as sweet and warm as he smells.

"I'm yours," I whisper, my voice catching with my words. "I won't leave again. I've learned my lesson. I promise."

Kase bares his teeth at me, his eyes glowing even brighter with the red light of his power. Scooping me up, he flips me onto his shoulder with a growl. "Promises mean nothing to me, angel-girl. I will determine whether or not you've learned your lesson when I'm through with you. You will wish you never uttered a call for divine help. You will wish it was me who you called. I will ensure it."

I hang limply on his shoulder, acting like the complacent heathen the angel thinks I am. I don't know what Kase's plan is exactly, but I know he's up to something. And who knows? Maybe it'll be something that could work. Maybe I won't be screwed after all. At least, not by Hell.

"Raven," a soft voice whispers through my mind.

I stiffen at the sound of the angel's voice in my head.

Arching my back, I peer where soft light shines the brightest and spot the expansive wings of the angel.

"This isn't the end."

I frown in confusion at the intruding voice.

The angel launches into the air without another word and lights up the night for a second. All that remains are his words swirling through my head. Whether it was a threat or a promise of hope for my eternity? I wish I knew.

Kase carries me away.

8

KASE

WRATH

I'M GOING TO kill him. I will cut off Micah's wings and eat them for being the fucker I knew he could be. What makes it worse is that Raven sought him first. She called to him, which means she still resists the place she belongs by my side. Her resistance pushed me forward, igniting a burning need inside me that yearns to prove to her that everything she knows of the universe is wrong.

At least Micah's rejection might've helped. The fucking idiot, completely lost in the light that blinds him. Just the thought of him touching Raven enrages me even more. It is my job to help finish what the brethren and I started so long ago. I know this. I thought I'd be okay with our mission and helping Raven seduce the angelic traitor, but I want to keep her far away. Lock her up so he will never be graced with her presence again.

"Kase," Raven murmurs, her voice breathy and sexy as fuck. Hearing my name on her lips is hotter than I could've ever imagined. I want to hear her scream it. "Kase, come on."

I ignore her, focusing on the world in front of us. It's all I can do to control the intense need inside me that wants to capture Micah and fuck Raven in front of him to show him that he'll never have her, especially knowing the soft sensation of her lips against mine.

If she didn't release the sexiest groan I've ever heard, I'd drop her on the porch and play a game of hunt the bird-brain bastard.

"You know I can walk, right?" Raven asks, smacking her hands to my back. "You're giving me a head rush like this. The angel is gone. You can stop flaunting your psychotic persona."

"Persona? Hardly, angel-girl. And no. Your naughty ass is staying right where I can smack it until we're inside. I will not risk the chance that Micah might be following us to steal you from me. It's already taking every ounce of my willpower not to tear the fucker in half." I consider proving my point by spanking her as she lies over my shoulder.

She squirms, trying to get down, but all it does is make me adjust my hand to squeeze her thigh. "Why? Are you mad that I'm capable of doing shit on my own? That yours and Dante's flimsy plan will fail?"

"Mad? Fuck no. You'd know if I was mad. You'd feel my wrath burn through you. I'm annoyed as fuck. You betrayed me, Raven, calling Micah out on your own. What were you planning to do? Beg him for mercy?" Heat burns in my palms, replaying the thoughts in my head. "I told you praying to the Higher Power was useless. If anything, you should fucking beg me for forgiveness."

Raven wiggles on my shoulder and huffs a breath. "Your forgiveness? Yeah, sure. Forgive me, you psycho bastard, for I have realized your true desire and don't trust you."

Damn, she sounds so hot all worked up.

"I was trying to get him to show himself, so I could make him fall. I don't think you're really down for helping me with this fucking task," she snaps.

I growl loud enough that I know she feels the vibration against her perfectly curved hip. She clenches her tight ass, squeezing her legs together. My cock hardens, her reaction eliciting the thought of her riding my fucking horns while I growl against her clit until she squirts on my face.

Fuck. I want that. My balls ache with desire, and it pisses me off.

"You are full of shit, angel-girl," I mutter, turning my head so she can feel the heat of my words on her leg. "You can't lie to me."

Flipping her off my shoulder, I set her in front of me and get her to walk by slapping her ass. She startles, but not in fear. One look into her wide blue eyes as she peeks at me from over her shoulder tells me exactly what's on her mind. She wants me to do it again. She loved it.

"I'm not lying." She stops in her tracks and turns to face me. Like she can't resist herself, she steps into my space and grazes her fingers against my palm, testing to see if I'll allow her to slide her fingers through mine. I do. "I know you would be okay either way. You want my soul forever. It wouldn't bother you if I failed. Admit it."

I smirk, turning my gaze to her pouty lips as she rubs them together. Fuck, I want to kiss her again. If I didn't know she was trying to use my lust against me, I would. "That's not what I was talking about," I say instead of telling her that of course I want her soul forever. I want more than just her soul. I want all of her. "You didn't pray to get him to reveal himself. You begged for help. He wouldn't have shown up to deny you otherwise."

She frowns, proving me right. Narrowing her eyes, she yanks her hand from mine and crosses her arms. "It was instinctual. I was being attacked by a demon."

I tighten my jaw. "I guess I'll have to remedy that."

I uncurl my tail from its hiding place camouflaged with my lower back and snake it around her, tying her legs together. She yelps in surprise and stumbles. Catching her, I lift her into my arms and graze her cheek with my tail, nearly moaning at the sensation of her soft skin.

She snatches my tail and squeezes her hand around it. "Can you put this thing away? It's weird."

"No," I mutter, tugging free from her hand despite how fucking amazing it feels. I can imagine her fingers locked around my cock just the same. "I plan to use it to tie you up. I wasn't joking about punishing you. I never, and I mean *never*, want you to ask for divine intervention again. You will only call to me or Dante, understand? We are your soul keepers. You need to trust us. I don't think this is a game, nor would I give up power just to control your soul."

Her frown deepens with my words. "Okay."

Is that disappointment in her voice? Fuck yeah it is. And I can't stop the smile breaking across my face. She wants me to want her and she dislikes that I won't give up the mission just for her, even though it's not what she truly desires.

"Don't sound so sad, angel-girl. I'll have you regardless.

You're mine, remember? I'd just rather you be my queen instead of my servant." The look she gives me sends a burst of energy through me, and I pick up my pace and stride the rest of the way to the apartment.

Her blue-green eyes stare off into space as she thinks about what I've said, and I wish I could listen to what's swirling through her mind. She's conflicted, but not over the fact that I just told her the reason I want to complete our mission. It's something else.

I open my mouth to ask her, but Dante flings the door to the apartment open. It breaks Raven from her thoughts, and her eyes glass over like she feels bad for her behavior. It gets under my skin. It's not the same as when I found her and she regretted breaking the rules because she put herself in danger and failed whatever she had planned to accomplish. No, it's far from that.

"Dante, I'm sorry," she says, blinking the sheen from her eyes.

Fuck. I knew it. Remorse adds a bit of a whine to her whispery voice. She feels bad for taking advantage of their deal and him.

Heat blazes across my face, and I summon power in my free hand and chuck it at Dante, getting him to move out of the way. "Don't apologize to the bastard. He should've known better."

Raven inhales a small breath. "But—"

"Go get cleaned up. I hate seeing and smelling that demon all over you. When you're done, go wait for me in my room." I set her on her feet and nudge her, guiding her to stroll past Dante without stopping. "Tonight, you're mine. Save your regret and apologies for Dante tomorrow."

She only nods, giving Dante one more look.

We watch her shuffle to where we dropped her stuff in the corner of the room. I wonder when she'll ask us for some place to put it. Standing next to Dante, we remain silent until she disappears into the bathroom and the shower turns on.

"Is she okay—"

Swinging my fist, I punch Dante hard in the gut, sending him reeling. The edges of my vision shadow, my rage consuming me. Raven might have left by her own will, but he is the one to have bargained with her over time that wasn't his to give. He's why she left in the first place. Had he just listened to me when I told him she needed to be around us if she's going to ever get used to us and stop resisting, she would've never been hurt, hunted, and almost sent right to Lucian for him to discover our shortcomings.

"Micah nearly sent her to Hell!" I yell, ramming my hands into his chest. "A fucking pest put his hands on her! This is your fault!"

Unfurling his wings, Dante expands them out to keep himself in place. "You better have killed the demon."

"Of-fucking-course I did! You should've seen her face, realizing who I was in my true form. You're lucky it didn't ruin it for me. Had Micah not pissed her off, she wouldn't have even kissed me." I summon red fire in my palms, replaying the moment in my mind. "Any chance of igniting his interest in her would've disappeared."

"Wait, she kissed you?" His eyes flash with his envy.

"That's what you've chosen to focus on? If you must know, I'll be banging the hell out of her later, too. She'll learn exactly what kind of beast I am as I make her beg for more." Was it petty of me to mention it? Who fucking cares. I'm pissed at him.

Dante flares his nostrils. "Until I get my time with her. I'll ensure she never thinks about you again."

The shower shuts off, and I take advantage of Dante glancing over his shoulder at the hallway and punch him in the gut again. "I'd love to see you try. Now, until then, get the fuck out of here and track Micah. I need you to see if he's still around. He's our first target."

"Fucking predictable. He was on the edge before Cassius yanked him back." Dante growls at saying another one of the traitor's names and scratches his beard. He glances over his shoulder, hearing Raven crack the door open.

Little eavesdropper. "My room, angel-girl. Make yourself comfortable."

She sighs and slams my door, only to crack it open. I let

139

it slide, grinning at Dante. He looks jealous as fuck, the vein on his neck bulging.

Stepping closer, he jams his fingers into my shoulder as he leans in to whisper, "You fucking take good care of that sexy troublemaker."

I laugh, and smack his back. "Well look at you, keeping your envy in check. If you get back early enough, maybe she'll let you watch. You know I will."

Dante groans deep in his throat, turned on by my suggestion. The damn voyeur. I shove him away and whip my tail at the back of his legs, making him growl. Storming toward the door, he flings it open and unfurls his black wings.

"Hey, Raven! Kase thinks he will get his way with you and get to bone you all night long. How about you deny him, and I'll let you sleep in my room by yourself tomorrow if you want?" Dante flashes his fangs at me with his cocky-ass smile.

Before I can lunge at him, he steps onto the porch and disappears. I grumble and shut the door, knowing damn well that the fucker got me good. There's no way Raven's going to let her guard down for some fun now unless I work twice as hard. It's a good thing I have all damn night. And even if she doesn't let me wet my dick in her hot snatch, at least I'll have her close enough to tease. She'll wear down. I know it.

I turn on my feet and hear Raven click my door closed.

She's probably anxiously waiting for me to meet her in my room, so I head to the kitchen. Throwing a grilled cheese sandwich on the stove, I quickly put together the best fucking dinner I can manage considering I don't eat anything besides pussy. Women like both things—someone cooking for them and getting their clits licked—and I gotta charm the pants off her if I want her lacing her fingers around my cock instead of having to use my own.

I grab an apple from the bowl on the counter and then pour a glass of water, holding it with my tail. Strolling down the hall, I listen as Raven messes with the blinds on my sliding glass door. I release a low whistle, giving her a chance to pretend she's not my little troublemaker.

I open the door and find her standing in front of my dresser, tracing her fingers across one of my favorite daggers. Picking it up, she spins and points it at me. A playful smile lights up her beautiful face as she carves something in the air.

"Put the food down nice and slow, and I won't hurt you." Raven points to the plate in my hand. "You guys suck at feeding me."

I bark a laugh and toss the plate on my bed. "Feeding you? You sound as if you think of yourself as our pet. Come on, angel-girl. That whole kitchen is stocked for you."

"It is?" she twists her lips to the side.

"Well, yeah. Food is the last thing I want to eat. But if

you want me to join you for dinner, you can shimmy your sexy ass out of those ridiculously modest pajamas and sit on my face. It'll make us both happy." I chuckle and kick my door closed, offering the glass of water to her with my tail.

She stares at it for a moment before taking it and clutching the cup in her hands. Her gaze follows my tail as I curl it behind me.

"You want to touch it some more? It's okay to be curious," I say, wagging my brows at her. "But I have to warn you, I'll want to use it to touch you back."

Something darkly delicious flashes in her eyes, peeking through the brightness of her angel-kissed soul. I can't stop thinking about which lucky bastard had fallen for her soul in another lifetime. Her mischievous expression pulls my attention from her light and back to her. I brace for what comes next from this naughty woman.

"I think the heat is getting to you if you think I'm letting your tail anywhere near me. So cool down." She chucks the glass of water at me with a laugh and risks turning her back to stroll to my bed. Snatching the sandwich, she plops onto my pillows, spreading out. I stand in shock, the water steaming against my hot skin. It takes her humming under her breath to get my brain to fucking work again.

"What the fuck? I hope you're planning to lick this off me, because if not, that's the last time I serve you something to drink." I swipe my hand across my wet face.

She laughs again. "Like you said, the kitchen is mine, so it was worth it. Maybe you should scold yourself. You looked in desperate need of a cold shower, and there is no fucking way I'm sitting in the bathroom with you while you take one since you won't leave me alone." Raven chomps into the grilled cheese sandwich and smiles as she chews, purposely trying to be messy. "You can sleep on the floor too. I don't trust that sneaky, weird-ass appendage of yours."

"It can still reach you from the floor," I tease. I don't care if she talks with her mouth full. Her pouty lips are still sexy as sin, all shiny with grease. They'd slip so sensually around my cock. I can imagine it already.

Glaring, she snatches a pillow and throws it at me. "Don't you fucking dare. I will break it in half or tie it into a dozen knots."

"Sounds fun. You'll enjoy the extra ribs you'd create. I'll risk it to find out." Locking my eyes with hers, I flick the button on my jeans open and shake them down, showing off the fact that I choose to go commando.

Her gaze rips from mine to devour the sight of my body, fully hard and throbbing for her attention. She notices the piercing on the tip of my cock immediately, her eyes narrowing like she'll get a better view if she squints. I stride forward and stand next to her, giving her the view she'd never ask for but I know she wants. Raising her hand, she looks ready to rub her fingers over my top ladder, and I hold utterly still.

"I have a ladder on the bottom too," I say, smirking. Her fascination leaves my balls tight and needy as fuck. I'm going to have to rub one out if she doesn't make up her damn mind soon.

She drops her hand to the bed and slides it under her ass like if she doesn't lock it in place, it'll reveal just how naughty she wants to be with me. "And I thought your tail was the only weird-ass appendage on your body."

"Just for that, scoot over or I'll tie you up with my tail and spank you. Hand or cock. I'll ensure either hurts that sexy bubble-butt of yours." I snake my tail around and slither it across the bed toward her legs.

She squeals instead of screaming and scrambles over. Snatching the pillow, she whacks it at my tail and then swings it at my head. I grab the pillow, but she doesn't let go, and I pull her to me until she can decide if she wants to punch my cock or suck it.

Yanking the pillow down, she uses it as a barrier, and I press harder to the downy-filled cock-block, testing the strength of the fabric with my aching boner.

Raven slides her hand up my bare chest and licks her lips before rubbing them together. "I know this must be the first time you've had a woman in your bed, but you need to calm down. I'm not fucking you tonight. I don't want to play with your tail, nor do I want to sit on your face. I have a massive bruise across my chest, and you don't seem like the gentle type."

"Says the horned angel-girl who manhandles me," I tease. "Plus, you're just saying it because Dante offered you his room, which is pointless, because you'll just want to sneak into mine."

"Is that so?" she asks, drawing her hands from my chest to neck.

"Mmmhmm." I grin.

Tugging me by my neck, she stretches closer, keeping her gaze locked on my lips. My muscles ripple and flex, imagining her tongue gliding over mine until I break away first to lick every inch of her.

She slaps her hand over my mouth, knocking some sense back into me. "Well, I can promise I won't. You're too cocky for your own good. I heard you gloating to Dante that I kissed you, and I want to make one thing clear. I only did it because the angel was watching."

I tug her hand away and lace my fingers through hers. "And to think I underestimated you, angel-girl. You played Micah so well, but now you have to be extra careful. He'll come for you again. I don't know if he craves you or craves sending you to Hell, so there's that. This is why I wanted you to follow our plan. You need to learn about the saviors before playing their games if you want to win."

Groaning, she shoves me away in annoyance and crawls to the side of the bed and lies on the edge like she needs as much space as she can get without giving up her comfortable spot to sleep. I follow her lead and plop next to her, bouncing the bed enough that she scoots a bit closer to me as to not fall off.

I prop myself up on my elbow and stare at the side of her face. "The saviors aren't as forgiving as we are. Once you're hell-bound, that's it for you. Most mortals can't come back from that."

She sighs and turns toward me. "You're lying. I know that forgiveness—"

It's my turn to shut her up. I press my finger to her lips and cut off the argument I know will spill from her mouth. She'll go on and on about things she can't possibly comprehend.

"How many times do I have to remind you that what you know is wrong? Shouldn't knowing that Lucian isn't the only devil prove that? Or how we're trying to get the appropriate balance to the universe? Do you know why we need the rest of the brethren, Raven?"

"To finish Hell's Kingdom," she responds, pressing her lips into a line.

"Yes, but do you know what that means? Why we need to in the first place?" I search her face, waiting for her to answer some of life's biggest mysteries not many think about. They'd rather focus on the meaning or themselves.

"You're asking me bullshit questions, Kase. Of course I don't fucking know. You two bastards have been too concerned with trying to fuck me, torture me, tease me, and ruin my life that you haven't given me any answers." She scowls and rolls over, balancing her body on the edge of the bed once more. "You know what else?" She doesn't give me a chance to respond. "You said you want to teach me about the saviors to play their games. But this isn't a fucking game to me!"

Her anger lashes at me, igniting mine, and I throw a ball of red flames at the wall, scorching the drywall. I can't stop my demonic side from peeking through, and I growl in rage, wanting her to get it through her blinding light that of course it isn't really a game, but someone has to win this war for power, and it sure as shit better be fucking us.

Gasping, Raven clutches the comforter and tugs it up like it'll somehow protect her from my wrath. Except I'm not mad at her. I'm pissed off at everyone else. Things would've been so much damn easier if the fucking mortal bastard ex of hers hadn't been drugging her and keeping her locked away. We would've come across her angel-kissed soul eventually and could've built her trust instead of throwing her into a deal with Lucian.

Things need to fucking change if we're going to get what we want. She can't be stressing over losing her damn soul so much that she can't focus on what's important.

I suck in a deep breath and turn away from her. "Raven..." One look at the tears streaming down her face steals the apology from my lips.

I've scared her. She won't even look at me.

Fuck!

I can't control the fury slashing through me harder than a thousand flaming whips to my back. A roar escapes my fierce jowls, and I catch sight of my demonic reflection in the mirror on my closet door. I swing my tail at it, cracking the mirror in my anger. I have to get out of this room. If Raven sees any more of the damned beast trying to change the universe turned me into, she will never believe anything I say. I'll always be her enemy.

And if that happens...

Shit.

Lucian will have more than a little Hell to pay.

9

RAVEN

PEEPING ANGEL

"I NEED TO get out, Dante. Kase said I'm not your guys' pet, but you might treat me better if you thought I was. I need more than half-assed groceries, water, and TV. I need fresh air. Exercise. More than two words of damn conversation." I lean on his doorframe and stare into his sex chambers—err, I mean room. "You've been purposely ignoring me...and I hate it."

Dante doesn't look up at me. "I've been giving you space, not ignoring you. This is the first time you've initiated conversation, pretty soul. You can't blame me if you found it torturous."

"Well, I'm done with space. Take me for a walk. I will be good," I say, drumming my fingers on the door.

He fiddles with the box on his lap. "Later. I'm busy."

I flick my gaze to what I'm sure is the biggest collection of butt plugs I've ever seen. Spraying something on each one, he cleans and organizes them into a case. He finally lifts his gaze and stares at me watching him as a dozen thoughts cross my mind. I've never had much experience outside of my hand and some less than stellar cocks, and I can barely comprehend what any of this is for.

"Come on, Dante. This can wait, can't it?" I shift on my feet. "I'm getting restless. It's been days since I've been out."

Picking up a medium-sized butt plug made from what I think is black silicone, Dante waves it at me. "How do you feel about this one? It comes with a remote. I thought we could eventually have some fun."

I blink a few times, trying to think of some sort of response since he ignored my complaint. I don't know why I expected something else from him. He's a horny fucker, and from his openly kinky room, of course he'd want to use his toys with me. He's made it obvious he thinks he'll wear me down, and I'm at the point that I'm getting bored enough to give in to his kind of entertainment.

I shake my head, pushing the thoughts away. I must resist. Dante already struggles with boundaries. If I give in, he might lose focus—or I will. "The only way you're getting that near my asshole is if you wear that one." I point at the biggest one of his collection. "And *I* get the remote."

Dante smiles and picks up the larger plug and wraps his fingers around it, unable to do so completely. "Damn, my pretty soul. I can't wait to play with you."

Shit. Of course he can't. "Seriously? You'd use that if I try one?"

"I'd use it even if you didn't." He motions me to come closer, and I peer down the hallway, listening to the TV blare. "Come here. Let me show you. You look far too curious for my liking, which means you've been deprived of what I can guarantee is immense pleasure. I bet you've been faking orgasms for years just to get that mortal bastard to flop off you."

I try not to react to his comment, but my cheeks burn with my blush.

He stretches out his hand until I finally get the nerve to take it. Pulling me closer, he turns me until I find myself sitting right on his lap. I don't get a chance to move before he sets the clear case of butt plugs on my knees.

"Don't be afraid of them. I'm the one who bites," Dante murmurs, picking up the smallest one. He sets it in my palm and lifts a remote, hitting a button to turn it on.

I screech and laugh as it vibrates in my palm and crawls across my hand. It falls back in the case, shaking around like a fucking rocket on a mission of ass-ploration. "That's intense."

"Wait until you see the other toys I bought just for you. I was going to surprise you, but I realize you hate surprises." He shifts the case back to the bed and lifts me with him, setting me on my feet. He doesn't let go and drapes his arms over my shoulders. Leaning in close, he hums in my ear. "You also look like you could use some extra self-love since you won't let me be your personal stress reliever. You'll feel better. Maybe then Kase will chill out. He's empathetic to anger, and you have a shit-ton of it."

"You think masturbating is going to fix things?" I ask, my voice rising as Dante strikes one of my many nerves. I spin out of his arms. "Have you even talked to Kase? Do you know why I'm mad?"

Dante doesn't let space linger between us for long and grabs my hands. Pulling me back to him, he locks my hands against his chest. "Look, whatever happened between you and Kase—"

The room shakes, cutting off Dante's words. I try to steady myself against him with the intense quaking rumbling through the apartment, but he chooses now to let me fend for myself. I stand frozen with my legs apart and arms wide. The last thing I want to hold on to is his sex toy display, because if I fall, I'll end up getting beaten by the top shelf of dildos as they rain on top of me. Dante rushes to catch the glass case of butt plugs he left on his bed and moves it toward the middle before it falls off and shatters on the hardwood floors.

I grimace at him, twisting my lips. "You abandoned me to save your butt plugs? What the fuck!"

"They're ours, and you're tough, pretty soul. If you fall, you don't break." Dante crosses his arms, unfazed by the trembling room. "Now ground yourself better. It's almost over. If you don't and you land on your ass, you bet I'll kiss it. With tongue."

I groan and fist my hands, hating that he put that image in my head. "Can you not threaten me with a rim job? Your tongue is as weird as Kase's tail."

"It's not a threat." Dante flicks his tongue at me, releasing what I can only describe as a playful hiss.

I glare. "I swear if you say it's a promise—"

A monstrous snarl sounds from the living room, cutting off my words. I jerk my attention to the open door as a rush of dread crashes over me. That's not Kase. His demonic roar is a bit deeper, though this one terrifies me more. I don't know why I didn't figure out that the apartment quakes because we have a visitor from Hell, and it feels as if Lucian wasn't summoned but instead broke through the gate to make an appearance. And from Dante flashing his fangs, I realize it must be an unwelcome one.

"It's been two weeks and you have no progress to report?" Lucian's voice booms through the hallway, and Dante locks his big hand around my wrist, pulling me closer.

I inhale a breath, trying to calm my nerves. His protectiveness prods at something inside me, and I hug my arms around him, feeling a bit ridiculous wanting him to pick me up and shield me with his breathtaking black wings like he had when Kase sent Joel where he belonged.

"What the fuck have you been doing?" The rotting stench of hellfire trickles into the room with Lucian's anger.

"You can only blame yourself, Luce. I warned you that bartering with her soul was a bad idea. It makes things complicated. You should've listened to my suggestion, but you let your damn pride get the best of you." Kase's voice remains even. "Now if you don't calm down, your wrath will fuck things up worse. Trust me. I know."

Another loud snarl pierces the air, and I automatically cup my hands over my ears to block the noise. Dante shifts me, inching closer toward the hallway. My feet remain frozen to the floor, and my soul screams that for the first time, it feels like there is too much space between me and Dante. My stubbornness doesn't want him to realize as much, and I dig my nails into the palm of my hands.

"Make things worse? I would get shit done," Lucian says, sending another wave of heat into Dante's room. "If I wasn't tethered here, this would have been finished centuries ago. You've lost sight of our purpose."

Something crashes with Kase's growl. "I have not. I just understand mortals far better than you. And Raven is different. Fear doesn't crush her into compliance. She puts up a fight. She resists even more."

"Then you're not doing your fucking best at putting her in her place." The glow of fire lights the hallway. The temperature rises even more the longer the Hell portal remains open. Sweat trickles from my hairline, and I try my best not to gasp in deep breaths as the air starts suffocating me.

"Her place is supposed to be by our sides. You know Purgatory can only be controlled by someone of light and dark, and if you push her too hard, she will fall into the abyss." Kase's voice grows louder. Instead of bowing to Lucian's anger, he faces it straight on. "If that happens—"

"We'll find another angel-kissed mortal," Lucian snaps, cutting Kase off. "Her soul will remain under my contract. I will not risk the saviors trying to get to her. You know that's why we need the contract."

Kase growls again. "I won't let that happen."

Lucian roars. "You already did!"

"Because Micah is the damn target, Luce. Now calm

155

GINNA MORAN

the fuck down and be reasonable. We know what we're doing," Kase says, his voice sharpening.

"You don't!"

Fire explodes in the hallway at Lucian's holler, and the disgusting rotting smell that comes along with the opening of Hell grows more intense. Glass shatters, and Dante pulls me away from the doorway, only to rush out into the hallway, abandoning me.

The floor rumbles again, and snarls and growls send goosebumps prickling over my skin. It sounds like Lucian unleashes Hell in the living room, and he and Kase fight, tearing the room apart.

My chest tightens with fear at the sound of unsettling yowls and screams, but the only thing I'm afraid of is if something happens to Kase and Dante. They might push my buttons and piss me off, but Lucian scares the crap out of me. He speaks of me like an object to gain power and not the being Kase and Dante claim I am to them.

Gathering my nerve, I stride into the hallway and to the case of weapons on display. I don't know what I'm doing, but I can't just cower in the room and hope Lucian doesn't rise against the other devils who fell with him, who are on the same mission as he is. If that's even the truth. Because right now, it sounds as if Lucian has something else in mind, and he's not including Dante and Kase.

I slide the glass door open and pull out a long dagger,

the weight of it surprising me. The smooth metal of the plain hilt cools my fingers. I practice lifting and jabbing it a few times like I can somehow face and conquer the worst devil of them all, but I have to try. I have to show that I'm not just a damn power source, and that he's wrong about me.

Rushing toward the glowing living room, I prepare to fight like Hell—or I guess against Hell, but Dante stretches his black wings out, blocking my path until he steps into the hallway. He shifts on his feet and motions for me to return to his room. Kase grunts, the pain in his voice stopping me from obeying Dante, and I shuffle forward, a bit slower, definitely more cautiously this time.

"You will not question me again. Do you understand?" Lucian bellows, sending another cloud of fire through the living room.

The crack of a whip startles me, and I cover my mouth at the sight of Lucian in all his demonic glory standing over Kase in his demon form. Jerking his clawed hand up, he summons a whip of fire and slashes it across Kase's spine. Black blood pours from the gashes, streaming to smolder within the blazing circle of hellfire.

"I understand, Lucian," Kase says, his guttural, throaty voice barely audible over the roaring flames and the crack of Lucian's fire whip slicing his back again.

"Never forget it. We might have jumped together, but I

am known as the sole devil for a reason. Don't think I can't turn your level of Hell into mine." Lucian slashes the whip over Kase's back over and over again until he falls to his stomach and doesn't get up.

My whole body trembles in anger. It was one thing agreeing to help Kase and Dante with this mission, but now that I've seen the true extent of Lucian's punishment, I'm not so sure I want to help him...but then what happens to Kase and Dante if I don't? What happens to me?

I realize I've been angry with the wrong devils all along.

Kase and Dante are trying to help me in their own twisted ways. We might not be on the same page yet, or even know each other at all, but they want to. They're trying despite my resistance instead of turning my life as hellish as it was before.

Summoning my courage, I shove past Dante's expansive wings and rush into the living room. Lucian stands tall on his hooved feet and blows a breath of fire toward me. I flinch at the heat, but it doesn't burn me like I expect. If anything, it ignites my bravado to face this demonic overlord with only a slight tremble to my hands.

I open my mouth to tell Lucian that I will get the job done, but the asshole disappears into a cloud of flames until the only reminder of his appearance is the scorch marks on the floor around Kase's badly beaten body, still stuck in his demonic form.

"Dante, take her back to your room," Kase mutters, shaking as he pushes up on his hands.

Spinning around, I aim the long dagger at Dante. "Try it and see what happens, Dante. I'm tired of being purposely kept out of things I should know about." I kneel beside Kase and hover my hand inches above his bleeding back. "Now tell me what I can do to help."

"Just leave," Kase mutters, turning his gaze to mine. "I can't summon my mortal façade, and I know you can't stand seeing me as I am now."

"That's not true. Yeah, it takes some getting used to, but come on, Kase. You saw Joel. At least you have a better personality." I smirk with my words and reach out, caressing my knuckles to his beastly face.

"All right, Raven. Kase won't tell you what he needs to heal faster, so I will. You know that little soul bonding you did with Lucian? That will help Kase. We get power from souls, and yours has enough to control Purgatory." Dante flaps his wings before folding them onto his back, hiding them completely from sight.

"I'm not fucking doing that to Raven," Kase says, struggling to get up. "She doesn't want my filthy darkness touching her light. She's made that clear."

I raise my eyebrows, unsure of how to respond. The way he says it makes me wonder if there is more to the soul bonding than I know for them. With Lucian, it was thrilling yet terrifying, especially when he demanded my soul. I already know it won't be like that for Kase. He might be a psycho with a temper, but it's the world he gets angry at. Not me.

Ignoring Kase, I turn to Dante. "Can you help him to his room? Tie him up if you have to. The last thing we need is for him to prolong his healing when we have shit to do."

Dante stands there without moving. "No. I'm not helping you." He and Kase share a silent look, annoying the hell out of me.

I frown. "What?"

"He regrets telling you how to help me," Kase says, groaning. He manages to get to his feet and wobbles. "The bastard envies me for facing Lucian's punishment."

I whip my attention to Dante. "Seriously? You're jealous that Kase got the hell beat into him?"

He shrugs. "I didn't think you'd offer to let him have at your soul. I thought we had a far better connection. It was supposed to be me first."

I nudge my hand into his leg. "Dante, we don't have time for your—"

Spinning around, Dante shakes his head and skulks toward the door. "Don't worry about it, Raven. Just do what you need to do. I'll be bird-brain watching."

I stare in shock as he slams the door, leaving us alone in the living room. Kase groans and stumbles away from me, using his tail to steady himself. My brain turns into mush, unsure what I should do. Kase needs me, but Dante's little fit makes me feel like he needs me too. It's strange to feel as if these two men each grip a part of my soul and neither wants to let go. They struggle to share though, their sinful sides getting the best of them.

"Just go after him, angel-girl," Kase says without looking at me.

"But you're hurt." I stride after him, knowing that I can deal with Dante later.

Kase waves his hand. "I'll heal."

"You were hurt because of me. I heard what you said about the deal with my soul. You can't keep pushing me out. You said I was to stand by your side, yet you won't treat me like that's where I belong." I race to his room, sneaking past him before he shuts the door in my face. "Come on, Kase. You owe me answers. Just stop being a dick, let me help you, and then we can figure out a plan. I don't want Lucian coming back here and threatening us again. I don't trust him."

"You don't trust me either," he says, easing onto his bed without lying down. "You sought a savior and begged to be saved, Raven."

I groan. "Can we just start over? These last few months have been like Hell on Earth for me, and I'm sorry if I have trouble believing you're any different than the assholes who want to ruin my eternity. You haven't given me much to convince me otherwise."

Hanging his monstrous head, he bows forward. "It's too late to start over, angel-girl. We've wasted enough time."

At least he doesn't blame it all on me.

Pushing away the blip of fear squeezing my chest, I reach over and touch his leathery skin, tough yet smooth and hot like he's just stepped out of a sauna. Kase lifts his chin, his eyes glowing red as they flicker over my face. Something dark spills over me, but it doesn't feel as I'd expect—his darkness doesn't scream evil. It radiates with mystery and intrigue and the dozens of answers to my questions hide somewhere in the shadows of his being.

My fingers travel up his sharp, protruding jaw until I reach the three horns on his head looking like a crown. He releases a groan as I lace my fingers around them, feeling the bone-hard density of his demonic features.

The world suddenly hazes around us with warm golden light until the room fades away, and Kase sits before me in his achingly handsome form—the same form he took on as an angel. He doesn't look much different apart from his lack of tattoos and piercings, and instead of the burgundy depths of his irises now shine golden brown like the sun glows on a jar of honey. His face lights with a brilliant smile, and I return my own, unable to resist.

It's in this moment I feel everything in his essence. I touch the light he's long since lost and bathe myself in the shadows dancing over my soul. Without thinking about it, I lean forward and brush my lips to his, savoring the sweetness of his mouth. My soul merges with his being, shooting energy through every molecule on my body. I gasp and kiss him harder, sliding my tongue into his mouth and running my fingers over his soft hair and down his neck until I feel the knotted, puckered skin of two long scars. Scars where he once had brilliant white wings.

"My beautiful angel-girl," he whispers, his voice swirling through my mind. "It's hard for me to let your soul go."

I hum in agreement. "Then don't. You're so— indescribable. I want to feel more."

"I must let your soul go, Raven. My darkness will get to you if I don't." Easing away from me, Kase's presence steals the warmth he brought to me, leaving me cold and shivering.

The light around us fades, and I blink my eyes, adjusting my vision to the dimness of the room. I expect to see Kase in his true form, but he sits before me as a man, light bruises covering his half-naked body that I just want to kiss and care for, showing him that his worry about his darkness affecting me are unwarranted.

Our eyes meet again, and I can't stop from continuing where we left off in our moment of bonding souls, and I slide onto his lap and cup his face, kissing him deeper, more passionately, like I can somehow merge my soul with his again if I try hard enough.

Kase tightens his arms around me and pulls me higher onto the bed with him, matching my desperation for his affection with his own. Heat blooms between us, and I reach between us and stroke my hand over the hard length of his shaft pressing into his jeans. He moans and grabs at my shirt, yanking it over my head. His hand roams up my back until he finds the clasp on my bra and unhooks it, letting it fall between us.

Breaking away from my mouth, Kase kisses down my throat and I arch my back, silently showing him where I want his mouth to explore. Heat flicks over my nipple with his tongue, and I moan and stroke the bulge in his pants faster. He unbuttons his jeans for me, tugging them down until all he wears is a pair of boxer-briefs.

"I want to fuck you with my fingers," he murmurs, kissing his way back to my mouth. "I want to feel what I do to you."

Kase rolls me off of him and kneels between my legs. My heart pounds like crazy as he drinks in the sight of my bare breasts. I bite my lip between my teeth and nod, easing my hips up to let him tug my pants off. Red light glows in his eyes, and I squirm under his smoldering stare. I half-expect his tail to sneak from behind his back to rip my panties off, but it remains hidden, and he uses his fingers to pull off my lacy thong like he knows I'm still nervous about things I've never dealt with before.

Lying beside me, he kisses me again, slipping his tongue into my mouth, exploring me with hot sensuality that leaves me breathless. His warm hand slides over my thigh as he grazes his hand up and between my legs at a torturously slow pace. I can't even remember the last time someone touched me like this and just the thought of him fingering me makes me wet in anticipation.

I ease my leg up, inviting him to do what he wants. Kase groans as he grazes his fingers over the soft folds of my body until he slides his finger inside me. Tingles burst between my legs, and I gasp in pleasure at the sensation of his warm finger fucking me how he said he wanted to. His thumb rubs over my clit in circles, the pressure making my legs shake. I haven't felt so wanted in a long time like I do now. Kase draws his finger in and out of me like my pleasure is all that is important to him in this moment. Instead of taking, he gives me the attention I had no idea I've been starved of, and I kiss him like he's all I need to survive.

"You're so perfect, Raven," he whispers between kisses. "You have no idea of all the things I want to do to you. You love my fingers, don't you?"

"Mmmhmm," I say in agreement.

He combs his fingers through my hair, locking me in

his gaze, increasing the pressure with another finger. "Just wait until you're brave enough to ride my horns. Get fucked by my tail. Only after that will I fuck you with my cock."

The only noise that escapes my mouth is another moan, my body suddenly not caring how he fucks me and only that he does. My mind on the other hand, well, shit. It's screaming to let go of my mortal hesitation and to give into the dark allure of one of the kings of Hell.

"You want that, don't you, angel-girl?" he asks, pulling me in to kiss him again. "To get fucked by me anyway I please over and over. You crave it."

I moan, my whole body buzzing as Kase brings me to my peak. I reach out and grab onto him as I scream in pleasure, the intensity of my orgasm shaking me to my core. He hums under his breath, continuing to stroke his thumb over my clit as my muscles pulse, refusing to let me go. It's like he ignited a bomb inside me and wants to enjoy the destruction for as long as he can until I can't take it anymore.

I grab his hand, slowing him down so I can finally breathe. My chest heaves and Kase caresses his lips to mine like he wants to ensure I will never get enough air again. And I don't even care. I'll suffocate if it means his lips never stop exploring mine. I'll burn under his touch as long as it means I'll never be cold from his absence. As for my soul? He already has it, so I might as well enjoy every delicious thing he has to offer. If I'm going to Hell, I'm going to embrace the darkness rising inside me. Because for once, I see things clearly. I've adjusted to the shadows unlike with the light. Staring into the light will always leave me blind. It'll leave me weak.

I'm ready to be strong.

Kase traces my jawline, drawing my attention to him. "I'll never get enough of you."

"You never have to," I say, smiling. "I'll make sure of it—"

A door slams, dragging my attention away from Kase. It's now that I realize the door to his room is wide open and Dante saw us like this. Sighing, Kase sits up and adjusts his still hard cock in his pants.

He touches my cheek. "I'll be right back. I'm going to talk to him."

I groan. "Maybe I should."

"No, you stay here and relax. You need to rest a bit after our soul bonding. I can handle Dante." Kase kisses my forehead. "He'll get over his mood, so don't worry. He knows the deal. You're ours."

I twist my lips, a dozen thoughts swirling through my mind. I know that they're both my soul keepers, but I don't know. I guess I didn't think much of it. Of course, I never expected to be naked in bed with Kase, either.

Kase offers me a reassuring smile and strides across the room without waiting for me to get my thoughts together to process. Groaning, I throw myself back on his pillows and inhale a few breaths of the delicious scent clinging to everything.

Something flashes in my peripheral vision, and I jerk my gaze to the sliding glass door. Soft golden light glows from between the blinds, but I know the patio light isn't on. It's already past sunset, so the light doesn't make sense.

And then I see him.

What a fucking creep.

"Kase! Dante!" I yell, grabbing at the sheet to cover up.

Through the crack in the blinds, I spot Micah staring silently at me through the glass. The second our eyes meet, he moves away from the slider.

The light fades with him, leaving me staring at the shadows of twilight.

He disappears completely.

10

RAVEN

REDEMPTION

"YOU WANT ME to what?" I ask, clutching the sheet around me. "No fucking way. He will try to stab me with his flaming sword again. You should've seen him. He was staring at me through the blinds."

"Probably watched the entire time Kase finger banged you too," Dante says, his voice deepening with the words.

"Even I didn't do that, despite how much I wanted to."

I furrow my brows. "Thanks?" My word comes out more as a question, because Dante sounds as if I should give him a cookie or some shit for not being on the same level as the pervert angel.

"Next time knock instead of getting mopey, and maybe Raven will invite you in to watch...or join," Kase says, bumping his shoulder to Dante's with a wide, cocky grin lighting his face. Turning to me, he caresses my cheek with his knuckles like he can't resist. "Isn't that right, angel-girl?"

"Focus, Kase," I snap, flicking him in his hard pec. The last thing I need crossing my mind is being in between these insanely creative, adventurous men who want to do things no normal person can ever comprehend. I'm nervous at the thought...but also curious as hell. "You need to go after the creep."

He smirks and leans in, kissing me without hesitation like we've been doing it forever. "Like I said, *you* have to be the one. He'll hide the second he sees us, but with you present, he won't." He remains ultra-close, his breath mingling with mine. "He can't even use his power to shift you temporarily through the planes without us seeing. Perks of being your soul keepers."

I swallow and lick my lips, my body craving another kiss. But I deny it. This is far easier than it should be. Who knew I could be so easily kissed into compliance. Kase was right about me. Lucian can't beat me into submission. I fight back. But with Kase? How he looks so damn hot watching me with his burning intensity, I'd probably drop to my knees if he asked.

"We won't be far," Dante adds, stepping closer to cage me between him and Kase. He rests his chin on my shoulder, silently begging for my attention. "We'll blast him into oblivion before he could even unsheathe his weapon. Trust us, pretty soul. We'll always take good care of you."

I never thought I would, but here I am, trusting the rulers of Hell.

Sliding out from in between them, I grip the sheet tighter because of the double entendre of Dante's comment. The two of them smile, enjoying my reaction, and I step back more to put space between us. My damn vagina reminds me of my moment with Kase, and I squeeze my thighs together, trying to get myself to calm down.

"Okay, fine. Give me five minutes to get dressed," I say, turning toward my pathetic clothes pile in the corner.

Kase snakes his tail around my waist and spins me back around. "That's not necessary. He needs to believe you've snuck out. The sheet will do."

I would ask if he's serious, but I already know the answer.

"Or you can just run out naked," Kase adds, tugging the sheet away from me, leaving me standing frozen as it dangles in front of me.

Dante whistles. "Good plan. Everything is better without clothes. Fucking modesty branded into mortal minds."

I try to snatch the sheet, but Kase lifts it higher and out of my reach. The fucker smiles, drinking me in. He wants me to jump to grab it, giving him a show, so I do the only thing I can think of. I close the space to him and press my boobs to his bare chest. It distracts him enough that he doesn't notice as I reach for his tail until I lock my fingers around it.

Tugging it to me, I hold it in one hand and stroke my fingers over the strangely soft yet tough appendage. Kase drops the sheet and moans, his cock hardening to poke me in the pelvis through his boxer-briefs.

I release his tail, only teasing him for a moment, and grab the sheet from the floor. "Pull that shit again, and you will never experience my hand around any of your appendages from now on." Fuck, that sounds like a weird-ass threat, but it works, because Kase leaves the sheet alone and lets me step away.

Dante laughs and punches him. "Don't worry, Kase. I'll give your tail a little rub while she jerks me off instead."

Kase tights his jaw and glowers at me. "Tease me like that again and you'll find yourself tied up with my tail, spread eagle, and on the edge of an orgasm I'll deny you until you beg me to show you mercy, angel-girl."

Fuck. Me.

I need air.

Blowing a breath, I ignore his threat and stride toward his room, knowing that if the creep angel is around, he'd be watching the slider. Dante and Kase don't follow me, remaining in the hallway and out of sight. Nerves bunch in my stomach at the thought of leaving the apartment by myself. I tighten the sheet and tie the ends in a knot, hoping it's strong enough to keep it in place. I feel like I'm on the ultimate walk of shame as I step onto the patio.

Damn it. I forgot about the wall.

I'm just glad the demonic bastards can't see me from this position. Because climbing a wall in a sheet won't be pretty. Grabbing the patio chair next to a small table, I move it against the wall and climb up. If the angel sees me now, he'll definitely assume I'm making a great escape from my soul keepers.

I hike up the sheet and stretch my leg, hooking my foot over the six foot wall. The rough texture scratches my knee, and I grind my teeth, realizing how out of shape I am. I can barely pull myself onto the wall. After a minute of huffing and groaning, I straddle the stone wall, wishing I was wearing some underwear.

Swinging my other leg over, I peer down at the grass, thankful the complex gave up on landscaping the back building of the apartments. Most have bushes or flowers growing next to the patio walls, which would be another fucking obstacle I would probably fail to avoid.

I drop down and fall forward, slamming my hands into the dry grass. Pain radiates in my wrists. I grind my teeth through the pain, trying to catch my bearings. This was the worst idea ever. If I didn't know that Kase and Dante would enjoy it, I'd punish them with a foot to their damn cocks.

Fuck, I still might.

Pushing to my feet, I dust off the dirt and grass from the sheet like it matters and peer around the dimly lit complex. It gets worse and worse each time I see it, and it really gets to me how I've never noticed how rundown it was before. Was it because I was thankful just to have somewhere to live or is it because I'm seeing things from new hellbound eyes?

The soft, familiar, now terrifying glow of Micah's presence steals my attention from my thoughts, and I straighten my back. He's an angel for fuck's sake. I shouldn't be so scared. A part of me really misses the idea that angels are these benevolent creatures in white robes with melodious voices and not the black-clad, sword wielding avenging righteous asshole I know waits for me.

Summoning my courage, I silently chant to myself that Kase and Dante won't let anything happen to me. They're psychotic enough to clip Micah's wings and eat them if he so much as touches me with one of his pure white feathers.

I clear my throat. "Hey, you perv. I saw you peeping into my room. What the fuck gives? Did you enjoy the show?" I wish I could ignore the fact that he was watching Kase get me off, but damn it. "I thought angels were supposed to be good. I feel violated by the intrusion, you sicko. Come face me."

The light grows brighter, sending my heart beating out of control against my ribcage. Shit. Shit. Shit. My soul stings at the mere presence of Micah's closeness, though he still stands a few feet out of my reach.

The second I meet his dark gaze, I snap. Something gets into me, and I stride the distance to him and kick him right between his legs as hard as I can.

He clutches his junk and flaps his wings, the force of the wind knocking me off my feet. I land on my back and heave from the air escaping my lungs. Micah recovers faster than I do, and he growls and launches at me. I screech and roll, trying to get away, but his boot lands on the sheet. My attempt to escape leaves me naked on the walkway, and I unsuccessfully try ripping the flimsy fabric away from him. The bastard is too heavy. He doesn't budge and just gapes at me, drinking in my naked body like I'm the first woman he's ever seen without her clothes on.

"Get off my sheet!" I yell, yanking at it again.

Where are Kase and Dante? Can't they see I'm in trouble?

Micah lifts his boot and finally averts his eyes toward the night sky. He doesn't threaten me like I expect and continues to stand there, waiting until I wrap the sheet around me again, and then returns to staring at me.

"What? You're creeping me out. First you try to kill me. Then you act like a pervert and peep into my room. Now, you just stand there and look like you wish I didn't cover up. Why are you here, Micah?" I ask, getting to my feet.

His eyes flash with golden light at the sound of his name coming from my mouth. "I...don't really know."

"Then fucking leave me alone. You made yourself clear of what you want to do to me." I inwardly cringe at my comment, because in this moment, it feels like it means something other than stab me and send me to Hell.

"Did I? How is that possible if I don't know, heathen?" His jaw twitches.

"You want to kill me," I say, hugging my arms over my chest.

Micah takes a step closer as I take one back. Pressing his lips together, he frowns, his brows knitting together. "I don't *want* to kill you. I *have* to kill you. You're a danger to everything. I know what Lucifer is up to, and if I don't send your soul to him, he will get the power he wants. No soul will be safe. Please, Raven. If I could help you find redemption, I would. But a deal with Lucifer? I can't save you.

You've been marked."

Hearing him say the words hurts me on a soul-deep level. No matter how many times I repeat it to myself, it still bothers me. I'm unredeemable. I can't be saved.

Fury snaps inside me, and instead of pitying myself, I get angry. Who is this asshole to say I'm dangerous? Unworthy? Who is he to define me based on something out of my control?

I close the space to Micah and surprise him by fisting the front of his shirt in my fingers. I shake him, trying to test his resolve, but he stands there without budging. Without blinking. The weight of his gaze penetrates my very being, stinging me like my body wants to repel him, but I'm too proud, too angry, too much of a glutton for this bullshit that I can't—no, I won't—back away.

"If you were going to kill me, you would've already!" I yell in his face, sucking in breath after breath of his dewy, crisp scent reminiscent of early morning fog in the winter. It hurts to breathe but I can't stop myself.

"Raven..."

"Tell me the truth, Micah! Tell me why you're stalking me. Why are you here? You're cruel for putting me through this. I thought the devils were the ones who thrived on punishment, but it's you and your righteous asshole attitude." Jerking my arm, I slap him across the face, expecting the sky to open up to strike me with a lightning bolt as Heaven smites me.

Nothing happens.

Micah doesn't flinch.

He doesn't respond.

Before I have a chance to react, he reaches behind him and unveils his flaming sword from wherever the fuck he keeps it along with his now hidden wings. My heart stalls, and a wave of panic crashes over me. I shove him hard, my hands slamming into his rock-hard chest. Two hands lock around my waist from behind, and Dante swings me away. I fly through the air, clenching my jaw to stop another damn screech from escaping me. I skid across the dead grass not far from our apartment and nearly collide into the side wall.

Red fire cascades through the air, turning the dim night crimson. I shudder a breath in relief at the rumbling ground. Kase's familiar monstrous form launches from the second-story apartment's balcony and lands on top of Micah. Swinging his arm, Micah punches Kase in the side, sending tendrils of smoke through the air. Bright light flashes from his hands, and I shield my eyes at the glorious heavenly fire burning far more intensely than Kase's hellish power.

"Stop!" I yell, pushing to my feet. "Don't hurt him!"

My voice distracts Micah so much so that Dante grabs him by the wings and spits something that smolders over the white feathers, burning them. Micah hollers and spins, wielding his sword. Kase shoots fire at Micah from behind, trapping him in between him and Dante. A hurricane of emotions rages through me as if the light of my soul battles with the darkness of my deal with Lucian, and it makes my head spin.

I drop to my knees in agony, my body turning against itself as I watch Micah fight off Dante and Kase. If I don't stop them, they'll ruin everything. I can feel my soul swaying, trying to send me to Hell. The two devils are lost to the sins they embody, and each of them enhances each other, creating the perfect weapon to destroy Micah. If he gets blown into oblivion, all is lost for me. I know it. There are five angels who must fall. They must bow to a new kingdom.

Dante hooks his arms around Micah and pins him in place. "Kase will tear you to pieces for even raising your sword at Raven. She is under our protection, and we will not allow you to hurt her."

Kase roars, standing up on his hind legs, his muscular body towering over everyone in his massive form. Whipping his tail, he lashes it across Micah's chest, shredding the fabric of his shirt. Light emanates from his bronzy skin, the deep color sparkling with a metallic sheen. Micah grinds his teeth, but he doesn't close his eyes. He faces Kase without fear.

And then I hear it. Micah's soft plea to the Higher

Power. "Accept my sacrifice for the greater good."

Holy shit.

"Kase, stop! Don't do it!" I yell, pushing on my feet. "Stop!"

I jump on his back and cling to him, grabbing onto the outer horns of the blunt, bone-like crown. He jerks his head back in surprise, I lose my hold and scratch my nails down his back, trying to hold on. I land on his tail, feeling the appendage slip over the sensitive skin between my legs as he tries to pull it free. The gesture startles me, the sensation sending tingles bursting over my clit, and I moan so embarrassingly loud that Kase and Dante both lose their focus on Micah.

Bending his knees, Micah launches into the air, lighting up the sky above us. My brain turns to mush, my hands gripping Kase's tail as I try to stop him from pulling it out from under me. Who knew such a thing could bring me to the brink of an orgasm so quickly. If I had allowed him to tug the two feet left of his tail free, I'd be lying in the grass, arching my back, and screaming my pleasure out to the entire complex. I don't even think the darkness protecting our place is enough to stifle my loud-ass mouth, fully prepared to get fucked by a damn demonic tail. What the actual fuck is wrong with me?

"You naughty, naughty pretty soul," Dante says, striding closer. "You're in so much trouble, giving the damn bastard some hellish intervention and using your sexy, sinful pussy to distract Kase to do so."

Kase blazes with red fire in front of me, revealing his human façade. I remain on the ground, my knees bent, still clutching his damn tail like it's my lifeline to save myself. Swiveling his torso, Kase peers at me, his eyes glowing red. Something dark, almost hungry, flickers in his expression, and I slowly ease myself off his tail without letting it go. I'm afraid of what he'll do to me with it if I do—and not because I'm scared. I worry about how much I'll like it.

Dante growls so lowly, I can feel the rumble of his voice over my skin. Grabbing the front of his jeans, he tugs the zipper down and pulls his massive cock out of his pants right in front of me.

"You're making me so jealous of his damn tail, Raven. Come touch me and watch me grow just as long," he quips, stepping closer. "Consider it your punishment for the angel."

I raise my eyebrows at him. "Or you could just take over for me. Maybe Kase will stop looking like he plans to eat me at any second."

I regret my words immediately, knowing exactly where both their minds wander.

"Not happening, angel-girl. What did we tell you? You once again broke our damn rule, so you know what that means?" Kase manages to curl his tail around me despite my hands clutching it. "You're in a helluva lot of trouble. I hope your little adventure was worth it."

Something mischievous lights Dante's green eyes at Kase's words, and the diamond shape of his pupils dilate wider. He shifts his eyes upward toward the roof of the building across from ours like he wants me to follow his line of sight. Without having to look, I know Micah hides just out of our sight. His soft glow gives him away. He isn't hiding from me, which means Kase and Dante can see him too, and they want to mess with him.

I clear my throat, trying my best to ensure my voice comes out pleadingly. "I'm sorry. It won't happen again. I know better now. I know the only thing he'll ever do for me is ruin my eternity."

"You're lying to us, Raven," Kase says, growling with his words. Damn it, does he sound convincing. "This is the second time he's pulled his damn sword on you."

"You're stupid as fuck if you thought he'd do anything but try to steal power from us. He doesn't want to save you," Dante says, grabbing my hand and dragging me to him. Locking his fingers through my hair, he manhandles me, yanking my head back to look at him. And damn it, does he look hot as Hell. "Do you understand?"

"Yes...sir," I whisper.

His eyes flicker with lust. He loved that. And shit. I might've just stepped through another one of his magical doors to Kinkland.

"She's lying again," Kase says, raising his voice. I expect him to whip my ass with his tail, but he doesn't. Am I disappointed? Shit. I might be. "Take her ass inside and lock her up. I'm going angel hunting."

Dante scoops me up, keeping me facing out. His raging boner presses into the sheet, trying to poke its way between my legs. It does nothing to staunch my desire from my unexpected tail rub from Kase. This whole night has been crazy. I might as well just climb aboard the crazy train and see the ride through. Maybe Dante is right and I'll feel even better. At least it will satiate my curiosity toward these sexual adventures I never in my life dreamed about. The two of them have opened my mind to a new level of delicious freaky kink that I know I'll embrace. I can feel my acceptance. If my vagina could talk, she'd remind me that I can take a good pounding. And with these sexy devils, I know I'll get off too.

"Micah might think chains are some sort of punishment, but they're your reward, pretty soul. You did great," Dante whispers into my ear. "He won't be able to resist his nature. I know it doesn't seem like it, but it drives him crazy that he can't redeem you. He sees the light of your soul chained by Lucian's darkness."

I only nod, because I'm afraid that I can't control the sound of my voice or how breathy it might be as his cock continues to tease me. On purpose. I know it. He's still thinking about me and Kase. If this is going to be a constant struggle to keep him from getting envious, I'm going to get exhausted. Kase mentioned the three of us together to help, but damn. Can I survive that?

Dante slams the door to the apartment closed, snapping me out of my threesome fantasy I never thought about having with two men. Adjusting me in his arms, he shifts me from being dangled in front of him to holding me like a blushing bride in his arms. Heat radiates from his skin, and I rest my cheek to his shoulder and breathe against his skin at the nape of his neck. Now that we're inside, my body relaxes.

We reach his room, and he doesn't set me on my feet and instead tosses me onto his bed. Now that I'm on it, I realize it's smaller than Kase's king bed. Hell, it's even smaller than a queen. He's given up a bigger bed to fit a weird chair with straps and what looks like a spot for some sort of sex swing.

Dante lifts the top on a huge chest next to his bed and starts pulling out restraints. I don't move, my mind finally realizing that he is taking Kase's order seriously. He's locking me up by restraining me to his bed.

Sitting on the edge, he snatches me by my wrist and stretches my arm toward the corner of the headboard.

I yank my arm, trying to break away from him, but he

tightens his hold enough to make me wince. A leather cuff encircles my wrist, and he adjusts a buckle to secure it. I never knew how exposed I could feel with my arm like this. It's the strangest thing.

"I thought Kase was joking," I say, narrowing my eyes at Dante. "Can't you just slap some fuzzy cuffs on me from your collection on the wall?" I realize I feel more than exposed. I feel vulnerable. Helpless, even.

"No." Dante moves to my feet and does the same thing with my ankles. He looks like he wants to pull the straps to spread my legs open completely, but Kase calls his name. Sighing, he glances at the open door. "I'll be back."

I shake my head. "Don't you fucking leave me here."

Ignoring my pleas and anger, Dante abandons me on the bed. He flicks off the light and shuts the door with a soft click. I glower at his absence.

"Dante! You can't leave me here! I have to go to the bathroom!" I yell, raising my voice. "Don't think I won't piss on your bed." I don't have to go, and I definitely wouldn't even if I did, but damn him.

"Do what makes you feel better," he calls, his voice muffled. "There's a mattress protector."

Of course there is.

"Dante!" I yell, thrashing. A blip of fear rises inside me, and I fight against the restraints even though I know it's pointless. He's demonic. He wouldn't have a damn quick release or something like that. "You're an asshole! I—"

Light glows from the window, and I freeze, snapping my mouth closed. I can sense Micah even before I see him, and I listen to the window scrape as he pries it open. Fear and anger cascade over me, and I fight the restraints again. There is no way Dante and Kase don't know Micah's here. They set me up without telling me. The fuckers.

"Raven, don't be afraid. I won't hurt you. I can't even come in," Micah says, his voice whispering through the cracked window. "Can you keep your voice down? I just want to talk. I'd do so telepathically, but your mind won't let me in."

"Thank God," I whisper.

"You mean the devils," he mutters. "Because of the mark, you have to be receptive to me. Now, please. I want to apologize. You don't deserve the fate you've been given. I wish we had found you sooner."

"Found me? You weren't even looking, so don't give me that bullshit," I snap, tugging at the restraints again. "Now go away. I don't trust you and your flaming sword."

Sighing, Micah sends a gust of his fresh fragrance toward me with a flap of his wings. It blows the curtain over, letting me see his sullen face peeking into the window. He truly is a damn peeping angel. I wonder if they're all like this.

Light flashes in his dark eyes. "Raven, please. Hear me

out—"

"No," I snap, cutting him off. "I've already decided redemption is overrated. Kase and Dante treat me better than anyone else ever has."

"You're restrained."

"It's a sex kink. I like it. I can't wait for Dante to come back and do whatever he pleases with me." I try to remain expressionless, because damn. My mouth needs to speak to my mind before opening. "Now stay away from me, creep. You have five seconds before I call for Dante."

Micah flaps his wings again, his frown deepening. "Raven, I—"

"Dante! He's here!" I shout, screaming as loudly as I can. "Kase!"

Micah disappears.

11

RAVEN

GLUTTONY

THE BED SHIFTS, pulling me from my twisted dream of Lucian. I have no idea how long I've been strapped to the bed, but I'm annoyed as fuck realizing it was long enough to have fallen asleep.

"Sorry I took so long, pretty soul. We were only going to be gone for a few minutes, but something came up." Dante grazes his knuckles over my cheek, shifting my dark hair from my face.

"Are you kidding me? Sorry isn't enough. You're a fucking bastard." I glower and pull against the restraints. "Now release me."

The corners of his lips quirk up in a smile. "You are in no position to demand anything from me."

"Dante!" I thrash, trying to kick him from my position, but the strap tightens to its full extent with him out of my reach.

"If you don't stop fighting, I will reposition you to your stomach and spank you. There's a reason I left you strapped here." His eyes search over my face. "I wanted the anticipation to leave you aching for me."

"What?" I blink a few times.

"You deserved the same kind of torture you've put me through tonight." Dante strokes my bare shoulder. "I heard what you said to Micah."

I inwardly groan. "I was just trying to get under his skin."

"Well, you got straight to my dick, pretty soul." He shifts and shows me his bulge, adjusting it in his pants. "It's making it impossible to think about anything else, despite knowing you didn't really mean it."

"So is this how it's going to be? You're just going to keep me restrained every time I give you a boner?" I tip my chin toward his cock. "That's not my fault. Maybe you should let me tie you up and punish you instead."

"You little tease," he says, his voice turning breathy. "You can't threaten such things unless you're willing to follow through."

"How do you know I won't?" I smirk, unable to resist the need to tease him as it steals my annoyance away. "You won't ever find out unless you release me."

Leaning close, he bows into me, sharing the same breathing space. "I will if you kiss me."

"What kind of deal is that? Both options only benefit you." I suck in my lips and press them together to hide them. I'm not even going to let him look at them.

A smirk plays on his lips. "I'd think your freedom was a benefit enough."

This cocky bastard. "I could just call Kase and make a deal with him. If I offer to let him slide his tail in anywhere, he—"

Growling, Dante pinches my chin between his thumb and index finger. "What do you want, pretty soul? I have many things I can slide into you anywhere too, you know." His tongue glides between his lips and he shows off his piercings. "I'd be willing to trade one kiss for anything you desire."

He hovers centimeters from my mouth. I expect him to steal a kiss, but he doesn't. He just peers into my eyes, unblinking. His diamond pupils expand and retract, and the scent of his smoky, warm scent envelops me. Heat radiates from his hands—one resting on my thigh and the other moving from chin and to my cheek until he pushes my hair behind my ear.

"So what will it be?" His fingers dig into my thigh, sending heat up and between my legs without him even moving.

I release a quivering breath. "I want to see you in your complete true devil form and touch your wings."

Easing away, he tilts his head slightly in surprise. "Out of everything you could ask for, why that?"

I stretch forward without responding and brush my lips to his, kissing him softly, sweetly, without getting carried away. He sits frozen like the last thing he expects is to find my lips against his, even though he already asked for it. Maybe he didn't think I wanted to kiss him. Maybe that's why he was trying to make a deal. But I don't know. Despite his flaws, psychotic tendencies in regards to others, and wild sex kinks, he's been...nice doesn't describe it. Neither does sweet. Whatever it is about Dante, I can't help my attraction towards him.

He slips his tongue into my mouth, deepening our kiss. I expect his forked tongue to tangle with mine, but the only difference I feel are the smooth metal beads of his double tongue piercing. I think he doesn't try anything adventurous with his kiss because he doesn't want to push me like Kase does. I doubt he'll ever admit it, but I also think the reason he never goes into full Hell-mode with me is because of my reaction to Kase when he startled me and broke the mirror.

I hum and lean back. "Release me and give me what I asked for."

He frowns. "You never answered my question."

Biting my lip between my teeth, I offer him a tease of a smile. "Because I want to see the real you. I want to get to know you as you are. Don't be afraid."

He chuckles. "Me, afraid?"

I nod. "Mmmhmm."

Narrowing his eyes, he studies me for a moment longer before unbuckling the restraints on my wrists. My limbs thump the pillows, and Dante starts working his warm fingers over my muscles, helping to ease the aches.

I can't stop myself from leaning into him, and he pulls me in between his legs and continues his massage of my shoulders, kneading his fingers into my skin. The heat of his fingers loosens the tension in every fiber of my being. A soft moan escapes my lips.

Tilting my head, I let my hair fall from my neck. "You're distracting me, Dante."

He hisses, flicking his tongue over the base of my neck. "I'm working you up to it."

His hands slide down my shoulders and to my arms. I squirm at the tingling sensation of his skin shifting into smooth scales the same color as his eyes. Flecks of gold color the ridges and grooves, traveling all the way down to his fingers, his nails lengthening into sharp points.

My breath hitches at his mesmerizing transformation. I gently trace my fingers over his wrists, working my fingers up his forearms and to his biceps. Shifting onto my knees, I turn to face him. He stares at the sheets, keeping his eyes down. I slowly raise my hand and trace his demonic features with the tip of my finger from his curved chin and wider mouth past the scales where his ears should be and to the short horns on his forehead. Two sharp fangs peek from his lips, and he flicks his forked tongue with another hiss.

I swallow my nerves and look past his beautifully monstrous features to his expansive black wings on his back. Neither Kase nor Lucian have wings, and it makes me curious as to why Dante does.

He remains utterly still under my exploration as I stretch higher and run my fingers over the inky feathers, glowing with an eerie light like the rainbow colors of oil on water in the sunlight. "What do you think, pretty soul? Do you regret wanting to see the real me and all my godforsaken glory?"

"Do you regret showing me?" I ask instead of answering him, drawing my hand back around to guide his face to look at me straight on. "Because you know...I have a lot of questions. Like about your wings. How do you still have them?"

Dante softens his features, shielding his demonic body with his human façade. Closing the space again, he kisses me softly like he needs to find out if I'll allow him to do so after seeing him in his hellish state. I run my fingers through his hair and back to his wings, wondering what it would be like to fly. Would I be scared out of my mind, or would I feel like the luckiest mortal on Earth for the chance to experience something beyond belief? Maybe both.

"After our jump, the saviors came for us. Kase lost his in the battle, the fuckers cutting them straight off his back," he says, ruffling the feathers of his wings like the thought hurts him to think about, even though it was Kase.

"And Lucian?" I don't know why I ask. I shouldn't want to know, but I do. The more I know about the devil who has marked my soul, the better prepared I can be.

Dante smirks, raising an eyebrow at me. "He hacked them off himself and fed them to the hellhounds."

"Hellhounds." I repeat the word again, my mind struggling to process it.

"Crazy little fuckers. You'd probably like them. I know they'd like you." Dante chuckles at my grimace. "If the rest of you is anything like your lips...damn. I want to taste every inch of you."

"Me fucking too." Kase's deep voice muffles through the closed door, and he taps his fingers on the wood. "I hope angel-girl is still restrained and naked, because I'm coming in."

He doesn't wait for a response and swings the door open, frowning at the sight of me still wrapped in the sheet and kneeling between Dante's legs, just playing with the downy feathers of his wings.

"Well, this is disappointing. You begged me to give you time with Raven and you've wasted it talking." Kase flops onto the full-size bed and slides his tail around my waist. "You could've at least gotten your dick sucked while going over the plan."

Dante growls and lunges, knocking me onto my back as he swings and punches Kase in the jaw. I lie frozen under him, his strong thighs straddling me, squeezing my torso to keep his balance. Kase laughs and raises his hands in surrender. It's now that I realize how close Dante's pelvis is to my face. If I arch up a little and he gets hard...

"Damn, look at how she looks at you. I think she's the one who wants to know what you taste like," Kase says, kneeling near my head. He grins at me. "You want him to fuck your face, don't you? Are you brave enough to swallow? I hear it gives mortals a buzz."

I don't even know how to respond, so I jerk my fist up and try to whack Kase in the junk. He catches my wrist and slides his fingers through mine. The weight of Dante's stare penetrates me, and I shift my glower from Kase's grin and peek at Dante. I was right about what would happen if he got a boner, and now, here I am, looking at his cock from two inches away, pressing against his pants.

"Hypnotic, isn't it? That's part of his demonic charm." Kase hooks his fingers under my arms and tugs me out from beneath Dante. "He might not be able to enchant your soul, but his cock? You'll be hooked."

I frown and shrug away in annoyance. I thought Dante was the envious one, but I'm nearly certain Kase is talking like this because he's jealous too. He's trying to put thoughts into my head that might make me question what the hell I'm doing. I thought that after our moment, he might act differently, but I guess he'll always have a demonic streak.

Instead of getting mad, I decide to play his game. He expects me to be embarrassed or to get mad and storm out. I can tell this by his cocky smile. What he doesn't expect is that I have my own devilish streak too, and I'm not afraid of showing either of them that I won't be messed with.

"I already am," I say, cupping Dante's hard-on through his pants. Summoning my nerve, I rub upward until I reach his button and pop it open. I slide my hand into his pants and nearly lose my resolve at how thick his shaft is. I can't even get my fingers around it completely.

Dante moans at my touch. "Raven..."

I tug his cock free right in front of Kase. "It's too irresistible not to play with, right?"

I keep digging myself deeper into this lust hole that I might get buried and never get out. Swiveling my torso, I glance over my shoulder at Kase. His eyes glow red, heavy with lust. I slowly continue my exploration of Dante as he flexes in my fingers. And then Dante kisses my bare shoulder, drawing my attention back to him.

I release a shuddering breath. "I think I've taken things too far," I murmur, staring down at his cock in my hand. Did I really just say that out loud?

Dante groans. I guess I did. "See what you fucking did, Kase? I should kick your ass."

"You should thank me," Kase replies, chuckling in my ear. "Doesn't she look so sexy with your cock in her hand? I'm the jealous one now."

Dante leans in and kisses my throat. "Would look even better if you let me paint your nails. Get you all dolled up for me, pretty soul."

Slowly releasing him, I slide out from between their two hot bodies and plop down on the edge of the bed. "This is why we shouldn't take things too far, you guys. I can barely control myself. You're both so damn attractive that I devour your attention, not even caring that you say weird ass shit or talk to me like I'm your play thing."

"You can play with me all you want, angel-girl," Kase says, twisting my hair in his fingers. "It's more fun that way."

I sigh. "You were right about my poor taste in men and terrible judgment. My ex was a serial killer for fuck's sake and you ripped him apart as a gift to me."

Kase scoots closer, tracing his fingers over the top of my hand. "You still need to thank me for that. Now's a good time."

I stand up and spin, shaking my head. "We're never going to get anything done. We have a damn mission, and it doesn't involve painting my nails for pretty hand jobs, fucking my face for your satanic jizz to get me high, or getting tied up to this bed naked."

Shadowing my every move, he envelops me in a mixture of vanilla and spice, the heat of his body warming mine. He catches me by the waist. "Want to bet?"

Dante snatches my wrist and pulls me to him, making me stand between his legs. "I'd let you restrain me and sit on my face if I thought you wouldn't leave after you cum to watch another three-day marathon of mortal trash TV. Haven't you heard of moderation? Save that for Micah and his gluttony."

His comment about Micah knocks all the lust right out of me. The fucking angel was peeping in the window, trying to apologize before I had fallen asleep. That's the initial reason Dante and Kase left. They're trying to figure things out.

I scrub my hands over my cheeks. "Why didn't you

start with the fact that you confirmed what will make Micah fall? Are you sure it's gluttony?"

Dante's jaw twitches, and he allows a few of his demonic scales to peek from his façade on his cheek. "Yes. He can't stay away from you despite what it means for him. We watched him leave and come back over and over again, just watching you sleep."

"He's taking away from those who need him, and not only mortals, to obsess over your devil marked soul." Kase straightens his back, clenching his fingers into fists. "That's what we need to focus on to break him. He will do everything he can to save your soul to prove what a righteous asshole he is. How greedy he is to be in your light. And once you fuck him? It'll be impossible for him to stop. He'll want more and more. It's perfect."

"It's insane," I mutter. "Do you really think he'll be a glutton for *me?*"

"And his mission to save you. That's how we'll get him. We'll put him in a position he won't be able to resist," Dante says, his lips curving into a wicked grin, showing off his fangs.

"What if it doesn't work?" Because really. It's hard to believe that Micah's downfall will be because of gluttony. I've only heard people called a glutton for two things—food and punishment—which I am neither. "What kind of position are you talking about? I went out in a sheet, and while it brought him out, he didn't bother to stay."

The two devils grin at each other, and then Kase says, "We're going to put you at risk of dying and going to Hell."

My eyes widen. "What? No. That's a terrible idea. What if he doesn't do whatever the fuck you think he will? I'm not going to risk failing and ending up in Hell."

Dante stands up and looms over me. "Either way, you'll be fine. You'll be with us."

"I'll be dead," I snap.

"It'll be better than living and failing. If you die trying, at least Lucian can't blame us." Kase gets to his feet, joining Dante like they can intimidate me with their sheer sizes.

"You guys are fucked up." I try to break away from them. "I'm not doing this."

"Sorry, pretty soul. We've already decided. You don't have a choice." Dante touches my cheek. "Now don't be afraid. You're worrying for nothing. Micah will come through for you. He's a savior, after all."

Too bad I have one unholy as fuck soul.

12

MICAH

SAVED

THE GOLDEN SUN rises in the distance, finally breaking the consuming darkness. I've never felt a night so long in all of my existence. I breathe in a crisp breath of morning air, finding relief. The confliction I face is unlike anything I could've imagined. Dealing with mortal souls should be easy. Light or dark. Pure with grace or tainted by the evils fighting the Higher Power every second and moment of their forsaken existence. Never have I faced a soul such as the one I can see shining through the blinds. It's the most beautiful one I've ever seen just like the woman who ruined it.

Beams of warm rays stretch toward the sky, illuminating the white clouds. It's a breathtaking reminder of why I'm here, standing on the rooftop of the unholy apartment complex destroyed by the presence of those fallen from grace. I've never seen a soul comparable to the light of the sun, bringing a new beginning each morning like I've seen in the mortal the devils keep. How they found her first? I wish I could go back in time and figure out how my brethren and I could've failed.

We've been waiting for her pure soul to return to Earth for too many sunrises to remember. And the fact that the dark betrayers got to her first? My very being weeps. It's why I couldn't do what I should've done the moment I realized what had happened. It's why I still can't. Why I'm here. I don't understand how or why I could've been given such an impossible test. My loyalty to the Higher Power shouldn't be tested in such a way.

The light of the soul fades from the window, and I flap my wings and jump from the rooftop, gliding my way down. Just losing sight of the glow makes my essence ache. My boots touch the dry grass with a crunch. Strolling around the building to the back, I hop the wall and stand on the patio.

"Put this on." Kase's command burns through me, making me tense.

"Will it even cover my damn vagina?" Hearing Raven speak is one of the most melodious sounds in the universe, no matter what comes from her mouth. "It looks like a shirt."

A throaty grumble reverberates through the air. "That doesn't matter. Consider this your uniform for being my pretty angel-girl. It'll stop the asshole from running at the sight of you. Our target has a hard-on for sexy little things, so unless you want to get hurt, put the fucking dress on. If you don't, and I have to do it myself, I will burn your pile of crap and leave you with only lingerie."

Shifting on my feet, I peek between the cracks of the partially opened blinds. Kase dangles a black dress from his fingers, swinging it back and forth in Raven's face. She snatches the flouncy fabric and drops the sheet from around her body, triggering me to focus purely on her soul. The last time she caught me watching her, her mortal rational put her on guard, thinking I was invading her privacy. I wanted to explain and apologize, but she's too far immersed in the darkness of demons that it'll take time for her to see I'm not her enemy. I never wanted to be.

"Touch my stuff, and you'll never get that tail any-where near me," Raven snaps, her soul swaying as she dresses in front of Kase.

I wish she wouldn't.

His darkness grows as he unleashes his human façade enough to let his grotesque demonic form peek through. Flicking his tail at Raven, he whips her with the filthy appendage and drags her closer to him. His presence overpowers hers, and I squeeze my eyes shut, pained by losing sight of her soul to him.

"Enough, Kase," Raven says, a musical laugh playing on her lips. "I want to get this over with. Any more distractions and you'll end up summoning Lucian again. I can't stand the thought of him hurting you."

I open my eyes, displeasure coursing through me at her admission. How can she feel even an ounce of sympathy for the beasts who imprison her soul is beyond me. If she's unfazed by their true bodies, I don't know what else I can do to show her how misguided she is.

Raven stretches up on her tiptoes and kisses Kase, losing herself to his charm. The poor, naïve soul. She has no idea how much she's being used. They play with her like the possession she is to them. If they cared even an ounce about anything besides their demonic needs and craving for power, they'd not ask her to do their bidding. From what it sounds like, they're sending her to collect on a debt from someone who bartered with their soul.

"I'd face all the agony of Hell to fuck you senseless, angel-girl. It would be worth it." Kase grins at her grimace. He feeds on the negative emotions he causes in her. Grabbing the front of his pants, he rubs his groin. "Leaving me like this is torture. More painful than Lucian's wrath."

She laughs at his audacious behavior. I wish her mind wasn't closed to me, so I could listen to her thoughts. I yearn to know what she likes about his crude attitude. If I understand her better, perhaps it'll be easier to gain her trust.

"Good. It serves you right," she says, patting his chest. Stepping back, she tugs at the short hem of the tight dress and tugs it down, only to accentuate her cleavage. "I hope you regret the decision to make me wear this too."

He has the nerve to whip her with his tail. "And they claim I'm the master of punishment."

I stare as the two of them share a passionate kiss, and an unfamiliar emotion washes over me. I dislike how it tenses my muscles and forces me to clench my jaw. Turning away, I inhale a deep breath and stare at the cloudy sky.

"Please give me the guidance I seek," I whisper, rubbing my hand over my cropped hair. "What is your plan?"

A door slams, interrupting my prayer to the Higher Power, and I launch into the air and hover above the rooftops. Bellowing laughter booms through the air from below as Dante and Kase circle Raven like the predators they are. Blush tints her cheeks, and she shakes her head at something

Dante whispers. Smacking his chest, Raven keeps him from lifting up her dress and darts away. Her stilettos click on the pathway with her brisk pace, and I follow along above them.

Raven remains ahead of the devils until she reaches the parking lot of the complex. Tipping her head back, she looks up and shields her eyes from the sun. Our eyes meet, and she raises her middle finger at me. I wave and force my mouth to smile, hoping I look okay. Her fear bothers me unlike I could have ever imagined. Maybe it's because of how she can face the rulers of Hell without an ounce of hesitation, or maybe it's because of the new feelings she arouses in my essence, but either way, she's pushed me into a territory I have no idea how to handle.

I fly higher, expecting her to inform her soul keepers of my presence, but she surprises me and turns her attention back to them, keeping her middle finger up while they laugh and tease her.

The three of them climb into an obnoxious bright red vehicle with Raven sitting on Dante's lap in the two-seater. Kase sends white smoke through the air as he speeds from the lot, cutting off a minivan in the process. I soar across the sky, flapping my wings harder and faster, pushing me to keep up.

About a mile away from their apartment complex, Kase pulls to the curb and Dante flings his door open. Raven stumbles out of the vehicle. She tugs down her dress and tries to yell at them, but Kase speeds off, leaving her in a cloud of smoke. Coughing, she waves her hand to clear the air. I glide toward the ground and wait until she struts toward an alleyway to land.

Peering around the garbage littered street, I meander after Raven, ensuring two dozen feet of distance between us. I don't shield myself from her, despite knowing she might react negatively. My need to watch over her and ask the Higher Power to help me protect her pushes me forward. The devils are either misguided to think that their influence on her soul will keep Raven out of danger or they lack any sort of consideration for her life because her soul is marked. It pains me that such a beautiful spirit will go to waste.

I turn the corner and crash into Raven. Grabbing her waist, I pull her into me, saving her from falling to the ground. Furrowing her brows, she glowers at me and scrambles away to put space between us.

"Why won't you just leave me alone?" Raven asks, peering at the alleyway behind her. "You're interrupting a job I must complete. If I don't, my ass will get restrained to Dante's bed again, and my shoulders still ache from last night."

I stare at Raven's beautiful blue-green eyes, unable to form any coherent words. The sun lights her hair, streaking it with a deep midnight color. She's even more breathtaking than before, now that I concentrate on her humanity instead of her soul.

She snaps her fingers in front of my face. "Hello? Did you hear me? I know your creepy ass has a thing for watching me be punished, but—"

"I'm sorry. I'm so sorry." Bending my knees, I launch into the air, my whole body buzzing from her closeness. I can't bear the way she looks at me as if I'm the bad guy, but I also can't bear to leave her. The need to protect her consumes me.

I land on the roof of the building and stroll along the edge, shoving my mixture of emotions to the back of my mind the best I can. I need to focus. I need a clear head. The task that Raven faces could help guide the brethren and I down the path to stop the devils from destroying the world we've cared after for so long.

Raven stops outside the backdoor of one of the businesses and raps her knuckles on the metal security screen. Stepping back, she crosses her arms over her chest, her face lining with worry. She rubs her lips together and peers in each direction of the alley. I follow her line of sight to the street and catch sight of the gaudy red car Kase and Dante are in idling nearby. Confusion washes over me. Why in heavens would they choose to send her alone only to sit back and watch?

"Hello? Mr. Tavern, I know you can see me on the security cam. Please open up. I'm here on behalf of Dante." Raven's voice steals my attention away from the devils.

She adjusts her dress, hiking it up a bit more. Turning her back on the door, she gathers her hair into a ponytail, revealing the smooth skin of her shoulders in the backless dress. My gaze travels down the length of her spine and to the sliver of lace peeking out from her waistline. I fist my hands and tip my head up to stare at the bright sun. I've never been so affected by a piece of clothing in my existence. Something is wrong with me.

Jumping from the rooftop, I land on the sidewalk not far from the red car, needing to concentrate on something else apart from Raven. If I focus on her any longer, I'll confront her again. I'll risk starting a fight with the devils because Dante and Kase exit the vehicle and stroll to the alleyway.

"I'm only a messenger, Mr. Tavern. Please don't make this hard," Raven says, her voice echoing through the air.

A door slams against the wall. "You want to feel something real hard? Come here. I have a message you can deliver to that bastard." The husky voice of the hell-bound man stiffens my muscles.

I keep my distance from the forsaken, hovering behind them as they huddle close and watch a man tower over Raven. He yanks a pocketknife from his jacket and aims it at her. Raven raises her hands in surrender and shuffles backward.

Her gaze flicks toward the street. "Stay back, Mr. Tavern. If you touch me—"

Raven doesn't have the chance to finish her threat as the man rushes her. Screeching, she hits her back on the opposite wall, getting cornered. My heart leaps toward the Heavens, and it takes everything in me not to intervene with the devils in front of me. Kase and Dante remain in their spots, doing nothing as a man towers over Raven and aims a knife at her throat.

"What are you going to do about it, bitch?" The man catches his blade on the bodice of her dress and rips the fabric.

Whimpering, Raven presses her back harder into the wall, not moving despite her undergarments showing. Tears brim her big blue eyes. Her chest heaves and her lips quiver. I turn and glower at Kase and Dante, waiting for them to react.

They do nothing, standing there with wicked smiles on their faces, enjoying Raven's humiliation and fear. Feeding on it like the most delectable thing they've ever tasted.

"Please, don't hurt me," Raven whispers, her voice shaking. "I'm just trying to do my job. You're the one who made a deal with the devil, as did I, and they're ready to collect on your debt."

The man growls through his clenched teeth and waves the knife at her. "You came asking the wrong man, sweetheart. If those bastards want me, they're going to have to come get me themselves."

"You don't want that." Raven blinks through her tears, turning her gaze toward the sky.

The man slices his knife at the front of her dress again. "I think I do."

My body hums with her silent prayer as her mind suddenly opens to me. I gasp at her thundering emotions booming through my essence. Her soul begs for help. Her body begs for protection. Her mind? Heavens, no. She silently begs for me. Hearing my name cross her mind opens a hole inside me that only Raven can fill. Her prayer cuts me deeply, stirring emotions I never knew were possible for me to feel.

I can't stop my feet from shuffling forward until I'm merely a yard away from the devils. Kase chuckles at Raven's distress and bumps his shoulder into Dante's. My blood cools at the twisted vocalization of his dark desires. It takes everything in me not to unsheathe my sword and shove it into his back.

"Show her what kind of man you are, Tobias. Cut that dress off her. Show her the kind of wrath you carry," Kase murmurs.

Dante hums under his breath. "Show her how much you envy us because she's ours."

Raven screams out as the dark soul grabs her hair and pins her to the wall. With a swipe of his knife, he cuts her bra down the middle, nicking her flesh in the process. She tries to kick him, but he stands too close to her, staring at her exposed breasts.

"Help!" Raven shouts, only to have the man slap his hand over her lips.

"If she can't handle one bad soul, it serves her right to die like this," Kase says, leering at Raven.

Dante rubs his hands together in anticipation. "I can't wait to rip that pretty soul in half and fuck her face like the cum dumpster I want her to be."

I break. I know better than to intervene in demonic affairs, but I can't watch Raven suffer like this. I can't bear to think of the rest of her eternity as the devils shred her soul to torture as they please. I just can't.

Drawing my flaming sword, I swipe it across Dante and Kase's backs, surprising them. Neither of them can unleash their hellish beasts before I launch into the air and fly towards Raven and the man. He rips at her dress, trying to cut it off completely while she sobs and begs for him to stop. Her emotions hurt me so deeply that I can barely see through the glassiness of my eyes.

Landing with a thud behind the dark soul, I latch my fingers onto his jacket and yank him away, sending him crashing into the wall. Raven gasps and screams, trying to run for her life, her body bloody and bruised, and the light of her soul twisting with a darkness that wants to devour her.

The ground rumbles with the growing shadow, and Kase charges into the alleyway in his wrathful form, his huge body towering over mine as he races to grab Raven.

"You can't have her, Micah!" he shouts, his guttural voice growling through the air.

A shadow streaks across the ground, and I charge faster toward Raven. If either of them gets to her first, there will be nothing I can do.

"Raven, please! Let me help you!" I yell, pushing off the ground to fly the rest of the distance to her.

I grind my teeth, facing Kase head on just like the day he turned his back on the Higher Power. The same day I took his wings.

I will take this beautiful soul from him too.

Nothing can stop me.

13

RAVEN

SAVING GRACE

"RAVEN, FIGHT HIM!" Kase hollers as he snarls and charges toward me in his hellish form.

My mind is clouded with fear from being left at the mercy of Micah. I knew what the plan was. I knew that things would get scary. But I can't help wondering how far Kase and Dante would've let things go if Micah hadn't intervened. Our ideas of what's fucked up are obviously nowhere near aligned.

I squeeze my eyes shut, my body refusing to do anything as Micah and Kase rush at each other with me in the middle. I could very well get torn apart in a battle of who will leave with me.

A cool arm hooks around my waist, dragging me from the ground. Roaring, Kase yells for Dante to grab me. My hair and torn dress whip in the freezing wind, and I force my eyes to open despite my burning tears.

Micah dangles me in one muscular arm, flying higher and higher into the air. My stomach twists with fear. I've never even flown on a plane before, and this is far more terrifying than I could ever imagine. If Micah drops me, I'm dead.

But I might be dead anyways.

He was supposed to intervene and save me from a trip to Hell, and in doing so, prove he was willing to endanger the greater good on my behalf. This whole fucked up plan was to get under his skin and get him to change his course enough to fall from the grace of the Higher Power, and not for him to kidnap and fly away with me.

"Micah! Let my pretty soul go or I'll tear off your damn wings myself!" Dante's deep voice reverberates through my body as he soars above us, his expansive black wings shadowing me from the sun. "She's been marked by Lucian. You can't change that."

Micah tightens his hold on me and drops a few dozen feet. My stomach feels as if it flies in my throat, and I open and close my mouth in a scream that doesn't come. The world spins and flips and drops, my mind unable to keep up with the aerial acrobatics Micah performs to avoid Dante. I feel so utterly helpless at his mercy, and I can't stand it.

Dante growls from above us and nose dives, falling like a speeding missile on course to detonate. Micah swings me up and against his chest, giving me no choice but to cling onto him if I don't want to plummet who knows how far—thousands of feet at least. The air around me stings my skin from the icy cold, and it hurts to breathe normally.

"Don't let go of me, heathen. I'm not going to hurt you, but your soul keeper will. He doesn't have any regard for your life and eternity like I do." Micah's voice drifts through my mind, igniting a strange wave of calming relief through me.

"Raven! Fight him! I'll catch you," Dante yells, darting past us as Micah dodges out of the way. "I can't go where he plans to take you. Please, you have to fight! I'm not ready for you to go to Hell just yet. Fight!"

Micah flaps his wings, shooting us upward. "He's lying. He doesn't care whether you live or die. He will torture your soul regardless. It's what he does. It's why he stood by and did nothing as the dark soul hurt you."

So many thoughts spin through my mind. I knew Dante and Kase were willing to risk my life because they knew they'd get my soul regardless, but I want to believe there is more to it. They know Micah. He was once their brethren. Deep down, they had faith in his inability to see harm come to me, but does it change the fact that there was no guarantee that it'd work? I have no fucking idea. There are only two things I know for certain about my existence, and my deal with Lucian and my Hell-bound soul are the only things I can truly count on to happen. It sucks, but it is what it is. I shouldn't be so conflicted about anything else.

"Raven, damn it!" Dante shouts again from below. "Fight! Let go!"

Dante ascends, stretching his arms to try to grab Micah's boots. Folding in his wings, Micah surprises Dante by freefalling instead of flying higher. I don't get a chance to convince myself to risk falling to my death to escape, because Micah summons a ball of bright light into his palm. Micah chucks it at Dante, hitting him in the chest. Dante hollers, letting the strange light eating at his flesh push him to fight harder. He flaps his wings and yanks Micah's leg, sending the two of us spinning in the air.

I scream and cling on to Micah, my survival instincts not allowing me to let him go. Micah twists his body as we freefall a dozen feet and manages to throw his flaming sword at Dante, sinking it into his wing. My heart plummets into my stomach as fire ignites across Dante's black feathers. He roars in anger and pain, twisting to try to get the flaming sword from his skin. I watch is shock and fear at his inability to keep flight.

"Dante!" I yell, stretching my hand out in disbelief.

From Micah's arms, I watch Dante fall until Micah shifts me, not allowing me to see the rest of his descent.

I can't stop the small sob from escaping my mouth as everything catches up to me. What the fuck is going on with my life? How did I get so unlucky to find myself in this position in the first place? What am I going to do now?

Micah's cool hand rubs the length of my back, trying to smooth the trembles from my body. "Please don't cry, Raven. This will all be over soon. Neither of them will be able to get to you where we're going."

I lick my lips and swallow the burning in my throat. "Is he..." My voice fades. I can't even think of the words.

"Unfortunately, it'll take a lot more than a fall like that to send him back to Hell where he belongs," Micah responds sullenly like he expects me to break down.

If anything, I'm relieved. "Oh."

"But I don't want you to worry about any of that. I'm taking you somewhere no one from Hell can go until I can figure out what to do," he says, tightening his jaw.

"I don't understand." I close my eyes, trying to calm my racing heart.

Micah adjusts me in his arms. "Please give me guidance. Tell me what to do."

His prayer trickles into my mind along with a swirling tornado of emotions I can't decipher. I've never felt anything like them, and a part of me wants to lose myself to the pureness of his light.

And then I do.

I should've known Micah would take me to church, but this one isn't mortal made as far as I can tell. One second I was feeling his essence wrapping around mine, awakening my soul as if I could siphon his purity to snuff out the Hell marking me, and in the next, everything grew tingly and cool like a misty morning in winter. When the fog cleared, I found myself alone and in this weird all-white stone room with a window that gives me a view of light. I can't see anything beyond it.

I move from the window and grimace at the bloody fingerprints I leave behind. Now that my adrenaline wears off, I can't ignore the stinging pain of shallow cuts from the knife the fucking monster Mr. Tavern inflicted on me. And my dress? Fuck. It's a reminder of how close that man was from—I can't think about it.

I shiver in the cold room and spin around, glancing at the arched doorway leading into a vast white room not unlike the one I'm in but far bigger with looming vaulted ceilings made of glass, shining the strange pure light over me, setting my filthy skin aglow.

Dressed in all black, Micah kneels in front of a crystal window pieced together into an intricate pattern that sends fractals of rainbow light glittering across the room. His striking contrast steals my attention away from the beauty of colorful light, and I shuffle forward on my bare feet. I don't even remember losing my stilettos.

"Micah," I whisper, afraid to speak too loud in this place of obvious grace. The Higher Power might smite me for just being here. "Micah, where are we?"

Micah remains frozen without responding to me. It's creepy as fuck, and all I want for him to do is to get to his feet, turn around, and tell me what he plans to do. The uncertainty digs deeply into my soul. It's hard to bear it.

I close the space completely and stand behind him. Glancing at the crystal window, I try to see beyond the intricate design to discover what is on the other side. My imagination wants to run wild and imagine the pearly gates of what I've been told is the entrance to Heaven, but there is no way I'd be just hanging outside them. For one, I'm alive. I know I am. If I died, I'd probably be kneeling at Lucian's feet. So this place? I have no idea.

"It's my sanctuary," Micah finally says, responding to my silent thoughts. "We're still on the Earth plane, but it's built from the grace of the Higher Power as a temple of reflection and prayer created solely for me. Consider it my home away from my true home."

"It's so...empty." I have no idea what else I should say. "Not exactly how I imagine Heaven."

"Because it's not, but also, you will never see what I see. It isn't intended for mortals." Micah remains gazing out the window without looking at me. "You're not supposed to be here."

"So why am I here?" I ask, staring at his folded white wings.

Like he senses I study them, he unfurls them, expanding them completely. Shuffling toward him, I close the space, soaking in the pure tranquility swirling through the air. Goosebumps prickle across my skin with each step I take. I find myself caught on an invisible line drawing me to his downy looking wings. Where Dante's are pure black, downy soft, and warm like the rest of him, Micah's sparkly wings illuminate like each feather contains a glowing lightbulb to shine from within.

"I don't know," Micah whispers, responding to me like it takes everything in him to speak. "I don't know anything anymore."

"Micah." I rest my hand on one of his wings. A burst of intense, fiery pain licks across my palm, and I scream and jerk away. Uncontrollable tears well in my eyes, blurring my vision and turning Micah into an inky blot among the brightness of his sanctuary.

Micah shoots to his feet and spins around, his dark brows lowering over his golden eyes. Grasping my wrist, he pulls my aching hand from my chest and inspects my palm. An imprint of his feathers sears across my palm, branding the hand opposite where Lucian's mark puckers from my skin.

"My wings are the one thing you cannot touch, Raven. They're sacred and blessed with the light of the Higher Power, created to repel the evils of Hell." Micah draws his cool finger along the edges of the feather branding. "You've been marked by Lucifer."

I sigh and tug my stinging hand away. "He goes by Lucian now." I don't know why I correct him or why I even humor standing before his righteous ass a moment longer without trying to escape. All I know is that I'm on the same page as Micah, neither of us feeling as if we know anything at all. "And maybe next time, you should warn an unsuspecting soul about the pain you can inflict."

"I'm sorry. I'm not used to kidnapping heathens from their soul keepers." A soft smile lights his pouty mouth like he enjoys the thought. "Nor am I accustomed to speaking to them, hosting them in my private quarters, or feeling the rush of emotions emanating from their souls."

"You're a righteous douche if I'm a heathen. I don't get you. You tried to send my soul to Hell, and then you stalked me, and now you kidnapped me. I thought angels were against doing all of this." I shift on my feet. "What do you plan to do with me now?"

Micah groans and kneels again, staring at the floor instead of the window. "I should send you to Hell to protect the greater good."

"But you're not." I might be testing my already bad luck by saying the words, but I need answers. I'm already living with a ton of unknowns. "You said you wouldn't hurt me."

"And I won't. I just—I need time. I need to know what the plan is and how to help you. I can't in good faith deny your request for salvation." Micah laces his fingers together in silent prayer. It's the strangest thing, experiencing what feels like an electrical current dancing across my skin as he asks for guidance and help on my behalf.

"Whatever it is you think you're doing...stop. I've accepted my fate, and I can't handle anymore disappointment. You said it yourself. Saving my soul isn't possible." I hate how even an ounce of hope leaves me breathless. "I'm a realist. Save the hope for someone who has faith in the Higher Power. Only Kase and Dante haven't let me down, despite their flaws. At least they're honest."

"Raven, it's not possible to save your soul now, but I want to try." His sincerity whips through me stealing my breath. "The devils don't deserve you. Look at what they put you through today. You were hurt." Micah turns his attention to me again. "The dark soul was going to defile you, and they found great amusement in the act. I've never felt such torture as I had in that moment. It was unbearable. I never want to experience anything like that again."

Anger sneaks up on me. His confession snaps me out of the tranquility settling down my soul. "What do you mean you felt tortured?"

"You prayed to me, opening a spiritual connection that I tapped into. It's why I reacted as I had." Micah straightens his shoulders, getting to his feet. "I couldn't bear it."

"*You* couldn't bear it? *You*? What about *me*? I know you were stalking me, Micah. You know I know. It's why I had prayed to you." The more the thought crosses my mind, the angrier I get. "But what I don't get is why it took so long for you to do anything? If I hadn't have opened myself up for you to feel my agony, would you have done nothing?"

He scowls at my question. "Raven, the devils—"

"Don't bring up Kase and Dante. This is about you, Micah." I yank the ends of my dark hair. "You know, all my life I thought of angels as being these sweet, loving beings who fought to protect the innocent and protected those who needed it."

"You must understand," Micah says, expanding his wings, filling the room with his holy presence. "I'm not supposed to intervene in demonic affairs."

"Bullshit! You're already intervening. Face it, Micah. Whatever this is—" I swirl my fingers around him. "It isn't about the Higher Power. It isn't even about Kase or Dante. It's about you. You're not doing any of this for anyone but yourself. It's why you waited to help me. Instead of intervening before anything bad happened, you waited until you suffered too."

Something shifts in his expression, and his wings droop. "Raven, I—"

"If you plan to apologize, don't." A new level of pain battles inside me. My soul weeps with my words. I'm angry, but I'm conflicted. I know I don't say everything I do because it's what I believe. Micah's purity, his grace, I know these things influence him. But I have to say them. It's what is required in my mission.

Because Micah's right. He can't save me.

I can only save myself.

It just hurts that it means I have to destroy him in the process.

"I want you to take me home, Micah," I add, crossing my arms over my chest. "This is pointless."

He tries to grab my hand, but I recoil. "Please. Let me—"

"Take me home!" I yell, spinning to find a door. The only way out of the room is through the crystal window, shining with rainbow light. "Give up on this self-proclaimed mission. You can't save me, okay? It's over. My life is over."

"Raven—"

Ignoring his pleas, I rush toward the window and crash through.

Light swallows me whole.

14

RAVEN

GIFT FROM THE DEVILS

"LOOK WHAT THE bird-brain brought home." A silhouette hovers over me, blocking out the yellow glow of the porchlight. "You owe me a fucking blowjob, Dante. I told you he wouldn't be able to handle more than a couple hours with angel-girl."

Dante groans, appearing next to Kase. "Damn it. She was pathetic enough that I thought for sure it'd be overnight." Squatting beside me, Dante combs my messy hair from my forehead. "You're fucking lucky I don't mind sucking cock, Raven, or I'd be pissed that you didn't even manage to seduce the angel."

Gathering my strength, I swing my arm and punch him in the thigh. "You guys are fucking bastards. You weren't even looking for me."

"Because we knew where you were. Micah would've only taken you to his house. What did you expect us to do?" Kase's voice lowers in annoyance. "You're mad at the wrong guys."

"What about Mr. Tavern? He would've fucking raped and killed me had Micah not intervened. You believe that you have my soul regardless, but rape? Are you fucking kidding me? That's far beyond forgivable. I'll not be put in that position again. I know you all struggle with right and wrong—"

Kase shoves his arms under me and scoops me up. I don't have a chance to react before he plants his lips on mine, silencing me. I jerk away and slap him. My emotions run hot and all over the place as I replay the last few hours in my head over and over again. The scratch down my chest still hurts. The branding on my palm isn't any better.

Tightening his jaw, Kase releases a low growl. "Raven, do you really think so little of us that we'd have allowed Tobias to get his dick anywhere near you? You knew that we were going to put you into a dangerous situation. You can't blame us that Micah waited for you to suffer. If we had intervened first, he'd have never fought for you. This is a good thing. The pain is only temporary."

This still feels so fucked up. He's right about me knowing how dangerous it could be, but it's still hard to process.

"And we plan to make it up to you," Dante adds, moving in close. "We have a present."

"A present? How will that help?" I shudder a breath.

"It's our way of apologizing and rewarding you for the bullshit you had to do. I didn't enjoy having to stand by and rely on fucking Micah." Kase leans closer, his mouth hovering near mine. "Please forgive us."

Is it messed up that I already do? Maybe. But I can't just let them think I will be so easy. It'll only make matters harder. They'll think they can get away with pushing me around.

"No. I don't think you understand. You can't just apologize and expect me to be okay. Today was hard. Micah somehow thinks he can figure out how to save me and—"

Dante bellows a laugh and shakes Kase's shoulders, grinning at me. "It won't be long."

"I told him it was pointless and to give up on me." I frown with my words. Hearing them out loud makes me feel as if I might've went too far. Like I fucked up. I groan and rest my forehead to Kase's shoulder, inhaling a breath of his warm, sweet scent. "Shit. I messed everything up, didn't I?"

"Are you kidding me, angel-girl? That's going to drive him wild." Kase rocks me in his arms and bounces on his feet. "Like Dante said, it won't be long."

"Now, it's time for your present. We've been waiting all day for this." Dante shoves the ajar door open completely, slamming it into the wall with a bang. "I think this will help remind you of what we're trying to accomplish. It'll also make up for that tit-slit injury. I will cut the fucker any way you please."

I grimace. "Huh?"

A deep sob answers me without Dante having to explain anything. Hanging from a brand new hook on the ceiling, Mr. Tavern flops like a fish on a line. He's butt-ass naked with his clothes torn and piled on the floor in a rancid mess of...ew. I don't even want to know.

I bury my nose in Kase's shirt, trying to stop my stomach from roiling. "What the fuck," I whisper, trying to look anywhere besides the man, but it's like I can't help it. I can only manage to keep my eyes averted for seconds at a time.

"Surprise!" Kase says, his voice rising with his excitement. "Look at this weak asshole now. To think I thought he was a tough guy."

"Far from it." Dante swings the door closed and rubs his hands together, strolling ahead of us. "He's so scared he shit and pissed himself. Twice." Circling the man, Dante shakes his head in disgust. "This is how much we enjoy having you around, Raven. We put up with this so you could enjoy his punishment too."

"Which is your choice, angel-girl. Tell us what you feel is appropriate for his wrongdoings. You're not his only victim. The fucker made a deal with Hell to keep his mortal freedom in exchange for his soul." Kase yanks me from him, not allowing me to cling onto him for dear life. Setting me on my feet, he spins me around to face Mr. Tavern. Kase wraps his warm arms around me from behind and presses his lips to my earlobe. "He was allotted ten more victims for the rest of his life. Just a little extra something to dirty his already vile soul the way Lucian likes."

My heart sinks into my stomach. "You let him hurt ten people? That's horrible."

"He went through them in...how long was it, Tobias? A year? Six months?" Dante stops in front of Mr. Tavern and grabs him by the chin, turning him into a blubbery mess. "Tell my pretty soul the truth. You don't want me to rip it from you."

"Two w-weeks," Mr. Tavern stutters.

My eyes widen at the thought. He's hurt ten people in two weeks. He hurt me. This fucker is more disgusting and vile than I could ever imagine.

"Please, I'll do anything. Tell me what you want," he

adds, jerking his arms, trying to tug the ropes down.

Dante swivels his torso and smirks at me. "Do you hear that, Raven? He wants another deal. What do you think? He could be useful."

Anger explodes through me, and I clench my fingers into fists, ignoring the searing pain of my nails biting into the brand from Micah's wings. "No. You guys should've never bartered with him to begin with."

Turning back to the man, Dante jerks his hand and grabs him by the throat. "See what you've done? My pretty soul is angry you enticed us with a deal to begin with. Now she might never let me fuck her brains out."

"Please! I'm sorry. Please!" Mr. Tavern hollers, fighting the restraints. "I'll do anything. Just give me more time. I can be of use to you."

Dante sighs dramatically and slides his fingers through his dark hair. "He makes such a convincing argument, doesn't he?" Twisting on his feet, he glances at us again. "He'll do anything for us."

"The options are endless," Kase murmurs, brushing his lips to my neck.

"Unfortunately, it's that pretty soul over there that has the final say. You'll have to convince her, not us." Dante wiggles his fingers at me.

The second Mr. Tavern's eyes land on mine, I lose it. Something dark and deadly sneaks from the depths of my soul to crash over my mortal rationale in an intensely hot wave. My whole body stiffens as if it sucks in the evilness radiating from this bastard man's essence.

His lips quiver. "Plea—"

"Send him to Hell!" I yell, heaving a breath. "He deserves an eternity of the same torment he put others through."

Kase rocks me in his arms. "Aw, come on, angel-girl. At least have us cut off and choke him with his dick. Show him what it feels like."

"Fuck his ass with it first," Dante says, pulling a knife from his jacket.

Mr. Tavern thrashes and screams his head off even though Dante doesn't get close to him, waiting on me.

As much as Mr. Tavern would deserve it, I'm not his kind of monster. I wish I could stomach inflicting what he's done to others onto him, but I'm not a devil like Kase and Dante. I can't agree to such a punishment in front of me. Knowing he'll spend an eternity in Hell is good enough for me.

Bringing my hands up, I cover my ears, trying to stifle Mr. Tavern's screams as best as I can.

The ground rumbles beneath my feet, and Kase's hands slide away from my waist. His shadow grows across the floor in front of me. I tip my head back and peek up at his monstrous feline form. Opening his wide jowls, Kase snarls, shutting Mr. Tavern up.

"I can sense you won't sentence him to any appropriate punishment, so I will choose it for you." Kase stomps forward, shaking the room with his heavy footsteps. "Go wait in my room. Know that justice will be served."

Using his long black tail, Kase nudges me toward the hallway. My body finally decides to obey my brain, and I shuffle forward. My heart pounds so out of control that I can feel it beating from my toes to the top of my head. Mr. Tavern continues to scream and scream, his voice imprinting itself onto my essence in the same vile way his actions earlier stabbed into me.

"Please, let it be quick," I murmur silently, turning my back on Kase just as he whips his tail toward Mr. Tavern's groin. "I don't want to hear it anymore."

Light glows from Kase's open door at the end of the hallway, drawing my attention away from the snarls and screams surely echoing across the universe as the putrid smell of Hell wafts through the air.

Silence suddenly falls over me, but one glance over my shoulder tells me it isn't because it's over. The fragrance of Hell still permeates the air as does the light from the fiery gates.

Whatever is happening now is because of...Micah. I can sense he lingers nearby. He probably never even left after bringing me back.

I want so badly to stop short and run back to the living room, but the bitterness of vengeance stops me. I don't want to know the twisted punishment Kase and Dante come up with for Mr. Tavern on my behalf.

Gathering my nerve, I stride into Kase's room and shut the door behind me. The familiar angelic glow radiates from the cracks in the blinds, Micah's light purposely shining brightly for me. I cross the room and yank the blinds open, not even stopping to peek out first.

I unlock and slide the glass door open. "You shouldn't be here, Micah."

He scratches the back of his neck. "I know I shouldn't, but I wanted to make sure you were okay. You unintentionally called to me. I'm not all powerful and can't make your soul keepers punish as quickly as you'd like, but I can envelop you in my shield, which can block out the noise of suffering."

I gather my nerve and step onto the patio and slide the door closed behind me. "You probably think I'm a hypocrite for denying the man mercy." Staring at his black boots, I refuse to meet his gaze. Why is it I feel badly about my decision?

"Raven, that dark soul was so far from redemption. Even if you could offer such a miracle, neither Lucifer nor the Higher Power would grant mercy to someone with a soul so vile. It would cause an imbalance in the universe, which is why I can't grant you the one thing I'd give anything for. I know you don't think you deserve it—or maybe you don't want it anymore—but I won't stop trying to figure it out."

"You really are a glutton, aren't you?" I say, twisting on the balls of my feet to glance at the back door.

Micah blinks in confusion, his expression hardening. His metallic gold eyes sparkle with the light emanating from his essence, and his long lashes cast shadows on his cheeks. "I'm far from a glutton, heathen. What have the devils been filling your head with? I can't overconsume anything in regards to you. You're not an indulgence to me."

He doesn't know—or maybe doesn't realize—what Kase and Dante see. Or maybe it's all in their heads, and we're going in the wrong direction. Either way, I'm starting to feel badly about it.

"I just want to help you. You deserve someone to fight by your side," he adds, slowly reaching to take my hand.

I let him. Something shifts inside me in this moment, and Micah's sincerity engulfs me in a pool of hope and the goodness that comes with finding it again.

Micah glides his fingers over my palm, tracing the brand burned in my skin from his feathers. "I don't think the Higher Power would've put you in my path if it were for any other reason than unchaining your soul from the darkness of the devil's sins. Look at my wing, Raven. We marked each other. It's like the Higher Power wanted us both to feel and see the reminder, so we don't lose faith. We—"

A loud hiss trickles through the air, and I jerk my hand away from Micah.

He glowers and unsheathes his sword, aiming it at the sliding glass door. Yanking it open, Dante bares his fangs at Micah. I raise my palm up, trying to get Dante settled down.

"You fucking marked her, Micah?" Dante asks, his deep voice reverberating through my bones. "You fucking staked your claim on a soul that doesn't belong to you. Raven is mine! I'm going to destroy you!"

Stepping closer to Dante, I try to steal his attention by gathering the front of his shirt in my hand. "Hey, calm down. He didn't mark me. It was an accident. I touched his wings."

Uh-oh. The second the comment escapes my mouth, I realize my mistake.

Dante's jealousy gets the best of him even thinking about me touching wings that aren't his. Fury lights his face and he grabs my wrist and spins me toward the door. His big palm spanks me right on the ass as he forces me inside and shuts the door in my face.

Micah launches into the air, tugging his flaming sword free, and Dante soon follows, sending black feathers drifting through the air in his wake.

"Get back here, you coward!" Dante yells, his voice muffled by the glass door. "I will teach you the first fucking lesson of this eternity. Raven is mine!"

15

RAVEN

PUNISHMENT

SOMETHING CRASHES FROM outside the bathroom door, and I quickly shut off the water and grab a towel from the rack. Kase's snarl shakes the flimsy door. Hot red light glows from the crack at the bottom. Wrapping the towel around me, I rush toward the hallway. I should've expected a fight the moment Dante would decide to finally return to the apartment, but it sounds far worse than I could've imagined.

"You've been gone for two fucking days!" Kase hollers, his voice bellowing through the air. "What if Lucian had decided to drop in? I haven't even seen Micah. You better not have fucking ruined this for us."

"He fucking branded her!" Dante shouts, his voice just as guttural and loud as Kase's. "Do you even care? What if he—"

A body slams into the door, shaking it on its hinges. Kase growls again. "Raven is eavesdropping on the other side of the door, so you better be fucking careful about what you choose to say next. I'm sure Micah's already put impossible ideas into her mind, and I don't need your envy to push you into believing in damn miracles, either."

Damn. I've been caught. I was hoping for at least another few minutes of their unfiltered anger to hear what is really on their minds.

"Now get your ass out here, angel-girl. We all need to talk." Kase knocks his fist on the door. "Hurry your bubble butt up, or I'll kick the door down. It's taking everything in me not to put Dante in his place my way."

I sigh and lock my fingers around the doorknob, tugging it open to confront the two of them. Kase stands in front of the door with his arms across his chest and his lips pursed in anger. Behind him, Dante glowers at the back of Kase's head and refuses to even look at me. The intensity of their moods digs deeply into my soul, burning me from the inside out.

"Can't you give me a couple minutes to get dressed?" I ask with annoyance lining my words.

Kase shakes his head. "No. We need to deal with this now."

Shit.

Pointing, he adds, "My room. Now. The both of you."

Like he doesn't think I'll listen, he snakes his tail from his lower back and laces it around me, tugging me from the bathroom. Dante skulks past us and stomps into Kase's room. I press my lips together and flick my gaze to Kase, wondering what the fuck this is about. I know he's just as mad as I am that Dante abandoned us to chase Micah, but I'm nearly certain our reasons vastly differ. Kase hasn't been his cocky self, mostly zoning out watching TV with me, and he hasn't hit on me once, not even complaining that I've been sleeping in Dante's sex chambers by myself.

The end of Kase's tail shifts the front of my towel, and I jump in surprise. Locking my fingers around the smooth appendage, I stop Kase from getting carried away. One look over my shoulder at him shows me he's no longer in his grumpy-ass mood. Who knew that Dante returning could affect him like this, but I guess when you spend eternity with someone...

"Join Dante's ass on my bed, angel-girl," Kase says,

nudging me toward Dante.

He sits on the edge of Kase's bed with his elbows resting on his knees. As much as I want to ignore Kase's command, I suck up my annoyance for Dante's sake. I know why he chased after Micah. I know he let his envy over Micah's mark on my hand get to him. So did the fact that I touched Micah's wings—wings like the ones on his back and the ones I loved touching. But where he sees the act as something to envy because it was Micah and not him, he can't comprehend that there was nothing behind my gesture with Micah—not like with Dante.

I shuffle the rest of the way to the bed and sit down beside Dante. Sitting ultra-close, I purposefully press into him, letting his weight ensure no space gets between us. Kase watches us from his spot near the door. His jaw twitches, and he crosses his arms over his chest, narrowing his eyes like he expects me to make the next move.

"Just get it over with, Kase. Show us your wrath, and let me go to bed." Dante scrubs his face with his hands. "I know I fucked up by leaving, but I'm back now and more clear headed."

"You think leaving was where you fucked up, Dante?" Kase asks, strolling forward. A smile plays on his lips, his sharp features turning more handsome. "Leaving and chasing Micah is something I get. I'd have done it myself. What I don't get is where in the fuck you got the idea that Raven is yours."

"Wait, what?" I ask, pushing to get up.

Kase flicks me back with his tail and plops down, sandwiching me to Dante. "Your soul is ours, angel-girl. If Dante's envious ass starts claiming you as solely his, there is going to be a huge fucking problem. Neither of us can help it. He'll start to turn into a little douche toward me, and then he'll fall to my wrath. You are ours, and he needs a damn reminder."

I swallow, feeling Dante's silent intensity as Kase's words sink in. "You better not be implying what I think you are."

"Don't say that like you're against punishing him for getting pissed off by your honest mistake." Kase turns and grabs my face. "You even slept in his bed, choosing to stop any progression you and I could've had while he was gone. Your soul knows it as much as you do. You won't have me without him."

My heart thunders in erratic beats. I hadn't realized the truth to his words until hearing them out loud as if he reads the warning on my soul. Whatever Lucian did to me, bartering my very being and threatening to split me between the two of them has fucked me up. And I don't even care. Kase is right. I've been lying to myself about the reason I've been in Dante's room. I have missed him. These last two days have been miserable without both of them constantly being within my reach.

"You also crave to show him as much as I do that you will never be his alone, isn't that right, angel-girl." Kase runs his thumb across my lips, stretching them with his finger. "That's why you're going to kiss me."

I raise my eyebrows at Kase, wondering where the hell he plans to take this. Dante quietly shifts next to me, the heat of his body warming mine. His soft breath tickles my shoulder as he bows closer to get a better look.

"Kase," I murmur. "This is fucked up. You only want to do this to get back at Dante."

"Get back at him? No. If I wanted to get back at him, I'd have fucked you over and over for the last two days in his bed, so he'd have to smell the scent of our passion without the benefit of getting to watch us how he wants." Kase eases away from me and smirks at Dante. I can't see Dante's reaction, but I can hear it, and the soft moan escaping his lips turns me on more than it should. Because Kase is right. Dante gets excited by the idea. "Isn't that the truth, Dante? You want me to remind you that Raven belongs to me too."

"More than anything. I need it. I'm afraid of what will happen if I forget," Dante murmurs, his breathing turning heavy.

Damn them and their ability to get me right in the clit with unsaid thoughts that get on all the thousands of nerves tingling between my legs in anticipation.

HER PERSONAL DEMONS

But a part of me hesitates. Can I go through with this? This is pushing boundaries that can't be rebuilt once they're crossed. Not that it's impossible. I just know that I won't want to. The thrill and excitement of truly cementing my damn soul right across Kase's knee for him and Dante to control me and do as they please leaves me wet and yearning. I crave their hot hands manhandling my body, yet I know that with their kind of control comes indescribable ecstasy. It'll be a waste to deny myself the pleasure. I'm doomed regardless, so I need to accept that if I'm going to Hell, I might as well ride the demons on the way down. Horns and tails, forked tongues and piercings, big cocks and metal accessories to dazzle me with? I've already signed my soul away. At least I can control my body.

Kase pushes my hair behind my ear. "You hear that, angel-girl? It's your choice. You can help the three of us get past this so we can move on and figure out the next step to breaking bird-brain—"

"Or you can watch me pay my debt to Kase and learn what it's like to feel just an ounce of what I feel," Dante finishes, rubbing his big hand down my arm.

My mind turns to mush at his words, and I sit frozen between them. Kase chuckles and stands in front of me. I can't take my eyes away from his pants as he unhooks the button and slides the zipper down. Warm fingers touch my chin, forcing me to break my gaze, and I meet Dante's glowing green eyes. His diamond shaped pupils expand and retract as he searches my face. Leaning in, he kisses me softly. I try to slide my tongue into his mouth to kiss him deeper, but he nips me with his fangs and eases away, leaving me buzzing and yearning for more.

"Look at her squirm," Kase says, dropping his pants to kick out of them completely. "She can't wait for her turn."

My mouth refuses to respond. I can't avert my eyes no matter how hard I try. Dante kneels in front of Kase and tilts his head at me, a cocky-bastard grin lighting his handsome features. Stroking his hard-on with one hand, Kase locks his fingers into Dante's dark tresses and pulls his head toward his body.

Tingles burst across my clit at the sight of Dante sucking Kase's cock into his mouth slow and deep. I never expected that watching the act would turn me on so much, but thank fucking Hell for the towel around me or else I'm certain I'd leave a puddle on the comforter.

"You can come closer, angel-girl," Kase says, stretching out his hand to me. "Don't think I want to leave you out. It's better from this view. Let him show you what I like."

Like my body takes on a mind of its own, I stand and stroll the few feet to them. Dante meets my gaze, his body rippling as he flexes his muscles, working Kase's cock in and out of his mouth faster and harder.

Kase pulls me close and locks his fingers through my

hair, tipping my head up to kiss me. The second our lips meet, I lose all reservation and slip my tongue into his mouth. Desire burns hotly through the bedroom, and Kase breaks away from my mouth to look at Dante. The two of them share a look, and I swear I can feel the heat between them shift to pour over me.

"You want a turn?" Kase asks me, tugging Dante by his hair until he pulls away from his cock and looks up. "Dante's had enough fun. It's time for him to watch."

Who knew I'd love the idea?

Kase scoops me into his arms, carrying me toward the bed and away from Dante. "Let this be a lesson, Dante. This could've been you had you respected the deal. Be thankful I don't paint her lips your favorite shade of red."

Setting me on the high bed where he can stand in front of me without bending down, Kase rubs his fingers over his shaft, drawing my attention to all of his piercings. I lick my lips and swallow, wondering what his dick will feel like in my mouth. Will the metal piercings be cold against my tongue? Will they tickle the roof of my mouth or hit my tonsils?

I lock my fingers to his hips, pressing my thumbs into the sharp V at the bottom of his abs and pull him to me, braving to satiate my curiosity. Opening my mouth, I stretch my jaw as wide as I can, taking him in. Kase moans at the sensation of my lips tightening around his shaft as I slowly bob my head, getting used to the strange feelings of his dick piercings.

Playing with my hair, Kase guides my head in the rhythm he enjoys, and I peek up at him, wanting to see his lust-heavy eyes watching me. Using his knee, Kase silently presses it to my leg until I ease my body open more. I expect him to get closer to stand between my knees, but something shifts my towel, allowing cool air to caress my body.

And then I feel it.

Kase sneaks his tail under my towel and tests my reaction by tracing the end along my inner thigh. I moan with his cock in my mouth, the vibration of my voice making him tighten his fingers through my hair. A rumbly growl of pleasure escapes his mouth. I peek up at him again, watching his devilish side ripple over his features, setting his eyes aglow with red light.

"Tell me you want it," he says, continuing to trace the naughty appendage up my pelvis and over my hip.

I clench my body as he maps his way around to my lower back and between my ass cheeks. "I want it," I mumble, sucking him harder.

Sliding his tail across the slick wetness of my excitement, Kase reaches my clit with his tail and rubs it back and forth with enough pressure to make me gasp in pleasure. I've never felt anything like it, the sensation turning me weak. Kase combs his fingers into my hair, guiding my mouth over his cock for me so I don't have to think about anything apart from the tingles building in intensity.

"You love this, don't you?" Kase asks, his breathing quickening. "Do you want Dante to see what I do to you?"

I hum my agreement.

"Come closer, Dante. Look at how hot our girl is. She's creaming all over me. I can't wait to taste her." Kase smiles down at me, slowing my movements. "You're so sexy. Beautiful. You want to ride my face, angel-girl? Show Dante exactly what to expect when he learns he can't have you all to himself?"

My whole body tenses with an orgasm, leaving me incapable of answering. Throwing myself back, I ride the wave of bliss, losing myself in the heat and passion Kase awakens in me. He doesn't give me space for long, joining me on the bed, kissing me hard while pressing his weight into me. I moan against his mouth and reach between us, trying to guide his cock between my legs but he stops me.

"I told you that you can't have my cock until you let me fuck you with my tail and horns," Kase says, rolling over to pull me on top of him. Lust lights his eyes as he thumps his hard-on against my pelvis, teasing me. He waves his hand at Dante. "Want to help our girl? She might thank you later."

Whoa. He's not kidding about screwing me with his horns.

He chuckles at my reaction and sits up, clutching my face in between his palms. "Don't be nervous. You'll like it. I'll only partially shift. Watch."

His eyes remain locked on mine as his skin ripples across his forehead and his three horns break through his skin a few inches. I reach up and caress my fingers over the blunt ends, seeming to have been smoothed and filed. The center one curves slightly more than the outer two, and I imagine the sensation of what it'll feel like inside me. Is this something I want? My sexual experience is going from boring to crazy as fuck in a matter of seconds.

"I've never sat on someone's face before..." I almost say, or horns, but the latter is obvious.

The bed bounces slightly and hot hands encircle my body below my breasts. Dante's scent engulfs me with his closeness, and he brushes his lips to the base of my throat. "I can't stand the thought. We have to change that now. And when my punishment is over...you're spending the next year riding my face."

I shiver at his comment and swallow, letting him lift me off Kase. Turning me around, Dante takes a second to slip his finger inside me, making me moan. Kase grabs Dante's hand, sucking his finger into his mouth like he expects Dante to sneak a taste of my excitement before him.

"Lucky bastard," Dante murmurs, waiting for Kase to position himself on the bed.

My mind whirls with so many thoughts. I can't believe I'm doing this—or that I want to. But Kase is who he is, and I'm so attracted to him on more than a physical level that my mind, body, and soul want to give him what he desires.

"Nice and slow, Dante," Kase says, digging his fingers into my hips. "I want her to enjoy every inch."

I give Kase and Dante my complete trust, allowing them to work together to position my body. Kase's outer horns rub against the sides of my legs first before pressure awakens every nerve ending inside me as Dante guides me onto Kase. I moan, thinking only about the pleasure and how hot these two men are wanting to give me the ecstasy I've been denied my entire adult life.

Something soft and hot slides across my clit, Kase somehow managing to extend his tongue to reach me. I moan so embarrassingly loud at the sensation. Dante whispers how much he wants to touch me. How much he wishes he were Kase. His envy grows with his tightening hands, his desire poking my back as he grinds me against him with his movements.

"I'm going to fuck her with my tail, too," Kase murmurs, kissing and sucking me in a way that leaves me on the verge of another orgasm. I've never had one during sex, let alone two, and I'm not sure I can survive. "Lick it for me. Get it nice and slick."

Dante releases me, locking me in place on Kase's face, his outer horns keeping me from squirming. I pant and moan as Kase flicks his tongue over me again, sending electricity zinging through my whole body.

"I want to fuck you in the ass, angel-girl," Kase says, his voice vibrating across my skin. "Show Dante what he's missing."

I lean my head back against Dante's chest, locking my gaze with his as he watches my face. Kase slips his tail between my ass cheeks, slow and sensually, moaning with the same pleasure that sends me over the edge as he makes me cum so hard that I soak his neck and chest. Dante inhales a breath and growls, and I hear his fangs click near my ear.

"Look how much she enjoys me, Dante," Kase says, a teasing lightness in his voice. "Now I'm going to enjoy her completely. She's going to scream my name."

I can't even catch my breath as Kase slides out from under me and shifts me onto my hands and knees. With a lash of his tail, he kicks Dante off the bed, growling that he doesn't trust him not to join in. My heart thuds against my ribcage, and Kase gets behind me, the two of us facing Dante. Flaring his nostrils, Dante heaves a few deep breaths, his jealousy testing his resolve. I expect him to stride closer to punch Kase, but he stands firm in his spot, crossing his arms over his chest. Dante unfurls his wings, blowing his scent at me, and I bite my lip as Kase aligns his body to mine.

Grabbing my hair, he tugs on it, keeping it out of my face to ensure Dante can see my reaction. Kase thrusts into me with a moan, and I close my eyes under the pressure of his thick girth stretching me in a way I've never felt, his jewelry rubbing my walls and igniting every nerve on my body ablaze.

"You feel so fucking incredible," Kase says, rocking into me hard and fast, his movements only allowing me to scream in pleasure. "Unlike anything I could've imagined."

Tightening his fingers into my hair, he stretches my neck enough to lean forward, kissing my temple. I grip onto the blankets, bracing myself with his powerful thrusts. Dante strokes his cock, drawing my attention to him, and I lose myself to their dirty desire to use me the way they please—a way I never knew would be something I want to experience again and again.

"Get out, Dante. You've seen enough." Kase points to the door. "It's my time with our girl, and I'm going to be the only one to enjoy this now."

Dante growls again, his annoyance sharpening his features, but he doesn't argue. The intensity of Kase leaves me at his mercy, and I close my eyes, my muscles tightening again as I explode with ecstasy. Without a word, Dante slams the door and leaves.

My emotions whirl through me, battling for my attention. I don't know what to think or how to feel. I never thought I'd participate in any sort of punishment, and from Dante's exit, I can tell this bothered him more than I realized. But I can't take it back. I'm not even sure that I would if I could.

I feel so amazing.

So wanted.

I feel as if for the first time in my life, I'm where I'm supposed to be.

"I'm going to cum. Brace yourself, angel-girl. You're going to feel it in your soul," Kase says, grabbing onto my hips, not even giving Dante a second thought.

I hang my head, panting and moaning, savoring Kase and everything he does to me. With a few more hard thrusts, he cums, sending a shockwave through my body that steals my breath. Sinking onto me, Kase presses me into the bed and kisses my shoulder, using his fingers to comb my hair out of the way.

"It's taking everything in me not to ravish you again and again," he murmurs, easing up enough to turn me over. A smirk lights his features as he caresses his knuckles to my cheeks. "You think you're the one in for an eternity of torture, but it's me and Dante. You're our punishment every second we can't be with you."

I can't stop the smile lighting my face. Stretching closer, I kiss him again, savoring the sweetness of his lips on mine.

"You like the sound of my suffering, don't you?" He chuckles at my nod. "You naughty soul. How did this happen? You weren't supposed to be the one with all the power."

"I guess this was destiny, huh?" Because it feels as much. "Maybe I'll be the queen of Hell."

"And as your kings, we will be at your mercy. The universe has no idea what is coming." Kase tilts his head back and looks up as if he speaks to the universe itself. "Just wait until the angels fall."

16

DANTE

ETERNAL PUNISHMENT

RAVEN'S SCENT CLINGS to me just from standing within her reach, and I can't stop myself from pulling my shirt up and over my nose, wanting to savor her for a minute longer. My cock throbs, my balls aching with need. I know why Kase had me bear witness to him fucking the hell into our girl, but it doesn't get any easier. All I can think about is how she's in his arms instead of mine. I'd gladly suck his cock clean if it meant I get to taste even a drop of her excitement. It kills me that I can't.

If I do it while I'm trapped in my intense haze of envy, I'll fuck everything up. I'd kidnap her, ensuring she fails to break the rest of the brethren. I'd tie her up and fuck her over and over again until she forgets who she even is and only believes she is mine.

It wouldn't be fair to drown her light in my darkness like that. If Kase didn't remind me who Raven is and who she belongs to outside of my raging envy to keep her for myself, I'd experience far worse pain than a pair of blue balls. One I can't take care of myself.

Swiping a bottle of warming lube from on top of my dresser, I tug my dick out and squirt the slippery liquid along my shaft. Usually I'd gather a couple of toys from my favorite chest and turn on some amateur porn, but my nuts feel like they're going to pop if I don't find fast relief.

I flop onto my bed and nearly bust a nut at Raven's scent lingering on my pillow. I can't fucking believe I missed her rolling around my bed, surely looking hotter than the deepest, fiery pit in the lowest level of Hell where Lucian rules over the darkest souls.

I snatch the pillow and hold it over my face, gasping in breath after breath of Raven's fragrance as I jerk myself off hard and fast, rubbing the ache away, imagining it's her mouth sucking my cock. Then me spreading her legs open to sink into her tight, soaking wet pussy, until I flip her over and finish in her sexy ass just how she'll crave.

My muscles tighten with the thought and I groan as I cum so hard that the fucking jizz splatters the mirror on the ceiling to rain down on me.

I growl and roll off the bed, my annoyance and need driving me fucking crazy as the ache continues to pulse in my cock. I'm going to have to jack off at least a dozen more times to satiate my desire. Maybe if I get a good massage on my P-spot, I'll finally settle down, though I really fucking wanted to wait for Raven to try my new plugs out.

Fuck this shit.

If only I didn't feel the damn familiar quiver of Lucian about to break open the gateway uninvited again. The disgusting smell of the gate splitting open under his intrusion kicks my ass in gear, and I rush to shove my junk into my pants. I really fucking regret agreeing to have a summoning circle in the apartment, especially now that Raven's soul allows him a tether to latch onto to drag his annoying ass out.

Snatching my favorite serrated dagger from the case in the hallway, I jog toward the living room. If Lucian interrupts Raven's good time with his needy bullshit, I swear to the bowels of Hell he'll regret every one of the decisions he's made throughout all of time. He's getting bitchier and bitchier, acting like the same know-it-all asshole he was while serving the Higher Power.

I drop to one knee and bow my head in time to feel the heat of hellfire swell through the room. The floor quivers and splits apart, burning away as Lucian rams his massive horns through the gate. The dramatic fucker snarls like always, the inconvenience of not being able to easily move from realm to realm always his biggest fucking complaint apart from being imprisoned in the kingdom he created. I have to admit though, I'd be a bitter fucker too. Had the rest of the brethren jumped like they were supposed to, Lucian wouldn't have to remain trapped to keep Hell going. He's a powerful son-of-a-bastard, but he's not the Higher Power.

A wave of heat encircles me, and I finally lift my head, staring at Lucian's scowling face. As hard as he tries to remain in his demonic form as if it'll somehow intimidate me, without mortal eyes in the room, he can't resist slipping into his former glorious form.

His muscular body ripples, his biceps flexing with his movements. Spinning on his bare feet, he peers around the room. I can't stop my gaze from roving over the red, fiery scars on his back. The slash down his shoulder blades, reminding me of the day shortly after our descent when I gripped his red-feathered wing in my hands while he sawed them off his own back with a blade forged from the depths of Hell.

"Where is she?" Lucian asks, rubbing his hands over his

shaved head. Tendrils of steam drift from his hot skin, and I kind of wish I had kicked on the AC to make his visit more uncomfortable. "I want to speak with her."

"She's out with Kase," I mutter, remaining unflinching and expressionless to my lie. After what Lucian did to Kase, trying to put Kase below him and doing so in front of Raven, I refuse to give him even a second of either of their time. I can handle him just fine.

Fire flickers in his black eyes, setting them aglow. "Then I'll wait. Time is up, Dante. I want five pairs of wings piled in front of me. If it doesn't happen in the next minute, I will start with yours. Don't test me."

Lucian rams his hand into his side and snarls as he yanks a jagged bone from his ribs. Blowing a hot breath on it, he molds it into a dagger not unlike the one I clutch at my side. He flips the newly formed weapon in the air, a grin lighting his face as he watches me watch him. We both know he's silently counting to himself, waiting for me to give in and admit that we're nowhere close to bringing the brethren to their knees at his feet.

"You and I both know you're not going to take my wings, Lucian. I can't summon Kase back here like I can summon you." I keep my voice even. "Why don't I blow you while you wait? You seem tense, and I'm already on my knees."

Lucian snarls and steps closer, toeing the barrier of fire

between us. His cock loves my offer despite his wrath threatening to test the chains of Hell to try to keep me on my knees.

"Stop stalling and bring me Raven!" Lucian's human façade flickers, revealing his devil form.

I square my shoulders. His wrath is nothing compared to Kase's. I live with the fucking embodiment of wrath. Lucian carries all the sins in his veins, which is why his bastard ass could use a good time. And in this moment, I'll do whatever it takes to keep Raven out of Lucian's path of Hell.

"Come on, Lucian. I told you, she and Kase are out. They're bringing Micah to his knees as we speak, so you might as well enjoy me while I'm on mine. I won't offer you this again." I raise my voice enough for Kase to hear. I know he's listening from his room. He'll keep Raven hidden and let me handle this bullshit now.

I'll do whatever and whoever to get shit done while Kase's approach is far more violent. But after tonight, this shit will change. I have the sudden need to only suck the cocks of the men Raven lusts after. Her soul is mine, yet I'm the one at her mercy.

"Trust me, Lucian. They'll be back with Micah. Let me help pass the time." I crawl on my knees through the hellfire, glancing once over my shoulder at the hallway.

Kase better fucking find Micah and force him here. I know he lingers nearby, because he refuses to give up on thinking about anything other than how he'll redeem Raven's soul. Angels love picking losing battles. They can't help it. Micah will find out soon enough that Raven isn't just bound to Hell by a deal with Lucian. Her pretty soul chose to tie itself right around my cock and there is no way she's letting me or Kase go. I felt it in her mind as she gave in to Kase's filthy fantasy. She wouldn't let him screw her any way he pleased otherwise.

Lucian growls deep in his throat and snatches my hair in his hand, yanking my head back to look at him. "I always knew Micah would reunite with us first. He never could truly resist the allure of free will and punishment."

"You were right. Like always." I force my mouth to grin and grab onto Lucian's hips, trying to pull his cock to my mouth.

Tightening his fingers through my hair, he stops me from molding my lips around his fat cock, far from being as sexy as mine or Kase's. A little manscaping would go a long way, but this fucker likes to repulse over seduce.

"And you were always overcompensating when you know you've failed." Lucian jerks me forward and rams his dagger right between my shoulder blades, forcing my wings to automatically unfurl and stretch from my human façade.

I holler in pain and annoyance, swinging my fist out to punch him in his knee. Lucian doesn't expect me to fight against him and stumbles back. I flap my wings, launching myself to my feet. Unsheathing my serrated knife, I flick my wrist and throw it at Lucian's chest. It sinks into the bone-hard armor of his hellish form, surprising him. It shouldn't have been able to penetrate him, but it crackles and hums with what looks like holy light.

Instead of slowing his rampaging ass down, the dagger sets him off into the powerful devil he is. I can't dodge away from him and out of the hellfire circle fast enough to escape his wrath. He grows several feet in height and slams his clawed hand into my shoulder, impaling me. I hiss and snap my fangs, putting Lucian's power and strength to the test. I only get in one bite to his muscular forearm. He's tethered to Hell, after all. His strength comes from the suffering souls he tortures, devouring their darkness to feed his power. To be on this plane, Kase and I had to sever the line to our levels of our burning kingdom, which is the only reason Lucian can overpower me in this minute.

Grunting, I take another blow from Lucian as he stabs me in the back again. He wasn't lying about taking my wings for failing to bring others as a gift to him.

"Lucian, stop," I snap, summoning my super strength. "You know I need my wings for the mission."

I lock my fingers around Lucian's ankle and squeeze, feeling his armor crush under my fingers. If I could get to my feet and do the same to his neck, I could force his ass back to Hell until he cools off.

He roars and jabs his blade deeper into my wing, twisting it in an attempt to leave me weak. Grinding my teeth, I suppress the pain he inflicts. It'll be nothing like the pain I plan to put him through once we return to our kingdom. He's let his power get to his head. His impatience turns him into the devil he's been painted as for as long as I can recall. If he doesn't remember what our plan was or that none of this is solely about him, it could fuck everything over.

"Lucian! Get it the fuck together! I'm not your enemy," I holler again, managing to jab my fist into his knee, forcing him back.

"You're worse." Fire ripples across his body, eating away at his former glorious façade.

Fuck.

I don't have to look over my shoulder to know Raven lingers nearby. Her soul calls to mine, the sudden whirlwind of her emotions pushing me to attempt to get Lucian in his place before she tries herself.

I flap my fingers, singeing my feathers on the hellfire as I stretch them past the summoning circle. Lucian smashes into my chest, knocking me against the fiery wall. If he wasn't holding me, I'd fall to the other side of the barrier alone. As long as he has his hands on me, I'm stuck within the circle with him. I can't go if he can't.

"I've waited far too long for my prophecy to come to fruition. This should've been easy, Dante. You let the mortal realm weaken you." Lucian grabs me by the wings and forces me to my knees. Punching me in the solar plexus, he winds me and stomps his hoof into my back. I fall forward, trapped under the strength of his power. "You don't deserve the gift I left with you. Those wings are too much of a reminder. They must go."

I grind my teeth as Lucian locks one hand to my wing and stretches it out. Searing pain explodes over my back, the heat of his dagger ripping into the base of my wing as he slowly saws through the top in his mission to remove them from my back.

I can't stop the holler from escaping my mouth, the agony of his torture consuming my ability to fight back.

"Lucian, no! Stop!" Raven's voice echoes through the air, cooling the wave of intense pain blazing through me. "Stop!"

A bright flash of light erupts through the room as Raven charges through the ring of hellfire. I blink through the haze of my pain, my vision faltering as it only allows me to see the vivid light of her essence.

Strong hands lock onto my ankles, dragging me from the summoning circle. I gasp at the wave of fresh air and relief, the agony turning into a more bearable ache. Kase towers over me in his hellish form. Roaring, he whips his tail at Lucian, trying to protect Raven from his wrath. I gape in awe, watching as our beautiful soul smacks Lucian in the face. I don't think I've ever seen anything so incredibly sexy in my life. No mortal has ever stood up to Lucian as much as she has, and my body awakens with a massive boner.

"You bastard!" she screeches, trying to slap Lucian again. "I'll cut your fucking dick off for hurting him. You have no right!"

Is it possible to fall madly in love with a soul in a matter of seconds? Who fucking knows. Whatever bursts inside me steals my breath and brings a strange emotion crashing over me. Her disobedient, protective attitude envelops me, strangling me the way I like. The light of her soul casts through the room so brightly that Lucian hollers in rage, throwing her at the wall with a thunderous boom. He tries to push his way through the summoning circle's hellfire, but it ignites, billowing higher, building a flaming wall he can't cross.

Raven hits the hardwood floor, knocked unconscious. That kills my boner, seeing as I can't rush and fuck her brains out, showing her how much I enjoyed watching her attempt to protect me from Lucian's bastardly behavior.

Kase jumps over me and charges across the room on all fours. Smoke billows from his mouth, a breath of fire escaping with his wrath. Lucian tries again to break through the barrier, hollering and screaming for Kase to stay away from his soul. I push to my feet and release a low hiss. Lucian spins to lash at the barrier in front of me, and I flip his ass off, turning back to Kase. He lies on his stomach next to our girl and nudges his big head into Raven's stomach, flipping her over to check on her. Her soul shines brighter than ever, though a chord of Lucian's darkness squeezes it so tightly I'm afraid she'll break at any moment.

"Leave her to suffer," Lucian bellows, his deep voice heating the room. "You two have failed to prove yourself worthy as my equals, and I will not stand idly by and watch my ungodly plan suffer because of it."

"*We've* failed?" I ask, fury burning me to the core. "How the fuck have we failed? Micah is moments away from jumping from grace head first and right where he belongs. The only fucker who will cause this whole damn plan to fail is you, Lucian. You treat Raven as an expendable soul when she is not. We need her—not just to break these fucking angels. We need her to completely cement our levels of Hell. There aren't many angel-kissed souls who will follow through. You've already endangered everything with your lack of patience."

Lucian snarls and beats against the barrier, shaking the whole damn apartment building. Fire blazes around him in bright orange and yellow, his power testing the strength of the Higher Power's cage that contains him.

"You've lost sight of our purpose just as you had for It." A deep rumble escapes Lucian as he opens his arms and tips his head back. "But unlike It, I will not just adjust my plans.

I will destroy you. You are replaceable. Raven can be broken by another."

His words lash out at us, shooting pain to my core.

He meets my gaze dead on. "Do not test me, my brethren. I would prefer you smarten up and rise as you should. But I fear you have given too much of yourselves to Raven. You have nothing to lose if you fail and if you remain on your thrones, so you have forced my hand. The contract does not include you specifically. I can and I will reward her soul to those worthy and willing to serve me if she fails."

"You wouldn't," I snap, fisting my hands.

"I already have." Lucian summons a fiery contract, unrolling it before me. I remain in my place, knowing he's not bluffing. I will not risk entering the summoning circle to have him attempt to drag me through the gates and back to Hell.

"You're making a mistake, Lucian," Kase mutters, standing on two legs, getting at Lucian's eye level. "Raven only accepted the task knowing that Dante and I would be here. If you test her, she will fight against you. She's not stupid. The angels will gravitate toward her, and if she knows you plan to give her soul away, she won't use her charm and the light of her soul to bring them to our side. I'm nearly certain she will use it to be saved."

"There is no saving a soul under my contract," he says, a shocked laugh escaping his mouth. "Either get yourselves on track or I'll send my personal army for you. You will be the ones burning like the weak, pathetic beings you're turning out to be. I'll give you one more week, but if you fail, you will never have Raven. You will never have your kingdoms. Hell will be mine."

I glower at Lucian without a word.

He's wrong.

Hell isn't intended to be ruled by one. I'm not afraid of his threats either. I'm a godforsaken devil myself. He's not the only one who can make the world burn.

"Hell is ours," I snap, flashing my fangs. "You will see, Lucian. You'll be the one bowing with your fucking foot in your damn mouth for not trusting us."

"I will gladly chew off my own hoof to see it. Now get it done or lose it all." Rubbing his hands together, he sends flames exploding over his body until he disappears with the fire of the summoning circle.

Kase groans and laces his fingers behind his head. "Maybe he's right. Maybe Raven's soul has gotten to us. I fucking refuse to jeopardize our plan over this, Dante. I can't allow someone else to get their hands on Raven's soul or our kingdom. We have to think of something. The light of Raven's soul makes it hard for her to do what needs to be done. I don't like seeing the darkness bloom inside her."

I tighten my jaw. "Then maybe we need to finish the task for her. Raven has gotten Micah close. Now we just have to drag him the rest of the way."

"You think so?" Kase shifts and looks at Raven on the floor. "She might not go for it."

"We can't give her the choice." I scrub my hands over my face. "What if she decides she doesn't want to risk losing her soul and the Higher Power grants a miracle?"

"That won't happen," he mutters. "We won't fail."

He's right. Angels have nothing on us, and neither does Lucian. We have power on our side, and a soul strong enough to bear it. Hell's kingdom will always be ours.

"I can't be around her right now. I'm too high on everything she does to me. I won't be able to focus." Kase strokes his hands over his outer horns as if he imagines her sitting on his face again.

And fuck. That's an automatic boner for me.

I adjust my throbbing cock. "You think I can do any better? I can't stop fantasizing about trying out the hands-free clit vibrator I bought for her before bending her over and spreading her tight ass cheeks apart, gliding in her new *spank me* plug. I want her screaming my name and soaking my sheets, so my cock can swim in her wet pussy."

I have every little detail planned out. She'll slip into the red lingerie that matches the shade of lipstick I can't wait to see on her that stains everything. I can already imagine how she'll squirm on my bed, tied up and at my mercy, begging for me to sink my teeth into her thigh as I show her what it's like to let me have her as my next meal. My mouth waters just thinking about getting her to squirt all over me like she did with Kase. I won't be able to do anything else until I experience her body.

Swinging his fist, Kase punches me in the jaw, jerking my head sideways. "You can't fuck her at all until Micah bows before Lucian."

"Then you deal with her," I snap, my demonic form sneaking through. "You saw how she tried to fucking beat that bastard down. She deserves a reward for that shit. I can't go in there and not give her the gift of orgasming until she walks funny."

Kase jabs his fist into my gut. "Figure something else out. I can't get my damn façade in control. She's going to open her eyes and cream at the sight of me. At least with you, all she'll think about is your bitch-ass on your knees. She'll want to coddle you instead of ride you like the beast I am."

I growl and thrust my hand out, striking him in the throat. Locking my fingers to his neck, I cut off his airway until he turns into his hellish form completely. Raven isn't that freaky. She's not going to fuck him unless he's mostly mortal-looking.

"Dante? Kase? Fuck." Raven's soft voice steals my attention. She hovers in the doorway to my room, which I'm fucking certain is hers now. "Are you okay? What happened?"

Kase takes advantage of my distraction and shoves me into the wall. "Dante will fill you in. I have shit to do and can't waste time on your crazy ass, angel-girl."

His comment wipes the concern from her face, puckering her features. Without giving Raven a chance to respond, he turns to me and squeezes my shoulders, giving me a look that says I better fucking keep my dick in my pants. He strides toward the front door and exits, leaving it open behind him.

"What's wrong with him?" Fucking Hell. Hurt laces her words, and her soul dims just a little. She doesn't have to say anything for me to know she expected Kase to give her more than a cold shoulder and attitude, especially after the fight we had over sharing her on every level.

It's torture that I have to be a complete dick too. If I'm not, I'll pull her into my arms and tell her how fucking awesome her crazy ass is, even though Kase made it sound like a bad thing.

And now I'm jealous as fuck that he left. He fucked her. He should be the one dealing with the strange tangle of emotions she unintentionally lassos me with.

"Dante? What happened? What did Lucian do? How long have I been out?" Stepping from my room, she closes the space and reaches out, stroking her fingers over my wing like she needs assurance that Lucian failed to cut it off. "Are you okay? I was so scared."

I close my eyes and sigh. "The only thing you should be afraid of is what's going to happen if you can't get your shit together and help us get the job done. The only thing Lucian did was remind us that this shit isn't about you, and you need to get your act together or let someone who is capable handle it."

I truly am the devil. Her expression says as much as a flash of darkness crosses her face. I steel myself for her wrath, her mood already playing on Kase's and how he just left her without so much as a second glance after their fuck fest.

"Get *my* act together? This is unbelievable. You were gone for days, Dante!" she says, raising her voice.

I growl and snatch her off her feet, spinning her toward the wall. "I was trying to get the job done when all you've been doing is trying to fucking figure out if Micah can save your soul or if you'd be better off to just do what you're supposed to."

"What?" She glowers at me, wiggling in an attempt to break free. "What has gotten into you? I thought we were okay."

I flash my fangs. "Nothing is fucking okay, Raven."

"Dante—"

I press my hand over her mouth. "Stop. I'm not finished. You need—"

Pain explodes in my back, and I stare at Raven's wide blue-green gaze. Fire reflects over the glassy surface as the demon shoves a blade deeper into my skin. I can't believe the fucker was brave enough to walk right in, and now I know for certain Lucian wants to test us before the week is over.

Shoving her hands to my chest, Raven tries to push away to make a run for it. I should fight. I could do it. I could kill this fucker with my eyes closed. But I realize this must be done. Raven won't push to succeed otherwise, not with thinking that she's our soul regardless.

So I drop to me knees.

I let the demon take her.

He steals away the one woman who feels like the sun I want nothing more than to orbit around for the rest of time.

I'm left alone in my suffocating darkness.

17

RAVEN

HER PERSONAL DEMONS

"MICAH, HELP!" THE words screech from my mouth, my mind and body feeling torn apart. He shouldn't be the one I yell for, but I can't help myself. It's like my soul knows deep down that he's the being best for me and the only one who doesn't want to possess my soul.

The demonic man adjusts me in his arms until he can slap his hot hand over my mouth. I had expected a disgusting, monstrous creature to be the thing dragging me away, but he looks mostly human apart from his pure black eyes and a glowing-red scar on his cheek. He leers at me and glides his black tongue over his lips. Shit. He knows I find him attractive. Double shit that it distracted me from fighting. What the hell is wrong with me? It's like as long as my attacker is hot, a part of me isn't as scared as I should be. I had no idea I was this vain. Maybe it's the claim Hell has on my soul. Maybe it's my obvious poor judgement in men. Whatever it is, my damn body relaxes and I even find myself smiling back.

"Look at you, my perfect little slut. You like my skin-bag look. I bet you'd suck my damn cock if I pulled it out. Wouldn't you?" The demon flashes a smile. "You'd swallow every last drop of my demon jizz like the cum guzzler you are. I can't wait to invite my contracts over and reward them with a good time with you. You look like a dirty girl who enjoys that, so I'll have to tell them to be rough if they want to hear you scream."

Oh. Fucking. No.

His comment triggers a shit-ton of fear inside me, and I finally snap out of my haze, seeing the man for the disgusting evil demon he truly is. His human façade falters, showing the beast lingering under his skin. His rotting body looks like it barely holds onto this realm, and green liquid oozes from clusters of holes that make my skin crawl.

Swinging my fist, I clock him in the cheek, regretting it immediately. The green ooze shoots from his pus clusters and burns across my skin. I screech and throw myself back, forcing the demon to release me. The world blurs with my fall, and I clench, expecting my ass to hit the ground.

Light blasts across my vision, turning the complex white, and the demon shrieks at a pitch intended for animals. I slam my hands over my ears, trying to muffle the noise. As quickly as it pierced my eardrums, it vanishes. My mind and body finally catch up to sync together, and I blink until I realize I'm in Micah's cool arms.

"This is why I didn't want to bring you back here," Micah says, anger lacing his words. "I've been watching over the apartment and felt Hell open. Lucifer—"

"I already know he was here, Micah," I snap, cutting him off. "He ruined my entire day and put Kase and Dante into bad moods. The demon interrupted an argument."

"So then you know something about your contract was altered? Lucifer put out a beacon, inviting demons here. He's using your soul to do so," he says, tightening his jaw. "Whatever happened...your binds to Kase and Dante have been severed. Your soul is basically free for any demon to take."

Confusion puckers my brows. "What?"

"You didn't know." It's not a question. "Of course you didn't know. The devils wouldn't have told you."

I shake my head, peering around the quiet world. Micah shields me in the weird dimension that feels as if time outside the two of us fades completely. On the ground a few feet away lies a puddle of burning goo, and I know without having to ask that it belongs to the demon Micah blasted with holy light.

Micah touches my chin, getting me to turn my gaze away from the mess and back to him. "I know you struggle to trust me, but I have to know, Raven. What kind of work are you obligated to do for Lucifer? What did he offer you? What was so important to you that you'd give away your entire eternity?"

I swallow, my mouth going dry. "You don't know?" I ask, my nose scrunching. How does he not? He was a part of the angels who were supposed to jump. "You were aligned with Lucifer at one point."

"That is untrue. I was always aligned with the Higher Power, Raven. I'd never betray it." Micah searches my eyes. "I don't know why you would think that? What have the devils said?"

Fuck. This could go one of two ways. Either Hell has been lying to me about finishing the kingdom and the brethren who were supposed to jump or Micah is playing dumb and will smite me the second he knows Lucian's plan starting from this point.

Either way, I'm in for an eternity of punishment.

"You can trust me, Raven," Micah says, his bottom lip puffing slightly with his words. "I know you were manipulated into this position. I know you did what you thought you had to do."

"I don't want to suffer for all eternity," I whisper.

"That's why you need to tell me everything. I can use it to help you. This could be what we need for divine intervention on a level no angel can manage." Micah tips his head back, staring at the dark sky above us. Flapping his wings, he stirs a crisp breeze around me, making me shiver. "Please. Trust me. I'm begging you. Whatever happened with Lucifer today—"

"Is none of your goddamn business, Micah." Dante steps from a shadow of a building, crossing his arms over his chest. "Nice try with the shield. You need more work on keeping it up if you're trying to take our pretty soul away from us."

That's strange. I was so distracted by the demon attack and Micah's help that I hadn't realized that Dante was taking longer than usual to interrupt. I thought he could always see me because of the binding of my soul, but with one look at his hard features, I'm no longer certain that is the case.

"She no longer belongs to you, Dante," Micah says, summoning a ball of heavenly light in his palm. "Were you ever going to tell her the truth, or do I need to?"

The truth? "What are you talking about?"

"Nothing," Dante snaps, stalking closer. "He's trying to get into your head, pretty soul. All he wants is to send you to Hell. Nothing more."

"That's not true." I turn my stare from Dante to look at Micah. I know it's not true. If it was, he'd have already done so. "You said it yourself that there was more to it. It's what we've been working on, so don't try to make me feel stupid."

"What have you been working on with the devils, Raven?" Micah asks, his voice a low breath against my ear.

"Don't tell him, angel-girl." Red light illuminates from the nearby parking lot, and I catch sight of Kase standing near his car. "It's important to our mission."

"Raven, let me take you away. We will get this all sorted out." Micah expands his wings, lighting the night with his ethereal glow. "I don't know what they made you believe, and maybe it was true at one point, but things have shifted. I can sense it."

A guttural growl echoes through the air, stealing my attention away from Micah's soft pleas. My stomach twists in fear, and I jerk my attention back to Kase. But the vicious noise doesn't come from him. The shadows behind him grow, looming across him with the appearance of a demon in all its demonic glory.

Kase spins around, unleashing his hellish glory, and guts the monstrous demon with his sharp claws. The innards spill across the roof of his car, and he slams his fist into the window, smashing it under the force of his hand. Whipping his feline head back toward us, Kase kicks off the ground to catapult in our direction.

"Give her to us," Kase hollers, trying to tie his tail around me. "It's not safe."

"She'll never be safe with you." Micah summons more heavenly light in his palm and chucks it through the air.

I expect it to knock Kase off his feet, but it barrels past him and engulfs another sneaky demon trying to best Kase as if he isn't one of the devils ruling the kingdom of Hell. Dante spins and strikes another demon, cutting the bastard in half before it can even make a sound.

"What the fuck?" I mutter, my mind and body whirring with panic. "Why are they attacking you guys? What aren't you telling me?"

"You don't have to worry, Raven. We are handling it," Kase says, moving closer. "Now come here. We need to go back inside." Snaking his tail around me, he tries to yank me from Micah, but I hold onto the angel tighter.

"She's not going with you. You deceived her after she trusted you," Micah says, unsheathing his flaming sword.

"We haven't. We've just hit a snag until she fulfills her part of the deal with Lucian." Dante shuffles closer, reaching his hand out to me. "Now, come on, Raven. Let us take you back to the apartment. We will sort it out."

"Not until you tell me what's going on." My blazing fear keeps my body locked to Micah's. It's like my soul can't stand the thought of being away from him. It hurts to even consider letting him go.

Kase groans. "Fucking fine, but it's nothing to worry about."

Why don't I believe him? "Then tell me."

"Lucian has opened the contract of your soul to the whole demonic population. He thinks you've weakened us and that we won't complete our mission because we've grown attached to you, and even if we fail, you were going to be ours." Dante growls with the words, his eyes flickering green.

My heart sinks into my stomach. "Are you joking with me? You can't be serious."

"You're going to be fine. Everything is in order. After Micah, things will be easy." Kase shifts closer, and I realize he and Dante are trying to trap us. "You'll know what to do."

"But what if it's impossible? I've just accepted the idea that even if we fail, I'll be okay. I've depended on it, Kase." My chest tightens. Air refuses to fill my lungs no matter how hard I breathe.

This can't be happening. I trusted my soul would be okay, even if I didn't fulfill my obligations to Lucian and became the ruler of Purgatory. I've grown to like Kase and

Dante. They aren't as horrible as I expected a devil to be. If anything, they're nicer than angels—at least how Micah was before. But if I fail and my soul ends up with a real dickish demon? Fuck my eternity. I can't risk it.

"Please, Raven," Dante says, his voice pleading. "Don't make this any harder. We don't want to give you up as much as you don't want to suffer at someone else's hands. You're ours, and we're not going to let Lucian take you."

Micah laughs in exasperation, shifting slightly to aim his flaming sword at Dante. "You don't have control over her soul. What kind of empty promises are those? Lucifer is known as the supreme ruler of Hell because he embodies all that is wrong with humanity to appropriately punish those who deserve it. You two are merely moths trapped in the pull of his forsaken flame. You have damned this beautiful soul which shines even brighter than Lucifer ever could've as an angel. Don't act as if you can save her. Only divine intervention from the Higher Power can help her, and it'll be me acting as the vessel who will be her savior."

Micah sounds so certain that I believe him. I believe in my very being that if I put my faith into him, he will find a way to sever the deal binding me to Lucian's fiery clutches. I want to believe Kase and Dante. I want to have faith that things will go as planned, and I won't be a soul damned and enslaved to demons for all eternity. But faith doesn't exist where hope is lost. Even if I could bring angels to their knees to have their wings taken by the embodiment of Hell, could I go through with it?

One look into Micah's dark eyes, so pure and full of everything good that I can no longer summon inside me, tells me no. I can't damn an angel. I can't go through with Lucian's plan. My soul is worth far less than Micah's, a being who can save more people than I could ever dream of. And maybe, if I pray hard enough, not just to God or the Higher Power. But maybe if I pray to the universe, to myself, to the light that could set the devil's darkness ablaze to push it away, I won't be doomed. All won't be lost.

"Raven, please. I know what you're thinking," Kase says, shifting completely into his mortal form. "But Micah can't save you. It's too late for that. Only we can."

Micah touches my chin, grabbing my attention. "There is only one person who can save you, and it's yourself. You have to make the decision to allow me to help you. I will do everything I can. Just say the word. Give me permission to take you away from here."

I heave a few breaths, knowing I have seconds to decide. Kase and Dante will attack before they ever let Micah take me again, especially knowing the thoughts crossing my mind. Is it possible that a decision can break not only my heart but my soul? Maybe. I hate that I'm in this position at all. My soul yearns to be close to Kase and Dante. My body begs for it. But the fear of the unknown. Of punishment. It screams that what I feel is only temporary, especially if I don't succeed.

I squeeze my eyes shut. "I'm sorry."

"Raven, don't say it," Dante pleads, the heat of his body warming the air around us. "If he takes you, the brethren will come. They will kill you. They will know what is happening. Micah will fall regardless. If he does so without us there to protect you, things will end for you. The angels will send you to Hell. You will no longer be ours."

Micah intakes a sharp breath at Dante's words. "They wouldn't. They'd see your beautiful soul how I do."

Kase growls. "Do you hear him, angel-girl? He's delusional. He will keep you even if it's not good for him or anyone."

Scowling, Micah jabs his flaming sword at Kase, trying to stab him. The world spins as Micah expands his wings, preparing to launch into the air. My head spins with a dozen thoughts.

What if Kase and Dante are right? What if Micah falls from grace with me, and he can't save me? It's possible that he'll accidentally doom me, because he can't see things clearly anymore. The devils—and Micah, for that matter—always talk about the light of my soul. Is it possible that it's blinding Micah instead of letting him see? Who knows. All I know is I'm suddenly terrified to find out.

"Raven, hold on tight to me. They're not going to let

us leave," Micah says, his voice deepening. "They just want to enjoy you for the little time they have left."

Kase roars, transforming into his hellish glory faster than I've ever seen as if his true body just bursts through his skin. Whipping his tail, he slashes it across Micah's wing, not even caring that it burns him. Micah jerks his arm, preparing to cut off Kase's tail, and I swing my hand out and grab Micah's wrist.

"Micah, I'm sorry. I really am," I say, tears burning my eyes, forcing me to rapidly blink to stop them from spilling.

"Catch her!" Kase shouts, locking his tail around my waist.

I release Micah and close my eyes, letting Kase throw me through the air toward Dante. I crash into his hard chest, gasping from the force. Fire and light illuminate the world as Heaven and Hell face each other, preparing for a battle no one can truly win. My heartbeat booms in my head, pounding hard enough to feel like it'll escape my body.

I can't bear to witness these two beings on a mission to tear each other apart.

Kase unleashes his wrath, pushed by the darkness of Lucian's threats still lingering even in my soul. Swiping his dagger nails, he shreds Micah's shirt, exposing the deep scratches he slashes across Micah's velvety dark skin. I gasp and cover my mouth, unable to even comprehend what unfolds before me.

Kase rams a ball of glowing Hell power into Micah's back, dropping him to his knees.

"You will not save her!" Kase yells, his deep voice reverberating through my essence. "She belongs to Hell just like you. Now agree to bow to the rulers of Hell and accept that Raven will be a part of the new order alongside us."

Micah shakes his head, clenching his jaw. "Never!"

"You'd rather see Raven's soul burn?" Kase asks.

"I can save her. Let me try." Micah holds his hands up in surrender. "Please. You know she doesn't truly belong there. Please—"

Whipping his tail, Kase slashes it across Micah's wing, sending white feathers dancing in the breeze. "Bow to Hell!"

Again, Micah refuses. His dark eyes turn to meet mine. "Raven, please." The words trickle into my mind instead of out loud, filling my soul with indecipherable emotions. They tangle with mine, sending my body humming. He's praying. Not to the Higher Power but to me.

"Bow!" Kase shouts.

Breaking away from Dante, I charge toward Kase. I jump on his back, throwing him off balance. His tail misses Micah, slapping the ground. Micah tips his head toward the sky, erupting in light.

"Go!" I shout. "Get out of here!"

Micah bends his knees and launches into the air.

Kase spins toward me and snarls.

I stand frozen, staring at Micah taking flight.

Closing my eyes, I send out a silent prayer.

I hope he gets away.

18

RAVEN

HELL-BOUND

"TAKE HER HOME. I'm finishing this shit once and for all. Micah will fall even if it's the last thing I fucking do. I will not fail our pretty soul." Kase snarls and barrels away without waiting for a response from Dante.

I don't know why I bother, but my brain screams that I better haul ass away from Dante. Kase might embody wrath, but Dante is still a ruler of Hell and can punish me just the same. What I did, intervening and allowing Micah to get away wasn't exactly the smartest thing to do, considering it guarantees my eternity at the mercy of some twisted demon, but I can't go through with this. I can't stand by and force Micah to jump from grace because of me.

Dante snatches the back of my shirt and jerks me into his chest. Hooking his arm around me, he lifts me up but keeps me facing out. A hiss tickles my ear, and I hang lifelessly with my head down. I'm beyond fighting. I'm beyond all of this, really. I can't win regardless, and I can't bear to take everyone down with me.

"I need you to give me a good reason why I shouldn't show you what true punishment from a devil is like," Dante mutters, keeping his voice low.

"Do whatever you think you have to do, Dante. I might as well get used to it. I'm going to be a slave to some fucking monstrous demon who will ravage my mind, body, and soul. I just hope you're right about the demon jizz. Maybe I'll be tripping for the rest of eternity because apparently treating me like a cum bucket is the top method of torture." I try not to think about being the target of a demon gangbang. Maybe if I can get over the freakiness and just accept that type of punishment, it won't be so bad. I mean, Kase ass fucked me with his tail. Hell pretty much lowered my standards.

"Now you're just making me jealous. I don't understand you, pretty soul. I thought we were on the same side, and then you go and fucking ask to be saved instead of trusting that we can and will complete this mission." Dante kicks the apartment door closed as he strides back inside. "I thought you liked me. Fuck, I thought you knew I was—still am—utterly obsessed with your sexy body, beautiful soul, and infuriatingly indecisive mind."

I sigh, still refusing to move a muscle. "I can't condemn Micah to Hell, Dante. I'm sorry. I thought I could. I really did. I accepted I'm destined for darkness and was going to fuck you on my way there...but I can't drag him with me."

"Raven, shut the fuck up. You haven't listened to one damn thing we've said. You can't drag Micah to Hell because he's already almost there. He's taking a goddamned elevator, for fuck's sake." Dante flings open his bedroom door. I expect him to carry me to the bed to tie me up again, but he moves me to his shoulder, dangling me upside down. "The guy is a glutton for you, and you can't blame yourself. Now, don't make me put a gag on you. I'm tired of hearing the damn bastards name on your lips. It's bad enough he marked one of my favorite things on your body."

"You're insane," I mutter, listening to what I think are chains rattling.

"And you enjoy it." Dante sets me in front of a contraption hanging from a couple anchors on the ceiling. I've never seen a sex swing in person, but I'm pretty sure that the straps Dante gathers are intended just for that. "Now watch. Stand here, and be the good girl you desperately want to be."

I plant my hands on my hips. "You are not hanging me from the ceiling. The bed restraints were good enough. You want to restrain me then you can do it there."

He quirks an eyebrow at me. Without a word, he grabs my shoulders and yanks me the two feet to the straps and spins me around. His fingers tangle in my hair and he bends my head to the side. Leaning down, he brushes his warm lips to the sensitive spot below my ear.

"You told me to do what I had to do, and it is this, pretty soul. You've already bonded bodies with Kase. You fucking let Micah brand you and put his mark on you. I've been patient and have obviously failed to realize that you don't even know what you truly want and only what you don't want." Dante clicks his fangs and nips me hard enough to make me clench in anticipation for a harder bite, but it doesn't come. "I'm going to prove to you that I am what you want and show you that you will fight for me by making every damn angel fall. I'll show you how I want you, and I will claim you as mine for eternity, so if you fail to suppress the lightness in your soul, you will know I will destroy Heaven's entire army to keep you. Do you understand, Raven?"

"Yes." Damn it. My rebel mouth needs to get its shit

together. So does my body. Goosebumps prickle over my skin, and I shiver as Dante glides his fingers along my lower back, circling around me to trace his way to my stomach.

Meeting my eyes, he remains brooding and stone-faced, allowing part of his devil form to peek through with his expanding diamond pupils. "I'm going to strip you down now. You want that, don't you?"

My heart thumps out of whack, battering my ribs violently enough to steal my breath. I can't even summon a response to his teasing question.

He drops his hands from my shirt and steps away. "If you don't answer me, then I'm going to have fun by myself." Strolling toward his huge collection of toys, he picks out a couple from the shelf and smiles.

My breath catches as he turns on a vibrator, the hum buzzing through the air. "What are you going to do with that one?"

Tilting his head up, a wicked grin stretches across his face. He crosses the room and stands in front of me. "I thought you might want to feel what you'll miss out on before I get started on myself. Just a touch through your clothes."

Warmth builds between my legs, my body humming as much as the vibrator. Slowly, I nod my head.

He licks his lips and leans down, kissing me to see if I resist. I don't. I stand on my tiptoes and caress my lips to his, my soul and body singing with anticipation. Dante teases the seam of my lips with his tongue until I open my mouth and let him in. The second I do, he rubs the vibrator over my thigh and between my legs, weakening my knees.

I moan and clutch onto him before I end up with my ass on the floor. Gripping my ass with one hand, Dante teases me with the vibrator while kissing me until I crave more. I want to feel the toy on my exposed skin and discover exactly what he can do with it.

It's in this moment I realize he was wrong about me. I'm not desperate to be good. I'm desperate to forget. I need to feel taken care of instead of constantly at battle with who I am and what Hell wants from me. I crave to just say fuck it and live my fleeting life, the short amount of freedom I have with reckless abandon.

I surprise Dante by hooking my fingers to his shirt and tugging it up until he bends enough for me to yank it over his head.

Dante releases a sexy rumble from his throat and pulls the vibrator away from my body, cutting me off from the pleasure. An annoyed gasp escapes my mouth, and I reach for his pants, wanting to teach him what it's like to bring me to the edge of ecstasy and then deny me, but he locks his hot fingers around my wrist, stopping me.

"I don't think so, pretty soul. This is about you, not me. I'm not here to play games with you. I want to teach you to trust me with every inch of you. That fucker of a mortal bastard really messed with you, and Micah's ignorance about what is happening to himself didn't help any. So now, I'm going to show you that I have only your needs at heart. I will not fail the mission. I hadn't realized what an effect your soul would have on me, but something about it—it's hard to explain. Angels aren't the only ones who your presence fucks up. You fuck me up. You make me want to do insane things. Ruin and destroy others on your behalf." Dante clenches his fists, flexing his muscles. His confession does something to my soul, and I want nothing more than what he wants.

I swallow and pant, trying to think of something to say that isn't begging for him to rip my clothes off and fuck my brains out. The heat of his gaze devours my face, and he remains silent like he knows I have something on my mind.

"I should slap you for giving me hope, you bastard," I finally manage to say. "I thought that kind of bullshit was saved for angelic pep-talks."

"Old habits." He unfurls his wings, expanding them out to touch the opposing walls of his room. "But I will fix it. Hope is for those who have nothing else to help them through things. You don't need hope, faith, or any of that shit. You have me and Kase. And soon, you'll even have Micah begging for you. It'll be so satisfying showing him that his mark means nothing to you. Not when you're going to have mine."

I can't stop the smile stretching my cheeks. "Is that so?"

He bunches the front of my shirt in his fingers. "Yes, you're mine."

The certainty in his voice sends energy zinging through my soul as if his essence tangles with mine. Haze crowds my vision as the electricity builds and something inside me cracks open, allowing him in. I gasp at the sight of Dante as he would've been as an angel, tattoo-free, his features softer, his wings as white as snow. His emerald eyes remain the same color but instead of fire in their depths, I catch sight of the purest light. I reach out and cup his face, drawn to him like his essence hypnotizes me. My whole body trembles with need, and I close the space to him, kissing him until it feels as if we become a single entity in a universe solely made for us.

"Do you trust me to take care of you, Raven?" Dante asks, his voice deep and husky with his question.

I swallow. "Forever."

The world shifts as the light from his eyes disappears. "Good soul. Now hold still."

My knees weaken, barely keeping me on my feet at his command. A flicker of darkness dances across his handsome face, and he takes his time undressing me like he gets off on seeing me squirm with anticipation.

He stands in front of me, roving his eyes over my naked

body, savoring every inch of me. The heat of his gaze awakens every nerve-ending on my body, and I squeeze my thighs together, feeling the slickness of my excitement wetting my legs. My nipples ache, so tight and hard, I bring my hands up to rub my breasts.

Dante tilts his head, amusement lighting his face. He enjoys everything he does to me. "I want to make a deal with you, Raven. If you want me to continue, you have to trust me. You have to agree not to pull any more of that soul saving shit. It's not angels who'll save you. It's Kase and me. It's you. Do you agree?"

How could I not? "I do."

"Apologize for doubting me, too. You fucked me up, Raven." Dante hooks his fingers to my waist and sets me into the cool seat of the swing. Tugging my arms over my head, he tightens soft straps around my wrists, restraining me to a thin bar above my head. "It still drives me crazy."

"I think you were fucked up to begin with." I can't stop from speaking my mind. I've lost all reserve with Dante as I sit naked and exposed, tied up and vulnerable in front of him, giving him all of my trust.

He narrows his eyes. "You're wrong. Even Lucian can tell what you've done to me. That's why he pulled this bullshit. But he was wrong. You don't distract me and put the mission at risk. You make me want it more."

"You should be thanking me," I tease, biting my lip.

"Maybe you won't feel the need to get on your knees for Lucian then. You know, you made Kase jealous. He doesn't want your mouth on anyone's cock but his."

Dante growls and grabs my ankles, tipping me back in the process. I can't even shriek before his palm spanks my ass as I hang before him. The sting of his hand radiates from my ass cheeks to my clit, and I brace for him to do it again. I crave it.

He silently denies me and adjusts my legs, placing my feet into straps that open my body completely for him. Moving forward, he stands so close that all he'd have to do is pull his cock out and he could have his way with me. I moan at the thought, my body going wild.

"Apologize, Raven. That's all you have to do, and I'll show you that you will never need Heaven when you have me. You'll forget all the shit Lucian pulled, and when I'm through, Kase will be back with Micah, and you'll never question our capabilities again. Is that clear?"

"Yes," I say. "And I'm sorry for...nothing. Serves you right. You were going to leave me in a dumpster to die."

Dante tightens his jaw, but I can see how much he wants to smile. "You know, for having such a pure soul, you're a naughty, naughty girl. I love it. Keep it up and maybe I'll let you mark me too."

I laugh. I can't help it. What started off as a shit day is now turning to be an adventure I never expected to be on board with. If he thinks this will help me trust him, I'm willing to try.

"Now pick your safe word. Make it easy for me to remember, because we don't use them in Hell, and I plan to see how far you'll let me go."

Fuck me. "Uhh...halo?"

A laugh escapes Dante's mouth. "I should be thankful you didn't say God. And just for that word choice, I'm going to pleasure the Hell into you. Kase likes to fuck with his tail, but just wait until you feel my tongue."

He flicks it out slowly, showing off the barbells on each side of the split in the middle that forks it. I swallow in anticipation as the smile vanishes from his face. I can't move much, but I rock the swing, my clit begging for me to squeeze my legs together to try to smother the tingling ache.

Stopping in front of me, he adjusts his bulge in his pants without pulling it free. He just teases me for a minute, tracing his index finger over my clit and between my lips, sliding it into me. He hums as he brings his hand to his mouth and sucks his finger, closing his eyes like he's been craving to taste me like this.

"You're so wet," he murmurs, adjusting the height of the swing, raising me up a bit more until he can kneel with me at his face level. He lowers the seat strap and adjusts the bar restraints until I can't see him completely. "So sexy. I can't wait to make you cum all over me."

Dante hooks his fingers to my legs and pulls me to his face, making me gasp and clench. The sensation his tongue makes is unlike anything I've ever felt, each side of his forked tongue massaging my clit in a way that it feels as if he strokes it between two lubed fingers while also sucking me hard enough to make my eyes roll back. My moan echoes through the room, the sensation bringing me to the edge of an orgasm faster than I expect, my whole body aching with a need for release.

Dante slows, cutting me off. "Not so fast. I'm just getting started."

The buzz of the vibrator sounds through the air, and I stiffen and jerk my body as the intensity of the toy sends stars bursting in my vision. I gasp and scream out in pleasure, the sensation stealing my ability to do anything else. Slowly slipping the toy inside me, he adjusts it just right that it hits my G-spot, sending tingles right to my clit as well.

"I'm going to leave my mark when you cum," Dante says, kissing me between my legs, stroking his tongue over my clit. "Just a quick bite right where any other fucker you might let enjoy you will see. They'll know who you truly belong to."

I moan my agreement, my mind fuzzy and my body heavy with lust and need. I'd probably agree to a tattoo right now if he asked, because if this is how the rest of eternity will be...where's the contract? Sign me up. I'm his.

"It won't hurt, but you will feel a bit high. You trust me, right? You know I'll take care of you," he murmurs, licking his tongue over my body again.

"I trust you," I say with a gasp. "Bite me. Fuck me. Do whatever you want."

"My pretty soul. You're too good for me, just how I like it."

I lose myself to the bliss he rouses, feeling my body build and build with tingles until I feel like I'll explode. My clit aches with my tensing muscles, and I feel myself squirt with my orgasm, the spasms so intense that I can't move or speak or breathe. My toes curl and I arch my back, riding the wave of mind-blowing pleasure. Dante grabs a strap on the swing that pulls me upright, and I watch through lust-heavy lids as he extends his fangs like a snake and bites into my thigh. He sucks his bite for a minute and presses his hot fingers on the circular marks until he staunches the bleed-ing.

My orgasm finally releases me, and I relax, enjoying the new tingles bursting through my body. Dante stands and brushes my hair from my face, smiling down at me for a moment before releasing my arms from the restraints. I moan and reach for him, brushing my mouth to his neck, and he tilts his head and kisses my lips.

"You're my perfect soul," he murmurs, carrying me to

the bed. "You have no idea how hard these next few hours will be."

I blink a few times, my vision hazy. My body sings with pleasure, still humming with the electric bliss Dante ignited in me. He curls on the bed beside me and plays with my hair, twirling it between his fingers. I expect him to unbutton his pants at any second, but he doesn't, just continuing to kiss me and play with my hair.

So I reach for him, yearning to feel his hard body in mine. It's all I can think about through the strange haze clouding the air. His fragrance fills my senses, and I inhale a deep breath near his neck, trying and failing to undress him.

It takes me a moment to realize he pulled my hands to his chest and pins them over his heart. "I want to give you everything you want, but you're probably seeing stars."

I force my eyes to open and peer at the strange glow coming in through the window. "Angels too," I murmur, trying to lift my heavy hand.

Dante stiffens and turns over. A growl escapes his lips, and he sits up and grabs something from his nightstand. "That's not a fucking angel. It's a flashlight."

The bed shifts as Dante gets to his feet and strides across the room. I can't focus on anything but the light. Yanking the blinds up, Dante hisses. I shield my eyes from the blinding light, but it only grows more intensely.

Glass shatters, and Dante roars.

My body refuses to react. To do anything.

I remain frozen on the bed and watch Dante drag in someone through the broken window. A holler rips through the air, piercing my ears. My muscles don't tense or anything. I know I should be afraid, but the strange haze and dancing lights lock my focus on them, not allowing me to process what's happening only feet away.

"You can't kill me," a gruff voice says, bellowing through the room. "I have a contract with Vik. If you hurt me, he'll—"

Dante hoists the man off his feet and squeezes his neck. I watch in fascination as the man's face changes colors. Growling, Dante transforms completely into his hellish form, unleashing his beast on the man until his body falls to the ground without his head. Dante throws the man's head at the window and shakes his head, heaving a breath.

I don't even react.

I couldn't care less.

Without cleaning off the blood, Dante returns to the bed and wraps me in his arms. "I told you I'd protect you, my pretty soul. Now try to sleep. There will be more assholes coming, so let me cuddle you while I can."

I sigh in contentment, my mind still spinning, the stars still dancing. "You promise to kill them all?"

He chuckles. "I'll hide the bodies. When the venom of my bite wears off, you might see things differently."

I laugh and kiss him, snuggling close. "Hopefully not, my psychotic devil. I want to know you will always protect me."

He chuckles and cups my face, capturing me in his gaze. "Always and forever. You're mine and Kase's soul. No one else can have you."

19

RAVEN

FIGHT LIKE HELL

I STARE IN shock at Dante mopping the blood from the floor next to several full black trash bags. If he knows I'm awake, he ignores me. Bright sunlight beams in through the front window, and it takes me a few seconds to realize I'm no longer in Dante's bed. But I'm still naked apart from the bloody sheet wrapped around me.

Sitting up, I wince at the ache between my legs. The

sensation shoots tingles right to my clit, reminding me of the crazy time I had with Dante last night. I shift the sheet and stare at the spot on my thigh, stinging slightly with my movement. The bite, which looks similar to one from a snake, glows an eerie red like light seeps out from my skin. I carefully caress my finger around Dante's tender mark and gasp, triggering an orgasm out of nowhere. I slap my hand over my mouth as I moan and hang my head.

"Good morning, pretty soul. It sounds like my mark is working as I had hoped. It's better than anything anyone else can give you." Dante props the mop against the door and strolls across the living room to me. "How's your head? Sometimes my bite can make a mortal feel hungover."

I rub the heels of my hands into my eyes. "I'm...great. Just disoriented. Why am I on the couch?"

"I told you I'd hide the bodies, and until Kase gets back, the only place to keep them is in my room." He says it so matter-of-factly that his words barely manage to register with me. "You don't have to worry, though. I promised I would keep you safe, and I am. They were all just a bunch of moronic flesh bags filled with false ideas of protection from their demon keepers. The fuckers can't come in here and face me, so they sent their contracted mortals."

Now I remember exactly what happened. Some ass-holes interrupt my cuddling session with Dante after he gave me the best orgasm of my life with his bite—a bite that also got me a bit high. The intruders also ruined any chance of getting him to fuck my brains out like I wanted because he was surprisingly considerate and didn't want to take advantage of my lowered inhibitions.

I grab his hand and pull him onto the couch beside me, surprising him by climbing onto his lap to straddle him. His fingers tighten around my hips, and he kisses me with hot passion, awakening my body all over again. Reaching between us, I rub my palm across the bulge pressing hard against his pants like at any second, his cock will penetrate through the fabric. He moans and slides his tongue into my mouth, deepening my kiss while helping me with his button.

"Help! My liege! Help!" The loud wail of a man explodes through the air. "Ouch, shit. What the fuck. Oh, God!"

I whip my attention toward the bloody man in the hallway, clutching his gut. Growling, Dante lifts me up with him only to set me down on the couch. The guy shouts and stumbles back, lifting his arms in the process. His bloody dress shirt bulges before something slides out from the crack between buttons.

"Damn it. I just cleaned this shit up." Dante jogs toward the man, scooping up a trash bag from the pile on the floor. "Here, aim for the bag."

My stomach flips as Dante holds the bag out and

whacks the guy on his back, sending his insides bursting through his shirt. I can't believe what I'm seeing or how Dante just folds the guy in half with his super strength and shoves him into the trash bag.

"What the fuck," I mutter, rubbing my eyes. I expect the disgusting madness to vanish, but Dante continues cleaning up innards off the floor. "How was that guy even alive?"

Dante swipes a bloody hand across his forehead. "Demon deals. Half of these assholes asked to cheat death...but it only works once. This guy must've not included anything about body damage. Serves the bastard right. You have no idea how much I want to fuck you."

I can't stomach looking at the gore like I could last night. I have to tip my head toward the ceiling to get my body to chill out enough to speak again. "Sorry. He killed my mood. That was the grossest thing I've ever seen, and now you're covered in blood."

"Oh, come on, pretty soul. You were fine with it last night. You wouldn't even let me give you a clean sheet." His soft footsteps thump across the floor as he returns to me. "Do you remember what you said?"

I groan. "I'm keeping it forever to remind myself of how sexy you were protecting me." The memory ping-pongs through my mind, but it doesn't feel like it belongs to me and more like I had an out-of-body experience and watched some crazy-ass monster possess me, cheering on Dante as he slaughtered at least ten people who were trying to abduct me.

He chuckles. "You were hysterical. Usually people freak out and hallucinate seeing Hell, but you were my perfect cheerleader. Next time I want to see you in a tiny pleated skirt."

"There isn't going to be a next time," I argue, pulling the sheet tighter around me. "I don't want to desensitize myself toward dismemberment or end up relating it to pleasure. My body is so confused right now. I'm so turned on but a bit sick. This isn't how I wanted to start my morning."

"Afternoon," he corrects, smirking at me. "You were on one helluva high until dawn."

My brows pucker in confusion. "Afternoon? Shit. Where is Kase? Shouldn't he be here already?"

A dozen thoughts spin through my mind. What if something bad happened to him? What if Micah called for backup and his angel friends took turns smiting my bossy, controlling bastard devil until he landed back in Hell?

Dante wiggles his fingers out to me, coaxing me to take his hands. "He'll be back eventually, so don't worry your pretty soul about him. Let's get cleaned up, maybe bang in the shower because I can't wait much longer, and then I'll make you dinner. How does that sound?"

It sounds fucking amazing. My mouth refuses to acknowledge it though. "Dante, what if something happened to him?"

Latching his hands around my wrists, he hoists me off the couch and dangles me in front on him. I automatically let the sheet drop and wrap my legs around his waist. His hip presses hard into his bite mark, and I moan so incredibly loud that I'm sure the demons circling could hear.

"Damn it," I say, gasping. "What have you done to me?"

"Gave you a temporary ignition switch to make your body explode. Fun, right?" A smile lights his face, and he nuzzles his nose to mine, acting more affectionate than I ever thought a ruler of Hell could be. Spanking me for some fun punishment? Yeah, that's what I figured would happen regularly. But sweet kisses, hugs, and nose nuzzles? It's unexpected, and damn it, do I like it.

"More like inconvenient." I pout my bottom lip with a sigh.

"At least you don't shoot semen. Now that would be inconvenient. A fucking mess." He chuckles at his thought. "Trust me. You can ask Kase."

I crinkle my nose, imagining he might have experience in that department. If Dante sucked Kase's dick, he probably bit him like this at one point too. The thought is almost enough of a distraction to make me forget all the bullshit. If a familiar whisper didn't drift into my head, coming from nowhere and everywhere, I would. Micah's soft plea of my name stiffens my muscles. He doesn't speak to me directly, but it's almost as if he prays to me, for me, for himself. My heart aches at how much grief comes into me. I nearly cry.

Dante notices my expression fall and cocks his head. "What's the matter? I won't do it again to him. You're our girl, and if we mess around, it'll be with you."

I blink my eyes, trying to suppress the sorrow. I turn my gaze to the front window, expecting to see the sky crack open in a thunderous downpour. It would be fitting for this moment as an angel cries and pleads for answers that don't come.

"Aww, come on. Let me show you how I'm all about you. I have a strap-on you might like. It has a vibrator you can wear while you peg me." Dante slides me lower until I feel his hard-on. "You look like you could use the feeling of power from being on top of me. The opportunity won't come often. Controlling you is far too addicting."

I don't even know how to respond to his suggestion. It sounds so...intriguing. I'm probably the first mortal to have ever been given the chance to fuck one of the devils instead of be fucked.

"Please. Give me answers. I'm lost," Micah whispers, his pleas seeping into me again.

The warmth Dante arouses inside me chills, and I ease

away from him and press my palm to his mouth, stopping him from trying to get carried away with his kinky adventure. "Dante, no. I can't. I want to know where Kase is."

Sighing, Dante peeks past me. "Pretty soul, like I said—"

"What is he doing to Micah? Don't lie to me. That's why you're not anxious like he was when you were gone. You know for certain he's good."

"Don't worry about it. He's taking care of things so you don't have to. Isn't that what you prefer? It was obvious that the light in your soul didn't want to steal Micah's, but we need him. You know this. He has to take his throne in Hell. It's the only way to ensure no one else gets you." His tongue flicks against my palm with his murmuring words. "It's what you want. You can't lie to me."

"But Micah's—"

Dante cuts my words off with a kiss as the walls of the apartment tremble. Kase's familiar heavy footsteps in his hellish form thud outside. I wiggle in Dante's arms, but he doesn't put me down, tightening his arms around me. Swiveling my upper body, I stare at the door. Kase's loud arrival draws closer. I expect him to kick the door open and drag a beaten and bloodied Micah into the apartment. I kind of hope for it. Except he doesn't come, and the thudding footsteps fade altogether.

Fuck. I'm certain it was Kase. I've heard him in his

hellish form enough over the last few weeks to recognize him. So where did he go?

I squirm harder in Dante's arms. "If you don't put me down, you'll never know what fucking me is like." I hate having to threaten it, but I don't know what else might work. He enjoys punishment, and I'm not great at arguing.

"Lies, pretty soul. You won't be able to resist me forever. Especially if I touch you right here." Dante digs his fingers into my thigh, sending an explosion spasming through my groin.

I throw all my weight back with my infuriating orgasm. Dante loses his balance, stumbling forward to stop me from eating shit on the floor. He hisses in my ear and flips me onto his shoulder. I expect him to slap me on my bare ass in punishment. I can tell he really wants to as much as I want him to.

"You're seriously in for it, Raven. I didn't want to fuck you in Kase's bed, but you need to have the wildness screwed out of you. You're driving me crazy. I want my good pretty soul back, not the one that can't resist gracing assholes with mortal intervention." Striding past the grotesque, bloody trash bags, he heads toward the hallway.

I try to smack his ass from my position. "Dante, put me down. I mean it."

"Threaten me with something that might make me, and I'll consider it," he snaps, jogging faster as the apartment trembles again.

What the fuck is going on outside? "Hey, God? It's me. Micah might've referred to me as heathen—"

A loud slap to my ass along with a sting that weakens my body cuts off my prayer. I shudder at the sensation, really wishing Dante wouldn't do shit like this—or that I wouldn't enjoy it. Because now I can't remember what I was going to pray for.

I stretch my neck, trying to peer into Kase's room as Dante carries me in. "God—"

"Raven, shut the fuck up. Now is not the time to call for saviors. They're circling like the damn demons." Dante tosses me on the bed and heads to Kase's weapon collection. "All the activity has them sniffing around, and as much as I want to send your sexy ass out there to bone them until they can't survive without you, we need to plan more thoroughly."

My eyes widen with his revelation. "Shit. If Kase's out there, he might need help."

"Damn it." Dante grabs a shirt from Kase's closet and tosses it at me. "Kase will be pissed off that you underestimate him, but I know you're not going to give up, so put that shit on. I'll show you he's fine. If you obey me and don't attract attention, I'll fuck you however you want when we get back."

I hurry and tug the shirt over my head. The hem

thankfully grazes just above my knees, so I don't have to risk flashing my vagina at any angels or demons. "You mean I'll bang you any way you want."

His eyes flash with desire. "This is why I'm not letting you get away from me, pretty soul."

Snatching a second dagger from the shelf, he offers it to me, and I look down, wondering where he expects me to keep it.

I end up grabbing a hoodie from the back of the desk chair, concealing it in the pocket. Dante doesn't give me a chance to search for bottoms and heads toward the slider instead of the front door.

He doesn't even have to stretch to set me on the wall, and I wait for him to hop over. I might be anxious, but I'm not careless. I'm not getting out of his reach outside the safety of our apartment.

"Do I look like an angel keeper to you, Andre? If you get your head out of your ass, you might see that Micah isn't with me." Kase waves his arms around the apartment complex. "Maybe you should ask the Higher Power for an answer."

"This is the last place I sensed his presence." The raspy voice coming from a hot as Hell...Heaven? Whatever. The angel's voice is far from angelic as is the rest of his black-clad presence in attire similar to what Micah wears. For being good, the saviors sure know how to give off some bad boy vibes.

"Until I chased him off. I told you. He only hung around long enough to see that his presence wasn't welcome. Now get the fuck out of here. I don't want to fight you, but I will." Kase flicks out his tail, wrapping it around the angel's neck.

"Tell me the truth. Where is Micah?" The angel's persistence doesn't surprise me.

Shit. I want to know the answer as well. Micah can't be that far since I heard him. I don't think he is capable of leaving completely. Not if Dante and Kase are right about him.

Growling, Kase transforms completely into his hellish form. He lights the angel off his feet with his tail and snarls in his face.

The angel scowls and flaps his wings, stretching out Kase's tail. I stare in horror as the angel unsheathes his flaming sword, preparing to cut himself free of Kase's hold.

"Please, no," I whisper under my breath.

Both Kase and the angel whip their attention to me. Kase recovers quickly and swings his tail, sending the angel whizzing through the air. The angel crashes into the side of the apartment, and the ground shakes under the force.

"Get her inside, damn it!" Kase shouts.

A light ignites behind Kase, haloing him in an angelic glow. Materializing before my eyes, the angel appears behind Kase with a flaming sword. I can't even get my mouth open to shout for him to turn around.

The angel sinks his flaming sword into his back.

My vision turns red.

20

KASE

BREAKING ANGELS

"OH, NO YOU fucking don't," Dante says, snatching Raven by the back of the shirt. *My* shirt. Fuck, she looks incredibly sexy, raging in fury on my behalf.

Burning pain sizzles across my back as Andre's heavenly sword slides free. If Raven wasn't freaking out, I might react with a grimace. The fucking wound hurts worse than anything from Hell, but I don't want her to know. She tried to attack Lucian to protect Dante. If she tries to attack Andre? I'll beat the shit out of the bastard for even touching her.

I wave my hand at Raven. "Hey, chill. What kind of devil do you think I am if I'd drop at this little flesh wound?"

Andre grumbles and shoves his sword into my back, sending it through my stomach. I stiffen and heave a breath, sliding my tail up and around Andre's hand. Forcing him to tug the damn blessed weapon from my body, I manage to rip it free. He punches his hand into my wound, trying to rip it wider. It's enough to drag my gaze from Raven.

"You son-of-a-bastard!" I holler, swinging my fist. I extend my talons and slice them across his chest. "Do you really want my wrath?"

Expanding his wings, Andre gathers his damn goodie light beams, threatening me with them. "Where's Micah, Kase?"

"I don't know, you fuckhead. I've already told you that. I don't want to break you in front of our girl over there, so this is your one warning. Leave or you'll lose those damn wings. Demonic affairs are none of your concern." I gather hellfire in my hand and throw it, not waiting for Andre to attack.

He launches into the air a second before it whizzes through the spot he was standing and explodes across the dry grass, setting it ablaze. If this wasn't my home, I'd leave it to burn, but we're established for business here, and I'm fucking tired of dealing with humans. Raven is my main focus now. Her pussy is too damn sweet to let go. I want to fuck her and feel my darkness tangle with the light of her soul. I get a high just being close to her. She doesn't know the extent of it yet, but the potential of her power as an angel-kissed soul is far greater than she can imagine. It's why Hell needs her, and Lucian wants to ensure she ends up nowhere else. Her very being can bring balance to Hell, and ultimately, fix the bullshit the Higher Power created.

I crack my neck and finish morphing, giving myself several feet more of height. Launching from my place, I land amid the fiery grass and put out the flames. Andre circles above us, his wings casting shadows on the ground. I hate how persistent the damn saviors are. I roar and jump toward him like a lion trying to snatch a falcon from the sky, missing him by inches. He tries to blast me away, and I hear Raven inhale a breath and smack her hands against Dante.

Suppressing my urge to pluck every last white feather from Andre's wings in front of Raven, I clomp my way towards her, transforming into my mortal façade. I greet her with a smile, drinking her in as she squirms against Dante, filthy with blood, smelling of him, and only wearing my shirt. Her perky tits harden at my closeness, and I snake my tail over her tight nipples, pressing against the cotton fabric.

She flutters her eyelashes and licks her lips, shivering

under my touch. "Angel-girl, there is a difference between being naughty and disobedient. I know Dante wouldn't have willingly brought you out here until you offered him a deal he couldn't refuse. Do you know what kind of trouble you're in?"

"I was worried," she whispers, her seductive voice striking me in my dick.

I probably shouldn't have touched her tits with my tail, because I now want more of her. Just the caress of our bodies hardening my cock, the reminder of how tight she was as I slid my dick into her hard and fast giving me the need to bend her over.

I step closer and grab her chin, sandwiching her to Dante. He keeps a firm hold on her with his arm around her stomach. His green eyes flash, and he mutters a growl under his breath. I don't have to ask him to know he wants me to hurry the fuck up and convince her to go back inside with him. I've been gone for hours, and it's obvious they haven't fucked and he's growing envious that she wants to give me her attention, but it serves him fucking right. It's his damn problem if he can't take what he wants from her like I did.

I slide my tail under the hem of her shirt to poke at his hellish side. "Are you sure you were worried, angel-girl?" I finally respond, purposely drawing out the silence. "Or did you just miss me and all the ways I can fuck you?"

Gliding my tail between her thighs, I hum under my breath at how wet she is. Dripping even. And then she tenses and throws herself at me, her moan so fucking sexy that I pull her from Dante's arms and into mine. I tug up her shirt enough to confirm my suspicions. Dante marked her in a way that will make her cream herself for at least another day. The fucking bastard.

I narrow my eyes at him and spin Raven away, leaning close to her mouth. "No wonder he's antsy. I bet he hasn't had the chance to blow his load. I know Dante wouldn't have fucked you when you were teasing Hell on his high, so his balls ache. Why don't you be a nice soul and repay him for the good time? Let me handle the saviors."

Flaring her nostrils, Raven inhales a breath. "Weren't you the one who said we have shit to do? What about Micah? I heard—"

I can't cover her mouth fast enough to shut her up. It's not her fault that Andre has super-hearing, but it is my fault that I didn't warn her that whispers wouldn't work. Spinning around, I toss Raven toward Dante and transform, letting my hellish beast side take over. Raven shrieks in surprise, but she doesn't resist Dante as he engulfs her in his arms.

"Take her home. Now! I mean it," I say, unleashing a guttural snarl.

Andre swoops toward Dante and Raven, pissing me off

even more. Spinning, Dante turns his back on the savior and shields Raven with his wings. Light explodes through the air, and Dante roars as Andre chucks his heavenly power at his wings. I leap from my spot and tackle the fucker mid-air.

We crash to the ground and skid across the dead grass. Dante runs toward the apartment with Raven, only making it a dozen feet before another savior arrives and lands in their path. Fucking angels. They flock together like the bird brains they are if they think something is wrong with someone in the brethren. Micah's already too far along the edge for them to communicate with them, even if he prayed. All it will take is another day at most to get him to bow before Lucian. The only reason I was returning to the apartment was because I wanted to check on Raven. Fuck her for a while. Make sure she knew I would take care of things. But then the bastard had to interrupt.

My wandering mind gets the best of me, and Andre lights up my face with his holy power, kicking me into action. I sink my fangs into his shoulder and rip him off his feet. I thrash my head and toss him at the wall of the building hard enough to crack the stucco. Pain explodes in my back, and I jerk forward and twist, flinging a flaming sword from another savior out of me.

"Get the fuck out of here, or you'll end up like Micah," I say, transforming into my human façade completely. "Five seconds, Cassius."

"Stop it! Leave him alone!" Raven's voice cuts through the air as Zade ravages Dante's wings with his heavenly light.

Mortals think demons survive on punishment, but they're wrong. It's the saviors. We're about serving justice to the souls too dark to even see the light of the Higher Power. Hell always gets shit on and blamed for causing such things, but mortals damn well make their own choices.

"Please! Please!" Raven screams.

I gather hellfire in my palms and dodge Cassius in an attempt to blast Zade away. Launching into the air, Cassius uses his power to knock mine off course. Raven screams again within the shield of Dante's wings, her desperation pushing me to fight harder. But the fucking saviors block me. Andre and Cassius won't let me get within reach of her.

"Where's Micah, Kase?" Andre asks again. "Tell us and we'll stop."

I flare my nostrils, summoning more fire into my palms. "Stay out of Hell's affairs."

Dante roars in pain, snatching my attention away from the assholes. My gut clenches at his guttural voice. I've never heard him sound like this, and it sets me off. Jerking my hands, I blast Andre with hellfire, launching it again and again, not caring that the ground shakes and the scent of Hell begins to permeate the air. If I unleash enough of it, I might open a portal to Hell, and it could suck Raven into it because she's the only Hell-bound soul nearby.

"Stop it, you fucking bastard!" Raven manages to get out of the protection of Dante's wings. Slapping Zade across the face, she sears the angel's cheek with Lucian's mark, her palm glowing with the fissuring portal.

Dante's body gives out on him, and he drops to his knees. His wings are unrecognizable, burned with holy light and barely hanging onto his back. Raven's fury turns her into a naughty fucking soul, and she tries to hit Zade again.

"Raven, don't!" I yell, ramming my shoulder into Cassius, finally getting through the angelic barricade.

She ignores me and snatches one of Dante's daggers. "I thought Hell was bad, but you're—"

Raising his hands, Zade lights up the world with his light, blinding her. I can't run fast enough as the angel hooks his arms around Raven's waist and bends his knees. I kick off the ground and leap toward Zade, but Andre flies at me from the side. I hit the grass and skid, not staying down for long.

"Kase!" Raven shouts, her voice drifting on the wind.

Dante attempts to get to his feet, flapping his charred wings. There is no way he can chase the fucking angels. Raven can't fight them off either. I roar in anger, throwing another ball of hellfire into the air. Nothing works to stop them.

Tipping my head back, I watch the silhouette of the three saviors ascend toward the sky.

They steal my angel-girl from us.

Micah hangs with his arms over his head, keeping his head bowed. I want nothing more than to make him suffer for his brethren kidnapping Raven, but I need him. He knows where they are, and he can take us to them. And when he does, those fucking saviors will break. I will take their wings and drag them to Hell myself for even touching Raven.

Striding across the empty apartment, I growl and summon red fire in my palms. The angels were stupid shits, not even realizing they were thirty feet from Micah.

Micah lifts his head, remaining expressionless.

"This could all be over if you just say the fucking word, Micah," I say, stopping a foot away from him. Shifting the fire from my palm, I light my finger like a candle and trace his jaw, searing his skin. "Bow to Hell, and you can have everything you desire. Just imagine how satisfying it'll be sinking your cock into Raven's tight pussy. If you think touching her soul feels good, you have no idea."

"I don't want to use her like you do. The only thing I desire is to save her soul and get her away from Hell. She deserves more from her eternity. You know she does." Micah locks his shimmering gold eyes on mine, pursing his lips. "It's why I'm here. You're afraid of what Lucifer plans to do. But I don't have to bow for you to save her. Just do the right thing."

Fury whips through me, and I jab my fist into his gut. Heaving, he rattles the chains and coughs. "You don't even know what that is, Micah. And saving her from Hell? Fuck that. You only want to save her to keep her for yourself. What happens if you somehow manage this impossible miracle? Would you leave her to live out her life, or would you stick around and stalk her? Hope she falls in love with you? Maybe let you get your dick wet until the saviors come for you?"

"It's not about sex," he responds, scowling.

"Soul fucking is basically the same damn thing. You won't be able to resist." I grab him by the throat and squeeze. "Admit it. You're a glutton for her. All these days you've spent obsessing and wanting more and more of her has left the brethren afraid. They took her, you know. They think it'll somehow get you to return to good grace."

Micah stiffens, his eyes bulging, but not from the constriction on his neck. His expression says everything. It's in this moment I realize that nothing I can do will cause Micah to jump. He was holding onto hope and faith that he'd figure this out. Now? I watch as that hope slips through his fingers.

"If they find out who she is..." Micah squeezes his eyes shut. "Please help us."

I punch him in the face, anger turns my vision red with hellfire. "Who are you praying to? You think the Higher Power listens? Do you think that someone will help you?"

Hanging his head, Micah doesn't respond, aggravating me even more. I grab the chains and rip them from the ceiling. Micah drops to the floor. He doesn't try to fight and accepts my wrath knowing he damn well deserves this punishment.

"If you would've had faith in our plan from the beginning, we wouldn't be in this position, Micah. You betrayed us. You betrayed me!" I whip my tail across his chest, slashing his skin. "Now look at all the pain you've caused Raven. We wouldn't have needed her if you and the brethren followed through, or has it been so long that you've forgotten?"

Groaning, he tips his head up at me. "It wasn't my path."

"But it was. It always has been. You've just prolonged mortal misery, and now Raven will see the wrong side of Hell because of your shortcomings." My wrath controls me, and I whip him again, wanting him to pay for failing the most intoxicating soul I've ever felt. The most beautiful woman I've ever kissed. Tasted. Fucked. He's failed his true mission, and in doing so, screwed over the woman who was going to help change things.

I want to kill him.

I want to cut off his wings like he severed mine.

"You have to let me go, Kase. I can't let that happen to her. Please. I'm begging you to give me the chance to save her soul. I know you want it, but it isn't yours. It's hers." Micah presses his palms together and holds my gaze.

Fucking angel tears.

It takes everything in me not to smile. This is exactly what I wanted. Micah is so convinced that he can save Raven that he might do anything.

"Tell you what, Micah. I'll make you a deal." I have to get something out of entrusting my angel-girl in his incapable hands. I don't need a deal, but it would be unlike me if I didn't get everything I wanted. "If you agree to my terms, I'll let you attempt to save Raven's soul."

"I'm not bowing to Hell. I know you don't want her sent to Hell as much as I don't," he mutters, ruffling his feathers, acting as if I slide my tail up his ass.

I groan and scrub my cheeks with the heels of my hands. "Fine, I guess I could accept something else." Twisting on my feet, I peer over my shoulder for no other reason than to prolong his torment. "How about when you save Raven, you bring her to me for one last fuck. I want you to see what you'll spend the rest of eternity wishing you experienced just once...could've been the best ten seconds of your existence, Virgin Micah."

"Agree. Now free me. I must find her." Micah rattles

the chains.

"You're taking me with you." I grab the chains and wrap them around my hands.

Micah tries to yank away, but I reel him toward me. Clenching his teeth, he looks ready to try to blast my ass to Hell with heavenly light. "You can't—"

The apartment door flings open, clattering against the wall. Dante's tall frame hovers in the doorway, the setting sun lighting him in a fiery glow. Cracking his neck, he silently tries to get me to leave Micah.

I shake my head. "The bird-brain has agreed to help Raven."

Flashing his fangs, Dante says, "It's too late. The saviors sent Raven to Hell. Lucian commands your presence. He wants to make a deal."

My muscles tighten at his words. "What deal?"

"One of us trades him places, and he'll let us keep Raven's soul." Dante shifts on his feet. "I'm willing to do it, but I wanted to tell you before agreeing."

Micah barks a laugh from his place on the floor. "And you say I'm the bird-brain?"

I spin and look at the fucker on the floor, gathering the broken chains to carry. "You have two seconds to explain before I choke you with my tail."

"Lucian is lying. Raven hasn't been sent to Hell. I've touched her soul. I can sense her on this plane. Once she wakes up, I'll be able to hear her too." Micah pushes to his feet and unfurls his feathers. "Now, if you'll please hold up your end of the bargain, I'd like to ensure Raven's soul lands in the proper hands."

I growl, swinging my fist to punch the wall. "We're coming with you."

"What about Lucian, Kase?" Dante asks. "He'll be—"

Launching at Dante, I shove him out of the apartment and get in his face. "He'll be fucking happy. I figured out how to make Micah fall."

21

RAVEN

HOPFLESS

"MAYBE WE CAN just leave her somewhere uninhabited by mankind." Bright light shines from above as three silhouettes surround me. The angel speaking bows forward, peering into my eyes. "Let nature take care of her."

The silhouette clears, and I gawk at a gorgeous angel, more beautiful than handsome, and most definitely the asshole who hurt Dante. The brand mark on his cheek, which matches the same as the one Lucian gave me on my palm, glows with light as if his holiness tries to heal it but can't.

A wave of fury pours through me, because of what he did to Dante. All three of these saviors deserve my wrath. I still can't see the other two apart from their heavenly glow, so I focus on Mr. Gorgeous Asshole. His turquoise eyes are a shade of blue only found in tropical waters near the shores of some Caribbean islands. They glow against his sun-kissed skin and blond hair with streaks of platinum dancing through the mop of short waves. His softer jawline curves to his oval chin, free of facial hair.

My gaze doesn't linger on his face for long because the angelic man's bare chest steals my attention. I don't know if he does it intentionally, but the fucker flexes each of his pecs like he wants me to check out how taut and smooth his muscles are. I don't think I've ever truly invested so much attention in a man's nipples, but his become the most fascinating thing as they move with his performance. They're tight from the chill in the air, and I have the sudden urge to pinch them in my fingers.

"I think it'll take the betrayers long enough to find her that they'll end up having to search Hell," he adds.

Jerking my hand out, I give in to my desire and snatch his damn nipple between my fingers. I don't know what kind of madness comes over me, but listening to his suggestion pisses me off. The angel's eyes widen, and he expands his wings but doesn't launch away. His wings knock the other two fuckers on their backs, and he finally gets his surprise under control and laces his fingers around my wrist, stopping me from trying to punish his pec for its distracting talent.

"What are you doing, Raven?" Hearing him say my name triggers something dark inside me.

I pinch him harder. "I don't know, but if you continue to recommend painfully slow ways to torture me to death, I will hurt you."

"By squeezing my nipple? Don't you think the Hell brand was bad enough? It's going to leave Lucifer's mark." He touches his fingers to the glowing spot.

"You're lucky I can't reach your dick to brand next." I glower and slap my Hell brand against his chest.

It doesn't mark him. Shit. I was hoping I could use it to my advantage. Whatever made it work before doesn't now.

"Really, Raven? Again? Your connection to Hell doesn't work here. Does this kind of behavior and threats work on the devils?" Amusement lights his gorgeous features, and his lips quirk up in the corner. "Or have those betrayers done this to you as punishment? I'm sorry if they have. No one deserves this kind of treatment."

White wings expand out in front of me and then vanish from view, leaving behind another shirtless man. "Stop, Zade. You shouldn't open a line of communication with her."

The husky voice fills the room, the angel sounding on the verge of bellowing. "She is the devils' vessel. That mark—"

Zade rubs his cheek again. "Is only a mark. Relax. She's been with the devils for weeks."

"So it is in our best interest to keep our communication to the bare minimum. We have never dealt with this type of situation. Who knows what Lucifer's mark can do or what she can do bearing it." The final angel strolls back toward Zade. At least he wears a jacket, hiding what I'm sure is a deliciously muscular body like the other brethren.

I jerk my attention toward one of the fuckers that hurt Kase outside the apartment—Cassius, I think. My vision adjusts to the light, or maybe the brightness of the room dims with the disappearance of their wings, but I can finally see my surroundings. Unlike Micah's home, this place looks normal—boring even.

Heavy curtains drape over the windows, the blue color the same as the stained carpet. In the middle of the room, a couple blankets are laid out in a row, and a small kitchenette with a fridge, microwave, and old cabinetry sits in the back. The studio apartment has seen better days, and even though these guys are angels, they live like...well, not devils. Kase and Dante put their clothes away, take the trash out, and live in far cleaner conditions.

"I suspect she's quite harmless outside of Hell's darkness. She's even already forgotten her attempt to hurt me."

Zade's comment draws my attention away from the messy apartment and back to him.

My fingers rest against his pec without pinching him any longer, and now that he points it out, I feel ridiculous. Who the Hell pinches nipples like this except maybe brothers messing around and annoying each other. I've seen it happen with some neighborhood boys growing up.

"But she—"

"She what, Cassius?" I snap, pulling my hand away from Zade. I don't know why I say his name, but it's like my mind wants to ensure I don't forget it. "Is one of Hell's pawns? Maybe. But do you think I wanted to ever be put in this position? I was left no choice."

Zade lets me go and stands up, rubbing his fingers over his nipple. I wish he'd put on a shirt or something, but I suspect the gashes whipping around his sides from his attack on Dante probably hurt. The same goes for the quieter angel staring at me from a few feet away.

"Mortals always have a choice." Cassius straightens his back and narrows his violet eyes at me.

I've never seen a color anything like them. They look like sparkling amethyst stones against his paler complexion compared to his brethren. His tousled black hair hangs every which way, wind-blown but not affecting how attractive he is. My gaze travels over his broad shoulders and to the heavy black jacket he wears, hiding his body from my attention.

"You obviously know nothing," I argue, getting the nerve to push to my feet. I hate feeling so small as they tower over me, but standing at my full height of five-seven doesn't make much of a difference. "And to think, I assumed you were all knowing like whatever higher power you—"

Sliding a sword from a sheath in his jacket, Cassius sets it ablaze with the touch of his heavenly light. I lose my gall and scramble away. Panic tightens my chest at the fierce angel. He doesn't look like the type to see any shades of gray in a situation—all or nothing sort of attitude—which reminds me of one of the reasons the devils jumped. They wanted away from that.

Cassius strides toward me, cornering me to the wall of the small studio apartment. I hit my back on the cool plaster and raise my arms protectively, trying to shield myself. Blinding light erupts through the room with the unfurling of his wings, and a bolt of electricity dances from one tip of his wings to the other. His smite mode supersedes how terrifying Micah was when we met—and maybe even Lucian, for that matter—and I can't stop the silent prayer from escaping my mouth.

"God, help me," I whisper, imagining Kase and Dante yelling at me for resorting to begging for mercy. Or for praying at all. I can't help it though. Maybe it's my soul's way of trying to show this angel that he should save his smite for someone else.

"Come on, Cass. That's enough. Look how you've frightened her. If she were completely consumed by Hell, she wouldn't pray." The quieter angel speaks up, coming up beside his brethren. "We'd have been able to take care of this problem as well."

"Andre's right," Zade says, staring down at me like I'm the most pathetic being in the universe. "She is Micah's mission, and we can't intervene."

Cassius scowls and swings the sword back. "But I can try."

Fear paralyzes me, and I scream and squeeze my eyes shut as Cassius chops down his flaming sword at me. I expect to feel the worst pain in existence. I hold my breath and wait for the fires of Hell to shoot from the door to swallow me whole. What I don't expect is for nothing to happen. No pain. No death. Yet I know Cassius stuck me with his flaming sword.

I flutter my eyes open and gasp at the sight of the flaming sword protruding from my chest. Cassius grumbles in agitation and jabs his sword into me over and over again like he expects it to hurt me eventually.

Throwing myself forward, I ram into Cassius's legs, surprising him. I don't know exactly how I manage to knock the angel onto his ass, but I don't question the universe for granting me the capability of doing something so satisfying, and crawl up the angel's body before planting my ass on his hard stomach.

"You asshole!" I shriek, clocking him in the face with my fist. "Why the fuck would you do that?"

Two strong arms grab me by my sides and drag me off of Cassius. I kick and buck my body, trying to break free. Spinning me around, Andre dangles me in front of him like an unruly child, but it doesn't stop me from trying to punch him next.

"Settle down, little hellion. Fighting does no one any good. That is the devil's way, and I won't tolerate it, even if I have to restrain you like this until you settle down." Andre remains expressionless with his words.

I huff a few deep breaths, wanting to test his threat, because really, how long can he actually hold me like this if I thrash enough? "Fuck you. Put me down!" The angel is delusional if he thinks I'm going to comply.

"I will when you settle down," Andre says, doing nothing more than continuing to hang me in front of him with my feet almost a foot off the floor.

Annoyance grips me so tightly that I fight for another minute, screaming and swearing at the bastard angel like my words might corrupt him after a while. He silently stares at me, waiting with the patience of a saint until I give up, or at least, pretend to. I'm betting on the angel being gullible and naïve. If he thinks I'll comply, he'll let his guard down. I already know there is nothing I can truly do to escape him, but I can make him wish I would.

Andre puffs a breath through his mouth, his tropical fruit scent reminding me of the coconut shampoo I used to like until Joel started using it too, treating my belongings like they were free for all. But the scent coming from the angel twists my feelings. From now on, I won't think of anyone except Andre with the fragrant scent.

I shake my head, knocking Joel from my mind completely. He deserves zero space in my head. So instead, I focus on Andre and imprint his essence into my being. I relax in his arms, letting the weirdly comforting emotions trickle through me. I know I shouldn't feel content, but it's like my soul recognizes he's not truly a threat.

His deep brown eyes with gold rings flicker with heavenly light. He meets my stare with his own, not averting his eyes away from me. I inhale slow breaths, wondering if he can listen to my thoughts like Micah. If he can, he doesn't say anything. But I realize despite not being able to read my mind, he's peering at my soul. In this moment, I'm not sure I even exist as a mortal. His essence seeps into mine. It feels a lot like when I let Kase and Micah merge with me. The intimacy awakens a deep-seated part of me that leaves my heart racing.

Cassius and Zade close in around us, but with the way I

find myself stuck in a staring contest with the unblinking angel, I know resisting any of this is pointless. So is fighting.

His expression breaks after another minute. Thick brows dip lower on his forehead in confusion as if he feels what I do. "Raven..." Hearing him whisper my name sends tingles all over me. "Your soul..." He can't form coherent thoughts, his confusion obvious. He might not understand or believe it, but his essence calls to mine. He's one of the angels that I need to break. Actually, the three of them might all be.

"What about it?" I search his face, waiting for him to drop me to run away.

But he doesn't.

He smiles and envelopes me in his wings, cutting Zade and Cassius off.

"It's indescribable." He leans in closer, leaving only inches between us.

Mapping features with my gaze, I savor his closeness consuming me. Andre is the perfect blend of rugged and beautiful, and I wonder why angels have to look so good. I turn my attention away from the weight of his stare, nearly burning my irises, and regret doing so immediately. A huge boner presses against his pants, pointing directly at me. Now that I see the angel pitching a tent, the dirtiest thoughts cross my mind. I have so many questions. What does this mean? Does my soul give him a boner or is it me?

I know I shouldn't do what my mind suggests at the mere sight of the angel's erection, but there are a lot of things in my life I shouldn't have done that I might as well just add to my pile of regrets. Swinging my body, I manage to lace my legs around his torso. He gasps in surprise and releases my sides to grab me firmly by my ass.

Andre blushes, his cheeks blooming with color. I can't stop the smile overtaking my face. Dante and Kase would crack up over this moment. I know these angels are so far removed from mortals and earthly experiences that they're virgins. His reaction proves he knows what's happening but he probably can't grasp as to why.

"I'm sorry," Andre whispers, shifting me higher, and in doing so, causing me to grind against his erection until it rests under my ass. "I didn't know this was possible."

"Did seeing my soul really just give you a boner?" I don't bother keeping my voice low. It would serve him right that the brethren overhear.

Andre swallows and purses his lips together. "It's out of my control and I apologized. What else would you like me to do?"

Heat blooms across my body. He walked right into my dirty thoughts. It's almost embarrassing that he doesn't realize that his question has a slew of inappropriate responses I can give him.

I channel my devilish side, now knowing that they

won't smite me. "Show it to me. Your dick looks huge through your pants. If you're going to penetrate my soul with your gaze, might as well let me see it. I think it's a fair exchange of intimacy."

Andre's eyes flicker with light, and he doesn't respond.

"Release her. Now!" Cassius yells from outside the privacy of Andre's wings. "She's trying to get to you."

"It's just a body, Cass," Andre murmurs, still keeping me hidden. "There is nothing wrong with curiosity."

Oh, shit.

Warm excitement slicks between my legs. He obviously doesn't know that nothing about him is just a body. He's like sex on a stick, and just the thought of seeing him in all of his naked heavenly glory turns me on.

What would Kase and Dante say? What would they want me to do? I mean, it was their plan for me to seduce angels after all, but now I really want to talk to them about it.

"Nothing wrong at all if we both agree," I say, smiling. My devils would want me to use this to their advantage. Bowing closer, I brush my lips to his ear. "Maybe if you get your brethren to give us some space, I will let you take a peek at me. I'm not wearing any panties."

His fingers tighten on my ass and a groan escapes his mouth. "Raven."

"Let Lucifer's seductress go, Andre. Now!" Cassius hollers, his voice stinging my soul. "Don't force me to make you."

Andre spins, sending the world blurring in white. My ass hits the floor, cushioned only by thin blankets. I whip my attention around the room, trying to orient myself to the sudden relocation from Andre's arms and onto the floor. Bright light explodes through the room, and I shield my gaze.

"I don't know what you think you're doing, but it won't work." Cassius stands alone a few feet away with his feathers ruffling on his back. Both Zade and Andre have vanished.

"What won't work? Getting you guys to realize that I'm not whatever monster you think I am?" I ask, pressing my palms to the floor to get to my feet. "You know if I was, you'd be able to kill me. Micah would've killed me too, but he hasn't. Nor will he ever. He wants to save me."

Cassius summons heavenly power in his palms, the ball of light reminiscent of what I imagine the sun looking like if he shrunk it and pulled it from the sky. "You're far beyond redemption, Raven, and Micah will find his way back. And when he does, you will see how wrong you are. Until then, you will stay here. I will not risk you falling into the hands of the devils again."

With his words, he throws the ball of light at me. I dodge out of the way as it engulfs the place in pure white nothingness. The light fades, my vision clearing.

Cassius is gone, and for the first time in a long time, I feel alone. But I don't feel hopeless. The angels have made a grave mistake.

Now that I know deep down in my soul that they are a part of all of this, I can use it to save my soul.

A part of Hell's Kingdom will be mine.

22

RAVEN

GRAVE MISTAKES

I WOULD'VE EXPECTED this torturous imprisonment from Hell but from Heaven's saviors? Fuck, I guess I should have. At least when Kase and Dante kept me under watch, they weren't mean about it. More annoying than anything. The holy light Cassius lit up the studio apartment with hums from the walls and ceiling. It buzzes over my skin, and I've shocked myself several times already trying to peek out the window.

It takes a good amount of my nerves to try the door again. I knew better than to try to walk out, but my stubbornness insisted that I had to at least attempt it once. Now blisters decorate my palm and fingers, the pain enough to make me hesitate.

Grabbing one of the blankets from the floor, I wrap it around my hand protectively. I stand a foot away from the rickety door, wishing I wasn't intimidated by the damn thing. The worn and weathered wood should be easy enough to kick down. I'm not even sure the lock works with the rust coating the door handle. The angels obviously don't need to use it to leave this place as they just vanished in their eye-stinging light.

"Just do it," I mutter to myself. "You've been hurt worse. It will be worse if you don't get out of here."

I grind my teeth and lace my covered fingers over the door handle. A burst of light knocks me off my feet, blinding me. I flutter my eyelids, trying to stop the stars from dancing in my vision. The spot where the blanket covered my hand now has a burning hole in it. I groan and shake my hand, jogging across the room to the small kitchenette. Flipping on the cold tap, I try to ease the burning pain with water. It helps a bit but not much. I think it's Lucian's mark setting off the room, trapping me. It doesn't matter which hand I use—fuck, any part of me for that matter—this angelic cage of an apartment isn't letting me out any time soon.

"You guys are assholes!" I shout, staring at the new blisters already forming. "If I didn't know any better, I would've assumed you were the devils and Kase and Dante were angels. They are far nicer, more caring, and they know how to treat a mortal. They went out of their way to make sure I had food to eat and clean clothes. Dante would even draw me a bath. Do you angels do that kind of thing or are you only here for the smiting? I want to speak to the Higher Power."

I know it won't get me anywhere, but I feel a bit better complaining. There has to be some sort of angel hierarchy, right? I know Kase and Dante said that the saviors ensured that mortals messed up and wrote things how they wanted, but they seem like they'd be the bragging type.

"God, can you hear me? Can't you do something about this?" I unplug the microwave and shove it onto the floor, smashing it. "What do I have to do to call on someone who can figure this out? Gabriel? Michael? Are you guys real?"

That's basically the extent of my angelic knowledge.

So instead of shouting some more, I start destroying what little the brethren have here. They live with the bare minimum, but I'm sure they can't go completely without on the mortal plane. I mean, Kash and Dante don't eat, but they shower and groom. They sleep. Feel pain. They even go through more laundry than I do. With the blankets on the floor, I know they at least want something to bring them comfort.

I stride from the kitchen and start scooping up the blankets. I have no idea what I'm going to do yet, but it has to be something enough to get their attention. I could light them on fire on the stovetop and risk sending myself to Hell or I can do something a bit more disgusting in the bathroom. Desperate times.

"Little hellion, what are you doing?" Andre materializes in front of me, blocking my path to the small bathroom with a standing shower, toilet, and sink.

I startle and step back, dropping the blankets to the floor. "Where did you come from? I didn't see your light."

Rocking on his heels, he peers around the small studio. "I'm on first watch and never left."

"You're a fucking creep. Why are angels so creepy? Micah watched me through the windows of Kase and Dante's apartment, but this is worse. I at least knew he was around." I hug my arms around me and wince at the pain of pressing my palms against the crooks of my elbows.

Andre's gaze travels from my face and to the rest of me, recognizing the pain that shudders through me. I don't get a chance to argue or brace myself before he snatches my wrist and tugs my hand to him. He tilts his head, inspecting the blisters with a frown.

"This looks like it hurts," he says softly, twisting his lips to the side. "It shouldn't have blistered your skin so intensely."

"You're lying. It's all part of your twisted plan to keep me here until I die." I jerk my hand away from him and flick my gaze to the floor, not wanting him to see how badly it hurts. If I could break down and cry, I would. I've never been burned like this and it's awful. It freaks me out, too. What if this is my eternity?

Andre doesn't respond and instead snatches my arm back to him. An embarrassing whimper escapes my mouth, my panic getting the best of me. He locks his fingers around my fingers and pries them open. With his free hand, he presses his palm to mine, causing more searing agony. I scream out, unable to control my reaction. Light glows between our hands, and I can't keep my legs working. But Andre doesn't let me go. He follows me to the floor and continues to bathe my hand in his holy light.

The pain vanishes with his power, and I half-expect my hand to be burned off and without pain due to the damage. Instead, Andre releases my fingers and reveals my healed hand apart from Lucian's mark.

"Better? I can't do anything about the brand, but I can summon the light back to me." Andre reaches for my other hand and hesitates, staring at the healed mark touching Micah's wings left behind. Flexing his muscles, he composes himself, turning expressionless. He doesn't ask me about it either. "Let me fix up your other hand now. It'll feel better."

I bob my head in agreement, wanting nothing more than for him to take the agony of the burns away. Tingles swallow my hand as he presses our palms together again, and I lock my gaze to his, wondering why he's helping me.

So I ask. "Why are you doing this? I'm assuming you weren't supposed to reveal you were creeping around here, right?"

He sighs and shrugs without response, focusing on siphoning the heavenly light from my skin. "Cassius thinks it'll be pointless, but I wanted you to know that I do hear you and you should know you're not alone."

"What exactly do you expect from all this? Cassius was right. This is pointless. You being here and listening to me does jack-shit. It doesn't make this better. If anything, it makes it that much worse. You know exactly what bullshit you're up to. Just being here pisses me off. The only thing that will make this even remotely better is if you let me go or you leave. And not just vanish from my sight." I tug away from him and lay down. I can't storm off, so I turn my back away from him instead.

Andre has the nerve to move and sit down in front of me. "I'm sorry, Raven. I truly am. The last thing I want is to see you descend into the depths of Hell, but you made an unbreakable deal with Lucifer. It is in the universe's best interest not to see exactly what Lucifer intends to do with a soul like yours. Did the devils tell you why you were targeted? Maybe Cassius will be able to use the information and—"

I glower and flip over, anger bursting through me. "Fuck off, feather-head. You're naïve to think I'm going to tell you anything. You don't care about me."

Once again, Andre moves, sitting in front of me. "That's where you're wrong. I care about all mortal souls. It hurts me deeply knowing your fate. It helps me understand why Micah hasn't completed his mission yet. Your soul is...indescribable."

"Well, apparently I've been angel-kissed or something. I don't really know. It seems kind of weird to think about I was making out with angels or some shit. You guys are assholes." I hate that I continue my conversation, but I can't help it. Andre feels so open. He seems like he would answer any question I ask.

"Not exactly kissing," Andre says, lying down beside me. He keeps his body propped on his elbow, but it doesn't make him look guarded. If anything, he appears more relaxed. Open. Fucking hot. "An angel loved you enough that its essence merged with yours. It's why your soul shines so brightly. It could've been romantic or platonic. I wouldn't know. Either way, you don't deserve to lose to Hell after receiving such a gift."

My head swims with a dozen questions. If an angel loved me so much, then why have I had such a shitty life? How did I end up attracting Joel? Nothing makes sense.

"Unfortunately, being so loved also puts a target on you. Darkness wants to ruin the kind of light you embody. Lucifer's essence tangles around you even now. It bothers me. Please tell me why you would agree to such a thing?" Andre's bottom lip pouts with his question. "What was worth it?"

"You can't expect me to bare my soul to you after this bullshit." I shift onto my back and stare at the ceiling. "You should spend the rest of eternity wondering why things are the way they are."

Andre arches up and peers down at me. It's like he can't resist trying to keep me locked in his gaze. I give up on avoiding him and return his intensity with my own. Who knew the eyes might be the windows to the soul. Andre doesn't make it feel pure and innocent as I expect an angel would. I shiver in anticipation. It's the same sensation I have before sex. The whole getting naked for the first time in front of someone new part. And right now? I like it. If Andre wants to soul fuck again or whatever, I won't resist. Maybe I can use it to my advantage. I mean, it worried Cassius enough that he went all psycho angel.

"I deserve your hostility, little hellion. I will accept the consequences for my actions even if it's denying myself the experience of learning more about how special you are." His admission throws me off guard. It's not exactly how I expected him to respond to my comment. The softness of his voice wraps around me like a whisper of despair. Instead of steeling myself toward his angelic innocence, I bathe in it. "I've failed you. I wish there was something in my power I could do to make it up to you or to change things, but things are out of my control and set forth by the Higher Power."

The urge to hug him consumes me, but I resist. It has to be the whole angel thing confusing me on a deep-seated level. He might be nice and feel bad for me, yet it doesn't change the fact that he won't do anything to help.

I stare at him without responding for a long while, wondering what it is I should do. Instead of the silence growing uncomfortable, it helps calm my racing heart. I can think more clearly with him sitting without talking or trying to reason with me over things I refuse to believe in.

"I want things to be different," he murmurs like he talks to himself. "It pains me knowing that Lucifer will get a soul that should've never belonged to him."

He's so open to me in this moment. I can feel the truth of his words as if it's just a fact of life and not his opinion. If only it didn't make me feel utterly and completely guilty. Because using his honesty against him is a total dick move, but this is my life and eternity at the saviors and devils' mercy. I never expected for things to get ripped from my control. As wrong as it feels trying to take advantage of an angel, it will be way worse if I go to Hell as a slave because of him and his brethren.

"Well, it is what it is, Andre." I shift my gaze down his perfectly muscular body and back to his eyes. "If you want to make things better, at least temporarily, I can think of something you can do. Cassius did cock-block me from peeking at your..." I motion at his pants, heat blooming in my cheeks. I can't believe I'm taking Dante's advice and being forward with an angel, trying to put dirty thoughts in his mind.

Andre's features sharpen with the change in his expression. Blinking a few times, I expect for him to turn me down. I expect him to shame me for even suggesting he whip out his cock for me to look at. What I don't expect is for him to push to his feet and drop his pants to his ankles. He stands before me in all his angelic glory—which should be completely sinful because of how sexy he is. Even though he's not hard, his dick is huge. Porn star status. Godly. Ungodly? I don't even care.

He stands a foot away and the intimidating appendage is within my reach. Heat burns through my body, and I just gawk at him. I don't even care that he's not man-scaped. Why would he be? He's an angel.

"You can touch it. It's not a big deal. Mortal bodies are

just that to me—bodies," Andre says, swiveling his hips and swinging his damn baby elephant trunk-sized member around.

The Hell inside me says this might be the only chance I might ever get to touch an angel's cock and that I shouldn't let the opportunity go to waste, but the human side of me screams I'm fucking ridiculous and need to chill.

"What about souls? What are they to you? You obviously liked seeing mine," I say, hovering my hand an inch away from his naked body. "Do you want to see it again?"

Damn. My monster-side wins, and I crush and scatter the pieces of my moral code to the hellish wind. Because with my comment, Andre's cock hardens and ends up tapping against my palm. I lace my fingers around his ethereal, heavenly dick and wonder if this is what it's truly like to call someone sex on a stick. A big stick. He is so attractive that even my soul hums with desire like I have a spirit boner for him.

His body ripples and flexes, and he moans deep in his throat. "Raven, what have you done to me?" He smiles with his words. "Your closeness—your touch. The light of your soul caressing me feels like Heaven. How can it be possible that such a wondrous thing can be destined for Hell?"

Was that an angelic pick-up line? It might sound like one, but the innocence in his words is rather endearing.

I can almost hear Dante encouraging me to offer a

blowjob. "Many people wonder that. If my soul is bad, then why does it feel so good?" The cliché feels more than fitting in this moment, because it's true.

Andre moans again as I slowly test his resolve and stroke my fingers along his shaft. I'm such a pervert enjoying how much the angel loves my hand—or soul—touching his body. His moans and rippling muscles, how he caresses his fingers through my hair and peers at me in front of him on my knees, encourages me to shove my hesitation away. Screw it. I want to ruin the purity of this angel.

I lick my lips and position myself closer, aligning my mouth with his erection. This is it. My very first angelic blowjob. I just hope if angels can cum that he doesn't blast me to Hell. What kind of end would that be? A fitting one for me, I guess.

"Can I taste you?" I ask, feeling especially naughty. I don't know what kind of knowledge he has, but I know he can't be that dense. He's been around mortals...forever.

"You want to lick it?" His eyebrows shoot up on his forehead with his question.

I nod. "Maybe suck it. It's called a blowjob...unless this kind of thing is against some sort of angelic law. I'm not an avid bible reader, but—"

"We don't have laws like the way you would think. It doesn't work like that." He smirks with his words like having to explain the ways of the universe is a silly concept.

"I'm nearly certain Cassius wouldn't agree with you." I keep stroking my hand over the length of his shaft instead of pushing things further. Andre is so open and honest, I don't want to miss my opportunity to figure out the other brethren.

Pursing his lips, Andre shrugs. "Just because he doesn't agree, doesn't make it untrue. Cassius just worries about the universe. He takes his mission to keep Lucifer in line very seriously. It still hurts him—the betrayal. Lucifer changed Cassius's purpose when he, Dante, and Kase turned their backs on the Higher Power and jumped, taking a part of humanity with them. Cassius and Lucifer were bonded by essence, created together, and intended to lead together. Mortals would refer to them as brothers. Fraternal twins."

Wow. Well, that was left out of the books.

"But that's enough talk about them," Andre says, combing his fingers through my hair. "I promised to do what I could to make you feel better, and from the looks of your soul, I see that I'm failing." His wings unfurl on his back and expand out before wrapping around me like a shield. "I don't want to fail anymore. And while I'm not sure how this will make you feel better, I think I would like to experience a blowjob from you."

Shit. His innocence is so damn pure, I feel evil corrupting him. I guess I truly do have to embrace my Hell-bound side. "Let's just say that I enjoy making you feel good."

"So selfless," Andre whispers, a blip of sadness lining his eyes. "Hell doesn't deserve you."

Oh, but it does.

Licking my lips, I part my mouth and lean forward, preparing to suck his massive cock into my mouth, uncertain I can even open my jaw wide enough to make it fit. I barely touch my tongue to his tip before he moans and tightens his fingers through my hair.

"Andre!"

I jerk away and throw myself back at the bellowing voice. My heart thrashes against my ribcage, and I expect Cassius to smite me for managing to get Andre's pants down. But it's not Cassius. It's Zade.

He whips his attention from me to Andre and frowns. "You told me to warn you when Cassius was on his way, but had I known it was because of this—" Zade waves his hand at me. "What exactly are you doing?"

"I was about to get a blowjob," Andre responds like it's the most normal thing to say. "You should experience what it's like to be so close to her. Her soul—she doesn't deserve to go to Hell."

Zade grabs Andre by the shoulders. "It's out of our hands. Now hurry, we must return to our posts."

Without even looking at me, the angels vanish in a flash of light. If only Cassius didn't glower at me, now standing in their place.

23

RAVEN

DEVIL IN DISGUISE

"STAY AWAY FROM me, you asshole!" I crawl on my hands and knees until I manage to get to my feet. The air hums with energy, sizzling static across my skin. "You can't kill me. I know you can't. So stay back!"

Cassius flaps his massive wings, hitting opposite walls with his wingspan. The gust of wind blows my hair in a tangled mess around my face. "You are like every Hell-bound mortal. You think you know everything. It's pathetic."

Spinning around, I search the floor for anything to protect myself with. I can't exactly lug the microwave around as a weapon and the blankets won't do shit. I can try to throw one over Cassius's head, but he'd just blow it away with a flap of his brilliant wings. Fuck, he could blow me into a wall if he wants.

"Maybe we wouldn't be so pathetic if you fuckers did your jobs. You failed me. I never wanted to be in this position. Do you honestly think I willingly made a deal with Lucian? I was trying to save myself because no one else would." I clench my fingers into fists as a dozen angry thoughts crash over me.

"Just like everyone else in Hell. Selfish," he snaps.

I glower. "Cut the righteous shit. If you were in my position, you would've done the same thing. Burn in Hell for eternity or rise up and claim Purgatory? You can't lie to me. Anyone with even an ounce of intelligence would choose the latter."

Cassius's eyes widen, and I realize I might've said too much. Fuck.

I give up on figuring out how to fight the righteous bastard and rush as fast as I can toward the bathroom. Cassius doesn't chase me or try to blast me off my feet with his heavenly light. His torment lies in his lack of doing anything except waiting. Like a snake, he'll rattle his tail but won't react until it's least expected. I know he's dangerous. He has immense power behind him and his cockiness proves it. This is nothing but a game to him. He wants to give me hope just to steal it away.

But he can't get to me on that level. I've accepted there is no hope for me.

Slamming the door shut, I press in the lock like the guy isn't strong enough to kick it down, but it makes me feel like I'm trying everything I can to keep him away. If I go down with a fight, maybe Lucian will relent and not hand my ass over to some twisted monsters for eternal punishment. He has to know the kind of power I face, and if I manage to get out of this alive, I will tell him as much.

"You can't escape me." Cassius's voice booms from behind me. "It's ridiculous that you even try."

I startle, my soul nearly jumping from my skin at him popping into the bathroom instead of attempting to get me to open the door. "How are you even an angel? You're a fucking monster with a god complex. Who needs the Higher Power when the almighty Cassius thinks he holds all the answers? You're a dick and an idiot if you think I don't know that," I snap, backing up to feel for the door handle.

His looming presence takes up the entire small bathroom. Claustrophobia kicks in with a wave of panic, and I slide to the floor, pulling my knees to my chest. The fact that he chooses to keep open a line of communication instead of just striking me dead proves that something is up. I just need to figure it out. Maybe because he can't kill me, he feels the need to act as if he can, flexing his power to try to put me in my place.

But what he doesn't know is that I'm partly a masochist. I'm not afraid to push him until he gives up or breaks. Kase and Dante's psychotic tendencies and justifications for some of the crazy shit they do has numbed me. Desensitized me. I will use it against this angel. He's obviously afraid of me if he tries so hard to get under my skin.

"You will be so fun to break," I add, summoning the darkness Lucian left clinging to my soul. "It won't be long. I didn't even have to do anything to Micah. I imagine all it will take is a bit of effort, and you will bow at my feet. It's inevitable. You'll see. I'm not the only one destined for Hell." I brace for him to slap me, blast me with power, or stab me.

Maybe pushing him into something he shouldn't do is the answer I've needed all along. Pushing them off the path set forth for them by the Higher Power is how angels fall. Cassius is so caught up on what he feels is right that he can't see anything else.

It's now that I realize where he will land in Hell's Kingdom. I've heard the stories about Lucifer and his pride, but the devil I know him as—Lucian—embodies all of the sins. It's Cassius, the one bonded to him through their creation, who embodies pride. Now that I know this, I can figure out his downfall.

I tip my head up and meet his glower. "You will go with me. You know you will. That's why you're acting like a shithead."

Cassius aims his flaming sword at my chest, stopping a mere inch from my body. If I so much as move, he'll stab me. "I don't know what kind of devil's work you're doing, but Heaven help me if you think you can poison me or my brethren with the dark chains of your soul. I would never turn my back on the Higher Power."

"You're crazy. Your righteousness not only blinds you from seeing the truth, but your cocky, know-it-all attitude will be what pushes your brethren toward Hell. Your inability to see beyond your light will send you over the edge." I should keep my mouth closed, but Cassius makes me so angry. I want nothing more than to prove to him I'm right. He will be responsible for his own downfall. Not me. "Is that what happened with Lucian? You couldn't stand that he wouldn't fall in line and would rather jump from Heaven and turn his back on the supposed Higher Power than spend even another second of his eternity with you? It's sad when someone would rather go to Hell."

Cassius's features sharpen with his fury, and he stabs his flaming sword into the bathroom door a few inches from my head. The heat of the angel fire radiates from the blade, stinging my skin. I screech and jerk away, the pain not unlike the burns Andre healed on my hands from attempting to open the door.

"How dare you speak of things you do not know." Cassius bows forward, baring his teeth with his leer. I never truly believed in avenging angels—never really thought much about them either—but Cassius is the epitome of all things divine out to destroy the unholy. And right now, it's me.

"Smite me and fuck off," I mutter, my body trembling. This damn fear will be the cause of my demise if I can't get my body to cooperate. "Do it and see what happens. Even Andre knows that you're an overzealous dickwad who refuses to see anything beyond his scope of knowledge. He thinks you act the way you do because you fear your brethren will abandon you once they realize you're the true devil in disguise."

"He would never," Cassius says, flaring his nostrils.

Throwing Andre in front of Cassius's wrath might be a bitch move, but I'm desperate. I need him to focus anywhere but me as I plan what to do next. Being locked in the bathroom is one thing. But being trapped with an angel, who will figure out how to send me to Hell, even if I'm not part of his mission or whatever, is basically a nightmare comparable to being a demonic slave.

I smirk, loving the sound of Cassius's doubt lining his

voice. "Then you obviously don't know him. He told me so right before he said he wanted me to suck his dick. I bet he's angry that you interrupted his desire for me to bring a piece of Heaven to this plane with only my mouth."

"He what?" Cassius snaps, his features morphing, the light of his flaming sword casting shadows over his face. And damn. He looks a lot like Lucian in this moment. If he shaved his head and grew out his beard, they would be a spitting image of each other. Except where Lucian's eyes are pure black, Cassius's are otherworldly amethyst. It makes me wonder how much Lucian changed with his creation of Hell.

"You heard me. He let me touch his big angelic cock and loved it. He wanted to put it in my mouth and fuck my face hard enough to feel it in my soul." My words both excite me and make me cringe. I never expected anything so twisted to come from my mouth, but the last few weeks with Kase and Dante let me find my psycho, monstrous side. "He would've if Zade hadn't come back to warn him you were coming."

If only my words could hurt his angel ears. I thought I wanted to corrupt Andre. But it's Cassius. I never thought I'd ever find pleasure in damning an angel, getting them to jump from grace to join Hell's Kingdom, but it suddenly seems like the best thing in the universe. I will bring this jerk to his knees instead. And when he's down, I'll enjoy taking his wings.

"You abomination!" Cassius shouts, curling his fingers into fists so tightly that light seeps from between his fingers. "Andre! Zade! Return to me."

He tips his head back and looks at the ceiling. I take his small distraction and manage to twist the doorknob to fling it open. Cassius's flaming sword flies from its place lodged in the wood, and I scramble toward it.

Light bursts through the air, and wind gusts around me, sending my midnight hair flying. I haven't believed in miracles until this moment, because Andre and Zade's arrival cuts Cassius off.

"Yes, Cass?" Andre says, squaring his shoulders. His gaze flicks to mine, but he remains expressionless. He obviously was eavesdropping and knows I threw him in front of Cassius to protect myself. How he feels about it? I guess I'll find out.

"Tell me what the devil's pawn told me isn't true. You didn't disobey an order and engage in despicable acts with the enemy." Cassius radiates with bright light, hazing the room with his ethereal glow. "You have a duty to the Higher Power and she wants to destroy us."

"Cassius, please calm down. Raven doesn't want to harm us. She's acting out because she's lost and has been denied help. I have neither disobeyed orders nor did anything despicable. All I've done was give her a moment to help ease the pain in her soul," Andre responds, his voice remaining even. "I was merely comforting Raven in a time she needed it. We've failed her, you know. If you would take a moment to see it, you will understand what I do. Her soul bears Lucifer's mark, but she's still so pure and good."

"It doesn't matter!" Cassius shouts, stepping closer to Andre. "What's done is done. There is nothing we can do for this mortal except ensure Lucifer can't continue to use her. We can't risk it. Her soul isn't worth more than every other one that would be affected if Lucifer's plans come to fruition. I know it's Micah's duty to complete this task, but I'm afraid he's been lost. She must end here."

Fuck.

"Cass, what aren't you telling us?" Zade says, finally speaking up from his spot across the room. He steps closer to face Cassius. "I know you work hard for the Higher Power, but if you don't let us see and know what you do, how can we stand together? What happened with Micah?"

Cassius groans and scrubs his hands over his face. How he can go from asshole angel to pathetic puppy with wide eyes? I wish I knew. "I suspect Micah will not be returning to us. I haven't been given confirmation, but there is no other explanation for his silence toward my calls. Even if the devils have him, he'd call. You both know this."

Andre swivels and looks at me from over his shoulder. Without him saying the words, I can feel his silent apology in the weight of his gaze. He doesn't agree with Cassius, yet he also isn't as naïve as I thought. He knows his place and where I stand. I guess I shouldn't have hoped that an almost-blowjob could knock him off his path. And damn it. I need better Angel 101. It might be too long since Kase and Dante fell.

Flexing his muscles, Andre turns around to face Cassius head on. "I don't think that's it. You know Micah. He will put everything into a mission. I'm sure he'll—"

"Micah has lost sight of his mission!" Cassius yells, expanding his wings. "The Hell-bound soul being here proves it. If you think there is even a small ounce of hope for her redemption, you are gravely mistaken, Andre. Look how fast she had you convinced that she was unjustly put in this situation."

Stepping forward, Andre tries to place his hands on Cassius's shoulders. "Cass, please. Relax. I've touched her soul myself. I—"

"You mean the same soul who nearly ruined us a century ago? The soul Raven carries is the same one responsible for Elias's fall! We lost him because of her." Cassius shoots heavenly light toward the wall, shaking the apartment with his burst of power. "How do you think she was angel-kissed? This isn't my first experience with this soul. It's why I know she can't be saved. Even if she was, she will keep returning to this plane over and over in a never-ending cycle that will only cause more damage in her wake. It's best to just let Hell have her. We can't handle any more losses. I won't allow it."

What. The. Actual. Fuck.

I have no idea what any of Cassius's revelations mean apart from that I'm screwed if he gets his way. Andre and Zade stand in silence, their bodies rigid as they process Cassius's words. If only the monstrous angel wasn't ready to send me to Hell, because I have a shit-load of questions that he might be the only one with answers to.

Processing that I have an angel-kissed soul is one thing. Discovering that Cassius knows exactly who loved me is crazy. I can't even fathom that there was an angel who fell because of me for something that should never be someone's downfall. Love is supposed to save the world. It is supposed to push people to do better, to be better. But this angel's love for me? It ruined him. Now here I am, on the verge of destroying the world because of his love.

I truly am a monster.

I know this because I don't even care.

No one can blame me for someone else's choices. How do I know this Elias guy wasn't a stalker angel? How do I know it wasn't one-sided? Cassius has a lot of damn nerve to blame me.

My rage grabs hold of me, and I let it control my being. Without thinking, I snatch Cassius's discarded flaming sword from the floor. It sears my hand, the smoke of my burning flesh billowing through the air. I don't know if my body shut down my ability to feel pain or it's something else entirely, but whatever it is, my soul and body experience a disconnection and I manage to get to my feet.

The three angels stare in shock as I stand before them with the angelic sword in hand despite the wafting smoke from my burning body. Andre brings his hand up to his chest, and Zade grabs his arm. Cassius shoves past the two of them, stomping toward me.

Fighting Cassius will be the death of me if I try, so instead of attempting the impossible, I rush toward the closest window. I might not be able to break it with my Hellbound body, but I'm sure Cassius's sword will do the job. I don't know how far I'll get, but if I can escape far enough to call upon my devils, they can come. They can help me. They're just as powerful as the angels, if not more, after all.

"Raven, don't!" Cassius yells, blinking into view by my side.

I screech and ram his sword through the window, sending fragments of glass exploding through the air. Light engulfs the room as the angelic energy dissipates, but I don't make it an inch out of the broken window. The world blurs around me, flickering with light and shadows until Cassius forces my back into a wall. He expands his brilliant white wings, glittering with what looks like silver tips. Cutting me off from his brethren and the rest of the world, Cassius gets in my face and pierces my chest with the point of the flaming sword.

"Please, don't," I beg, my whole body rolling with pain. "Please."

I send my prayer to the universe, knowing these angels will not listen or give a shit about my plea for mercy. I just hope there's something more out there willing to hear me. Maybe the Higher Power will see things untarnished by hurt feelings from a past that don't belong to this life.

"I never wanted to be in this position. I thought you were saviors. I thought you fought for the good in the universe. How can you stand here while I beg you for help and for your mercy? You can't hold another life against me. You can't. This is far from fair." I press my palms together, continuing to pray on the floor before Cassius. "Please, God. Please don't let him do this to me. Haven't I been punished enough?"

Bright light blinds me, stealing my vision and dulling all my senses. "In the name of the Higher Power, I send you to—"

"Cassius, no!" Micah's deep voice bellows through the room, flooding me with relief. "I command you to stand down. She is my charge and purpose. You will not intervene."

I've never been so thankful for his intervention. Cassius's light dims, leaving shadows in my vision. Bruised and with a split lip, Micah stands on the broken glass just inside the window. His white wings ruffle with the wind coming into the apartment, sending his crisp sea breeze scent through the room.

Cassius drops the blade to his side, but he doesn't step away from me. "Where have you been, Micah? We thought something had happened to you. The betrayers—"

"Imprisoned me. Kase was trying to use force to break me and get me to turn my back on the Higher Power." Micah shifts on his boots and turns his gaze to me. "He doesn't want to lose Raven's soul to those more inclined to serve beneath Lucifer and grows desperate."

My stomach knots and twists, hearing Micah reveal what Kase had been up to before I found him arguing with Cassius as he searched for his missing brethren. Am I angry? Maybe a little. But I already knew what he was capable of, and I can't hold it against Kase's psycho ass because his heart is in a good place. I don't want to go to Hell as a servant as much as he doesn't want me to be someone else's plaything.

"Now please, Cass. Back down. I will handle Raven," Micah adds, strolling closer.

Some indecipherable expression crosses Cassius's face, and he jerks his sword forward and points it at me again. The holy metal heats up the skin under my chin, turning from uncomfortable to painful over a dozen seconds. I grind my teeth and cry out, trying to get space between my body and the angel's blade.

"Cassius, stop! You're hurting her." Micah expands his wings, unsheathing his own sword from beneath his billowing jacket. "Step away from my soul."

"*Your* soul? *Your* soul?" Cassius asks, chanting the comment like he can't process the words. "I think you're mistaken. That soul belongs in Hell. I command you to fulfill your mission, so we can move on. This is an order. I will not stand here and watch you destroy everything you worked for to ensure the balance of the universe." Twisting toward his silent brethren, he points at Andre and Zade. "Stand ready. I think we have a devil amid us."

Micah laughs in shock. "You surely can't be referring to me."

Cassius twists and aims the flaming blade at Micah. "Finish your mission, Micah. The soul must be sent to where it belongs," he repeats, his body rippling.

Micah slowly puts away his sword and raises his hands in defeat. My heart sinks into my stomach as he surrenders. I can't believe Cassius will get his way and that my prayers were denied after all. Why I even carried an ounce of hope is beyond me. I knew better than to expect anything less than a gruesome end to a shitty life and now a doomed eternity.

And why? Because an angel loved me?

Because Lucian needed me?

Because Heaven and Hell are fighting a never-ending battle, putting me in the middle?

This is fucked up. It's unfair.

I refuse to sit here and just let it happen.

Cassius tightens his jaw, easing his sword away from my aching throat. It's the second I need. Jerking my fist out, I punch Cassius right in his angelic cock, praying it is as sensitive as mortal men's.

Scowling, he swings his attention back to me and locks his fingers to the front of my shirt, hoisting me up the wall. His amethyst eyes light up with holy power, sending purple beams around me.

"May you get the punishment you deserve," Cassius mutters.

His eyes widen, a soft groan of pain erupting from his mouth. The light around us dims, and Cassius drops me back to my knees. A growl rumbles through the air, shaking me to my core. It comes from Micah, the guttural sound unlike anything I've ever heard. It's sexy and scary, and the one thing that keeps me from turning into a crying mess.

"I warned you, Cass. Raven's soul is mine. She is my mission, and I will not let you use your divine intervention to change my purpose." Micah slides his sword from Cassius's back. "Do you understand?"

Cassius closes his eyes. "You must accept what needs to

be done. If you cannot, then I am sorry. Neither of you are leaving." Stretching out his arms, he silently whispers something under his breath before snapping his eyes open again. "Zade, Andre. Prepare yourselves. Micah is lost to us. He has fallen. He has lost his light."

Micah stabs Cassius again. "You're wrong. I haven't fallen. I've been in this position all along. But now, I don't have light blinding me. I can finally see."

24

MICAH

FALLEN

JABBING MY SWORD, I sink it into Cassius's gut and kick him back. I rush to Raven's side and scoop her into my arms. She groans in pain, her skin seared and bruised. An intense, horrible feeling crashes over me unlike anything I've ever felt in my existence. It's dark and deadly, all-consuming and born from the unforgivable actions of Cassius.

"Hold on, Raven. I'm getting you out of here." I smash

the door open with my shoulder and charge from the apartment. "Be strong for me. I know you hurt."

"Where's Kase and Dante?" she asks, her voice whispery and trembling. "They will help us."

"We don't need them. They have put your soul in my hands to protect until I figure out how to save you. But don't worry. I will take you to them before we vanish." Expanding my wings, I bend my knees and prepare to launch into the air.

"What?" Sliding her warm hands around my neck, she hugs me and nestles her face into the crook of my throat, shielding her eyes from the brightness of my essence.

"I will explain everything. But we have to leave." I flap my wings, shooting us into the air. As long as I can get us to my home, we will be safe. No one—no angel or devil—except for me and my achingly beautiful Raven can enter the place made solely for me.

She shivers at the icy wind blowing around us, and I adjust my jacket and pull it around her. Her lips brush the base of my neck with her shuddering breaths. Her pain and fear sink into me as she opens herself and lets me into her being.

Fire burns from my core, working its way through my essence. She thinks about the brethren over and over again and how terrified she is of Cassius but also how much she hates him and craves to see him destroyed. Just the hours he had her broke her pure soul into pieces, turning her toward Hell in her pure desperation. Cassius fed the darkness clinging to her, helping it bloom. Where he should've tread lightly with understanding, he allowed his hurt and need for justice against those who betrayed us get the best of him. Raven doesn't deserve to be on the receiving end of his vengeance.

"Micah! Micah, bring her back! We can fix this. Please, I can't lose you!" Cassius shouts from below. I look down and catch sight of him flying beneath us, zooming toward me.

"She needs me. All you want is to send the most brilliant soul I've ever touched somewhere she doesn't belong." I flip and nosedive, soaring past Cassius before he can reach me.

Raven shrieks and clings onto me, whispering a prayer in my ear. It stirs something fierce inside me. Summoning my heavenly sword from my inner light, I adjust Raven in my arms, getting her to wrap her legs around my waist.

A shadow crosses overhead, and I swoop and spin, slashing my sword.

"Micah! Please. I understand what you see. I saw it for myself. Don't abandon us. We have a purpose—"

"And Raven is mine. Take her away, and you steal my purpose. Don't you get that? You have to stop Cass. Please, Andre. Just give me a chance to lea—"

Fire cuts across my wing, sending me spiraling out of control. Raven screams in terror as we freefall toward the ground. Fifty feet, a hundred, a thousand—if I can't catch myself soon, we'll plummet and smash into the earth. I can survive it, but Raven can't. This is Cassius forcing my hand. If Raven dies because of me, he thinks it'll fulfill whatever path he claims I'm on. But if I lose Raven, I lose everything. I can't let her go.

Pushing away the pain, I expand my wings, trying to slow our descent. I catch an air stream and use it to glide another hundred feet, slowing my fall. Raven heaves a breath, clutching onto me, her heart thumping against mine in a lively melody I'm afraid of losing.

"Micah!" Cassius shouts, nosediving from above.

I need to make it to the ground before he can get to us. We're still too high. If I drop Raven, she might not survive. I refuse to let Cassius do this. He's lost sight of our purpose. We're not to damn anyone. We're to do everything we can to save those deserving of the glory of the Higher Power.

A heavy body crashes into me and fiery agony scorches across my other wing. I automatically fold my wing in, sending us spiraling. Raven cries out in fear, her voice disappearing on the wind. The world zooms closer and closer to us.

"Raven, I'm so sorry. Please forgive me," I whisper, clutching her to my chest. I tilt my body back to stare at the sky above and stroke my hand up and down Raven's back. She trembles and prays, her body, mind, and soul open to me.

Anger snaps through me. This can't be it. I refuse to let the brethren take my beautiful Raven from me too early. I made her a promise to save her soul, and I intend to keep my promise even if it means facing Hell myself and changing it from below instead of above. I can't imagine an eternity without this angel-kissed soul. She'll change everything. I know it.

Black feathers scatter around me, the fire searing through me lighting me with a new light. The kind of light that pushes away darkness. The kind of light that brings me clarity and reminds me of the souls I've given my existence to protect. Lucifer might have Raven's soul, but it means nothing to me. I will fight the universe until she's free.

"Let her go, Micah! Don't take her with you!" Kase's voice bellows through the air.

I stare at the four silhouettes of angels above me—not all angels. Fire blazes through Dante's skin, allowing me to see his features from above. He punches Andre, sending him crashing into Zade. The two brethren spin away and soar upward. Cassius swings his blade, scratching it across Dante's stomach. The devil spits his hellish venom, smoldering Cassius's wings.

"Micah, let her go!" Kase shouts, throwing a red orb of

Hell energy high into the air.

I brush my lips to Raven's forehead. "I'm so sorry. You deserve better. You deserve more. I've failed you."

She blinks through the wind whipping around us. "You're wrong. You saved me."

Kase roars. "Now!"

Bowing forward, I use all my strength to throw Raven into the air, praying to the Higher Power to show mercy on her when the brethren won't. She screams and flails, trying to grab the empty air for anything to hold on to. Her soul calls to me, begs for me, but all I can do is stare at the azure sky and her soul lighting the world like the sun shines from her very spirit.

The world shakes and quivers, and thousands upon thousands of whispers cry in my ears. My eyes water with tears, my body seeming to split open under the wave of darkness and despair threatening to swallow me whole.

I reach my arms out, imagining Raven bracing me in her pure light. She screams my name through the air and into my mind. Sadness rips through me, but the foreign emotion doesn't belong to me. It's Raven's grief and regret. It's her soul weeping as I fall away from her.

Like a dark shadow cutting through the brilliant light, I watch Dante catch Raven in his arms and soar away. Heat burns at my back, and I ignore the sensation licking and biting my skin, tearing through my clothes until I'm as exposed as my being to the unfair world. A world I yearn for—no, I need for—it to find the justice it deserves.

Shadows engulf me, stealing away the light from the sky, and I close my eyes and give silent thanks for the devils saving Raven, for the world for sparing her from Hell. I lose myself to the pitch darkness and try to summon my holy light to push away the shadows, but nothing happens. I exist in a world of nothingness. I'm nowhere and everywhere, nothing and everything. An electric sensation sparks through me, starting at my fingertips to zap over my hands and up my arms. The energy flares through the void, cracking the foundation of this strange realm on in-between. Bright light shoots through the fissuring world until the darkness vanishes, and my world turns white.

I press my palms into the cool floors of my home, my body weak and broken, but my being pulsing with the energy that dragged me from darkness. I kneel on one knee and stare at the crystal glass, reflecting my image back to me. My sanctuary suddenly feels so empty. So bare and lacking everything I had loved. The window that once gave me a view of the light I've spent my eternity fighting for now only shows the blood and bruises from Cassius...and black wings in place of where my heavenly light once shone through in feathers of pure white.

I bow forward and hang my head, a flurry of unfamiliar emotions bursting through me. How could this have happened? I followed my path. I fought for and obeyed the divine mission. I don't understand how everything I spent my existence fighting for could've just abandoned me, leaving me in a quiet world without love and grace and the one soul I felt so destined to save.

"Why?" I ask, voicing my question out loud. "Why give me a path I couldn't take? Why abandon me and the most brilliant soul in the entire universe?"

Silence greets me.

If the Higher Power listens, it doesn't give a response.

I'm alone.

Heat bursts through my body, and I slam my fists to the floor, cracking it with my strength. All the love I had for my home away from the heavenly kingdom vanishes with the last ounce of light I had left. Pushing to my feet, I stride toward the crystal window. In place of myself stands a towering creature standing on two hooved feet. Thick cords of muscle twine around my limbs, pulsing a strange fiery light through my body. I no longer have hands and fingers, but in their place is another set of hard bone structures like the hooves on my feet. Tusks jut from my massive head and sharp teeth fill my wide mouth. A tail with strands of tough skin swings from my lower back and it's strange to feel like as if it's just a normal appendage on my body, though when I reach to touch it, my back is as smooth as always.

I drink in the features of the strange beast—the beast I

know lingers inside me, and see myself as the devil the world will now know me as. I run my hands down my body, watching the hooves drag across my torso, despite feeling my fingers touch over my muscles as they work down to my penis and scrotum—things that were just a part of me for no other reason than to mimic a mortal...but now.

I groan at the pleasure exploding through me, taking in the strange sight of the fat, twisted appendage between my legs. I look down and inspect my body. The only monster is the reflection in the mirror, but it's like the creature sets me off. I can't stop myself from stroking my hand over my shaft, watching it grow with the addicting sensation tingling through my groin.

"Micah...?" The softness of Raven's voice trickles through my mind, the call of her soul like an unsung melody playing my soul strings. I feel it deep inside me, and all I can think about is her.

"Raven, I'm here," I call out, spinning to look around the empty sanctuary.

"What's happened to him, Dante?" she asks, her voice turning into a whisper. "Is he going to be okay?"

"If he makes the right choice," Dante responds. "If he doesn't, he'll be lost. I don't know when we will ever find him again."

A wave of despair crashes through me, coming from Raven. "Micah, please. Please don't leave me. I'm lost without you. I need you. Please. Please."

"Sorry, pretty soul. Prayers don't work on him any longer." Dante's words ignite something inside me. I don't need prayers to guide me back to Raven. I have the light of her soul, even here, in this place of loneliness.

Raven sighs. "I'm not praying. I'm begging."

"It's making me jealous," Dante says, growling.

Laughing, she says, "Good. It should. He saved me. He—"

A scream rips through my world as Raven's anguish explodes through my sanctuary, stealing my breath. The world shakes around me, and I rush toward the crystal window again. My fiery eyes glow orange, and a haze of black mist kisses my dark skin. Fury unlike anything I've ever felt burns through me at the sound of Raven screaming again.

Swinging my fist, I shatter the crystal window, sending rainbow light beaming through the air as the shattered pieces reflect my burning firelight. I climb through the broken window, the icy wind blowing through my black feathers and pulling me toward the ledge leading into a dark abyss.

I stare down into the black nothingness, searching for something, anything, to focus on. A pinprick of light snags my attention, and I narrow my gaze, watching the light grow and devour the shadowy world until all I see is the familiar light of Raven's breathtaking soul.

"Micah, please!" Raven calls.

HER PERSONAL DEMONS

Desperation hooks me onto an invisible line, and her voice reels me forward until I toe the edge of the cliff. I overlook the only thing important to me. Raven's soul shines like a beacon of everything good in the universe. Her essence stirs something wild inside me, and I know as long as I lose myself in her light, I'll be okay. We'll be okay.

Cassius and the brethren were mistaken about Raven.

She's not going to destroy the world or bow beside Lucifer. If anything, she will shine brighter than the Morning Star ever could. Peering over my shoulder, I glance at the empty room that used to bring me comfort. What I loved about this place is now gone.

So I turn my back on it.

I close myself off from the world that was supposed to be everything good and pure but now feels so unjust and wrong.

Bending my knees, I jump from the ledge of the cliff overlooking Raven. Instead of falling, I fly. I soar.

Bright light and pitch blackness strobe around me as I glide toward Raven, letting the warm winds carry me to the only place I want to be. By Raven's side, there will never be darkness. Her light will never blind me.

"Micah, no!" Cassius's booming voice thunders through the air, and I close my wings and plunge toward Raven's soul faster than I have ever moved before.

The world blurs around me, the light and dark turning

into a dazzling blue similar to the depths of her eyes. Bursts of energy fly around me, but as hard as the brethren try to throw me off my mission to be with Raven, they can't try to force me off course again.

Tensing my muscles, I brace for the impact with the ground, and land so hard on my feet that the ground splits and breaks. The world quakes from my force, and I open my arms and catch Raven before she can fall into the fiery abyss surrounding me. As quickly as the world breaks open from my descent, it seals up, leaving me standing in the middle of a parking lot.

Cool fingers clutch my face, and Raven guides my head up to look into her eyes. Her brilliant soul shines and grows until I can see her angelic face clearly. Tears sheen her gaze, turning her blue depths into pools like the ocean. Her emotions hit me like a ton of concrete blocks, and I reach up and press my fingers to her trembling lips, leaving her skin pink with my heat. Throwing her arms around me, she engulfs me in a hug that wraps me in her very essence, sending my body tingling under her touch.

"Micah, behind you!" Kase calls, his voice echoing through the world as he chucks an orb of red energy over my head.

I don't get a chance to move or let go of Raven. Thuds sound through the air, the brethren landing around us. Kase roars and shifts into his devilish beast and attacks Zade, getting him to back away.

Lightning strikes the ground beside us, and Raven cries out, the heavenly energy crackling close enough to burn. Cassius expands his wings, blocking out the sun, and I shove Raven away.

"Run!" I shout. "Go!"

A shockwave of white electricity slams into me, knocking me onto my stomach. I holler and buck my body, trying to summon my sword, but it doesn't come. Cassius stomps on my back, forcing me to stay down. His angelic power sizzles across my skin and locks me into place.

"How could you do this to us? We were family," Cassius says, towering over me. "And for what? One soul? What about the rest? How many lost because of this? You've betrayed us."

I grind my teeth and jerk my arms, trying to knock Cassius off me. Turning my head, I catch sight of Raven as Dante and Kase surround her protectively, trying to drag her away. "Raven, it's not your fault, okay? I chose this. I accept the consequences of turning my back on the Higher Power because you should've never been in this position. I wasn't the only one to fail you. The Higher Power did nothing, so I will do things myself. I will still save you, but for now, go with Dante and Kase. I don't want you to see this."

"The only thing you'll ever do is damn her," Cassius says, digging his fingers into my wings. "It's all you'll ever do from now on, betrayer."

I don't fight Cassius as he instructs Zade and Andre to hold me down.

Instead, I close my eyes.

They can do anything they want, and it won't break me.

The only thing I will ever do now is rise.

25

RAVEN

WHEN ANGELS CRY

"CLOSE YOUR EYES, Raven. You don't want to see this." Dante envelops me in his arms from behind me. "I wish I could take you away, but we can't leave. So please, just close your eyes."

"You have to stop them!" I scream, shoving my palms into Kase's back. "Don't just stand here."

"It is up to him to fight." Kase rubs his hands together,

sending sparks of red glowing light smoldering through the air.

"We can't fight for him. He must earn his place." Dante attempts to cover my eyes with his hand, and I jerk my elbow back, hitting him in his hard abs.

Pain swells through my arm, but I do it again and again, panic stealing away all my sense of reason. I don't know how I can face three avenging angels to save Micah. I've given up on miracles. On hope and faith. The only thing I can do now is test my Hell-bound soul to see if I can somehow summon demonic intervention. I refuse to stand by and watch this monstrous act. Micah is here because of me. I have to try, even if I fail.

"No! Cassius, don't do this! Micah, fight! Fight for me! You must fight!" I scream the words, thrashing and fighting until Dante's grip around me loosens. Dodging past Kase, I bolt forward toward the angels.

Cassius whips his head up and scowls. "This is your fault, you dirty, dark, abomination. I will ensure you go to Hell." Chucking a lightning bolt of energy at me, Cassius tries to strike me with his vengeance.

Kase roars and deflects the power with his own. I use the chance to keep running, knowing that Kase and Dante might not fight for Micah, but they will fight for me. Blasting Hell power at Cassius again, Kase manages to get him to send Zade into battle to stop Kase. Micah remains on his knees, his face bowed. He doesn't fight. He doesn't respond to my screaming his name. It's like with his fall from grace, he's lost his hope for an eternity at all.

Cassius locks his fingers onto one of Micah's now black-feathered wings and forces him to expand it out. My heart crashes around my ribcage, threatening to beat me to Micah. Kase and Zade fight, sending heavenly light and Hell power through the air. Kase snarls and gnashes his fangs, blocking the angel from trying to stop me.

"Micah, fight!" I scream again. "If you don't, you will have failed me. I know you don't want that. I need you."

Micah scratches his fingers into the ground. "But I can't save you."

"You can! You can save me from breaking my contract with Lucian. You can save me from demonic enslavement. It was never a choice between Heaven and Hell for me. It's a choice of where I'll land when I fall into the fiery abyss." I push as hard as I can on my feet, feeling the gust of Dante's flapping wings behind me.

Andre twists on his feet, letting go of Micah's arm. Cassius yells for him to finish what Micah couldn't, and I tense and smash into Andre, praying that his touching my soul is enough to stop him from murdering me.

Flipping me over, Andre slams me onto my back, and I cough and heave as he forces the air from my lungs. Sparkling tears sheen his eyes and trickle down his face, the grief of this moment hurting him like it hurts me.

Dante's looming shadow casts over me as he rises above Andre and stabs him in the back with his long sword. Fire sears the front of Andre's shirt and he hollers and throws himself forward, kicking me in the process, trying to escape the power of Dante's blade.

I land on my stomach feet away from Micah, and he lifts his head and opens his eyes. His irises glow orange in color, the golden hue they were before more beautiful than ever. I stretch out my arm to him, begging with my entire soul that he can siphon my strength and determination into him.

Cassius slams his boot between Micah's shoulder blades, ignoring me completely. He doesn't see me as a threat, but he's wrong. His underestimating me will be his downfall.

If only I could get up fast enough.

If only Cassius's flaming sword didn't blind me.

"Micah, fight!" I shout, shaking with anger and fear. "Micah!"

Cassius swipes his flaming sword through the base of Micah's wings, severing them from his back. He hollers in pain, his body crumpling on the ground. His black feathers explode in flames, his wings turning to ash around him, creating a silhouette to remind the universe of the angel he once was before Hell claimed him as one of its devils.

Silence falls over the world as if time stops. Kase and Dante stop fighting Zade and Andre, and Cassius lowers his sword. Micah remains on the ground, burning and bloody and broken, the light from Heaven vanishing from his skin completely.

"Say your goodbyes," Cassius says to Zade and Andre. "Let this be a lesson. None of us are immune to the darkness of Hell."

Tears glitter on the angels' cheeks as they stand around Micah, crying for their fallen brethren. I grind my teeth and push through the exhaustion and pain to get to my feet. How dare they cry for Micah. They did this to him. Cassius pushed him into choosing a side when all Micah wanted was change. He wanted a chance to see if beyond his world of good and evil if there was something in between, hiding in the shadows. He wanted more than to discover the shades of gray in a world so black and white. He wanted to find all the colors of the rainbow. But most of all? He wanted to help me. How can the saviors and Higher Power fault him for that?

"Raven, its over," Kase whispers, sliding his fingers through mine.

Dante comes up on my other side. "We should go. We still have time to figure out Lucian's contract."

I yank my hand from Kase and snatch a dagger from a sheath on Dante's back. This is far from over. This shit has just begun, and these saviors will learn that I'm not a soul to be messed with. Hell might not intervene to help secure Micah's place, but I can.

Cassius aims his sword at Micah. "I'm sorry, Micah. You've turned your back on Heaven, but I cannot let Hell have you. It has taken enough from me."

My stomach twists at the realization. Cassius would rather destroy Micah's very essence rather than see him go to Hell.

"No!" I scream, throwing Dante's dagger at Cassius.

The hilt hits him in the face, my knife throwing skills non-existent. It surprises him enough that he launches toward me, his sword blazing. His fury sparks through the air with bolts of electric energy, but I don't run away and cower behind Kase and Dante. I remain tall in place, bracing for the worst.

"Micah belongs to Hell, and you can't change it. It is fate," I say, holding steady as the wind from his wings tries to knock me on my back.

Zade and Andre shoot power at my devils, keeping them a foot away. A war erupts between the angels and devils with me in the middle.

Cassius leers, aiming his sword at my chest. "It's time to go where you belong."

I do the only thing I can think of.

I pray to Micah. I pray that he realizes this isn't the end

for him, and that just because he lost his angelic light and turned his back on his brethren, doesn't mean it's over. I pray that he realizes his purpose is still here, and his path awaits, one where we will travel together.

The ground shudders and shakes. I kick my feet into the ground, shoving myself away from Cassius and his flaming sword. A looming figure towers over him, fire blazing from cracked and burning skin of a monstrous beast. Tusks jut from the chin of the demon, and the ground sinks under its weight as it charges toward Cassius.

"That soul is mine!" the beast yells, dropping onto four legs.

It still towers over Cassius, the boar-like demon the size of an elephant. Fire billows from its mouth, its fangs glistening with molten saliva. The ground scorches around Cassius, the fire clawing toward the sky, trapping him. Ramming its head into Cassius's stomach, the demon impales him with a long tusk and flings him into the air so fast that Cassius spirals out of control before smashing into the ground.

Zade and Andre abandon their fight against the devils and take flight, scooping Cassius up and launching into the air. I tip my head back, staring at the sky, watching the angels disappear from my sight completely.

A deep, guttural growl sounds from in front of me. My body trembles in uncontrollable fear, the world quaking as the ferocious demon clomps closer, cracking the concrete beneath his hooves. Fine, wire hair prickles across its massive body, and it rises onto two feet, towering fifteen feet into the air, taller than Kase and Lucian in their devil forms. I remain frozen in my spot, my heart thudding in erratic beats. The beast might look animalistic, but the humanoid features like bulging muscles and abs, oval eyes and black curls of soft hair trigger something familiar inside me. This isn't some demon here to drag me to Hell. It's Micah in his Hellish glory.

"Look at that perfectly monstrous cock," Dante says, stepping up beside me. "That thing looks like it was made for your g-spot. Feeling brave, pretty soul? Micah looks like he could use a good time...actually, we all can."

As Dante says his twisted words, Micah morphs into his mortal façade and falls to his hands and knees. The ravaged skin of his back bleeds down his sides as he bows naked before me. I ignore Dante and Kase and crawl toward the fallen angel, hovering my hand over his body like I can summon some sort of miracle that can fix him.

But I'm helpless.

Micah's fate lies with the universe now.

All I can do is wait to see what damage his jump from grace left behind. Or what Lucian will do now.

"Micah, I'm here, okay? So are Kase and Dante. You are not alone," I whisper.

Dante strides around me and hooks his hands to Micah's sides, flipping him onto his shoulders. "All right, pretty soul. We've been out here long enough. It's time we take this fucker home."

"Give him space, angel-girl. He needs to rest and heal." Kase tugs me away from Dante's messy room, still caked in dried blood from the demon-bound mortal invasion. "And we need to talk. Come on, Dante's waiting."

Kase laces his fingers through mine and leads me across the hall to his bedroom. Two heavy blankets hang over the window and slider door, blocking the view of anyone who could attempt to spy on us. Dante rests his back against Kase's headboard, offering me a whisper of a smile, his green eyes dark with something indecipherable. He pats the spot next to him, and I climb onto the high bed, letting him pull me onto his lap. I straddle his legs, and graze my fingers across his bearded cheek, feeling as if it's been forever since I've been so close to the man who has sworn to protect me for the rest of eternity. One of the men who staked a claim on my soul.

I lean in to kiss him, my body begging to give my affection in hopes of softening his hard features. A hot hand grabs my neck, and Kase tips my head back and steals a kiss first, arching my body back to bend to his desire. There is nothing soft and sweet about the heat of his mouth against mine. His lips start a fight I can't win, and he nips and sucks, and explores the taste of my tongue through his heated passion.

I clutch Dante's legs, feeling his desire awaken as he watches me kiss Kase. Like he can't stand it a moment longer, Dante pries Kase's hand from my throat and pulls me to him. Flipping me onto my back, he sandwiches me to the bed under his weight, using his wings to keep Kase away. Dante slides his tongue into my mouth at the same time he rubs his fingers between my legs, exciting me through my jeans. I gasp and pull away, and Kase shoves Dante off me.

"We agreed there wouldn't be any foreplay or sex until we get the important things out of the way," Kase says, pinning Dante beneath him on the bed. And damn, do they look hot. "Will you be able to control yourself?"

Dante licks his lips and nods, not putting up a fight. "As long as she does."

Heat blooms across my cheeks, my body going haywire.

"Knowing that she nearly had Andre's cock in her mouth drives me crazy," Dante adds, reaching over to stroke his fingers along my jawline. "You have no idea how hard it is for me not to pin you down and fuck those pouty lips of yours."

I smirk at him. "It was your idea to start with. I was taking advantage of the situation. You have no idea just how naïve and easy that angel was. I think he'll be the one to lose his wings next."

Kase chuckles and hugs me from behind. "You love the idea of screwing the Heaven right out of the bastard, don't you?"

Blush warms my face. "It's so wrong, isn't it?"

Dante caresses his fingers over the top of my hand. "Far from it. I'd love to watch you bang the Hell right into Andre." He traces his fingers up my arm and back to my mouth, stretching my bottom lip. "But these lips? They're mine and Kase's."

Kase slips his hand under me and squeezes my buttcheek. "This ass is ours too."

"The fuckers must earn their share of our pretty soul." Kissing me again, Dante smiles against my mouth. "Isn't that right, Raven."

"Mmmhmm," I murmur. "They must know their places."

"It's the only way we'll ever share you." Combing my hair behind my ear, Kase meets my gaze. "They must be worthy."

"Don't think we won't punish the hell into you if you make a mistake. Understand?" Dante asks.

Damn. All that does is make me want to fuck up. I like his kind of punishment, and we both know it.

"Now that we all agree, we need to figure out how to handle Lucian. He's ready to break free from Hell over this, and we can't let him. Neither of us are willing to take his place." Kase shifts on the bed, the lust gone from his eyes with his words. "I was thinking of cutting ourselves off from Hell, but we need access to complete our mission."

"Then what do you think we should do?" I ask, pursing my lips.

"We need to give him Micah, Raven. Lucian must be reminded of what our mission is—"

I shake my head. "What? No."

"This was always the plan. He must learn his place and claim his throne in Hell. If we don't, we'll go to war. The saviors will take advantage of the unrest between us. Lucian will do whatever he can to get you to break the contract. But giving him Micah? It'll prove you are capable of the task. He will be required to back off. The agreement says you must get the brethren to fall, and now one has. There isn't a time limit on the others." Dante swings his legs off the bed and gets to his feet. "If he tries to say otherwise, he'll be breaking his own terms. Either way, this is our chance to keep him at bay."

But can I just hand Lucian Micah? I knew he'd take a throne in Hell, but I didn't consider what it meant to do so. What if he resents me or tries to refuse? What if the angel—the devil—I started to feel a connection to vanishes?

I guess I will find out.

A groan sounds from the hallway, and Kase stands beside Dante. The two of them share a look and abandon me on the bed without another word. They obviously want to beat me to Micah to tell him what they expect from him now.

If a soft glow didn't illuminate from the window, I would chase after them. Grabbing a dagger from the case on the wall, I pad my way across the room to the window and fling the blanket away. I expect to face Cassius's righteous, asshole scowl, but no one is there. The angel, whoever it may be, is too afraid to face me.

Fury burns through me, and I rush to the slider and yank the blanket down. I refuse to let the saviors think I'll hide in fear. That I'll stay in the protective shadows of my devils. No, that's not happening.

I slide open the door and step onto the patio, feeling the sensation of someone watching me. I glower and search the sky for the silhouette of wings, for bright light, or anything that alerts me to angels.

"You cowards!" I shout, fisting my hands. "Show yourselves. Face me!"

But nothing happens. The angels stay hidden.

"This isn't over, you assholes. I will show you what it's like to be denied mercy. You are unworthy of any power. I'm going to prove it, even if it's the last thing I ever do. You can try to send me to Hell, but it won't save you from me. You'll see. This isn't over. You'll be the ones weak and

useless at my feet. Only then will I ever help you rise again."
I spin around, glowering at the sky.

"You tell them, pretty soul," Dante says from the doorway inside. "It's fucking over for them. They're going to enjoy every second of your punishment."

Dante's right, but it's not just the brethren's purpose that is over. It's the saviors' divine rule over humanity and the world.

It's done.

Things in the universe are about to change, and it starts right here in this apartment. With my angel-kissed soul.

The change starts with me.

26

RAVEN

DATE WITH THE DEVILS

I KNOCK MY knuckles on the doorframe of the bathroom. Micah sits on the edge of the tub with his elbows resting on his knees. I hesitate for a second, seeing that he's completely naked, his towel draped over the shower curtain rod above his head.

"Micah? Can I come in?" I whisper the words as if speaking them out loud might cause the room to burst into flames. I don't even know what to do or say, but I want to be here for him.

He nods in silence, keeping his gaze trained on the tile floor. I shuffle into the bathroom and stop short of him, catching sight of his ravaged back where his wings used to be. I inhale a soft breath and grab a washcloth from the shelf of clean linen. Micah tips his head and peeks at me. I press my lips into a thin line and climb into the tub behind him.

Turning on the faucet, I warm the water and soak the washcloth. "Is it okay if I help you clean your wounds? I doubt Kase or Dante will. I imagine they hurt, which is why you haven't showered."

"I can handle pain just fine. I was just...I don't know what I'm doing. I feel lost yet free. If that makes sense." Micah straightens his back and groans, reaching over his shoulder to graze his fingers over the still burning and bleeding jagged wounds. It looks as if Kase or Dante cut the remaining pieces of his wings away, but didn't do much else.

I carefully squeeze warm water over his back. "It does. That's how I felt after breaking up with Jo—with my ex before I lost my job and had to crawl back to him for help. I was scared to death of being on my own but finally getting away from his intolerable ass..." I let my voice trail off. "I guess it's not really the same."

Micah shifts his torso, trying not to move too much, but it's obvious he's in pain. I stop cleaning his wounds and rest my hands on his shoulders, bending forward to look at him. He clenches his jaw and blinks his orange flickering eyes, offering me a tight smile.

"I think you were very brave for choosing to create your own path despite the obstacles set before you." Micah's features soften and he reaches up and rests his warm hand on mine. "Far braver than I ever could be. Look at where you are. You're tending to the wounds of a disgraced man without even an ounce of hesitation despite his failures."

I frown. "Micah, you didn't fail. I've told you that already."

"I could've prevented putting you in Cassius's path. I should've accepted that the Higher Power turned a deaf ear to my prayers. The silence wasn't because it was listening. Nothing was there." His face twists with his anger, and he growls, unleashing a glimmer of his devilish side.

I grab his face and turn him to me, trapping him in my gaze. "Stop it, Micah. I'm fine. Better than ever. Facing them made me realize how frightened they really are by the extent of our power. They know it will only be a matter of time."

I can't stop smirking with my words. I never thought such a thing as teasing angels and planning for their falls would be so sweet. How twisted is that? But what can I say? Kase and Dante make bad feel so incredible. I want more.

His eyes roam over my face, and he finally graces me

with his handsome smile. "You beautiful heathen. I think I need you to teach me a couple lessons on how to enjoy this new eternity."

I suck my bottom lip between my teeth. "I might have something to start with. You're a bit too pure still."

Cocking an eyebrow, he laces his fingers around my wrist and pulls my hand to his cock, the bold move sending an excited thrill through me. I laugh and pull my hand away, wagging my index finger at him.

"Careful, Micah. Kase and Dante have rules around here," I say, getting to my feet. "You don't want them to punish me, do you? I kind of like it."

Hooking his fingers around my waist, he pulls me to stand between his muscular thighs. My eyes wander down the length of his body, feeling his arousal brush against my leg a few inches above my knee. Even standing, I feel small, his presence enough to fill the room even if it's me who peers down at him. Micah digs his fingers into my hips, the heat of his touch sending a jolt of crazy desire through me. But I know I shouldn't give in to him. I'm still high on adrenaline and nerves, and I know once I give him an inch, he'll take a mile. He's a glutton for me after all.

"My beautiful heathen, you can't honestly think I believe you are one to obey some rules meant to keep you compliant and a plaything at their disposal? You're not enslaved to them. You are not their soul." Micah smirks as he says the words, but I glimpse a shadow of darkness crossing his features. The soft gentleness he once embodied hardens as he pulls himself from the imaginary crater I envision he left in his wake when he abandoned his brethren. It's the same level of Hell I assume awaits him to claim the throne. The fierce angel who couldn't let me go so easily is now a powerful devil. I should be nervous about the thought of him raising Hell around me. I shouldn't even humor his words. But his darkness tangles with my light, drawing me closer and closer.

He stands up, lifting me off my feet. I gasp at the sensation of his hard shaft flexing and thumping against the seam of my jeans. He hugs his arm around my back and combs his fingers into my hair, holding my head. His skin trembles, his jaw tightening. His inner beast threatens to break free, wanting nothing more than to have me any way he pleases.

"Micah," I whisper, his name a breath of a moan as he slides his hot hand lower toward my ass.

"They think they own you, but your contract is open to two devils who take a throne. Maybe I'll teach them a lesson and show them who you truly belong to. I didn't abandon the Higher Power for nothing, Raven. I did it for you. For your soul. It can be mine forever. Don't you like the sound of that?" Micah bows closer, his fiery heat radiating through me. "You want me to claim your soul."

The sudden shift in his demeanor lights a curiosity inside me. I should be afraid, but Micah doesn't scare me. I've learned over the last couple of weeks that I have a thing for possessive devils, and I want to discover the new dark side of Micah.

I lick my lips and slowly shake my head. "Just because you jumped for me doesn't mean you can have me."

"Is that so?" he asks, leaning closer, his lips inches from mine. "Do you really think this is how it's going to work? You're mine."

The room rattles and quakes, and I dig my nails into Micah's shoulders. The putrid smell of the gates of Hell opening wafts into the bathroom, knocking my sense back into me. It's now that I realize why Micah suddenly changed. As Hell opens, it'll tease his devil side, awakening something in him he must learn to tame.

Glowering, Micah spins and kicks the door closed. He shoves the free standing cabinet onto its side, blocking the door. I gasp as the world blurs. Micah presses my back into the cool shower wall and bows forward, parting his full lips to kiss me.

Kase roars from the hallway and kicks the door open, sending toiletries scattering across the floor. The apartment rumbles, igniting a blip of fear in my heart. I thought I'd have more time with Micah. I thought I'd get at least another day.

"Time to go, Micah. Lucian will not be kept waiting," Kase says, his deep voice booming through the room. "You know what must be done."

Micah flares his nostrils, grinding his teeth. "I'm not leaving without Raven."

Oh shit.

I don't get a chance to react before Micah laces his fingers around my throat and squeezes. He cuts off my airway, crushing my neck, and I try to gasp and scream, but he's too powerful. Punching my fists against his head, I fight with my slipping strength. My heartbeat thuds in my ears. The edges of my vision shadow. Micah's lost himself to Hell, and he plans to take me with him.

Kase snarls and Micah's grip on me releases. I fall and land on my ass in the damp bathtub, my mind whirling and my thoughts mush. My body goes to war with itself. A part of me wants to get between Micah and Kase, stopping them from attacking each other. Yet, another part of me enjoys seeing them confront each other over me.

I don't have to make the decision about what to do, because Dante unfurls one of his wings and cuts Kase and Micah off from each other. The tips of Dante's feathers caress my cheek, and he smirks at me in amusement.

He ruffles his black feathers, purposefully rubbing them in Micah and Kase's faces. "You two bastards need to get your shit together. Kase, get our pretty soul. She must be

411

the one to give Micah to Lucian."

Dante lowers his wings and steps into the small bathroom, towering over Micah. He grabs him by the shoulder and sinks his fingers into the wounds from his severed wings. Micah drops to his knees and scowls through the pain, but he doesn't fight Dante.

"And you, Micah, you son-of-a-bastard glutton. This is your one and only warning. You cannot claim what doesn't belong to you. Get your Hell side together and remember who she will be to our kingdom. She is not a doll to fuck and own. That addictive, sweet, glorious pussy of hers must be earned." Dante flicks his forked tongue at me, sending tingles between my thighs with just his words. "Plus, there is no fucking way I'm going to let you get your dick wet by her before me."

Micah shifts his jaw and offers a sharp nod. Turning his gaze to me, he bathes me in all of his silent intensity. "He better work fast, because the second I can escape Hell, your body is mine." His lips don't move as his voice drifts into my mind. His ability to speak telepathically to me remains the same, reminding me of just a day ago when he was whispering a prayer to me. Who knew I'd like his telepathic promises more.

"I think you've forgotten already, Micah," I think back to him, "but I'm the one who brings men to their knees."

Firelight flickers in his golden gaze, and he remains expressionless as Dante manhandles him, shoving him out of the small bathroom, not even allowing him to dress. Though I don't think earthly possessions last long in Hell. I never thought much of it.

Kase strides the short distance to the tub and lifts me into his arms. Brushing his lips to mine, he kisses me for a moment like it's all he craves to do. And I can't blame him. I'm sure Micah's comments got to him. The two of them have bitter history, and it might take more than losing his wings for Micah to get into a neutral place with Kase.

"This is harder than I expected it to be," Kase murmurs against my mouth. "You need to stop being so damn tempting. Every single one of these bastards will try to take you as if you belong to them and them alone."

I ease away and meet his gaze. "Do you feel threatened by them?"

"Far from it. More annoyed than anything." He kisses me again. "You have to realize that I've only ever shared anything with Dante...and occasionally Lucian before coming to this plane. But I also know mortals. I can't expect you to hit it and quit it with the saviors because they're hard to get. I've always known you could get attached, especially letting them near your soul."

I pout my bottom lip, a wave of emotions rising through me with Kase's admission. I knew behind his total possessive, asshole façade lingers the softness he carried as an angel. I don't point it out though. I know he'll shut down if I do.

Instead, I brush my fingers through his hair, playing with the soft strands. "I honestly don't know what to expect from any of this. It's hard for me to even grasp the idea of eternity. But I want you to know that whatever happens from here, I'm already attached to you and Dante. You think I belong to you, but you psycho bastards are mine."

He smiles. "I love when you think you have power over me, angel-girl."

I shake my head with a laugh. He won't admit it, but I do. He wouldn't have gone through such lengths if I didn't. Lucky for him, the feeling is mutual.

A snarl rips through the air, Lucian's arrival stealing away the sweet emotions I wanted to savor for the rest of time. Tensing, Kase carries me the whole way to the living room where a flaming circle sets the room aglow. Dante stands tall, his skin rippling with his hellish beast, and I stare in fascination at his blossoming scales.

"Give me one good reason I shouldn't call upon Hell's army to send you back to me," Lucian says, his massive hooved form standing tall, caressing his horns to the ceiling. "Where is the soul? She has failed to follow through with our contract, and I will not wait any longer."

Kase sets me on my feet and spins me around to face Lucian. The devil keeps his back toward me, focusing his vicious rage on Dante. He's so consumed by his desire to drag Dante and Kase to Hell that he doesn't notice Micah standing silently just outside the flaming circle.

Caressing his lips to my ear, Kase whispers, "Go put that dickhole in his place, angel-girl. Don't let him scare you."

I swallow and nod, gathering my nerve. Squaring my shoulders, I saunter across the room as quietly as my bare feet allow. Micah crosses his arms over his chest, refusing to even look at me. A part of me aches for his attention, but another part of me knows it's best for the both of us if we remain clear-headed. This can't be easy for him, facing the angel he rejected so long ago.

"Where is she?" Lucian asks again, his voice shaking through the room.

"I'm right here, Lucian. Open your damn eyes." Yeah, it's probably not the best way to respond, but his demands and high and mighty attitude grate my nerves.

Lucian spins around, and the hellfire explodes toward the ceiling. His black gaze glows with flames and he jerks his head from me to peer at Micah by my side. A growl escapes from Lucian, and it takes everything in me to obey Kase's comment about not being scared of Lucian, but how can I not be? He looms over me, his beastly form looking on the verge of devouring me, and instead of smiling that I have brought him Micah, he looks furious.

"I did not fail to fulfill my contract, Lucian," I say, keeping my voice low to stop it from quivering. "I've brought you the first angel, and in doing so, I get as much time as it takes to hold up my end of the deal."

Lucian flexes his bulging muscles. "The fallen angel must bow to me. If he doesn't, your soul is mine..." Clomping toward the fiery barrier, he meets Micah's gaze. "And I'm willing to offer it to you, my dear brethren. You have no idea how happy I am to have you home. You will serve me well."

Micah growls and transforms into his new Hell beast form and crosses through the hellfire. My heart stalls as he faces Lucian, towering over him. Micah has to bend slightly to stop his head from hitting the ceiling.

"You have always been a traitorous fool," Micah says, sending billowing fire into Lucian's face. "I know my rightful place and will not accept anything less. Why would I serve you when a throne in Hell is mine? Or have you forgotten? That soul isn't worth such a trade, *brethren*."

His words get to me in a way they shouldn't, but I can't help it. I'm really fucked up by thinking I want him to prove how much he wants me by accepting Lucian's offer even if I don't mean it.

"I knew you wanted to be mine," Micah thinks to me, his voice drifting into my mind. "Don't worry, my beautiful heathen. That is still my plan. I will not fail where Kase and

Dante have, letting Lucifer know how much control you have over them. I plan to change things and soon. Don't miss me too much."

Micah drops on all fours in front of Lucian and bows, touching his head to the floor. I watch in awe and fear, half expecting Lucian to try to break him with his fiery power.

"You may rise," Lucian mutters, turning his attention to me. "Make no mistake, Raven. You have four more angels to go, and it won't be easy. Hell's army will test my brethren as much as they test you. Slip up once, and your soul is mine."

Grabbing Micah by the shoulders, Lucian sets the two of them ablaze in hellfire. Kase steps up beside me and drapes his arm over my shoulders. I heave a few breaths, feeling the darkness of Hell coursing through me, messing with me on a soul-deep level. The ring of hellfire disappears with Lucian and Micah, and I hang my head.

"This is a good thing, pretty soul," Dante says, coming to take his place at my other side. "We will no longer have Lucian breathing down our backs."

I groan and scrub my hands over my cheeks. "Only all of Hell's demons."

Kase growls. "I hope you didn't just insinuate that we're incapable of handling a few pesky bottom feeders."

I tilt my head up to meet his gaze. "I just don't want to mess up. I can't lose my soul to Lucian. I can't."

"You won't," Dante says, sandwiching me to Kase. "Your soul is ours."

Kase pushes my hair behind my ear. "And we'll never let it go."

EPILOGUE

RAVEN

ANGEL–KISSED

"YOU BETTER WALK faster or I promise I won't be able to control myself." Dante's footsteps pick up pace as he strides behind me. "Did Kase put you up to this? That's my fucking favorite shade of red. The bastard got into my things."

I tip my head back and laugh. "It was sitting on the dresser. You told me to dress up a bit, so you can't hold it against me."

Locking his fingers into my hair, he pulls me against his chest and restrains me. "I said doll up, not paint your mouth fuckable red. I can't stand it. You need to take it off.

No one but me should see you so sexy."

"If you want it off, then take it off yourself," I tease, daring him with my words. He's been tense all morning since Kase called with a lead on the brethren. We're supposed to meet with him at a restaurant downtown to discuss how to proceed.

Dante bends my neck to the side, extending his fangs with a click. "Don't push me, pretty soul."

I reach behind me and grab onto his cock through his dress pants. "What about pull?" Tugging down the zipper, I slide my hand into his pants, turning myself on in the process. He's commando and so hard he throbs against my fingers. I want to give him whatever he desires.

Dante moans and flaps his wings, launching us into the air a few dozen feet before landing in an alley. Turning me around, he brushes his lips to mine, sucking my bottom lip between his teeth. I break away from him and press my finger to his mouth, stopping him from kissing me again. I rake my fingers down the front of my shirt as I lower myself to my knees, not even caring that gravel digs into my skin.

"You naughty soul. You're going to make me mess up your lipstick," Dante murmurs, tangling his fingers into my hair. He curls his wings around me, blocking me from the rest of the world. "Is that what you want?"

I smile to myself at his comment, knowing he wants me to play his games. "No, Dante. I want to keep my fuckable lipstick on for everyone to see."

He growls under his breath and grabs my chin, tilting my head up to look at him. "The only way anyone will see those fuckable lips is if your lipstick is smeared across your face."

I lick my lips and pull his cock from his pants completely. "If you smear my lipstick, I'm going to ride your face."

Dante moans as I part my lips and slowly suck his tip into my mouth. A taste of cinnamon blooms across my tongue, and I squeeze my thighs together, incredibly turned on how he already drips in excitement for me. Heat sizzles across my skin, and I work my mouth over Dante's cock, stretching my jaw to fit his girth in. The taste of him makes my mouth water, and he guides my head, taking over my movements.

"You're so sexy, Raven," he murmurs, rocking his cock into my mouth, taking control. "I can't get enough of you."

I hold onto his hips, humming in my throat as I breathe through my nose. He tests my gag-reflex—or really, lack there of—by gliding himself all the way in until I feel his tip in my throat. The spicy cinnamon flavor of his pre-cum trickles over my tongue. Tingles dance over my lips and work their way through the rest of me.

"Look at you, taking me all in. It feels so incredible. I want more of you. My pretty soul, so sexy and satisfying.

I'm going to take good care of you. You're not going to be able to walk right, but it's okay. I'll carry you and fuck you over and over until your pussy soaks me more than those pouty lips." Dante moans and caresses my cheek, his eyes never wavering from mine. He murmurs my name and plays with my hair. I feel so incredibly sexy, loving how much he enjoys my mouth around him. "Are you going to swallow, my pretty soul? You know what happens if you do."

My body already sings, just the taste of his pre-cum turning the world into a state of euphoria I'm not ready to let end.

I hum my agreement, tightening my lips and rolling my tongue, deep throating him hard and fast until he cums in my mouth, his release far more powerful than I expect, hitting the back of my throat. I automatically swallow and gasp, my tongue buzzing and his cinnamon-spice flavor making my eyes water a bit. I laugh and peer up at Dante, a smile stretching across my lips.

"Your turn, Raven, I can't wait to find out how wet you are for me," Dante says, guiding me to my feet and steadying me against the wall of the building so I don't wobble.

Hiking up my dress, he moans at the sight of my g-string as he stretches my leg onto his shoulder. I tighten my fingers through his hair and gasp before his tongue even touches me. A strange haze fogs the world around me, and I blink at the glowing light emanating from a blurry figure at the mouth of the alley.

"Dante?" I moan, my voice barely managing to escape my mouth. "I think I'm hallucinating."

"It's my venom. Some escapes me with my cum," he responds, stopping to peer up at me. "What do you see?"

"A wingless angel." I blink my eyes, trying to force the figure to disappear. "Or maybe he's angel-kissed like m—"

"I cast you back to Hell, demon," a sharp voice snaps, cutting off my words.

Cool water splashes over me and Dante, and Dante launches to his feet, transforming into his hellish beast. Aiming a strange gun at me, the glowing man pulls the trigger and sends an arrow into my upper arm. Agony bursts through me. Locked to the end of the arrow hangs a rope that tightens as the man tries to reel me to him. Dante growls and locks his fingers to the rope, setting his hand ablaze.

"I cast you back to Hell," the man repeats, shaking more liquid at us, burning Dante.

My head spins, dizziness washing over me. I can't open my mouth to scream. I can't even raise my heavy arms to fight. I blink again, and the world shifts. I stare at Dante fighting against a flaming barrier. Why is he so far? What's happening?

A car door slams, and it takes a few seconds to process

that I'm sprawled across the backseat of a piece of junk car. I sit up, my senses returning to me. I thrash, trying to free my hands from a pair of cuffs, but I'm not strong enough.

The world speeds by as the man stomps the throttle.

"Where are you taking me? What have you done to Dante?" I ask, focusing on the rearview mirror, but I can't see anything except the man's glowing skin, far too bright to see his features.

He ignores me and jerks the wheel, sending me crashing into the door. "Hey, it's Elias. I have her. Text me the drop off point. I'll be there soon."

Elias? Drop off point? Fuck. "Elias? You're Elias?" I ask, trying to unscramble my thoughts. I've heard the name before, but where?

And then it dawns on me. He's the savior responsible for my angel-kissed soul. He loved me in another life until he fell...which means he's a devil.

The vehicle screeches to a stop, and the man flings open the door and grabs me from the backseat. I scream in pain, my soul lighting with my anguish. I don't understand any of this.

"Elias, please. Tell me what's going on? Why are you doing this? Don't you know who I am?" I lie helpless as the man drags me across a rundown parking lot.

Releasing me, he drops me on my back and glares down at me, the sun haloing him in light. "Of course I know who you fucking are. You're the woman who's going to get me back into God's good grace."

"What?"

He shoves a wadded piece of fabric in my mouth. "No talking. No crying. No calling out to your masters. If you can follow those rules, I won't hurt you. Understand?"

Tears burn my eyes, and I nod my head.

"Good. Now don't move." Elias leans down and grabs my chin, peering into my eyes. "I need to get everything ready."

To be continued...

Thank you so much for reading Her Personal Demons! To find out what happens to Raven and her devils next, check out *Her Deadly Angels*, the second installment in *The Seven Sinners of Hell's Kingdom*!

OTHER REVERSE HAREM NOVELS BY GINNA MORAN

THE VAMPIRE HEIRS WORLD

The Divine Vampire Heirs
Blood Match
Blood Rebel
Blood Debt
Blood Feud
Blood Loss
Blood Vows

The Royale Vampire Heirs Series:
Rebel Vampires
Rebel Dhampir
Rebel Match
Rebel Heir
Rebel Fight

Academy of Vampire Heirs Series:
Dhampirs 101
Blood Sources 102
Coven Bonds 103
Personal Donors 104
Blood Wars 105

THE MATES OF MAGAELORUM WORLD

ABOUT GINNA MORAN

GINNA MORAN IS the author of over fifty novels, including the popular The Pack Mates of Lunar Crest, The Divine Vampire Heirs, and The Royale Vampire Heirs Why Choose novels.

She always carried a fascination for all things paranormal and wrote her first unpublished manuscript at age eighteen. Her love of the supernatural grew stronger through her adult life, and she now spends her days with different creatures of the night. Whether it's vampires, werewolves, dragons, fae, angels, demons, or mermaids, Ginna loves creating and living in worlds from her dreams.

Aside from Ginna's professional life, she enjoys binge watching TV, crafting and design, playing pretend with her daughter, and cuddling with her dogs. Some of her favorite things include chocolate, mermaids, anything that glitters, learning new things, cheesy jokes, and organizing her bookshelf.

Ginna is currently hard at work on her next novel and the one after, and the one after that.